THE RAVEN DECEPTION

Michael Murray

ibooks

DISTRIBUTED BY PUBLISHERS GROUP WEST

An Original Publication of ibooks, inc.

Copyright © 2006 Michael Harreschou

An ibooks, inc. Book

Distributed By Publishers Group West
1700 Fourth Street, Berkeley, CA 94710
www.pgw.com

ibooks, inc.
24 West 25th Street
New York, NY 10010

ISBN: 1-59687-310-8

10 9 8 7 6 5 4 3 2 1

Printed in the U.S.A.

Prologue

August Street had begun today's game with a double bogey on the easy first hole, doubled again on the treacherous fourth hole, played decently until the ninth, then took yet another double bogey. He was six over par for the front side and his erratic swing did not cause him to think that his score on the back side of the Village Country Club would be any better. But it was exercise with one's friends, he rationalized.

The days on California's central coast were idyllic, its weather a cause for local inhabitants to smugly regard their home as the best kept secret in the country. Halfway between San Francisco and Los Angeles, Lompoc had none of the heavy industry that attracted larger populations, while nearby technical research and manufacturing firms supplied just enough tax support for city and county residents to want for nothing. The temptation to remain forever in this seductive location had all but succeeded in making Street forget about strong winds that lashed the seaside town from February through July and its cold, pervasive, fog that precluded cocktails on the patio after five P.M. year around. Real Lompocians were expected to receive these minor discomforts as very small prices to pay for life away from the crush of cities.

His year of sabbatical was up. Decision time was upon him.

The H. P. Carlisle Foundation, a research institute located in Virginia, was funded mainly by the federal government who needed wide-ranging studies done, mostly war-related. Chief among them was intelligence services—both military and political—regional and world geopolitical estimates, and other data foreign and domestic. While the Carlisle group also did evaluations of national education, health systems, and crime in America, those were neither Street's areas of interest nor his expertise.

Street's work over a period of twenty years with the foundation had never been boring and, still affected by yin and yang, copies of his latest book, *Raven*, were beginning to sell in significant numbers. Where else could one gather the kind of data needed to produce such a book and get paid for it than the H. P. Carlisle Foundation?

While there was strong appeal to take up the full-time life of a golf bum punctuated by an occasional publication of a book, it was his third round of golf in as many days that began to clarify his thinking. Not only had his game not improved much in the past several months, but missing three-foot putts had pushed him into a state of mild depression.

A very strong factor in any decision was that the woman he loved, Linda MacTaggart, lived and worked in Lompoc. That was easily solved, even as he gulped at the thought, by marriage. Linda, an attractive Canadian nurse, brown of hair and tawny of body, was everything he ever wanted in a woman, and in that assessment he included her head, which was almost always in the right place. She never lost her temper, she enjoyed beauty in all of its forms, and she seemed to love him as much as he loved her. They could sell the Lompoc house, marry, and move to Virginia.

So, he thought, chuck the golf. Unlike his playing buddies, he had a life.

But Street was wrong. He was about to have his life taken from him.

Book I
The Present

Chapter 1

"How's the golf?" Bradley Wallis asked over the telephone. Street could picture the aging spy sitting behind his oversized mahogany desk, feet propped upon it, perusing the patterns of his argyle socks. The quintessential old-school spook, Wallis despised all things more technical than a fountain pen, so Street knew that the ex-SIS executive was talking to him over a land line, not a cell phone.

"I've mastered all parts of the game," Street lied, knowing that Wallis was a frustrated hacker himself. "As a matter of fact, it's getting a bit old and I'm giving some thought to coming back to work."

"You say that as though you had, in your past, actually worked. But I like your spirit. I'll talk to our office manager about finding something for you to do."

"I don't like the direction this conversation is going. It's my intention to demand shorter hours and far more money than I've been paid in the past."

"Demand away. But remember unemployment figures are high," Wallis said.

"Bradley, I'm getting married."

"Well, blast it all," Bradley said, his tone changing dramatically. "Congratulations, I mean that, August. You're a different man when Linda is around. Not so stiff and boring."

"Thank you, Bradley."

"Has the date been set? Will you marry there or here?"

"Virginia, we think. After all, I have more friends there than here. I'd hate to throw a reception and have no one show up."

"Good point. So when will you two arrive?"

"Probably this weekend. I want to get the place settled before Linda comes. She has to give thirty days notice," Street said.

"Then you'll have time to drop by the factory on Monday?"

"I will indeed."

"Morning tea, then. Does that suit you, August?"

The H. P. Carlisle Foundation was situated in a charming country setting west and slightly south of Washington, D.C. It was horse country, the sort of neighborhood where horses live better than most American families. It featured long fences painted white, their mazelike configurations inevitably leading to the stables and to the main house. Some years ago the Foundation had remodeled the paddocks by pouring reinforced concrete walls five feet thick and had substituted high-tech communications equipment inside, while leaving the outside of the building a freshly painted white.

The windows were still in place but no one but Superman could see through them. The doors were now blast proof, but there were no more deliveries of oats and hay.

The main house was treated in much the same way. The three upstairs floors were converted from accommodating a large family and frequent guests to office space sufficient for what one would expect for a modest campus composed of scholars and their assistants. Indeed, there was a collegial air about the Foundation that was not only intended but which in fact was quite genuine. The top floors, however, were the virtual tip of the iceberg.

Below ground level were six more floors, again set among thick, blast-proof concrete walls and hardened-steel doors. About two hundred people worked at any given time in what was euphemistically called "the hole," but they labored in comfort. Special effort was made to create the environment of a normal office building, short of real windows. It was well lit, extremely well ventilated, and the walls of the building were decorated with carefully chosen works of art everywhere one looked. In each workstation, comfortable furniture was de rigeur. The third floor housed a cafeteria that served outstanding dishes twenty-four hours per day at no charge. The only thing excluded from the cafeteria menu was alcohol which, while it could be found in the executive offices above ground, was forbidden in the hole.

There were a substantial number of military as well as civilian staff attachéd to the foundation. These were Intel types along with a specialized group of "event" planners, EPs, whose job it was to interpret current-stream Intel products that were too hot to be processed through regular channels. Worldwide rivers of data flowing twenty-four-seven were so great that assessment specialists in the Pentagon, the CIA, NSA, and other such organizations were deluged. The Foundation's EPs would make their assessments and, after adding their recommendations for action, make sure the correct command authorities received the material.

Across the Atlantic SIS (or The Firm), at 85 Albert Embankment, Vauxhall Cross in London, also widely referred to around the world as MI6, was and always had been listed under, and reported to, the Foreign Secretary. Ironically, it was SOE, founded in 1940, that was the child of SIS. While it was not unusual for the chief of Military Intelligence to brief a Home Office minister, it was usually in an expanded setting where a number of cabinet members needed to know intelligence information of a general nature. Christopher Brooks, chief of SIS or, simply "C" as he was referred to in the trade, was mildly at sea when asked to meet with John Cheaves, secretary of state for Home Office. A youthful-appearing man with intimidating size, Brooks carried with him a mind that was the envy of all government officials inside the Intelligence community. He forgot nothing. He instantly analyzed all information that passed within his sight or hearing and did it with ease. He had lost one eye as a young officer in combat during Desert Storm, the result of a land mine explosion that took the life of his best friend and former college roommate from St. John's. "It opened my eyes," he observed later in a speech, "to the dangers of war."

Ms. Lucille Vickers caused his desk phone to flash. "Yes?"

"Minister Cheaves is here."

"Send him right in," Brooks said, rising at once from his desk and walking with athletic grace to his office door, which had been left ajar in anticipation of his important guest.

"Ah, there you are, John. What a thoughtful man you are to come to our part of town," Brooks said, extending a massive hand. The minister's sacrifice of driving time from Westminster to Vauxhall, however few minutes that might be, was not lost on Brooks. John Cheaves's hourly value to the Crown could only be guessed but it had to be quite high.

In contrast to Brooks, Cheaves was of average height, but his habitually slumped shoulders made him appear even shorter. He was bald, also in contrast with his youthful appearing host. Ironically, Cheaves's bald head made him appear more intelligent than he was, so his lack of sex appeal was a reasonable trade off. Below his shiny pate was a florid glow of red skin that gave everyone who knew him the impression that he was a man who pushed himself to his limits in dealing with vital tasks. His intensity created the impression that everything he undertook was of dramatic importance to the kingdom.

"Have you read the book?" Cheaves asked without preamble, settling into the nearest leather chair. He unbuttoned his overcoat deliberately while maintaining unblinking eye contact with Brooks.

"Tea, Minister? You are one of Ms. Vicker's most admired men and I know for a fact that she keeps your favorite brew in her personal supply."

"How good of her. Yes. Well?"

"Tea for two, Vickers," Brooks said wryly into his desk telephone. Then, turning back to Cheaves, Brooks loosened his own suit coat before sitting near him. "Book? I assume we're not talking about the Holy Scriptures."

"I'm talking about *Raven*. Surely you received my memorandum."

Cheaves always managed to imply that others were far behind his fast-operating mind. This was at least one of the reasons Brooks could never quite warm to the minister and that seriousness compelled him to tweak the man.

"The novel. Yes, of course. Thank you for the excellent tip. Good read. Edith is into it now, to my great surprise. She's something of a literature snob but I noticed only this morning that her attention to it has been avid."

"Christopher, surely you know why I told you to...asked you to read it. Eh? It has the gravest consequences for the Crown," Cheaves said, leaning forward in his chair, biting off his words as though each was protein.

"I don't follow you, John," Brooks said, deliberately naive.

"Good God, man, think. If this bloody thing is true then..."

"But it isn't true. If you don't mind me saying, John, it is nonsense to think so. Ah, here's our tea. Sugar? Milk?"

Cheaves flung himself back petulantly against his chair, mouth agape, one hand making small circles in the air as though assembling his musical score with an incomplete orchestra.

"C, I don't understand your dismissive attitude about a book which has been authored by a respected academic and put out by one of the world's most esteemed publishing companies. And is, as we speak, causing a small but growing media tsunami."

Brooks was amused by the minister's metaphor. He wondered what a small tsunami might look like.

"The book is fiction, Minister," he said, sobering.

"Thinly disguised, obviously. The oldest literary ploy in the world to reveal secrets and get away with it. The author winks his eye by hiding behind the disingenuous position that he invented the entire story, while the mountain of his supporting historical evidence stares the reader in the face."

Brooks pursed his lips. John Cheaves's complexion was evolving from beet red to dull purple. C briefly wondered if he should not call for oxygen lest the Home Secretary gasp his last breath before his very eyes. He was also aware that Cheaves was probably the prime minister's closest friend.

Cheaves seemed quite serious.

Brooks sighed. "I've apparently not given enough serious attention to the book you recommended, John. At least not in the sense that it might not be fiction. After all, the notion that an actor, a British actor, might have insinuated himself into the highest reaches of the Third Reich during..."

"Hitler himself!" Cheaves blurted, heaving himself out of his chair. "Not just high up in the government, for God's sake."

"Yes, of course. That's the problem I have, right there. If he had been anyone else. Göring. Goebbels. Or..."

"Hess."

"Yes..."

Hess. Why did the man's name not roll off Brooks tongue easily? It was one of the few genuine perturbations that Brooks had suffered during his eighteen years in SIS. There were enough inexplicable loose ends connected with the Intelligence business to go around without the Hess conundrum.

"Well," he continued, "let me take another look at those pages, Minister, then I shall come to your office with a fresh point of view."

"Don't put it off, C."

"Of course I won't. Not a bit."

"You and I have a meeting with the Prime Minister Saturday morning. And please keep your staff out of it."

"If you wish," Brooks said, not sure if he was appeasing Cheaves or agreeing with him because it was a wise course of action. Either way, it comported with C's sense of management style.

When August Street arrived at the front gate of the foundation, there were two differences that he immediately noticed. The first was a new brass plate set into the stone gate support that, however new, said exactly what the old one had said: H. P. Carlisle Foundation. Nothing more. No address and no year that it was founded.

The other thing Street saw was that the white, heavily foliaged fence that surrounded the complex was now several feet taller.

"It's the times we're in, Mr. Street," offered the aging Mr. Bucks, the gardener whose duties included tending the wrought-iron gate. "Nobody's comin' in unannounced. That's the way Mr. Wallis put it. This here is Jimmy." Mr. Bucks said, nodding to a much younger man who was also wearing work clothes and standing not far from a wheelbarrow "My new assistant gardener."

"I'll bet you have lots more assistants around here, somewhere," Street said to Mr. Bucks.

There was a twinkle in the old man's eyes as he nodded. "Goin' inside today?"

"Tea with Wallis," Street said.

"Have a nice morning, then, Mr. Street."

"Good morning, Mr. Street," Cletis said, the wisp of a smile touching his pouty British lips. Street wondered if the man had opened the doors of British SIS when Bradley Wallis was deputy chief there. He supposed, now that he thought about it, that he must have done so.

"Good morning, Cletis. You haven't gained an ounce in the past year," Street observed.

"Kind of you to say so, sir. You are looking very fit yourself. Please come in. Mr. Wallis is pretending indifference but I think he's anxious to see you."

The weather was warm enough that Street had not bothered with a topcoat. He wore a plainly tailored, modestly priced suit made of gray Italian wool. He favored east coast establishment ties that never went out of style. A blue broadcloth shirt completed an ensemble he believed would signal sobriety and dedication.

"And how is Bradley's health, Cletis?"

"Sound as ever, I should say. He has always been a vigorous man, of course."

"Would you tell me the truth if you knew otherwise?"

"Certainly not," Cletis said, allowing himself the suggestion of yet another smile.Cletis rapped softly on an inner office door before opening it and sticking his head inside.

"Mr. Street is here, Mr. Wallis," Cletis said, immediately moving aside for Street to enter the spy master's inner sanctum.

"So he is. Hah! I hope you brought your clubs, August. I've been working on my short game since the day you left," the older man said, using both of his hands to firmly hold Street's.

"I couldn't beat you even when your short game was average, Bradley. You've just talked your way out of easy money." Street, genuinely fond of the cagey spy, grasped Bradley's shoulder with his free hand.

Street was aware of someone else in the room.

"You know Jean Scheerer, of course," Bradley said.

Scheerer extended his hand to Street, his smile warm.

"Good heavens," Scheerer said theatrically, "could it possibly be only twenty-two months, four days, and seven hours since last I saw you?" Scheerer laughed at his own joke, one he might have prepared for the occasion.

"Well, if it isn't the grand conspirator himself," Street said. "Aren't you supposed to be off in Egypt or somewhere at your mythical dig?"

"I just happened to be in town. Bradley said you were here so I thought we could visit a bit. You're always such fun," Scheerer said.

"What's the Egypt thing?" Wallis asked.

"That's his cover," Street said dryly. "Or at least that's what it was almost two years ago when I was trying to communicate with him all over the world, ready to fall on my knees begging for help."

"What you needed least of all, August, was help from me. Congratulations on the book. I couldn't put it down."

Cletis had returned to the room pushing a tea trolley. The cart contained cookies and scones as well as butter, marmalade, and jam. After serving the men in the room he placed a decanter of Irish whiskey at Scheerer's elbow.

"Ah," Scheerer said, pouring a healthy amount into a tumbler for himself without offering any to the others, "the rewards of retirement."

"Scheerer, for God's sake, cut the crap. I can see that you're moving and if you're moving then I know you're not dead and if you're not dead I know that you are still at work," Street said.

"To the Queen," Scheerer said, knocking back the whiskey.

Wallis sniffed at his cup. "This is green tea."

"Indeed it is," Cletis admitted.

"I don't like green tea."

"Green tea contains antioxidants. You should cultivate a taste."

"If I want medical treatment I'll visit the physician. Right now I want a simple cup of tea and I shouldn't have to mewl like a bloody kitten to get one!"

Cletis sniffed, then quietly left the room closing the door behind him.

Wallis sipped his green tea, pursing his lips in distaste.

"Mind what Cletis tells you, Bradley. Drink your green tea."

"I have vivid images of Asian tea plants being fertilized by human feces. I doubt the bloody things are even rinsed off before they are shipped straightaway to the West," Wallis said, his eyes tightly closed to the horror.

Street found that he was no longer interested in finishing his own tea. He glanced at Scheerer out of the corner of his eye. Scheerer nudged the whiskey decanter toward him. Street did not hesitate to pour a healthy splash for himself into another tumbler. Wallis, watching the action, clanged his tea cup noisily into a saucer and reached in turn for the Irish product.

"I hate to admit that Scheerer has ever come up with a good idea, but this seems to be the exception. Cheers, all."

"Now then," Wallis continued, visibly more focused after a throat-clearing swig from his glass, "you will be pleased to know that your employment agreement has been revised, August. It is now open-ended and you will find…" Wallis located a manila folder in his desk drawer from which he extracted a number of neatly typed pages clipped together. He passed the pages to Street. "You'll find that there is a substantial increase in your pay and benefits. Far more than you deserve, if you ask me. I suspect that the personnel director worries about Linda's well being."

Street leafed quickly through the twelve-page document, making no serious attempt at reading it all, yet his eyes rested long enough on the fourth page that contained his salary figures to ascertain that his increase was indeed substantial. "I'll have to go through this later," he said, aware that Scheerer was still nearby and making no preparation, so far as Street could tell, for excusing himself from the room.

"Of course. Well, I think that's all. Ah. I almost forgot," Wallis said, reaching for yet another folder among many on his desk. He withdrew a three-page document, glanced at it as though to make sure he had the right papers, then passed them over the desk to Street. This time Wallis included a pen along with his offering. "We'll need your signature."

"What's this?" Street asked as he began to read the pages.

"Confirmation that your book, *Raven*, is fiction," Wallis said.

"It's published as fiction. It's a novel. What do they need this for?" Street asked, suddenly reading more carefully. Street used the pronoun *they* fully understanding that Wallis presided over the foundation at the pleasure of the White House.

"Clarification. That's all, August," Wallis said, minimally. Wallis and Scheerer briefly made eye contact.

"It says here," Street said, referring to the paper in his hand, "that the characters in the book do not and never did exist in fact. That isn't true."

"But you admit the book is fiction," Wallis pressed.

"Well, yes, but that doesn't mean that all of it is fiction."

"Make up your mind, August. Is your book fiction or is it nonfiction? It can't be both things at once."

"World War II was a fact. Thomas Ross MacQueen was a commando in that war and I spoke with him. That's a fact. Rose Smythes Hawkins is a real person, the daughter of Archie Smythes. I interviewed her, too. I can't discredit those people and others by signing this thing." Street dropped the pages onto Wallis's desk.

Wallis leaned back in his chair, an index finger crooked over his pursed lips.

Scheerer remained silent.

It was beginning to become clear to Street why Scheerer was still there— why, indeed, he had been there at all. Nothing happened by chance in his business.

"Steven Dietrich has communicated with the department of state through his attorney. He is outraged that his name and his family's name has been associated with those you used in your book," Wallis pushed.

"I don't believe it."

Wallis shrugged, found still another letter from his inexhaustible supply of documents atop his desk, and passed it to Street.

Street quickly read the brief letter, which appeared under Dietrich's letterhead and which bore his signature. Street dismissively wafted the paper back to Wallis.

"And this, this, nonsense about how I dreamed up the whole thing. How the events never took place except inside my head. What the hell is that supposed to mean, Bradley?" Street demanded, agitated. "That isn't how I work and you know it damn well."

Wallis rolled his eyes before settling them once more upon Street. "You're acting like a school girl. Most authors would be delighted to be accused of having enough brains to invent their own plots. So what is the bloody problem, here? The money? Afraid of killing off the book sales? August, don't you understand what is involved here?"

Street leaned back in his chair. "I suppose I don't."

Wallis placed a withering glare upon Street. "Because the foundation is not officially part of the United States government or its agencies, I turned a blind eye to the publication of your book without prior approval. But you violated the spirit if not the letter of the Official Secrets Act. You had better show your contrition now and sign the document before you leave this room."

"Like hell I will," Street said before closing the door behind him.

Brooks thought Prime Minister Clay Waldon was an amazingly tenacious competitor on the tennis court. Waldon gave the impression that whether or not he won the contest was of less importance than the amount of energy he brought to the game. He ran for every shot, however impossible to reach, and he dove onto the hard grass surface more than once, racket flailing, even as an overhand shot was well past. His clothes soaking in perspiration, he never pleaded for mercy, never asked for a rest, and never complained when his own shots that he thought were in were called out.

Clay Waldon was the consummate gentleman, Brooks noted to himself as he sipped hot Scotch and milk while the PM wore down his opponent, a better player in form and arm strength but perhaps unequal in heart.

John Cheaves wordlessly took a chair next to Brooks. Cheaves was wearing sweat pants and had a white towel draped around his florid neck.

"Hello, John. I'm early so I put my drink on your bill."

Cheaves only nodded. The Lion's Head never accepted money from anyone except its members.

Brooks snuck a glance at his watch. He did not want to be rude but Saturday was a regular work day for him and the time he could be away from 85 Vauxhaull Cross was limited. As though the Prime Minister could sense C's need to press on with his department's always urgent matters, Waldon stopped his game with a mock bow to his opponent and begged to be excused. A young club staff member quickly supplied Waldon with a towel as he strode to the sidelines, his mouth widening into what Brooks thought was a genuine smile for the SIS man.

"Good morning, C. I see you have a drink. Good. Hello, John. You must have slept here last night."

"I've been admiring your tennis game, Prime Minister. You've improved a great deal since the last time I saw you play. Probably a year, now," Brooks said.

"Do you think so, really? Damn, that's nice to hear. I do work at it and now that you've brought it up, I have been winning more of my matches lately. There must be hope for me yet. Are we ready to eat? You look like you could use a bite, John. You've never neglected the crying needs of your stomach but you seem a bit piqued today. A poached egg would help, eh?"

"It can't hurt," Cheaves said, rising from the table to follow Waldon's lead to the club's west dining annex. The annex was a glassed-in patio extending out from the outer brick wall of the main building, with green potted plants from floor to ceiling artfully placed among tables covered in crisply ironed white linen. Games of tennis could be followed from most locations in the annex, but Waldon directed the maitre d' to seat them in a remote corner of the room. They were essentially between meals, breakfast and lunch, so that only two other tables were occupied with club members, all of whom greeted Waldon and Cheaves ineffusively, as club discretion required.

Even with his host's studied casualness Brooks noticed that the prime minister betrayed a certain anxiousness with the way his eyes soared over and beyond the menu without seeing it, the tips of his fingers impatiently flicking at its edges. Waldon and Cheaves in turn declined the waiter's offer of coffee, while Brooks asked for the club's darkest brew, Italian or French roast. There was a well-tended buffet offering of eggs in various forms along with toast, sausage or bacon, potatoes grilled in fresh rosemary, so the decision by unanimous consent was, in the interest of time, to avail themselves of ready-cooked food.

Instead of small talk while filling their plates and resuming their places at the table, there maintained among them an asseverated climate, one with which Brooks was not yet in accord.

Waldon cleared his throat. They had hardly touched their food and the room was now thinning of its members so that they would have had to raise their voices to be overheard, but old habits die hard and his level of volume was subdued.

"Well, C, John and I have given considerable thought to the book we've just read. We are in complete agreement about its potential impact on this country should world opinion believe there is much truth to it. You've not been asked here to comment on those ramifications, that is, what policies Britain should adopt, but rather to inform us of the facts surrounding this so-called 'operation Raven'."

"I understand completely, Prime Minister," Brooks said, the strip of bacon on the end of his fork suddenly unappealing.

"So," Waldon said, "if you would give us your opinion as to the book's factual content and its central premise, I'm sure John and I will follow up with questions." The prime minister arched his eyebrows as he glanced at Cheaves who, without speaking, waved his assent with a radiantly white linen napkin in hand.

"Of course. At John's request," Brooks began, lowering his knife and fork gently onto his plate, glad to quit his pretense of appetite, "I read the book once more, quite completely, making notes as I went along. I must say that the writer was up to his job. I've never met August Street but I understand the man is a professional researcher and report writer. He is a senior fellow at the H. P. Carlisle Foundation in America. The Carlisle people are well known to us and highly respected. Point of fact, we've used them once or twice and have participated in joint efforts..."

"Joint?" interjected Cheaves.

"Yes. War planning scenarios, Intelligence capability studies, and military equipment projections going back as far as forty years. It isn't unusual for us to work with the Americans and share the cost on those kinds of studies. They can be very expensive. We only have to pay for the portion of them that we might need for our defense—somewhere around fifteen or twenty percent."

"Sure," Waldon said, slowly pushing his plate to one side, as though by so doing he would be able to focus more attention on his chief of SIS.

"Right. So the man knows his business," Cheaves prompted.

"He does. I've only had two days to dig into our records and I should tell you that the job is enormous. In the first place, many of the records that go back sixty-five years are buried in various locations in the basements and vaults around the city and the world, so digging them up is literally a physical challenge. Then, there is the secret aspect. World War II was conducted in compartmentalized confidentiality. The more secret an operation was, the more it was intentionally obscured. Secrets were in such abundance that the lifestyles of many were heavily influenced by the secrets they kept. Then there was the deliberate obscuration of those secrets. Every department of war in those days took pride in not only keeping secrets, but in misleading the enemy in the process if possible. So we come along more than a half century later and try to sort through them. No easy task."

"I hope, C, that you are trying only to explain away the difficulties you encountered within the past forty-eight hours and not suggesting that those problems will be with us tomorrow and in the future?" the prime minister said.

"Yes. I suppose I am, but only so that you, by facing issues in the real world, can more perfectly construct your national policy vis-a-vis the events referred to in the book, *Raven*," Brooks responded dryly.

"Let him talk, Clay," Cheaves said, correctly resigned to the inevitable bad news that arrives with any meeting with SIS types.

"Of course. Go on, C," Waldon said.

"We have a very large task, or tasks, before us if we are to discredit the contents of this book. For example, just within the Intelligence community we have to locate and review all radio logs, message priorities, and personnel who, if living, sent or received those wireless transmissions, and we have to do the same with any field controllers, if living. The same is true for all SOE records. We need to locate and interview SOE survivors. The three principals named in the book, I am given to understand, are no longer living but they had aides and assistants who are still surviving. All of their memoranda have to be located and read. We have to locate the code word logs used in that time and vet them and cross-check them for reference to the entire Raven operation..."

"Good lord," Cheaves said with a groan.

"And then there is the military. RAF flew SAM flights, Special Air Missions, for five years depositing hundreds upon hundreds of clandestine personnel throughout all of Europe. Their mission records have to be checked, aircrew who survive located and interviewed, as well as a number of the maintenance people who took part in supporting that mission and others. We'll have to locate all of the records of Third Para Commandoes and as of now, I've found nothing about the unit. Still, every unit regardless of size has a long wake of support and supply trailing behind it. They provided food, ammunition, medical support, transportation, military pay, and there will be vouchers for all of that. Where they trained and where other commando units trained—a good deal of that took place in the Scottish highlands so we'll need to travel there. Medical units always generate a mountain of records and we need to see it all. The trail continues after the war. There will be Social Security numbers, continued disability payments perhaps, insurance paid to relatives. In fact we'll have to locate and interview relatives of anyone connected to Third Para personnel and perhaps other commando units. We'll have to locate and examine the TOEs. Those are the Table of Organization and Equipment. Then there is that entire Rudolph Hess business and the transcripts of his..."

Brooks halted at the prime minister's upraised hand. "Hess."

"Yes. According to the book he arrived in this country uninvited. The *Raven* book says that he discovered our fake Führer and wanted to make a deal."

"Of course I remember that. I just never..." Waldon waved his hand in helpless resignation.

"Well, we kept the man incognito for some reason, didn't we?" Cheaves suggested gloomily. "The whole world wondered why we kept the poor devil locked up for life. Including me."

"We blamed that on the Russians, too," Brooks reminded them. "Then there are bank accounts, driver's licenses. The list goes on and on and we haven't begun to talk about family people like the Dietrichs, or Rose Smythes Hawkins, or others."

The prime minister had, by now, lost his appetite. His knife and fork rested on his plate.

"You might be interested to know that the Hess transcripts are gone," Brooks said.

"What do you mean?" Cheaves asked, leaning forward in his chair.

"I mean they are no longer in the same vault system into which they were placed, or where they should have been placed, after his completed questioning."

"How is that possible?" Cheaves asked, incredulously.

Brooks shrugged. "They could have been stolen. The Mossad once stole the plans for the French Mirage fighter plane and took them to Israel. The blueprints filled an entire boxcar," Brooks pointed out, casually.

The prime minister sank back in his chair, letting the painful silence creep ever more deeply into his psyche.

"And after we accomplish all of this?" he asked no one in particular.

"Well, I would think that part of your grand strategy would be to cover it all up. More exactly," Brooks said, "at least muzzle those who are alive and could talk."

"No question," Waldon said, beginning to pull at his lower lip for the second time in the past hour. He leaned forward again in his chair as he addressed Brooks, his voice falling even more softly as he began to speak. "This nation, in its recent history, did nothing less than order the deaths of twenty-seven million Russians. Twenty-seven million. And it allowed the deaths of more than six million Jews. We, C, are the direct cause for our friends having to endure unspeakable tragedy, far more extreme and on a scale unrivaled in world history. Why? So that we could ensure the survival of the British empire."

The prime minister paused so that his words would have the desired effect on his chief of SIS. Obviously Waldon and Cheaves had already exchanged their thoughts about the subject and it was Brooks alone, an integral part of whatever strategy Waldon developed, who needed to be brought totally aboard.

"If any part of the book can be verified, if the history of Britain has to be rewritten to show that we Britons caused the annihilation of nearly forty million souls in order to save our own skins, we would become a leper nation. Our elderly population would live in shame and, almost certainly, there would be an even more dramatic effect in our foreign affairs. Our prestige around the globe would be nil. As a nation of influence we would all but cease to exist. Even the United States would want to distance themselves from us. And I submit to you that our trade exports would suffer grievously. Our manufactured goods and textiles would simply sit on the docks and go nowhere. Foreign trade, C, is as much dependent upon good will as necessity. The whole affair, if proven, could be a calamity of giant proportions."

After a very long moment of quiet reflection it was Brooks who cleared his throat. "No question that your assessment is, ah, very likely close to the mark, Prime Minister. Assuming as much, what would you have me do?"

"Do? We have no choice, do we? You and your agency have to begin to work on the horrifying litany you just outlined. You have to chase this thing down, find out if we're dealing with fact or fiction. If it cannot be verified then we can ignore it. But if any of it can be verified then we have to do whatever is necessary to suppress the facts."

"Burying paperwork is one thing, Prime Minister, but burying people who are not yet dead is something else, if I make myself clear. Unfortunately for us there are a good number of people who fall into that inconvenient category. What do you propose we do with them?"

"I'm not sure."

"Well," Brooks examined his fingernails theatrically, "with respect, sir, when do you suppose you will firm up your thoughts along those lines?"

"I'm even more aware of the exigencies we face than you, C," Waldon said, his testy response barely a whisper. "Do what needs to be done. We must see that none of them are able to confirm even a single fact in *Raven*."

Chapter 2

Bitterly disappointed and at somewhat of a loss of what to do next, Street used his Virginia condominium telephone to call his pal Westbrook Claridge. Wes agreed to join the researcher for dinner. Street then made another call, this one to Linda in Lompoc. It was early yet and he was not surprised when she did not pick up. Street left a message.

"Don't pack, darling. Seems I ran into a little problem at the foundation that calls for some rethinking. I'm coming home in a day or two. Sorry to ruin your day but I promise to make it up to you. I'm having dinner with Wes tonight so I'll feel better afterward. Love you."

His call to Linda reminded Street of other pressing calls he needed to make. Consulting his palm secretary, he began looking up numbers. He notified local utility companies that he needed to discontinue their services two days hence even though he had only ordered them turned on days before. He called a national moving company and made adjustments to his plans to cart certain furnishings from Lompoc to Virginia, and asked if he couldn't instead arrange to have a few pieces of furniture shipped from the east to the west. He looked in the yellow pages for a real estate agent, intending to put his condo on the market, but hesitated before dialing the number. It would probably be better to get a referral. Besides, might he not be acting in haste? It could wait until the next day.

He took his time driving to the Bailiwick Inn, a distance of about twelve miles, but having forgotten the hazard of rush-hour traffic from the interstate to Highway 236, he arrived almost a half hour late. He gave his name to the maitre d' while surveying the crowd over his shoulder where he thought Westbrook might wait.

"Mr. Street," the maitre d' said, having briefly referred to a scribbled note on his service stand, "Mr. Claridge called. He said that he was terribly sorry but he would have to miss dinner tonight. He said that the Martians were landing and he had to be there to greet them."

"Got it. Thank you, Peter," Street said, responding to the man's name discreetly etched on a placard attachéd to his workstation.

"I still have your table, Mr. Street. Would you…?"

"No, thanks. I think I'll go into the bar."

Although the Bailiwick dining room was elegant and pleasantly quiet, Street became aware of the heightened noise level inside the bar as he raised a martini to his lips. Twenty years before he might not have noticed, but now the crush of packed bodies and the racket they produced annoyed him. He downed the gin in two gulps and ate the two stuffed green olives that came with it. He was hungry but knew he couldn't eat, at least not alone.

He returned to his condominium and a frozen TV dinner.

By previous arrangement, Street returned the next morning to the H. P. Carlisle Foundation to clean out his office. At the front desk he did not ask for Bradley Wallis nor was there a communication from him. Although Street believed he had cleaned the place thoroughly before going on sabbatical he found that twenty years of accumulation had become part of the very fabric of his ten-by-fifteen space. Working through cabinet drawers and various piles of papers was slow. Except for a late lunch, he continued long into the evening before returning to his condo.

There, he showered, drank a bottle of beer, went to bed, and immediately fell asleep.

He awoke the next morning feeling refreshed. He shaved, microwaved a cup of day-old coffee, and ate two shortbread cookies. Breakfast of researchers. He worried that the high dose of sugar and butter in the cookies would savage his brain cells. He wondered if science had a device that could measure the destruction.

The Foundation supplied him with heavy boxes suitable for shipping. He had made arrangements for them to be picked up the following day. There wasn't any rush since nothing he had in them was part of a current project. He was careful to avoid including any classified information with his outgoing material and he took nothing from his computer station that operated off a mainframe machine in the bowels of the building. His personal material was scrupulously maintained on his laptop. He went by Westbrook's office before noon hoping to join him for lunch. Wes, according to one of his colleagues, had not been in that morning and probably would be gone most of the day. Street took it as a compliment that the foundation assigned no security person to oversee his cleanup and packing, which was standard operating procedure in most cases of an employee leaving.

It was late in the day when he finished, and he still hadn't seen Wallis. There was little to say, he supposed. Wallis had made it clear that he thought Street was being totally unreasonable, even unprofessional, in refusing to clarify his position about his novel. While Street could understand his point of view, he admittedly had not and would not retract any part of his work just because it might embarrass the British government. That's what it was all about. Well, they made all of the mistakes, not he, and if they hadn't tried to deceive not only their own people but the entire world as well, they wouldn't find themselves in this kind of mess.

Street's stance on this issue was one of principle and personal integrity. He saw no way to retract his work that would not betray not only himself but others.

The next morning he used his cell phone to call Westbrook at the

Foundation but got his voicemail. He clicked off the connection with his thumb, deciding he would talk to Wes later from California. Street carried his suitcase in one hand, his hang-up bag over the opposite shoulder, and locked the door from the inside before leaving. He left his office keys and picture identification at the security desk and drove into the city in his rental car. He returned the car to Avis at the airport and boarded a plane for Los Angeles.

Street's plane had been delayed over an hour before leaving the gate at Washington Dulles Airport, causing him to miss the last commuter bus from LAX to Santa Barbara. He was tired and decided to get a room at one of the many convenient hotels on Century Boulevard, then catch a shuttle north in the morning. He almost fell onto the bed at the Airport Hyatt and was asleep within minutes. He awoke the next day late for him, but his schedule was now his own and northbound shuttles left LAX several times throughout the day. After a shower and change into comfortable clothes, Street called Linda in Lompoc. To his slight annoyance there was no answer. She had said she was taking the rest of the week off so that the two of them could spend time together when he arrived home. Street then called Linda's work place only to be told that indeed she was off and not expected back until Monday. Was anything wrong?

No. Of course nothing was wrong. She's probably just out shopping.

The LAX/Santa Barbara commuter bus departed at noon and by 2:00 P.M. he stepped off the bus at the Santa Barbara airport. From there he called his home again. This time Linda answered.

"Hello."

"Linda?"

"Oh, August, is that you?" she said, her voice cracking.

"Sure it's me. I called this morning but… Hey, what's wrong?"

"Where are you? Oh, hell. August, they're deporting me! Can you believe it?"

Street had a sudden urge to laugh. He had often teased her about putting off becoming a U.S. citizen. Part of the tease was that she might someday be deported. She would smile at the notion. When they start deporting registered nurses, she once said, this country will be in a lot of trouble. The fact that Linda was still a Canadian citizen hardly entered his mind. She had lived in the United States all of her adult life using only a resident alien card. There had to be a mistake of some kind.

"That's silly. What do you…"

"Silly!" Linda's voice cracked again.

"Darling…" Street hardly knew how to begin calming her. "I'm in Santa Barbara. On my way home. I'm going to rent a car so just stay calm. I'll take care of everything when I get there."

"They're here," she said, heaving the words from deep within her as though she was sick to her stomach.

"Who's there?" he asked, fingers tightening around his cell phone. For a moment he thought he might break the plastic case.

"I don't know. Two men and a woman. She's from the Canadian consulate, I think. God, August, they're making me pack."

"Okay," he said in a voice he hoped sounded steadier than the pit of his stomach caused him to feel. "All right, I'll be there soon."

He was on the road within ten minutes, weaving in and out of traffic like a man on his way to a fire. When he arrived forty minutes later, there were two unmistakable government vehicles parked in front of his house. One of them had Canadian consular license plates, while the other car was a U.S. government vehicle with federal tax exempt plates. Both cars were adorned with several aerials sticking outward like the spikes on a sea mine. Street parked his rental car in his driveway. He marched across his front lawn to the door and, trying the latch, found the door unlocked.

"Mr. Street?" a large man in his late thirties wearing a gray suit and acetate necktie stood in the center of the hallway making transit around him impossible.

"Who are you?" Street demanded, biting off his words.

"I'm Agent Howard Hogan, Homeland Security." Agent Hogan held up a small I.D. wallet containing a pictured card.

"Take it out of that wallet and let me see it," Street snapped.

Agent Hogan tried not to reveal a smile that wanted to come to his lips. He liked the reaction from Street so far. With any kind of luck at all Street would become more belligerent until the big government agent would have to physically restrain him. The agent enjoyed every step along the way in these confrontations.

"I'll hold on to the wallet and the identification card, Mr. Street, but you're welcome to look at it as long as you want," he said very calmly, maximizing the insolence in his voice and holding the card closer for Street to see.

Ignoring the card and the man, Street started around Agent Hogan but the big man had only to adjust his shoulders slightly to keep himself between Street and the walls of the hallway.

"Get the hell out of my way," Street said. "This is my house."

"Yes, sir, it is. And I have a warrant to be in it. Now, here's the way things are going to go, August. The woman that lives here with you," he began, instantly and casually degrading the loving relationship between Street and Linda, "is going back to Canada. Deportation proceedings are all done and she's got the paperwork. She's packed her things and we're going to drive her to Los Angeles, where she'll be put on a plane back to Ontario…"

"I want to see the goddamned paperwork," Street interrupted. "This is outrageous."

"To Ontario. There isn't anything you can do at this time, Mr. Street. I'm going to let you see her for a few minutes…"

"Damn, how kind of you."

"You can say goodbye. That's about it. I don't want any interference, understand? Okay, raise your arms. I'm going to pat you down."

"You're going to *what?*"

"Have any weapons of any kind on you, Mr. Street? Pocket knife? Needles?" Agent Hogan was well into the search process before Street could object.

"Of course not," he said in a defeated voice. "If I did I would have used it by now."

Agent Hogan moved inches closer to Street's face. "What did you say? I'm not playing a game with you, Mr. Street. If you threaten me you're going to go down hard. Understand what I'm saying to you? All right, now go in and see Ms. MacTaggart."

There was a hint of disappointment in the agent's voice that he had to bring Street up too short too soon, but he moved aside enough for Street to get by. Inside the living room Linda was already on her feet. At the sight of him she rushed forward and flung her arms around his neck and held on tight. The two embraced for a long moment, his hand gently touching her soft brown hair. Her eyes were red from crying, a very hard thing to cause Linda to do, Street knew. In her life in hospitals she had seen more than her share of human carnage and psychological damage. She was not stoic but she was courageous and it angered Street all the more that strangers could enter their home and wreak this kind of havoc. He was aware that two more people were standing inside the room, a woman and a man. Street hardly glanced in their direction, unwilling to give them the satisfaction of producing their omnipotent paper and cellophane blackjacks. Two of Linda's suitcases were standing near the French doors, presumably packed.

"Did you call the Canadian consulate?" he asked her, holding her in his arms.

Linda nodded her head.

"Well? What did they tell you they're up to? What did they say you did?

Break a law?" Street wanted to know, not willing to ask either of the officials who were looking on.

"Something about associations in Canada and in this country. They said some friends of mine are terrorists. I said they were crazy."

"What friends?"

"They didn't say who. What terrorists could I possibly know?" Linda said, fighting back more tears.

"None, of course. There's a huge mistake happening here. We'll figure it out. I'll make some phone calls right now."

"We have to be leaving, now, Linda," the other woman spoke for the first time.

"Her name is Miss MacTaggart," Street said in measured words, "and she isn't ready to leave yet."

"We'll take your bags," the woman addressed Linda, ignoring Street.

The female Canadian agent, or consular official, took Linda by the elbow while the man picked up her two bags. Linda offered no resistance but Street stepped in front of them both.

"Did you hear what I said? She's not under arrest," he insisted.

"Stand over there, August." The voice of Agent Howard Hogan. His tone was the way a cop would talk to a perp. First name, facetiously, patronizingly personal.

"You again," Street said, his lips compressed into white strips of flesh.

Agent Hogan nodded to the two Canadians officials who proceeded to the door with their "terrorist" in tow. The two, with Linda's luggage, made their way down the cement path to their cars parked at the curb. August started toward the four of them but was restrained at the door threshold by Agent Hogan who placed a large hand on his chest.

"Right there, August," Agent Hogan said.

"You asshole," Street spit through clenched teeth.

The smile was gone from the agent's face when he gave Street a little extra restraining push, this time with a knuckle right under his breast bone. It was not a debilitating blow but it took all of the air out of Street's chest leaving him gasping. And it hurt like hell. If he had any further insults to direct toward agent Hogan he could not have made them heard.

Street drove his own car, an XK Jaguar, down Highway One, right behind Linda and her quasi-legal kidnappers.

The government cars were moving at a good clip as they hurtled down Highway 101 and Los Angeles. It was tempting on Street's part to run his $90,000 Jaguar right up their tailpipes but he forced himself to remain calm. This was no time to antagonize law enforcement officers, no matter their personality defects. He was determined to use good reasoning. Dropping back a quarter mile from the two cars that convoyed Linda, Street placed the automobile telephone adapter into his ear and autodialed a number.

"Law offices of Haskins, Knowles and Vass," a cool female voice said at the other end.

"Steve Haskins, please. This is August Street calling."

"Mr. Haskins is not in the office today, Mr. Street," the receptionist said.

"Where is he? This is an emergency."

"I don't think he can be reached, Mr. Street. Is there anyone else in the office who can help you? Mr. Knowles is here…"

"No. It has to be Haskins. He's… wait. Ed Knowles? All right, put him on."

"He's with a client, Mr. Street, but I'll go into his office and ask him if he'll take the call. I'm sure he will. Can you hold?"

"Yes. Please hurry," Street said.

After several moments a man's voice came on line. "Ed Knowles, here."

"August Street, Ed. You, Steve and I played golf…"

"Sure, I remember you very well, Mr. Street. I'm sorry that Steve isn't here himself. I guess you're stuck with the junior varsity today."

Street recalled Ed Knowles as a heavily built but well-maintained man who had once played college football. He would be in his early fifties, only a fringe of hair remaining on a large head, and he wore gold-rimmed glasses. He was a cheerful, unfailingly polite man who, in his earlier life could make short work out of opposing ball carriers from his defensive tackle position.

"I know who I'm dealing with, too, Ed, and I know it isn't the JV."

"Kathleen said you had an emergency on your hands. What can I do for you?"

Street shorthanded the story for Knowles, talking clearly enough to have confidence that the attorney was keeping up with him entirely. "I don't know what the hell they're up to or why they're picking on Linda but there is one massive mistake, somewhere."

"So where are you on the highway now?" Knowles asked.

"We're north of Santa Barbara. At this rate we'll arrive at LAX in about two hours."

"Okay, I'll make some phone calls. First thing we have to do is keep her off that airplane. I know a federal judge who should be able to issue me a restraining order. I'm going to send one of our men, Ernie Cardena, to the courthouse, then he'll go directly to the airport. If they're going to Canada they'll be leaving from the Tom Bradley terminal. Agree?"

"Figures."

"You stay with them. I'll be at the front door before you arrive. I'm going to give you my cell phone number. Ready to copy?"

Street speeded up to close the distance between his car and the car that contained Linda. He was a tenth of a mile behind their two-car caravan as they exited the 405 Freeway onto the airport off-ramp. Traffic slowed substantially as the route to departure terminals and incoming autos from Sepulveda Boulevard intersected. Street had a good view at all times of those he was following and, so far as he knew, they had no idea what kind of car he was driving or, for that matter, that he was driving at all. As he suspected they would, the officials escorting Linda halted directly in front of the Tom Bradley terminal and left their automobiles at the curb. A nearby LAPD officer strolled past but the federal plates gave them unrestricted parking.

As Linda was escorted into the terminal building, Street left his car behind the federal officers, willing to take the ticket that was sure to come. From the sidewalk he used his remote door key to lock the XK then walked quickly through the wide terminal entrance. He fell into step well behind Linda and her escorts who were moving at a deliberate pace deeper into the terminal. The female official still had one hand gripping Linda's arm as though, Street thought, Linda were a common criminal being marched to a jail cell.

"August!"

Street paused to look over his shoulder. Edward Knowles was hurrying to catch up, his sizable stride closing the distance easily. He wore the lawyer's uniform of a blue suit and black loafers, effectively letting people know that he was a serious man going about his business.

"Hello, Ed. You got here just in time. Did you get the writ?"

Knowles grinned wickedly as he tapped his hand against his breast. "Right here. Let's nail 'em. Where are they?"

"Right up there," Street said, the two men turning as one toward the far end of Tom Bradley Terminal. They walked at a quick pace but even as they moved along, faster than other passengers around them, Street no longer had them in sight.

"I don't see them," he admitted.

"They'll probably use Air Canada," Knowles said, nodding his head in the direction of Air Canada's ticket counter. Knowles guided Street, hand touching his elbow, to the front of the ticket line. He commanded the attention of a ticket agent by the force of his size and businesslike demeanor.

"This is Mr. August Street and I am Ed Knowles, Mr. Street's attorney. We have a restraining order to serve upon Linda MacTaggart, who we believe will board one of your aircraft. Will you please verify that for us?"

The ticket clerk had listened carefully to Knowles's request and had made a judgement about whom he might be dealing with. A roaming supervisor had been within hearing distance and followed his curiosity toward the ticket seller.

"Moment, please," the ticket clerk said while he and his supevisor briefly exchanged words.

The ticket clerk, with the supervisor looking over his shoulder, quickly typed in commands to his computer, then studied the screen. The ticket seller shook his head but it was the supervisor who spoke to Knowles.

"We have no reservation for Linda MacTaggart."

"Do you have any seats reserved for Canadian officials?" Knowles asked.

"On which flight, sir?" the supervisor said.

"On any flight!" Street snapped.

"Mr. Street is right. We have no idea which of your aircraft they might board," Knowles said, calmly.

While the ticket clerk did not appreciate Street's rudeness, he again punched the keyboard in front of him. "Nothing," he said, scanning the screen.

"How about another airline?" Street appealed to the supervisor.

"Possible, of course," he said, punching yet another set of keys then peering into the fish-tank-like green environment before his eyes. "Continental services parts of Canada, landing at Toronto, Ontario. So does Northwest and United Airlines."

"Damn," Street mumbled, turning toward Ed Knowles. "What do you think? Would they answer a page?"

"Not if they were smart. You take Continental Airlines, I'll go to Northwest. If we don't find her there we'll meet at United."

Street had more trouble getting the attention of a helpful ticket clerk at Continental Airlines. Their personnel were struggling to service long lines of passengers at each of four open ticket positions. He presented an annoyance to people waiting in line and, when a female supervisor finally attended his increasingly loud demands, the airline official was not eager to be of service.

"What kind of legal document did you say it was?"

Though still on the sunny side of forty, the supervisor wore her hair tightly against her temples and fastened firmly behind her head. Her heavy lipstick had been mashed onto her lips as though she wanted to finish off a nearly exhausted tube and start a new one. She had small eyes set close together and a nose that reminded Street of a beak.

"A restraining order. It is signed by a federal judge," Street said.

"Let me see it, please."

"Well, I don't have it on me…"

"Then I'm sorry."

"My lawyer has it. Ed Knowles."

"We are not allowed to divulge any reservation or ticketing information to the public, sir. If your attorney presents us with a legal document—"

"He's at the Northwest ticket counter," Street said, interrupting.

"Well. When he finishes there, you might want to come back and we can—"

"Hey, come on, lady, all I want to know is if my wife is being put on one of your airplanes. Is that asking too much?"

Even as Street was pleading he knew he had chosen the wrong approach to an already hostile woman. As he watched her retreating toward the far end of the ticket counter he knew that if he came back he would have to have Ed Knowles do the talking. Worse, he had wasted their time without learning whether or not Linda's name existed in Northwest's reservation system. He crossed the building's vast lobby toward United Airlines. He could easily make out the broad shoulders of Knowles as the attorney, leaning on the ticket counter, pleaded their case to a ticket agent.

"Nothing here," Knowles said.

"We'll have to check the passenger waiting areas," Street said.

"I've already got Ernie Cardena working on that," Knowles said, even as he retrieved a small cell phone from his jacket pocket. He glanced down at the machine and pushed the necessary dial button. "What've you got, Ernie?" he said into the phone. "Uh huh. Yeah. Okay, go ahead," Knowles said before closing the device.

"Only one woman with a man that was near the description of Linda MacTaggart was at the Continental waiting area. Ernie talked to her but no joy. He's on his way to Northwest, his last stop."

"What happens next?"

Before Knowles could answer there was a distinctly audible sound that came from his coat pocket. "Hello?" Knowles said, holding the phone to his ear. He continued to listen for what seemed to Street a very long period of time which, in fact, was under a minute. The attorney at last closed the phone cover again and returned it to his pocket. "I've got to get to a landline phone."

"I'll wait here," Street said, impotently, as the larger man turned on his heel and walked away in search of a public phone. Street was jostled from the side and, his short temper getting even shorter, felt like pursuing the rather diminutive man who had been careless and discourteous enough to walk by without so much as a "sorry." But what was the use? Frustration, he reminded himself, was the source of anger. He wasn't really angry at the little man already swallowed up by the crowd, but at himself for letting events spin out of his control.

It was no longer daylight when Street, without Knowles, retreated slowly toward the entrance of the huge terminal building. There had been no sign of Haskin's legal partner who had not returned. Linda was gone.

He absently patted his coat pockets to locate his cell phone before remembering that he had left it in the XK, still attachéd to its auto mount. As he exited the building and turned slightly to his left he saw his car but there was a difference from when he had parked it. A policeman was there, a ticket tucked under the windshield. He was also facilitating a tow truck driver so that the Jag could be hoisted onto the bed of the truck.

"Officer," he said, "do you really have to do that? Can't you just hand me the ticket and let the car down?" Street could imagine that within minutes he would be sitting in the seat next to the tow truck driver on the way to the police impound, then waiting in line to pay the hundreds of dollars in towing fees, fines, and all that goes with it, before getting his car back.

"This your car?" the policeman asked.

"Yes, it is."

"What's your name, sir?"

"Street. August Street. I live in Lompoc."

"May I see some identification, Mr. Street?"

"Sure thing," Street said, reaching into a back pocket of his trousers. Even before his fingers made their way into his pants he realized that his wallet was gone. He checked the same pocket on the opposite side of his pants, again, knowing that it would not be found there, either. Same with his coat pockets, inside and outside.

"My wallet's gone," he said, stupidly, vaguely connecting the small man who bumped him in the terminal with his missing wallet.

"Uh, huh. You realize this is a stolen car, don't you, Mr. Street?"

"No, I don't realize that and no, it isn't a stolen car. It is my car and I lease it from Gateway Leasing company. I've been leasing cars for nine years from the same people and if you'll look inside you'll find corroboration in the glove compartment."

"We've already looked inside. Do you have a firearm permit, Mr. Street?"

"What kind of a question is that? Firearm... no. And I don't need one. You mean to carry a gun? I have a gun at my house but..." Street stopped talking. He could hear himself and it did not sound good even to him. The policeman had rattled him and he prattled back like a child in a room full of people who discovers his fly open.

"Stay right where you are, Mr. Street," the policeman said. His voice betrayed the fact that in his mind the issue was settled. Stolen car, no ID, and not a rational answer to his questions. The next thing that would happen is that the policeman would put Street's hands behind his back and snap cuffs around them. When the cop turned his back momentarily to have the tow truck driver sign a receipt, Street stepped into a group of people exiting the terminal. The crowd was moving in the general direction of the parking structure entrance. Street did not dare look back over his shoulder lest he draw attention to himself. He had little more than thirty paces to go when he heard a voice behind him, possibly the tow truck driver.

"There he goes!"

Street immediately quickened his pace into a near run. It was not unusual to see people hurrying in one direction or another in travel terminals, late for a plane, train, or a car service. Street made it to the pedestrian entrance of the parking area and, still without looking backward and moving even faster, passed an "up" ramp and continued on the main street level, running toward the rear of the concrete building where automobiles entered to park. He might have turned right to place himself back on the sidewalk but well away from the last site of the policeman, but movement out of the corner of his eye made him veer in that direction. A man was just dropping the trunk lid of his car and reaching for the driver's side door.

"Hi. Hey, I'm really sorry to bother you but I'm wondering if you could do me a favor. I'd really appreciate it, just a lift to Century Boulevard," Street blurted. "They just towed my car away and I tried to pay 'em for it but there was a cop there and he got pretty mad and, I don't have any way of getting out of here to get my car back…"

"Aw, hell. Get in. Been there done that." The man started the engine of his late-model BMW, pulled it out of its parking space, and began to increase speed down the exit ramp.

August Street's savior wore white painter's pants complete with pockets to hold tools. Under a well-worn but fine-quality suede jacket was a yellow and green polo shirt. The man had thick sandy hair, except for a spot in front that was just beginning to thin. Under a large, aquiline nose was an outsized moustache, which was twisted theatrically upward at each end. There was little body fat on the man, Street noted. A construction worker? He had green eyes that lit up at first sight of the policeman.

"Aha," a smile broadened across his face. "You must have said nasty words to your pal in the blue suit, eh? Should I slow down so you can step out and pop the son of a bitch? No?"

Street slid low into the BMW's passenger seat as the mustachioed driver left the smile on his face and cruised smoothly by the trotting policeman. Once outside the parking structure, the BMW joined outgoing traffic moving counterclockwise, six lanes abreast. Rush hour for Los Angeles. All hours were rush hours in Los Angeles. Traffic moved along at an agonizing pace for Street, who imagined that they would run into a road block at the airport's exits.

"Don't worry, pal," the driver said as though reading his mind. "Just a parking ticket, right? You can sit up, now."

Of course it was not just a parking ticket. Or at least it should have been nothing more. Stolen? Totally wrong. But why? There were two mistakes working against him: the biggest was the move against Linda and the second was listing his car as stolen. Street was an empiricist. As a man of reason he found it unlikely that two weighty anomalies could have fallen onto his person purely from chance. Someone was pulling strings.

"So, where to? I'm not driving into the city or wherever the hell they keep cars. I'm going to make a right pretty soon. Manhattan Beach is where I live."

They were now on Century Boulevard where, Street reasoned, there were hotels, cars to rent, telephones. "Let me out right here," Street said when the driver slowed for a light. "And thanks. I appreciate your help."

"Like I say, pard, been there, done that."

The driver waved as Street closed his passenger side door and dodged his way to the curb. The BMW had pulled away by the time Street had crossed with the light to the opposite side where he continued walking up the pedestrian walkway to the Regency Hotel. Inside the building, as he approached the registration desk, he suddenly remembered that he had no wallet. He jammed both hands at once into his pants pocket. His worst fears became real as his hands came out of the pockets with nothing more than a few crumpled bills and some loose coins. He never liked the feeling of a money clip banging around in his trousers, choosing instead to keep cash, along with credit cards, in his wallet.

Yes? May I help you?" a cheerful young lady asked from the other side of the registration counter.

"No, ah… Public telephone?"

"Right around the corner, sir," the girl said, pointing.

First making sure he had the necessary coinage, he followed her directions to a row of public telephones separated from each other by sections of glass. He was relieved to see that there was at least one complete directory. His list of telephone numbers remained in his cell phone, which by now was either at or on its way to a police garage. Street flipped through the yellow pages of the book under attorneys. He found Haskins, Knowles and Vass and dialed the number. Before it began to ring an automated operator asked that he deposit one dollar. After the required number of chimes were set off in the machine's electronic innards the reassuring ring on the other end could be heard. It rang again, and again. Eventually an answering machine clicked on and a female voice announced that the law offices of Haskins, Knowles and Vass was closed for the day. The machine voice suggested that the caller might like to leave a message and assured him or her that their call would be returned as soon as possible.

Street had less than six dollars. That was not enough to rent a room of any kind and he had no way to pay for one. The only people he knew in Los Angeles were business types who, even if he knew how to reach them after office hours, he did not feel he could ask for money or a car. Steven Dietrich lived in Santa Monica, he recalled, and Street sensed that Dietrich might be just the man who might help. He found Dietrich's number easily enough but the only response was the omnipresent answering machine. He hung up quickly enough to get a refund from the telephone. Still dressed in the clothes he had worn on the airplane from Virginia the night before, Street needed a shower, a shave, and a change of clothes. It wouldn't be long before he would begin to smell. Harking back to his teen years when it seemed problems were far simpler, Street had done his share of hitchhiking. There was no other choice.

He caught a city bus that ran east and asked the driver for a transfer. At La Cienega Boulevard he transferred to another bus which, he was assured by the driver, would take him out Sepulveda to the Valley. The bus was packed with people and for several miles of starts and stops he remained standing. By the time they had reached Santa Monica Boulevard, the crowd had thinned enough for him to sit. When the bus swung to the south at Sherman Oaks, Street left the bus and walked a distance of about two miles until he reached highway 101 north. He was exhausted and when the first car pulled off the high-speed freeway in response to his outstretched thumb, he was also shivering cold. Even so, his eyes remained painfully open until when, three rides later, he arrived in the early morning hours at his front door in Vandenberg Village.

The door was locked. There had not been a resident burglary recorded in the village in more than two decades and for that reason he and Linda had seldom felt it necessary to lock all of the doors except at night. When they went out of town they paid a house sitter to feed the dogs, drink their wine, and watch TV. He went around to the back and tried all three doors. They were locked as well. His office in the back of the property was above the double garage with access to a side door and this, he found was locked as well. It popped open on the third kick. He mounted the stairway to the loft, a roomy place with large windows facing east and west. While he was not the neatest housekeeper in the world, there was no question about what had caused the mess he saw before him. His two filing cabinets had been forced open, their contents strewn about the carpeted floor. Stacks of miscellaneous books, maps, and papers stored in cardboard boxes had been dumped. Books that were on shelves had been tossed around and his many notebooks, most filled with pages he had written or downloaded from the Internet, were opened, tossed, and left wherever they fell.

He looked under a seat bench where he kept two document travel bags, a stack of unused mailing envelopes, and a fireproof valise made by Brinks. The lock on the valise had been forced open, the contents opened. It had contained most of his legal documents, including credit card and driver's license photocopies, and his banking information.

He knew before he bent over to examine the scrambled papers once filed in his cabinets that his and Linda's passports would be gone along with the house deed, mortgage activity and insurance records. His auto file, complete with maintenance records and lease agreements, was not to be found. A glance at the north wall told him that his decade accumulation of monthly bank statements would be gone.

They were. His computer's hard drive was removed and his backup discs were gone as well.

Street made his way downstairs into the garage. He lifted a pry bar from its hook on a wall. He decided that forced entry into the kitchen would be the least destructive route, Street jammed the steel bar between the French doors and struck the bar sharply with the heel of his hand to gain a firm bite. He slowly began pulling, feeling increasing strain as he put his weight into it. He suddenly felt a sharp snap along with the unmistakable sound of panes of glass breaking. He did not want to look to find out how many had shattered. Inside he stood motionless, listening to a deathly silence, unbroken even by what should have been the friendly greeting by Jasmine, the Dachshund, or Jack, the Fox Terrier.

Tired beyond caring what needed to be done next, Street fell upon their king-sized bed and, barely managing to kick his shoes off, fell immediately asleep.

It was light when he opened his eyes again but he only finished undressing, then climbed under the covers once more to resume his deep sleep. It was noon when he was able to rise with a clear head and take a long shower. He shaved, then dressed for a trip to the bank. Linda's car no longer occupied the other space in the garage, so after a moment's hesitation he crossed the street and knocked on Vivian Irvine's house. When she came to the door Street simply said that something had happened to his car and wondered if he couldn't use hers for a run to town. Vivian was not her normal cordial self, Street thought, but she nonetheless gave over the keys to her Ford Taurus.

The bank's main office was only moderately busy and the teller lines were short. He looked for a face he might know and who might remember him, then stepped into one such line. When it was his turn he was aware of how his facial muscles might send signals to the lady on the other side of the service counter. He did not want to appear overly desperate but, rather, concerned.

"Hello, Joan," he said. He didn't know her but there was a nameplate at her window.

"Hi," she said, neutrally.

"Joan, I just got back from Los Angeles and I lost my wallet," he began, and was pleased to see her concern immediately register on her face.

"Bummer."

"Yeah, so I need to get some cash from my account. I'll just sign a counter check or something."

"Sure, we can do that. What's the name?"

Not good. "August Street."

Joan efficiently tickled the keys on her computer, looking carefully.

"One thirty-eight Inverness Avenue?" she asked by way of confirmation.

"That's it," he said.

"Hmm," she said, her brows furrowing. "That account has been moved."

"What do you mean, moved?"

"You account. It's been transferred to…" Joan clicked more keys. "To The Mercantile Bank and Trust in Cleveland, Ohio."

"That's not possible. I didn't move my account. I gave no one authorization to move my account or to do anything else with it." Street could hear the tone of his voice beginning to rise. He could not allow this confrontation to get out of hand. He lowered his voice.

"We better talk to the branch manager," the teller said, locking her money drawer.

"Good. Ron Mau?"

"Ray Downs," she said.

"I don't know him. Where is Ron Mau?"

"Mr. Mau has retired."

"When?"

"A month ago. Gee, I guess it's been a couple of months now."

"He said he'd never retire," Street heard himself say, weakly. "He couldn't afford it."

The bank teller smiled. "I'm sure Mr. Mau was kidding."

Of course he was. God, how stupid that must have sounded.

"What can I do for you, Mr. Street?" Ray Downs was an affable man with an expanding waistline, carelessly trimmed mustache, and a warm dry handshake that was intended to put Street at ease. At any other time it would have worked. Street sat at a chair near Downs' desk, approximately the same position he was often in while being lectured to by his fifth-grade teacher, Mrs. Bodenhammer. He had never seen Ray Downs before nor had Downs ever met him.

"I lost my wallet. No, actually, my pocket was picked. Last night at LAX. Naturally my credit cards were in it, driver's license. You know."

"Oh, hell," Downs said, learning back in his chair. "Did you call the credit card companies?"

"No. Not yet. As a matter of fact..."

"We better do that right away. Who did you have cards with?" Downs said, pulling a scratch pad in front of him.

"American Express," Street said, his heart sinking. He had ill feelings about canceling sources of credit in his name, but the banker was right. It had to be done. "Visa, and a MasterCard. I don't know the names of the issuers. I banked online and the checks went out automatically each month."

Downs waved a hand dismissively. "Doesn't matter. We have a clearance system here. All we need to do is give them your name and all of your cards will be cancelled all at once. And we'd have a record of your online payments here on our computers." Downs, like the teller, accessed the computer terminal on his desk top. Street watched the man's face frown.

"You didn't tell me you moved your account," Downs said, his lips pursing.

"But I didn't. That's why I'm sitting here at your desk."

Downs reviewed his files via more key punches. "Well, it shows here that according to your directions, and your signature given to one of tellers at the head office, we electronically moved all of your funds from checking and savings accounts to your new account in Cleveland, Ohio."

"Look, Mr. Downs, I ought to know what I did and what I didn't do. I didn't come into this bank and request that my account be moved. I haven't been in Cleveland, Ohio, for ten years, and frankly, I don't want to go back there. And I sure as hell don't want to keep my money there. I mean, why the hell would I?"

Ray Downs regarded Street for a long moment, his chin in his hand wondering what kind of response to make. "Could you stop by the bank tomorrow, Mr. Street? Just before noon, maybe?"

"Yes." As Street rose to his feet he was somewhat at a loss for a place to go. "I guess I'm going to report this to the police."

"Didn't you do that in Los Angeles?"

Street shrugged. "I... I had to get away."

He could feel Ray Downs's eyes on his back as he left the bank.

***

"Yes, sir?" chemist David Glowd asked of a customer whom he had never seen before. There were few families in the hamlet of Abergritch that he did not know. He was third generation in this very shop and he prided himself on knowing the town just as well as his great grandfather knew it.

"Sodium cyanide, please, sir. Seems that I have a problem with..."

"Rats! Eh? Yes? Ach, the little bastards, 'scuse the language, are everywhere. How much will you need, Mr...... ?"

"Blanch. Roger Blanch, Mr. Glowd."

"Blanch, of course," the chemist said, covering his embarrassment with a little white lie. Terrible when a man knows you but you don't know him. You know him, that is, but his name slips. Flips right out of mind. Not a function of age at all. "And how much do you think will do you, Mr. Blanch?"

"Oh, I should think an ounce. 'Tisn't like I need to kill every rat in Ireland now, is it?"

The two men shared a chuckle at the thought of Ireland's legendary rat problem. Of course, that's all it was. Legendary.

"Very good. Now, let's see," Chemist Glowd said, going directly to his supply of powders. "Ah, here it is. You want to be very careful of this stuff, Mr. Blanch."

"I have some experience," the man said.

"Of course you do. I'm only concerned for the welfare of a good customer." He carefully measured an ounce of the powder into a brand new electronic scales. Very sensitive. Nothing like the old ones his father used and even he had used before the store went modern. It never ceased to amaze him at the machine's ability to weigh one hundredth of a gram. Gingerly, he transferred the chemical to a vial, which he capped and securely taped closed.

"I'll just use a bit on cheese for the little darlings," the man smiled to the chemist.

"The last meal, indeed, for those vermin. Will there be anything else, Mr. Blanch?"

"Yes, come to think of it. I fancy one of those gas lighters. For cigars. Friend of mine has one."

"Step right over here. We have a fine selection."

The butane-loaded tanks that the druggist offered to his customer were cheap and, of course, refillable.

"Very nice," the man said. "Why don't I take two?"

Twenty miles away, at the Mugarow motel, bungalow number four, the man who called himself Blanch stood in the bathroom wearing a plastic apron with rubber gloves nearby. Within reach was a second set of gloves. In front of him was a glass tube, a roll of cotton, and the small bottle of sodium cyanide. He applied a small screwdriver to the recently purchased butane lighter and removed the screw valve. He pulled a small amount of cotton from the roll and shaped it in his fingers, wetted it, then inserted it well into one of his nostrils. He repeated the process for the other nostril. He donned the rubber gloves. He then carefully removed the tape and cap from the sodium cyanide bottle and, using a hollow glass tube of the kind used in laboratories, he placed a thumb over one end to produce a crude vacuum seal. He placed a good amount of the acid into the cigarette lighter.

The man then dipped into a traveling bag to produce a small plastic bottle of household astringent. He rinsed the glass tube in clear water, dried it, then used the same tube to dip into the second bottle. Despite the number of times the man had done this operation, he was aware of sweat upon his skin at the scalp. He placed the glass tube and its contents above the open chamber of the cigarette lighter and allowed two drops to fall.

Very quickly he replaced the screw valve into the lighter. As he tightened the valve he could not help but turn his face away from the threat of what was now prussic acid, instantly deadly if even a minute quantity were to penetrate the cotton filters in his nose.

When the valve was tightened firmly he almost staggered backward from the lethal canister. But there was one more operation. From within a small kit he found a CO_2 cartridge. He pushed the cartridge firmly against the gas valve until he heard compressed gas flowing into the now-deadly cigarette lighter.

Finished, he pulled off his rubber gloves, tweezed the cotton from his nostrils, and collapsed on the bed. He now needed nothing more than an innocent appearing newspaper.

Chapter 3

"Happy birthday to you, happy birthday to you, happy birthday dear..."

"Argghhh. Stop that now!"

"..dear Thomas, happy birthday to you!"

Customers along with employees of The Wise Pelican surrounded the elderly man like he was their pet cat who might run away and hide. For their enticing bait they held a large devil's food cake topped by vanilla icing, with a single candle burning brightly in the middle. The table was set by one of the big tables overlooking Carmarthen Bay, Wales. It was a perfect day to party inside because the weather in the bay was its usual dark and gloomy self.

"Make a wish!"

"Bet the old man can't get it blowed out!"

"Eh? Who said that? Was that you, Dicky boy? I'm going to blow you clean out, is what I'm gonna do next," the white-haired old man said through missing teeth, while switching his cane about the air with his one good hand. The crowd, including the patrons, laughed heartily, their great fondness for the old man glowing in their eyes.

"Tell us how old you are, Thomas."

"None of ye'r business."

Laughter.

"Come on, man, the ice cream's meltin.'"

"Damned if I'll be the cause of meltin' ice cream. All right. You, Beth, stand back or the force o' me mighty blowin' 'll knock ye down."

Thomas MacQueen huffed and puffed like the wolf in the fairy tale and delivered more than enough wind to extinguish the candle. But the flame remained.

"What the...!"

The old man blew two more times before taking the candle from its place on the cake and examining it more closely. It was a trick, of course, and everyone had been in on the joke except Thomas.

"Very funny. Very funny. Louis!" he called across the pub to a man standing behind the bar with his arms crossed over his chest. "Pour these rotten sods the worst we've got in the house. Go on, now. Get away," he waved at those gathered around him, pulling at the arms of young ladies who clutched at his neck to plant kisses on his pink cheeks.

Thomas MacQueen's birthday party continued late into the night with people of various ages stopping in to pay their respects. Customers included those who had practically grown up in the place when Thomas first opened in 1958 and had done all the work himself. He had tapped the ale kegs, made sandwiches from bread he and his wife baked in their home, and they had lived on the floor directly above the pub. In the early morning hours he swept the floors and mopped up the spilt drinks, and he cleaned the lavs until they shone. He worked daily and had been in business four years before he hired his first full-time help. So the whole town of Saundersfoot plus a good many who came there for sea and sand knew him well and they filled the place. More than a few customers had met their future spouses in his pub.

That night, his birthday night, Thomas MacQueen did for the others what he seldom did for anyone other than his wife, Michele, when she was living. He sang. He held the room in thrall with his rich baritone for the longest time while he sang a Scottish lullaby as well as "These Are My Mountains", "The Bonnie Banks of Loch Lomond" and "Will Ye Go Lassie Go". There was not a dry eye in the place when the last amazingly clear note came from the old man's throat.

It would have been the perfect end of the evening had not a man no one had ever seen before, holding a rolled newspaper in his hand, crowded among those squeezing through the doorway leaving the pub. There was too much vocalizing, laughter, goodnights, to hear the faint, brief, release of pressurized gas. Thomas MacQueen fell to his knees like a bag of wet sand. He clutched at his chest, closing his eyes tightly, before slumping the rest of the way to the floor.

There were shouts for someone to do something, to call emergency medical assistance, and plenty of volunteers leaped forward to pump on the old man's chest, but Thomas MacQueen would never wake up.

Street started the engine in his neighbor's Taurus and sat for several minutes considering his next move. He needed papers, duplicates of what he had lost, at least a driver's license, Social Security card and the like. He would go to the police and report the crime so he could begin afresh.

At the police station he told the desk sergeant who he was and that he wanted to report a theft.

"My pocket was picked at LAX. They got my credit cards, driver's license, money. Everything."

"LAX? In Los Angeles?"

"Yes."

"You're just reporting it now? Why didn't you report it there?"

"Because... I... There wasn't time."

"Oh. Well, I can take your report but I'll just have to send it down there. There's nothing we can do about it here. Out of our jurisdiction."

"What I really need is some identification."

"We don't do that here, either. There's a DMV in town. You can talk to them about getting a duplicate driver's license and in Santa Maria there's a Social Security office. I suppose that would be the place to go for a new card, too."

Street couldn't bring himself to say thanks to the sergeant so he just walked out.

The following day Street got an earlier start. Another friend and member of his golf foursome loaned him his ten-year-old pickup truck.

In Santa Maria he arrived a few minutes after nine o'clock when the Social Security office opened for business. There was already a full house, people of all ages occupying several dozen chairs. He signed his name to a numbered sheet and took a number from a large roll that hung from the wall. There was still an available chair so he sat. Three hours later, after having moved only once to visit the men's room, and after closing his eyes for what he thought was just a few minutes, he finally heard his number called. He arrived at workstation number two, of four such windows, and faced a woman of indefinite years. She had dyed her hair black and was so scrupulous about tending each root that might betray her real age that her hair appeared to be a wig colored black. Street told her his story about the stolen wallet and his need to get a replacement card. With no visible change of expression she countered with a form for him to fill out. When he finished he handed it back over the counter.

"Mr. ...?"

"Street. August Street.

The government employee regarded him thoughtfully.

"Can you prove that?"

"Beg your pardon?"

"I said, can you prove it?"

"That's why I'm here. I want you to help me prove it."

Her eyebrows, plucked and replaced with a pencil line, knitted into a frown as she stabbed at yet another series of buttons on her computer keyboard. In due time a printout clicked its way upward from a space on the left of her workstation. She ripped it off with practiced boredom and scrutinized it.

"Is this your Social Security number?" she asked. "You're sure?"

"I've had it all of my adult life. Even before I was an adult, I think."

"Well, she said, referring to the computer printout in her hand and which she was clearly not going to share with Street, "the number belongs to August Street who resides at 1207 Justin Street, Cleveland, Ohio, and who—"

"That's wrong! There is no such person. I live at One Thirty-Eight Inverness Avenue in Lompoc, right down the road!"

"And whose former address <u>was</u> One Thirty-Eight Inverness Avenue, Lompoc, California?" The woman delivered each word clipped and as dry as a desert twig.

Street was back at the bank for his appointment with Ray Downs with minutes to spare. As Street approached the man's desk he could tell the news, whatever it was, wasn't good.

"Sit down, ah, Mr. Street. Right on time."

"Yes."

"I don't have good news for you."

"Why did I have the idea that you might say that?"

"I tried calling you this morning."

"I was running errands," Street said, irritably. "Police station, Social Security office, DMV."

"7335510? Is that the right number?"

"Yes, it is."

Downs dialed the number carefully, then leaned over his desk to hand the instrument to Street.

"The number you have dialed, 8057335510, is no longer in service and there is no new number. If you feel you have reached this number in error, hang up and dial again."

"I don't know what to say," Street muttered, slowly lowering the receiver from his ear. But he knew there was no mistake.

"We couldn't cancel your credit cards, Mr. Street, because they weren't stolen. At least that's what the man in Cleveland says. He claims you've been impersonating him for years. He has all of the other documents you say are yours, too. Do you have a lawyer, Mr. Street?" Downs asked.

"Yes."

"I mean a good one. A criminal lawyer. Know what I think? Hell, I'm sure of it. You're the victim of identity theft. Fastest growing crime in America. And you know something else? The police won't even take a report about it. It crosses jurisdictional lines and it usually comes down to he said, she said. Sometimes it can take years to get straightened out."

"Not this time," Street said, almost under his breath. "It's my death warrant."

Chapter 4

It had been an exhausting day for Prime Minister Waldon, made especially so by the strain to make the day seem anything but exhausting. It is essential for all trade officials and politicians at the ambassadorial ranks to exude rock-solid confidence, and that appearance is not only for the benefit of those with whom they are dealing, but also to anchor the Crown's never-retreat position. Waldon had "dropped in" to give his regards to his old friend Sir Frederick Burckhardt, minister of foreign trade, who was in shirtsleeves negotiations with Vlada Luskatov, Russia's ambassador for foreign trade. The cocktail party to which Clay and Margaret Waldon were invited was going on at the opposite end of 7 Kensington Palace Gardens, so there was no reason why Waldon should not pop in and say hello.

"Enjoying yourself, Freddy?" Waldon asked his trade minister.

"Are they giving you plenty of vodka over there? I could use about a quart of it right now," Burckhardt said, his receding forehead glistening.

"You're beginning to sound bitter, old man. Not like you."

Burckhardt was a hard-nosed onetime rugby player who, legend had it, once broke a striker's ankle with his nose. The name Burckhardt, Freddy was proud to relate, meant *stone* in German, and Frederick Burckhardt might have used the literal translation to shape his life. Of average height, Burckhardt had the heart of the British lion and the guts of a Liverpool street fighter. He never lied, so far as Waldon knew, and he wasted little time in idle conversation. Burckhardt was left-handed. Waldon had once read a magazine article that said left-handed people had a distinct advantage over the rest of the world, and true or not, Waldon had watched Burckhardt in utter fascination while the man did mathematical calculations in his head.

"Not bitter. Not at all. The sons of bitches are leaning on us for whatever reasons they have. I've never liked them, you know."

"Hush."

"They're like dogs," Burckhardt said, ignoring the prime minister's admonition of caution. "If you touch them while they're sleeping, they'll bite you. If you go near their food they'll bite you. If you try to reach out to them in kindness they'll take your bloody hand off. Or they might not. They have no hearts. They act only out of self preservation."

"That's why you're the man to deal with them, Freddy. No heart of your own." Waldon dropped his hand easily on Burckhardt's shoulder but did not get the expected release of tension nor hint of smile from his trade minister. "Sorry, Freddy, I'm just trying to be funny."

Burckhardt shook his head as he leaned against the edge of a window sill, facing the prime minister in their small corner of the conference room. Behind them was a large table around which men and women of the trade ministry tended to piles of papers and portfolios. There were any number of small conversations rippling up and around the table where items were discussed with the Russians and numbers attachéd to each. Millions of metric tons of crude and trillions of cubic feet of gas were tossed about with prices quoted in pounds, dollars, Yuen, marks, and euros.

"I could use a laugh."

"Is it all that bad in here?" Waldon asked, lowering his voice even more.

"Hmm."

"Hmm? What do you mean, leaning?"

"I don't know. Maybe it's just me. I'm tired of all this stuff, really."

Waldon waited a protracted minute while Burckhardt put his thoughts together.

"This Luskatov, fellow. Know him?" Burckhardt asked.

"We've met, of course. A hockey player, as I recall."

"Yes, Olympic team twice. Probably doesn't remember the last time he chewed food with his own teeth. So many stitches on his face you could use it for a road map."

"And?"

"I've known Vlada for only three years but he is uniformly vicious. A Russian dog that I could always count on to bite my hand. Now there's no bite. I have to ask myself why."

"So?" the prime minister replied. "What does he do?"

"Passive aggressive. Lots of aggression, lots of passive."

"He won't make a deal on our terms?"

"He won't make a deal, period. We had this business all but done months ago. You know my technique of trading. Take care of the little things first, get them out of the way, and get on to the thornier issues later when we all have a position to protect. Everybody knows I work this way."

"It makes sense."

"Yes, I think it does. But nothing is working. Not the little things. And how do we get to the big things without the stepping stones? I suggest, he listens, nods. And nothing."

"No disagreements?"

"No. And you see, without disagreements there are no positions and where there are no positions, no deals will be made—not big, not small."

"There you are, Clay," the familiar voice of Alexander Khoklov, could be heard distinctly above the incessant murmur of table dialogue. "What are you British bulldogs planning, eh? Plotting against the poor peasants of the North?"

Sasha, as Khoklov insisted he be called by his circle of friends, which Waldon was tacitly invited to join, was a Princeton underclassman when Waldon, an Oxford graduate student, gave his first of five lectures on the period of European Enlightenment. Khoklov had insinuated himself near Waldon that evening at the local drinking house and introduced himself. He was never out of arm's reach, as Waldon remembered later, until Waldon returned to England two months later.

Khoklov was a large man, almost three hundred pounds, a state of corpulence he once confided to Waldon was the result of an unfortunate medical condition. Khoklov was well known to SIS, of course, and their arcane medical experts advanced the opinion that Khoklov's obesity was a product of simple gluttony. Luckily for the Russian ambassador he was six feet, six inches in height, so that if that amount of weight could be carried with grace, Sasha was the one who could do it. He was also, Waldon noted, left-handed.

"Sasha," Waldon choked out the word. He felt a chill; his knees became momentarily shaky as the Russian seemed to have bored through their skulls into their brains. His face must have shown embarrassment because the Russian ambassador immediately threw his long arms around Waldon's shoulders.

"What have I said, Clay? Did I interrupt you and Sir Frederick at a bad time?" he clapped Burckhardt on the back with a free hand. "I only wanted to take you away from work. This is Friday!"

The Russian ambassador, in conversation, had a way of mocking British titles. Burckhardt cringed at his form of address.

"Tuesday," Waldon corrected, without thinking.

"Ah. You see? We worked right through the weekend. Come, Clay. You, too, Sir Freddy. Put away the pencils and let's have a drink and something for our blood."

"A transfusion?" Burckhardt asked, unamused.

"Caviar. It turns the blood bright red, you know."

"No. I didn't know that," Waldon said. He turned toward Burckhardt. "I'll get out of your hair, Freddy. Why don't you take Sasha's suggestion and chuck it all early?"

Burckhardt did not answer with words but with a knowing glance at the prime minister.

"Yes, Sir Frederick," Khoklov said, his lips upturned but his eyes not smiling. "Go home and read a book. Relaxes and enlightens, I find."

"Jordan remains in a high state of emergency," Brooks revealed to Prime Minister Waldon while only glancing at the notes he had made in the margins of the neatly typed daily intelligence briefing SIS delivered to Number 10 Downing Street. It was customary for at least two other PM staff to be present during these briefings, usually to record the meetings and, if necessary, execute follow-up assignments. But this morning there was only the prime minister and Brooks. "King Abdullah and the royal family were moved out of the capital last week for their own safety. Jordan's JID intelligence service was somehow tapped into The Falluja Returnees, as they call themselves, but they are part of al Qaeda."

"Saudi Arabia has declared its own state of emergency in the north due to Intel information that the kingdom is being overrun with al Qaeda aiming at overthrowing the royal family. Nothing new in their goal, Prime Minister, but the intensity with which they are going about their business is noteworthy," Brooks pointed out.

"Hmm."

Brooks hesitated in case Waldon had something more profound he wished to add. There being nothing forthcoming, Brooks turned to another page of the report.

"We have a communication from American Department of State intelligence sources who say they do not see Abbas enjoying a long career in his newly elected post. Hardly an insightful piece of information except that it appears that President Bordine will not deal with the man. He has no intention of inviting him to the White House or consulting with him in any way above second or third consular level. He is, not to put too fine a point on it, a dead fish."

Again Brooks paused over his notes, skipping ahead to something more dramatic, at least an item that Brooks felt carried exceptional intelligence gravis.

"The Chinese-Russian relationship seems to be heating up, Prime Minister. Plans for those countries to cooperate in building an air superiority fighter aircraft that will meet or exceed the specifications of the American F-22 are proceeding beyond the planning stages. We've spent considerable time and pushed our best Asian assets to—"

"Christopher," the prime minister interrupted, his leg bouncing nervously under his desk, a pencil twiddling between his hands, "what is being done about the *Raven* matter?"

"Do you mean specifically, Prime Minister?"

"Yes. No, not the minutiae, but are you progressing on that assignment? What have you been able to come up with?" The prime minister's eyes were well focused on C.

"We're working assiduously on the problem, of course, Prime Minister, even to the point where I'm forced to delegate far more work in other areas than I'm comfortable doing, but your directions were forcefully framed—"

"That's exactly right, C. Go on."

"It's the old bad news, good news tale at this point. Bad news is that we've come across nothing that disproves the premise of the book and, I might say, we've come across circumstantial evidence to support the story. But one would expect that in any yarn that is intended for an elevated audience, so to speak. We're certainly not alarmed. It's just that we can't yet roll out a banner in Kensington Park with the word 'fraud' painted upon it."

"And the good news?"

"I hope I haven't enunciated that part too dramatically."

"Well, whatever it is, what is it?"

"We've, ah, contained various people who might be able to, ah, help us unravel the details."

"Contained."

"Yes, sir."

For some very long moments, a pendulum clock was the only sound in the prime minister's office. The two men sat listening to it, their hearts near to its meter. As it seemed to become louder to their ears the prime minister cleared his throat.

"I see."

Of course he did not see nor did he want to see. He only wanted to be reassured and Christopher Brooks had done that.

"Things are not going well with the Russians," Waldon said, drumming the fingers of one hand lightly on his desk.

"In what way, Prime Minister?"

"I'm not sure. Not sure at all. But something is going on. About that, I am completely sure. Their attitude is, well, quite dark."

"Ah. And you believe their attitude is being shaped by the Raven Operation?"

"I think it is more than possible."

Brooks waited.

"Press on, C, will you?"

Brooks knew the meeting was over. He closed his notebook and rose to his feet. The prime minister, remained uncharacteristically seated as Brooks let himself out of the room.

The elderly gentleman with a full head of snow-white hair wore corduroy pants tucked into his mud boots as he fed the swans at St. Margret's Loch. He shivered slightly under a constant drizzle despite wearing an undershirt, a cableknit Scottish wool sweater and a rain slicker.

"Come, darling," he wooed a bashful swan with a piece of dark rye bread. "Here princess. That's it, little sweet." The secret way to a swan's heart was the addition of chopped walnuts to the bread dough. She swam toward him but in the wake of the male swan who was not only larger than the princess but determined to be treated first and fullest.

"There you go, King Ghotha," the old man said, as he tossed a goodly sized chunk of bread to one side and a bit away from the course of the princess. "Eat well, you old honker." Then, turning back to his favorite bird now just a few feet from him, he tossed her choice morsels. She might well have eaten from his hand but he respected the strength of the swans' beaks and did not relish the thought of bruised or even torn fingers. The birds were beautiful enough to appreciate from where he crouched. He broke his second loaf of bread into smaller pieces and strewed them onto the water for the other swans and miscellaneous birds who were making their way shoreward to join the feast.

The man pushed himself to his full height with great effort, the pain from an arthritic joint taking its full toll in his tenth decade of life. He used a crude but strong stick to help himself from water's edge to the ridge above where he had parked his bicycle. There were times when a car was a tempting creature comfort but he believed that when he could no longer move his own weight by pedal he would die.

"Beg your pardon, sir..."

"Yes?" the old man reacted to a voice nearby. It was a rich Scottish brogue combined with the hoarse crackle of a long-term smoker. He had heard a car behind him disturb loose gravel and now he turned to see who it was that had parked nearby. He was a rawboned chap, not tall, but one of the first things one would notice was his very thick fingers and thumbs. The man had an oversized nose, turned bright red on a blustery day like this, and he produced a leather folder which, when opened, identified the man as Scotland Yard.

"Are you Edward Wiles?"

"Sorry, no. Looking for a white-haired bank robber, Constable?" the old man chuckled.

"No, sir, nothing of the sort. Er, the name would be...?"

"Coronet. Robert Lockhart Coronet," the man said with a slight nod of the head, as though punctuating a certainty.

"Er, would you mind showing me some identification, Mr. Coronet?"

"Wouldn't mind at all. If I had it, that is. When I'm out riding I take nothing but raisins for me and bread for the swans."

"I see," the constable said, retrieving a notebook from his pocket and a ball point pen from the inside of his well worn brown wool overcoat. "And your place of residence, Mr. Cornet?"

"I live at four zero nine Hope Terrace, number six," the man said.

"A fair piece from here, Mr. Coronet. Might I give you a lift home?"

"I have my bicycle, thank you."

"No trouble at all putting the bike in the back, sir. No trouble at all," the Constable responded.

The old man fixed the policeman square in the eye. "No trouble at all, eh? Tell me, constable...?"

"Furgus, sir. Roy Furgus."

"Furgus. Have I committed a crime? Am I under bloody arrest, then?"

"No, indeed not, sir."

"Well, in that case Constable Furgus, I'll continue on with my habit of exercise and if by any chance later in the day we should meet at four oh nine Hope Terrace do feel free to knock on number six and I'll be happy to show you my identification."

The old gentleman turned deliberately from the Scotland Yard man and, with an easy push, mounted his bicycle and pedaled toward the city. The Constable watched the old man slowly diminish into the gloom of late afternoon before stepping back into his car.

The old man was wet and chilled as he lowered his head into heavier rain, dropping his ten-speed bicycle into a lower gear. He estimated his trip time back to the city as slightly over an hour. He considered where he should go once there. He could stay at the Drummond House, he fancied. He had looked forward to a meal and pint at the Rat and Parrot pub but now he had to avoid any of his favorites. He briefly considered rescuing his research books at Canongate but rejected the idea at once. He had to assume it would be watched. He would leave Edinburgh first thing in the morning. A train from Waverly Station during rush hour would have been his first choice, but since returning to his apartment was now out of the question, he would first need to purchase a set of clothes in which to travel. Too bad, he thought. He would miss Edinburgh. Maybe it was time to visit the Continent.

Chapter 5

Street got one hundred seventy five dollars from Lompoc's lone pawn shop on a gold braid bracelet that Linda had given him years ago. He was not much of a jewelry man so he would not miss the bracelet, and he never wore an onyx ring that he dropped into his pocket. He could not return to his house because, he was told that morning by a deputy sheriff who arrived at his door, that the new owners were asking him to leave without violence.

New owners!

Intense fury rose in his gut but passed almost as quickly as he realized that the latest act of his intended removal from the face of the earth could have been predicted. If he had the power, that's how he might have done it.

He considered his next move as he sat at a city bus bench on H Street, a small suitcase nearby containing the bare essentials of an overnight stay. Suppose, he thought as warm sun and fresh air bathed his face, that he returned to the H. P. Carlisle Foundation with hat in hand. Suppose he prostrated himself before Bradley Wallis or whoever Wallis was acting on behalf of, and agreed to all of their demands. He would agree to disavow any facts contained in the book and sign whatever document they put in front of him. He might even get his old job back. The problem with that logic was that it was too late. They didn't need him anymore. They had the "real" August Street. In Cleveland. In fact, to reverse themselves at this stage of the game, to suddenly expunge that August Street and reinstate yet another August Street was much harder and far riskier than simply finishing off the final little detail: disappearing him.

Coming to that stunning conclusion, and there could be no other, caused Street to look around him 360 degrees. Was there even now a sniper on a rooftop placing him inside the crosshairs? He did not want to appear, even to himself, melodramatic, but after the years he had spent in and around the intelligence business, he was aware of the various ways to kill a human being without making a ripple in the surrounding social fabric. Well, then, to run or to fight back? Street cared little for the prospect of running. In the first place, it was not the kind of life he cared to live and in the second place, and more crucial, he believed in the end they would finish him off, probably sooner rather than later.

No, one had to fight back. And to win. But with what? Ironic but both he and "they" had as their goal in victory the same treasure. They had to discredit his book, while he had to prove it was true—or at least prove that the facts he had written were true, not necessarily the conclusions they presented. If these were the parameters of the game, he needed to provide himself with the necessary equipment to play. He would need to travel, mainly to Europe where his research had begun, and he would need to find people and records to support his original assertions contained in the book. He would need the accoutrements of the researcher, such as communications, transportation by air, automobile, rail, and he would need a new identity. If they were looking for August Street, the real one, he would have to make it hard for them. Most of all, he would need money. He shuddered at the irony. He had never taken the time to examine his net worth but he thought it was about two million dollars not counting the value of his home. But none of it was any longer his.

He wore designer jeans, Nike running shoes, a blue T-shirt with "Cornell" emblazoned in red letters across the front. He carried a fabric bag full of other clothing over his shoulder as he stepped from the bus on Interstate 10 in Indio. It was still early enough in the afternoon to begin his plan. He purposely did not shower. Instead he changed his running shoes for golf shoes with soft rubber cleats on their soles. He changed his Cornell T-shirt for a golf shirt and, because it was still 80 degrees outside, he carried only a cardigan sweater over one arm. Satisfied that he looked like a player, he left his room.

He waited most of an hour for a local bus. He had to transfer once, but the local line took him to within a quarter mile of the PGA West gated community.

He walked toward the golf course complex but turned away from the main entrance where security guards regulated auto traffic into the residence area. There were still homes in one stage or another of development and it was no problem to pass unnoticed through these lots and onto one of the five golf courses. He was quite familiar with them all, having, over the years, played each several times.

The later afternoon players were still finishing their games while August Street strolled through the electric cart service area and up the double flight of stairs to the clubhouse. PGA West was a semiprivate golf club but its members included an exclusive group who have preferential tee times, and private locker facilities for showers, spas, weight rooms, and the like. There was a sign on a door that said MEMBERS ONLY through which Street confidently walked, as though he belonged.

He stepped up to one of a dozen sparkling clean wash basins that sported expensive polished brass fixtures. Walls and cabinets were made of faux mahogany and burnished oak. Fresh cotton hand towels were stacked neatly in two locations within easy reach for members. Hair combs bathed in antiseptic solutions, razors, shaving creams, and aftershave lotions were placed at each wash basin. Street washed his hands and face, then walked rather slowly into the locker area. There were several members of the club who had recently arrived from playing the great game. Street chose one of them who appeared most like him in general size. The man he selected was about the same height as Street, his cheeks a bit fuller and with considerably less hair. He also appeared a bit heavier than Street, and seemed to be relieved to take the weight off his spiked feet. Street sat down a few feet away.

"Hi," the member said.

"Hi," Street said, feigning a tired smile.

"Which course did you play?" the member asked.

"Stadium," Street said, wiping his face with the white towel. "Too much for me."

The member laughed out loud, displaying gold teeth in the back of his mouth. "Hey, aren't they all?"

"I suppose so, but my club is a little more humane," Street said.

"Oh, you're not a member here?" the man asked, genially. In all of Street's years of playing various golf courses it was a pleasant fact that the members of private clubs went out of their way to extend a warm welcome to members of other private clubs.

"No. We're at the Valley Club in Santa Barbara," Street lied, easily. Dropping the name of the prestigious Valley Club had the desired effect as the man's eyebrows shot up.

"Never played the Valley Club but I've sure heard about it. They say it's beautiful. Tough, too, huh?"

"I think they're all tough. What's tough is getting the club on the ball. At least it is for me. Tim Cousins," Street said, extending his hand.

"Art Brightmeyer, Tim. Glad to know you," the man said, pleased to shake Street's hand. "So, what brings you out this way? Down here slumming with us poor folk?"

Brightmeyer hauled one leg up to the opposite knee where he could untie his shoe laces, an expanding stomach beginning to challenge his dexterity. Between Brightmeyer and Street was a folded bath towel.

"Actually I'm just tagging along with Pete and Craig. They're still out on the driving range playing for twenty bucks a shot. Closest to the one fifty yard flag." Street made a show of leaning back against the row of lockers, still too tired to begin undressing.

"That's kind of high rolling if you hit enough balls," Brightmeyer said, genuinely impressed.

"Not for those guys. I don't know how much Pete made producing *Murder and Housework*, but it had to be jillions. Just a guess," Street said, closing his eyes.

"Ah. Yeah, I've seen that show. What's Pete's last name?"

"Flescher."

"That's it! My wife never missed that show when it came on every Thursday night. To be real honest I didn't miss it very often myself. You in that business?" Brightmeyer asked.

"No. Investments. Like I said, I'm just tagging along with those guys. Known 'em for years. How about you, Art? Still working for a living?"

"Retired about two years now. I sold a steel fabricating business in Pasadena. Pasadena Wire and Iron. Ever heard of it?" Brightmeyer asked as he struggled with his socks. He pulled each of them inside out, nearly sliding off the plank bench.

"No, but that doesn't mean anything. I've been easing into retirement myself. Just looking after my own stuff."

"You look too young to be retired," Brightmeyer said.

"Thanks, Art. Truth is, my wife has got so much money I feel kind of silly wasting my time at work. I should spend that time with her."

"Hey, that's nice. That's what Irene and I are trying to do. We take a lot of cruises. We got a nice place down here, too, right in the community," Brightmeyer said, jerking his thumb over his shoulder to indicate their home was nearby.

Art Brightmeyer opened his locker. He stripped off his damp golf shirt and stepped out of his trousers, hanging them on a hook inside his locker. While he was doing this Street casually picked up the folded towel between them and began wiping his arms and face. Then, as Brightmeyer turned away from his locker standing quite naked, Street feigned embarrassment.

"Oh, hell, Art, was this your towel? I'm sorry, I wasn't even thinking... Let me get another one. Where do you keep them?"

"Don't be silly. I'll get it," Brightmeyer said, starting to walk away, then remembering that his locker was wide open with his personal possessions inside. He hesitated, glancing at Street who now had the large towel draped around his neck, his eyes half closed. Because it would be insulting to his new acquaintance to lock his locker for the few seconds he would be gone, Brightmeyer simply continued his short trek to the towel cache.

The naked country club member had hardly turned the corner around a row of lockers when Street reached into the locker and lifted Brightmeyer's wallet from the trousers. He dropped it quickly into his own pocket and resumed his position of languor on the oak bench. When Brightmeyer returned, a fresh towel now securely wrapped around his waist, it appeared Street had not moved.

"Why don't you join us for a drink, Art?" Street asked, looking up from his place on the bench.

"Well, Irene is playing tennis and—"

"Great. When she gets through she'll come over here, won't she? She can join us. I get tired of listening to these guys talk about movies. Television and movies. To be really honest with you, I'm a book reader, myself. I don't think Craig Wilson has ever read one."

"Craig Wilson? The actor in that cop series?"

"The same. Very nice guy. So is Pete, but I've heard all their stories." Street complained.

"Well I haven't! Irene would love that."

"Perfect," Street said, getting to his feet. "By the time you get out of the shower and get dressed they should be finished at the driving range. If they aren't I'll drag them in."

"Okay. Meet you at the bar," Brightmeyer said, tripping off toward the showers.

Street made his way upstairs, and walked purposefully to the bar. He leaned over and spoke into the bartender's ear, then continued through the lobby and out the front door of the clubhouse. In the portico he approached one of several young employees of the club dressed in white polo shirts and white shorts. There was a small armada of electric carts of all sizes used not only by golfers but also by employees to pick up newly arrived or departing players and their bags.

"I wonder if you could run me out to the gate?" he asked the bag boy.

"Yes, sir. Hop in," the white-clad young man said.

The run to the gate took only a couple of minutes. Street reached into his pocket and came out with a wallet that bulged pleasantly in the middle as did its former owner. Street extracted a twenty dollar bill for the bag boy as he stepped out of the cart. "Thanks."

"Thank you, sir," the lad said, turning his near-silent vehicle back toward the clubhouse.

Street had the cab driver take him directly to the Cabazon Indian Reservation between Palm Springs and Banning on Interstate 10. On the way to the casino floor he stopped at the souvenir shop and purchased the weakest pair of reading glasses he could find. He put them on as he crossed the casino to the main cashier's cage. When the person in front of him finished his business Street made sure the cashier had her attention fully on him when he took his wallet from his pocket. He opened it deliberately on the counter, allowing the cashier to see that it was fat with credit cards, a driver's license, and some cash. He took some time sorting through his plastic until he found an American Express card. He dropped it in front of the cashier.

"Five thousand," he said. "Two in chips, three thousand cash. Put it on the card."

"Do you have one of our preferred player's cards, Mr. Brightmeyer?"

"No. This is my first time here. Can I get your card later? I'm kind of anxious to play."

The cashier examined the no-limit American Express card, then said "Driver's license, please, Mr. Brightmeyer?"

Street removed the license from his wallet and passed it to the cashier. The cashier compared the photo with the man standing before her. "I like your old glasses better," she said, smiling.

"So did I. My wife didn't," Street said, conscious of perspiration that was beginning to soak into his golf shirt under his arms.

"One moment, sir," she said.

Stepping off of her elevated chair she turned toward a man wearing a dark blazer and necktie as well as a brass nameplate over the pocket. He glanced at the American Express card, then at Street, then scribbled what might have been his initials on a small piece of paper before turning nonchalantly toward another part of the cashier cage.

"Hundred-dollar and fifty-dollar chips, Mr. Brightmeyer?"

"Just fine," Street said before his throat went dry.

The cashier expertly counted out the cash and chips in the denominations requested by Street. Street assumed that he would be watched by the casino's security personnel located, among other places, in the ceiling spaces above the gaming floor, but he did not look up. Affecting a certain disregard for both as he directed his gaze out at the tables of the casino, Street dropped the cash into his jacket pocket and, holding $100 denomination chips in his two hands, headed for a blackjack table. He chose a table that required a $10 minimum bet. There were too few players at the $25 minimum tables, only two of which were open. He took a seat among three other players and dropped a $50 chip in front of him. On the first deal he caught an ace and a five and went down for double, dropping another $50 chip on top of the first. When it was his turn he looked at his down card and it was a four. The dealer hit his own pair of sixes with a third six, raking in Street's bet as he picked up the cards.

Street played at the same table leaving his bets in the mean $50 range. He purposely hit middle numbers like thirteen, fourteen, fifteen, thus helping the dealer along on his edge. Street had dropped several hundred dollars but it had not gone fast enough for his comfort. He anticipated that the real Art Brightmeyer would wait for Street and his imaginary friends for at least an hour before giving up on them. Chances were good that he would be putting all of his drinks and food on his club membership account, thus having no reason to reach for his wallet while he and Irene waited. At the end of the hour, Street assumed, Brightmeyer would miss his wallet. He would retrace his steps of the day, guessing that he had either left it in his golf bag or possibly in the electric cart. He would be irritated but not alarmed.

Brightmeyer would begin the process of searching for the misplaced wallet. He would locate the golf cart that he drove today and search through it. Next, he would check with the club's lost and found. It might even occur to him that the wallet had been dropped somewhere out on the golf course, but it was now dark and there was almost certainly no hope of finding it until morning.

Street had bought valuable time but his business in the casino was not yet finished. He still had more money to lose before he could slip out without the eyes of the security people following him. This time he took a chair at the $25 minimum table. It took him a little over an hour to lose the twelve hundred dollars in chips leaving him with three thousand in cash.

Street used a Visa credit card to rent a mid-size car off the main lobby of the casino. The name he signed was Art Brightmeyer. He drove along

Interstate 10 at moderate speed, neither too slow nor too fast, not wanting to draw attention from police cruisers. At El Monte he pulled into a strip mall that contained, among other businesses, a chain-operated drug store. He bought hair tint, a hair dryer, shaving gear, and a pair of thinning scissors, and he selected yet another pair of 1.00 power reading glasses. This time he used care to buy those with frames that more closely resembled Art Brightmeyer's driver's license photo.

He stayed on the 10, now called the Santa Monica Freeway, arriving in West Los Angeles before midnight. He checked into a hotel off the 405 Freeway, leaving instructions with the night clerk to wake him at 6:00 A.M. Inside his second-floor room Street emptied out the entire contents of Brightmeyer's wallet. There was four hundred fifty-six dollars inside which, added to the three thousand in his coat pocket, provided Street with maneuvering room. But he was after much more. Spreading the cards out on the table he found a driver's license, a health insurance card complete with plan number, a private pilot's license, five personal cards that revealed Art Brightmeyer's name, home address, and telephone number, and three credit cards, all from different issuing credit grantors. There was a debit/ATM card as well. Street's initial urge was to destroy the ATM card since it was of no use if he did not have the PIN number, but on second thought he decided to keep it. There was a photograph of a woman Street took to be Irene, but it could also be a picture of Brightmeyer's daughter, if he had one. Better not to take a chance on complications, Street thought. He burned the picture and he burned the American Express credit card. He kept everything else.

He diluted the bottle of hair rinse even more than the directions called for, then applied it vigorously to his hair. While it was still wet Street used a safety razor to trim back the hairline on his forehead to approximate Brightmeyer's. He used the electric blower to dry his hair. Looking at it appraisingly in the mirror, it appeared to him about as close to the picture as he could get. Add to that the fact that government photos were less than perfect and he believed he could pass in both color and cut. He used the thinning scissors on the very top of his head with several extra bites on the back and sides. He combed the sheared pieces out from his scalp and looked again. It looked out of balance to him, one side being thinner than the other, but the pattern of baldness was not always symmetric.

Street returned to the front desk and asked a semi-alert night clerk for a $20 calling card. He found a public telephone in the lobby and, using the dialing access number on the calling card, dialed Westbrook Claridge's direct line at the H. P. Carlisle Foundation. As expected, Westbrook's phone was answered electronically and his recorded voice invited the caller to leave a message.

"Wes," Street said without identifying himself. "Call me back at this number when you get to work. Use a public phone." Street gave the number of the hotel, added his room number, then replaced the handset. It was possible, though unlikely, that Westbrook's telephone was being monitored at H. P. Carlisle Foundation. He and Wes were not known to be friends. If social connections were to be the criteria for tracing Foundation calls in hopes of finding Street, Wes would be near the bottom on the list. Street badly needed rest and the bed in his room would provide it. The risk seemed worth taking.

Street was sleeping soundly when, as he had calculated, Wes returned his call at 5:00 A.M.

"Wes?"

"Yeah. I'm at a doughnut shop buying doughnuts when we've got a zillion of 'em at the strip mine. Not too cool, huh?"

"I need your address."

"Dropping by?"

"Maybe, but first I need a place to send mail."

"Got it," Westbrook said, repeating his home address and zip code.

"Thanks, Wes. I'd, uh, appreciate it if you could keep this conversation just between—"

"That guy in your book. MacQueen..."

"What about him?"

"He's dead."

Like two low-voltage electrical wires touched, Street's stomach muscles spasmed. And just as quickly, his heart hurt.

"How?" he said.

"I don't know, but I can tell you something interesting. The guy hardly hit the ground before his body was bagged and removed. Four EMTs arrived in three minutes. Like they were parked down the street."

"MacQueen," Street said, remembering every crease and scar on the man's craggy face.

"It's funny, isn't it, August, that the news about an old man who owns a pub in Wales comes on a satellite downlink to the foundation on a Level 5?"

Level 5 was the highest level of top secret message transmissions.

Street needed sleep but would not get it. He could only think of Rose Hawkins who still lived, he hoped, in Burton Heath, England. Having lost his notes and his computer to the burglary of his house, Street would have to find her telephone number by overseas information. He pulled on a pair of pants, wore shoes without socks and a lightweight jacket with a T-shirt in which he had been sleeping, and returned to the lobby of the hotel. He bought $50 worth of calling card time and approached the public telephone with dread.

It took him thirty minutes of working with three operators to get what he thought was the correct number for Hawkins at Burton Heath, although he could not rationalize the number given him by British information and her rural address as he remembered it. Nor was the telephone listed under Rose Hawkins but rather a man's name. With nothing to lose he followed the dialing instructions and heard the telephone ring on the other end. After the phone had rung six times he was about to replace the handset when he heard it answered.

"Hello?"

There was an eight-hour time differential between Pacific Coast time and Britain. No need to apologize for waking the party in England.

"Yes," Street said, raising his voice slightly, the subconscious reaction to a very distant connection. "This is August Street calling. Is this Rose Hawkins?"

There was a discernable hesitation on the other end of the line.

"This is Mrs. Hawkins, yes. Who did you say this was?"

"August Street. Rose… Mrs. Hawkins, surely you must remember…"

"You must have the wrong number. I'm sorry," the woman's voice betrayed the sound of stress, the effort of speaking somewhat forced, breathing impaired.

"Ah, yes, apparently that is so. I'm calling from America. I only wanted to tell Archie's daughter that she is in great danger. She should immediately return from whence she came. A long time ago. Immediately. If you see her would you tell her that?"

"Yes," the word came to him almost as a gasp. Then the line went dead.

Chapter 6

After a nervous shower and a bran muffin with tasteless lobby coffee, Street drove north from the hotel on the 405 to the Olympic Boulevard off-ramp and turned west. He had only a few blocks to travel before finding Butler Street. Despite the early hour there was a large number of people waiting for the Social Security Administration to open its doors. His fellow waitees were mostly Latino, with only a few Caucasians sprinkled in. When the doors opened, Street, now knowing the drill, pulled a numbered ticket from a roll suspended from a wall and had a seat. While he waited he filled out a form that he knew would be required. It took him only an hour to be called.

"I need to replace my Social Security card," he said to the middle-aged man on the other side of the counter. He pushed across his completed form.

"Did you lose it?" the public servant said as he scanned the form for errors. Apparently there were none.

"I guess so. I haven't seen the card for thirty years."

Street's candor brought a tight smile to the Social Security employee.

"What's the number?"

Street told him the number that was contained in the stolen wallet. The clerk entered the number into the federal computer.

"Name?" the man asked.

"Arthur Brightmeyer," Street replied.

"Identification? Driver's license will do."

"No problem," Street said, retrieving Brightmeyer's license from the wallet.

He passed it over the counter. The Social Security man hardly looked at the card or the photo before pushing it back toward Street. The clerk tickled the computer keys again, then rose from his chair to retrieve the printer's output.

"Here you go," he said.

Street examined the page. "You're going to mail me the card?"

"Within two weeks," he was assured.

"Send it to this address in Virginia. I'll be there for several months," Street said, passing Wes Claridge's address to the civil employee. "Also, do you have anything I can use in the meantime? Uh, the bank needs a document that shows my Social Security number."

Another entry was made on the keyboard and again the government worker retrieved a work product from the printer. Street read it. At the top of the page the document said:

> Social Security ADMINISTRATION. Social Security NUMBER VERIFICATION.
>
> OUR RECORDS INDICATE THAT Social Security NUMBER 544385121 IS ASSIGNED TO ARTHUR SEBASTIAN BRIGHTMEYER.
>
> YOUR Social Security CARD IS THE OFFICIAL VERIFICATION OF YOUR Social Security NUMBER.
>
> THIS PRINTOUT DOES NOT VERIFY YOUR RIGHT TO WORK IN THE UNITED STATES.

He folded the document carefully. "I appreciate your help," he said, sincerely.

Street returned to the 405 Freeway and drove south to Washington Boulevard, a street that started at water's edge in Marina del Rey and ran through south Los Angeles almost to Whittier. Street needed to drive only three miles from the Social Security office to the California Department of Motor Vehicles on Washington. He stood in another line.

He was number seventeen in line when he arrived but things moved along apace. When it was his turn he faced a pleasant young lady who had not yet been on duty long enough to become soured by auto supplicants.

"Hi, I lost my driver's license. Bet you haven't heard that one before," Street said, in an effort to calm his larcenous nerves.

"Only about twenty times a day. More on Mondays," she said, then rose from her stool behind the counter and fetched California State form DL44.

"Fill this in," she said, "then come back here to my station. Next, please."

The form was straightforward. He placed an X in front of *Replacement*, then entered the name of Art Brightmeyer in the following block along with date of birth, copying directly from Brightmeyer's license which he held in the palm of his hand. It took no more than five minutes to complete the form. He returned to the young lady's workstation where the form was checked and the computer verified the information on his new application. He was required to pay $25.

"Step over here, please, Mr. Brightmeyer," the lady said, leading him down the counter to an area where, at her direction, his photo was snapped. Again at the DMV employee's direction, he signed the document on the bottom and, within minutes, was given his "new" driver's license.

That same evening he boarded a redeye flight to Washington, D.C., the ticket paid for in cash.

He found the key to Westbrook's first-floor apartment, as promised, in a flower planter. It was probably the first place a burglar would look for a way into the place so Street did not expect that Wes was living in a high-crime area. Like a lot of bachelor pads this one was sparse. Furnishings appeared to be bought for the purpose of comfort only, with no interest in color coordination or theme. The apartment was on one end of a condominium complex that overlooked a quiet street. The view from the living room was at least 180 degrees. He dropped his travel bag near a small, gas-assisted fireplace and quickly toured the other rooms.

A large counter surrounded most of the kitchen. Four stools provided a barlike atmosphere for serving drinks or food. Two bedrooms and two bathrooms were located in the rear of the place, each large and comfortable. After removing his jacket and pouring a large glass of tomato juice from Wes's refrigerator, Street returned to the library room. Wes had not locked his computer, although he had denied access to many files by use of passwords, so Street sat down to compose a letter to Linda. In the note he related all of the facts of the jam they found themselves in, omitting the part about stealing someone else's identity. Nor did he describe where he was or where he was going other than to say he was safe for the time being.

He explained that certain people in high positions in various governments were clearly dedicated to silencing him as they were equally devoted to the task of discrediting his book. While he did not want to alarm Linda, he also did not want to mislead her about the danger she might be in. It could be, he said, that since she was in Canada and out of active touch with him, "they" would leave her alone except to watch her. She would not be able to communicate with him, nor would he be in touch with her until this thing, whatever it was, was finished. He advised her not to go anywhere with people she did not know, not to go out alone at night, and stick to well-traveled places when she moved around outside the house—and, if possible, get a roommate.

Street assumed Linda was staying with her mother, Helen, age seventy-three, but when he had finished writing he addressed the letter in care of one of Linda's two sisters. He stamped the envelope then placed that envelope into a larger one onto which he affixed the address of the Postmaster, Washington, D.C.

He was extremely anxious to get to Europe but he needed money and documents. The first thing he did was to speak to a customer service representative at a nationally known outdoors clothing company. He ordered two sleeping bags and a large tent, the total for which was $572.49. For payment he gave the service person Brightmeyer's credit card number and was asked to hold. Within a few seconds the salesperson was back on line to say that the number was not good, that the account had been closed. Street apologized and said that he had mistakenly used an old card. He said he would call back soon with the new account number, and hung up the telephone.

So the real Art Brightmeyer had finally closed out his accounts.

In Westbrook's kitchen Street found a number of *Washington Post* newspapers, the most recent of which was a day old. That didn't matter. He found the classified section and with very little searching located just the advertisement he was looking for.

Credit Repair. Flat Rate. Proven results. Same day service. Turn your life around. Today!

In addition to a telephone number there was an office address. Street tore the advertisement out of the newspaper and put it into his pocket. It was still early enough in the day to begin his credit repair business. The distance from Wes's apartment in Manassas was only thirty-five miles.

Personal and Business Credit Repair was located in Suite D on the second floor of a strip mall on the edge of the city. In a breezeway that bisected the mall with a dry cleaners on one side and a liquor store on the other, cluttered with fast food containers and ice cream wrappers, was an elevator door. There was also a set of stairs behind a fire door. Calculating that the stairs would be faster than a hydraulic screwlift elevator car, Street chose the stairs. Someone had tried to minimize the graffiti tattooed onto the stairway walls by covering them with even more paint but did not always choose matching colors. The net result might have been Salvador Dali's first mural, done at age two.

Suite D was easy to find, its faux oak door at the end of the hall was out of place among cinderblock construction. Street opened it without knocking. Inside was a small office occupied by a secretary's desk, a cheap photo reproduction of a Yankee clipper ship, an indoor plant with plastic leaves, all provided, Street guessed, by a rental agency. There was but a single chair in the outer office.

Behind the desk was an overweight girl who looked to be around age thirty, wearing hiphugger pants and an abbreviated top, which would have exposed her navel were it not riding on a roll of fat over the pants and pointed downward out of Street's view. Her hair was a neglected red that was allowed to flow around but not hide large plastic loop earrings. A desk plate announced that her name was Felicity Lourdes. Felicity's desk was completely bare of anything that looked like work except for the computer terminal on which she was surfing the Net.

"Hi," the girl chirped as Street closed the door behind him.

"Hi," he responded. "Is the manager in?"

The girl's eyelids moved almost imperceptibly behind a flash of suspicion.

"He's busy right now. Would you like to fill out one of our forms?" she said.

"Not really. What's his name?"

Felicity hesitated just long enough to assess whether Street might be an investigator of some kind. His faded jeans and open collared shirt indicated nothing. People wore whatever they needed to wear to get their jobs done. She evidently decided that Street was an acceptable risk.

"Guy Virgil," she said.

"I'd like to see Mr. Virgil. My name is Art Brightmeyer."

"If this is about your personal or business credit report, Mr. Brightmeyer, I can help you—"

"If Mr. Virgil is too busy to see me right now I'll go somewhere else."

Felicity's eyes narrowed, conveying to him that what she was about to do was done only in the spirit of bending over backward for a customer. She spun her wheeled chair half around as she pushed herself out from under her desk. With this thrust against inertia she rose to her feet and opened a door behind her, disappearing inside. She was back shortly with a benevolent smile on her face.

"Go right in, Mr. Brightmeyer," she said, stumbling over the last name. Street decided it didn't matter.

Guy Virgil was near one side or another of forty, wore a gray pinstriped suit that might have been made from real wool but not in this country. He wore a necktie that Street hoped was not acetate because they exploded when lit and Guy Virgil was a smoker. Like his ashtray, his lips were full. He almost no hair on the top of his head, leaving a damp wreath of curly brown frizz above the ears. Virgil stared at Street from behind thick plastic glasses, remaining seated as he, like Felicity, attempted to make a snap judgement of the man before him. He did not offer his hand nor did August Street.

"So, Mister ah, Brightmeyer?"

"That's right," Street responded. Virgil spoke in a high voice, but it was neither squeaky nor particularly unpleasant. He sounded rather like Marlon Brando in his early movies.

"Okay, Brightmeyer. So what can I do for you?"

"I read your ad in the newspaper," Street began.

"Yeah? Which one?"

"Which ad or which newspaper?"

Virgil chuckled in appreciation. "We only got one ad, Mr. Brightmeyer. We're a low-overhead business here, passing on our savings to customers."

"That's good to hear. *Washington Post*," Street said, producing the small piece of newsprint from his pocket. Virgil hardly glanced at it.

"All right. You're at the right place. You must have a problem."

"I do, indeed, Mr. Virgil. Somebody stole my identity. They took my wallet, my bank account, my car…" Street opened up his hands to indicate everything. Guy Virgil's thick eyebrows shot upward.

"Heavy," he said.

"Yes, well, luckily I recovered some of the documents. I was able to get my California driver's license replaced and my Social Security card. But of course I had to close down my credit cards. And I still can't access the money in my personal bank accounts."

"Because?"

"Good question, Mr. Virgil. It's complicated."

"These kinds of things are always complicated," Virgil said, waiting.

"Well, the other man, the one who stole my identity, is still in California pretending to, ah, be me. Still."

"It's your word against his?"

"That's right."

"Real common."

"So I gather."

"You want us to help. The problem is that the other guy, the one who stole your identity, is in California, like you say. I know you're in the right because you told me you were. But, it isn't like we can go out to the Coast and, ah, convince him that he should return your possessions. It could be done that way, but it'd be very expensive."

"Naturally, like any consumer, I'm looking for ways to save money," Street agreed.

Virgil interlaced his fingers and rested them on his stomach as he leaned back in his all-vinyl swivel chair. And said nothing.

"I have to travel. As soon as possible. To do that I need credit cards. Can you help?"

Virgil remained motionless for several extended seconds while he continued to appraise his new, potential customer.

"What do you do for a living, Mr. Brightmeyer?"

"I'm self-employed."

"Sure about that?"

"I'll make this as straightforward as possible for you, Mr. Virgil. I'm not a cop, not an investigator, I don't work for the government or any agency. As of the moment I'm unemployed."

Virgil inhaled deeply as though he were about to jump into a January lake.

"Let me have your wallet," he said, holding out his hand.

Without hesitation Street gave it to him. He said nothing as Virgil emptied it entirely of its contents. He noted with a fleeting smile Street's new driver's license, his temporary Social Security number. He took his time examining all of the other cards, one of which he held up to light shining through one of his two small office windows. There was about five hundred dollars in bills, Street having held back one thousand still in his luggage. Virgil paid no particular attention to the cash, merely riffling the bills with his thumb.

"You changed your place of residence from California to a local one?"

"Yes."

"So your I.D. and Social Security cards will arrive here pretty soon?"

"That's right."

"You make out a police report yet?"

"I reported the theft of all my stuff in California but the police weren't interested. They said that they wouldn't investigate, anyway, so a report was a waste of time," Street said.

"That's a fact, Mr. Brightmeyer, that's a fact. But this time your going to report it to the police and you're going to fill out a form and sign it. Tomorrow morning, you're going downtown to D.C. Metro police. They're at 300 Indiana Avenue NW," Virgil said, scribbling the address on a yellow Post-it pad and handing it over to Street. "When you get to the desk ask for Sergeant Dean Minor. There are two Sergeant Minors so make sure you get Dean Minor. If he's out, wait for him. Get the form from him, fill it out, and make sure you give it back to him. Understand?"

Street nodded.

"See, once you've registered a report of identity theft then it damn sure is your word against the other guy's word. The credit card companies and the retail credit reporting agencies are going to check with the police. If you have a complaint already on file, we can roll. But if you just say somebody stole your stuff and you didn't bother to make out a police report the credit card folks are going to think you're the bad guy. We don't want that to happen. Mistake like that."

"For sure," Street said.

"This'll take a few days. Hope you weren't figuring on hopping a plane tomorrow," Virgil said.

"Guess not."

"You figuring to leave the country?"

"Yes. I have urgent business in Europe," Street said.

"Hmm. You'll need a passport."

It was Street's turn to be mildly surprised. "You don't happen to keep a drawer full of blanks in there, do you?" Street nodded his head toward the only file cabinet in the room.

Virgil's face soured, but only slightly. "Something like that."

"The price goes up."

"Sure."

"How much for everything?"

"To turn your credit cards back on, six thousand dollars, Mr. Brightmeyer. I add a passport that works, another five thousand. If we want special delivery, it's another three thousand. See, then we got to have somebody walk everything through. Want my advice? Take the special delivery. It's a bargain at fifteen thousand."

"Adds up to fourteen thousand."

Bemused, Virgil did not blink.

"But I wasn't a math major in college," Street conceded. He withdrew the cash from his wallet. "Need a down payment, Mr. Virgil?"

"Hey," Virgil said, laying on the patois of a crime figure, "what do we look like, here? Some kinda fly-by-night joint?"

"Not at all," Street said, rising to his feet and offering his hand across the desk.

"You remind me of someone my brother went to Yale law school with," Virgil said.

"I never went to law school. Do you even have a brother?"

"Nope."

Virgil opened the door for Street. "But I've seen you somewhere. Right? So, tell me where."

Street considered. His face was shown from time to time on the inside dust covers of books. He had also appeared occasionally on television, mostly obscure, public programming. He had never written a bestseller. In a short period of time he had come to trust Virgil, if that was his real name. But he thought it might be best for all concerned, including Virgil, to keep his real name buried.

"Doesn't matter, Guy. Maybe someday we can have a drink."

"Take your money, leave your wallet. You'll get it back."

Chapter 7

Steven Dietrich was a West Coast boy, if he could still claim that warm self-description in his mid life, but he had spent two years in Boston on the campus of Harvard during his graduate studies. There were more than ninety colleges and universities in Boston, so it was said, like the number of golf courses found in Palm Springs. From UCLA he had been drawn to Harvard for his graduate work based on the reasoning that if one wanted to shoot crap the place to go was Las Vegas where there were a lot of crap tables. But Dietrich had spent the past three days in New Haven, Connecticut, on the campus of Yale university. Yale had been his grandfather's choice.

There he looked up the class of 1937, the one his grandfather should have been in but wasn't. It was almost as though he name had been expunged from the records. But Steven Dietrich picked up a name that made a connection with his grandfather. That name was Warren Alsop.

With some difficulty Dietrich was able to locate a telephone number and address for the man whom he believed knew his grandfather in college. Dietrich was put through to Mr. Alsop and asked if he could speak with him. Mr. Alsop was curious and gracious enough to grant an interview. When Dietrich arrived at the Carlyle Hotel on Madison where he was staying in New York there was a telephone message waiting for him in his room.

"Mr. Dietrich," the female voice said from the recording machine, "Mary Ellen Paige, calling. I urged uncle Warren to postpone his visit with you this evening but he wouldn't listen to me. He isn't well at all and he is eighty-six years old. I would ask you not to make your visit with him a very long one for that reason. With that in mind I look forward to meeting you later in the day."

He arrived at six o'clock, an early hour in New York for much of anything but conducting last-minute business or beginning the cocktail hour. Mary Ellen Paige was waiting for him on the fifteenth floor as the elevator doors opened.

"Mr. Dietrich, welcome. I'm Mary Ellen Paige."

She was over forty, Dietrich guessed, and not a natural beauty, but she had a definite presence about her. She probably worked hard at presenting a strong physical appearance. Her manufactured aura made her attractive and Dietrich found himself a bit thick of tongue.

"Oh, hi," he responded vacuously while taking her hand, suddenly self-conscious about the great amount of weight he had gained on his short stature. Nervous eating was a habit seemingly impossible for him to shake. "I'm, uh, glad to be here."

"Really? After that rude message I left you at your hotel?" she asked, leading him easily toward a door standing ajar in the hallway.

"Oh, please," Dietrich waved dismissive hand in the air as if he were disinvited to people's homes every day.

He looked for an apartment number on the door as she guided him into a well-lighted hall, which then gave way to a large, luxurious living room. The walls were done in gold wallpaper that looked like real gold thread was used in its fabrication. Large windows along the east wall were trimmed in regal red tapestry. Three chandeliers hung from the ceiling, each lighting stem also trimmed in gold. Furniture pieces were almost certainly period, Dietrich thought, but he would not have been able to guess which period or even whether the design was European or early American. Carpet and furniture colors were subdued, managing to set off the walls and ceiling of the apartment rather than clash. There were two doors leading off from the living room: one, partially open, led to a dining room, the other, toward which he was still directed by gentle pressure of Mary Ellen's hand on his arm, led deeper into the dwelling rooms.

A man materialized out of nowhere as Mary Ellen stayed their progress through the door. Even Dietrich knew at first glance that the man was a household servant. He smiled and nodded almost imperceptibly as Dietrich's eyes met his.

"Before we go in to see uncle Warren may I offer you a drink? Warren isn't allowed to have alcohol these days but we'll bring him a soft drink while you have anything you like."

"Bourbon would be nice. Just a little ice," he said.

"Spring water for me, Grantham," she said to the butler before leading Dietrich by a half-step past several more closed doors to yet another in front of which she paused. "This is Warren's suite."

"Big place," Dietrich said.

"We have the entire floor. I wish we had the time to give you the guided tour but I have a dinner and—"

Dietrich stopped her with the palm of his upraised hand. "No need to explain. This visit is just as much a surprise to me as it is to you. I'm sorry to barge in like this."

Before he could turn his head away he felt her hand touch his forearm. "Mr. Dietrich..."

"Steve."

"Thank you. Steve. My sister and her husband and I and my husband have been taking turns away from our homes out of state, occupying this mausoleum so that we can take care of uncle Warren. He should really be in a place where he could get better care but he refuses to leave..." she moved a hand in a swirling motion, "...all of this. It's his home and his refuge."

Dietrich followed her through a door upon which she knocked first but opened almost without waiting. The room had once been ornate, Dietrich thought as he glanced about, but now seemed cluttered with items that were never meant to be located in a sleeping room. There were photographs of men and women, individually and in groups, that might once have been found on an office wall. There was a large coffee table piled with a week's worth of unread city newspapers, including the *New York Times*, and several rows of magazines, all current, and all unread.

"Uncle Warren doesn't see well, anymore," Mary Ellen whispered as she seemed to view the room through his eyes. "Uncle Warren," she called, raising her voice and injecting cheerfulness.

Dietrich stayed at his hostess's side as they entered the bedroom area of the suite. It contained an impressive array of medical support paraphernalia, only a few items of which Dietrich recognized. There was an idle EKG machine on rollers in one corner of the room, a heart monitor nearby, an oxygen tank in still another corner. Even with all of the machines that forecast doom the atmosphere was hugely uplifted by two large windows that offered a panoramic view of the city's west side and its skyline.

"That's why I like it here," a surprisingly strong voice came from the man in an oversized bed. "One can't help but feel a part of the city from here. Its beauty and its vitality. You can't get it from that box." The man nodded toward a large but unobtrusively placed television set.

"Warren, this is Steven Dietrich. Mr. Dietrich is here from California," Mary Ellen said.

Warren Alsop held out a hand which trembled slightly. Dietrich stepped forward quickly to take it. "It's a pleasure to meet you, Mr. Alsop. I know it's short notice and you..."

Dietrich realized he was about to suggest that Warren Alsop surely had more pressing obligations but realized that he would sound trite. The old man's eyelids drooped downward momentarily. It was enough to finish Dietrich's thought and move on.

"I enjoy company. I used to have a lot of it."

Grantham arrived with the drinks, which he wordlessly began to distribute. Warren Alsop's drink was served in a gold-trimmed, long-stem wine glass with a flexible straw sticking out of it.

"There's a bottle of Jack Daniels in that armoire," he said to Mary Ellen. "Bring it to me."

Their eyes locked for a very long moment; neither wanted to argue but neither would give in to the will of the other. At last Mary Ellen sighed, rose from her chair, and fetched the bottle. She made no effort to pour a small amount into the old man's glass. On the contrary, she put in a generous amount, forestalling any possible objection the octogenarian might have raised. He did not reward her with a smile as she handed him the glass. Instead, he snapped the straw out of the cola and dropped it onto a side table. He took several large swallows of the mixture and smiled.

"Damn."

"Cheers," Dietrich said, pleased at the sight of the old man so clearly enjoying himself. A quick glance at Mary Ellen's down-turned mouth told him that not everyone in the room was ecstatic.

"It isn't that I disapprove of you finishing off your liver, Uncle Warren, but how anyone on Earth can drink that rotgut mixed with cola and still smile about it is beyond my understanding."

Warren Alsop's smile increased. He took another deep swallow of his drink.

"You a pilot, Mr. Dietrich? Navy pilot, by any chance? Well, I can tell you that Jack Daniels and Coca Cola shot down more Jap planes than fifty caliber machine guns. Any man in our squadron who didn't consume a lot of the stuff we would have thrown overboard. Thank God we didn't have to do that."

The old man finished off his drink and held out the glass. "I'll have another."

With only the slightest hesitation Mary Ellen made the round trip to the bar, returning with the same mixture.

"There wasn't any ice," she said, dryly.

"All the better to delight the taste buds," Alsop said, taking another swallow but more slowly, savoring the flavor. "Well, I suppose I know why you're here, Steven. Mind if I call you Steven? You know that your grandfather was my friend. Close friend."

"That's right, Mr. Alsop. I never met him. I want to find out about him."

"Then you came to the right man. I have to smile every time I think about Steve Dietrich. He was a heller. I'd come up with the ideas for getting us in trouble and Steve was the guy who had the guts to do it." The old man's eyes did indeed light up at the memory of his friend.

"Tough kid. Wasn't much of a football player because of his size and weight but he made all the teams. He could take more hits than the tackling dummies. Great swimmer. And diver. That was a sport that didn't require size. Outstanding student. I should have gone to Berlin with him."

"In nineteen thirty-six?"

Warren Alsop nodded slowly. "Four of us were going to go. Steve, me, Dick Miller, and John Hersey. Dick Miller was a track man at University of Oregon but a friend of Hersey's. When John dropped out Dick did, too. Then I met a girl, later to become my wife. Sue Katherine Nance. Her picture hangs in the living room. Sue was Mary Ellen's aunt."

Dietrich only then realized that Mary Ellen had quietly left the room. If there was to be any further drinking by the old man he, Dietrich, would have to be the bartender.

"Did you see him when he came home?" Dietrich asked.

Alsop drained his glass of bourbon. He leaned his head back into his pillows and closed his eyes. Dietrich waited for a long moment, wondering whether the old man might have suddenly drifted off to sleep. Then Alsop's eyes fluttered open again.

"No. At least not… Not until well after the war was over."

"Do you mean that he simply stayed in Germany from nineteen thirty-six?"

"Didn't your father tell you about his father?" Alsop asked.

"He never talked about his father. Even when I was old enough to insist he dodged around me."

"Yes. Steven Dietrich stayed on."

"And, do you know, Mr. Alsop, what my grandfather did in that war?"

Another wisp of a smile. "What so many children ask of their seniors, eh? What did you do in the war, Daddy?"

Warren Alsop touched his glass once more and for a moment Dietrich though he might have to mix another. Looking up, the old man seemed to read his thoughts.

"I know when I've been lucky. I'll submit to limiting my booze intake, at least for today. Yes, your grandfather stayed there. Before the war he met a woman and they later married. I don't know her name but she was German, I think. I never met her, but of course she would have been your grandmother. It was all so…"

"So?"

"So long ago."

Steven was certain that Alsop was going to say something else, something different.

"Mr. Alsop…"

"Call me Warren, my young friend. My new pal who has brought with him the luxury of liquor without a fight."

"Warren, did you read the book *Raven?*" Dietrich asked.

"No. I only read periodicals these days. Why do you ask?"

"The book is fiction, or so the author says. It's a story about World War II in Europe. A character in the book sounds very much like my grandfather. The character's name is Steven Dietrich and in the story he joins the Luftwaffe and becomes a fighter pilot. But the Dietrich character is spying for the British. The book goes on to tell the most bizarre story about an actor, a British actor, taking Adolf Hitler's place after the dictator was assassinated. The character of Dietrich becomes the link between London and Berlin."

Dietrich paused at the sound of gentle chuckling from the bedridden man nearby.

"I..." Dietrich continued, clumsily, "I can have a copy sent to you."

Alsop waved a feeble hand in the air, indicating the negative.

"Too late. Doesn't matter, now. Well, well. I never believed all the garbage that was floating around about Steve."

"I don't understand. Who told you? My grandfather?" Dietrich found himself leaning forward in his chair. His heart might have picked up a beat or two.

"In nineteen forty there were newspaper stories about him. *Time* magazine, too, as I recall. The American who flew for the Germans. Steven Dietrich. At first no one put together that it was Steven Dietrich, Yale, class of 'thirty seven. Then, before anyone could get interested enough in the story to poke around for the facts, there was nothing more. No articles, nowhere. Stopped. But the rumors persisted. His family was embarrassed. Got so bad they moved across the country. I suppose that's why you grew up on the coast, eh?"

Dietrich only shrugged.

"The Nazis were hated, of course. Anyone helping them was hated as well. I never believed it, myself. I knew Steven well and he was no Nazi. He could have flown an airplane here, too, you know. On our side. But, Jesus, his family suffered. His parents thought they had spawned a traitor. I saw him when the war was over. He came back in nineteen forty-seven."

"My God."

"I spent the war flying Hellcats in the Pacific. We didn't get a lot of leave in those days so when it was over I spent a year drinking and playing as hard as I could. Sue was always on my arm, never said a word about my damn excesses and my selfishness. Investment banking was the last thing I wanted to do. Maybe she knew something about me that I didn't know myself but at some point I got the clue that the family had run out of patience and that I had better begin earning a living. In November or December of 'forty-seven into my office walked Steven Dietrich. Thought I was seeing a ghost. Or maybe I was having DTs from alcohol. But there he was. We went out to lunch and after that I took him home and we talked for two days. He told me that he had flown for the Germans. I tell you, what he went through would curl your hair.

"But he said nothing about being a spy. Nothing. He said that he had embarrassed his family and hoped someday that they would understand. When I asked him what it was they were supposed to understand he only shook his head and dropped his eyes. He said that he was changing his name and that he and his wife were going to live abroad. I asked him where and he said maybe Spain. Maybe Italy. Maybe even France. I never saw him again."

Dietrich noticed that it was dark outside, that all the lights in New York were now on. It truly was a beautiful sight. He could understand why the old man could never tire of it.

"You didn't see him? But did you hear from him? Did he write or call?"

Warren Alsop merely shook his head slowly.

"I never got a thing from Steve except what he told me. But I got something else. A man came to see me. He said his name was Lyles. Or Miles. No, it was Wiles. He gave me a box he said contained papers written by your grandfather.

This Wiles character, Englishman he was, asked that I open it only after Steve's death." The old man sighed deeply, slowly turning his eyes toward the window. "I could never bring myself to do that. Open it, that is. I don't know that he isn't still alive, do I? Maybe I believe that as long as I'm alive the box should stay closed, too. Well. That's nonsense, I suppose. You should have it. I'll look for it, Steven. If I can find it I'll send it to you."

The following morning Dietrich awoke early. He sat, an unopened newspaper at his side, looking into the infinity of the hotel wall ten feet in front of him, and wondered what he would do next. He had no clue. He was trying to run his business in Santa Monica from his hotel room in New York, talking almost non-stop on the telephone with his office manager when there was a knock on the door.

"Yes?" he said near the unopened door.

"Delivery for Mr. Dietrich," the voice said on the other side.

"Hold on." Dietrich promptly got off the phone and opened the door. Before him was a uniformed young woman wearing jacket and gloves. In her hands she held a package wrapped in plain brown paper. She also carried a clipboard.

"Steven Dietrich?" she asked.

"That's me."

"Sign here, please," she said, offering her clipboard.

He closed the door and looked at the box in his hands. There was no return address, only his name and, under that, the name of the hotel. Under brown wrapping paper he found a plain box. It was old and appeared that it might have once held stationery. But it was now well stuffed with pages, some of which were typewritten, others written in longhand. The pages were often dated and Dietrich could see that they had been written over a period of years. It was done in the first person. Written by Steven Dietrich.

Chapter 8

There were more than a few advantages that went along with Street's free room at Wes Claridge's apartment. The most obvious was worldwide telephone connections made possible by Wes's satellite telephone. It was a difficult intercept even if the super secret National Security Agency (NSA) was looking for it specifically. The problem for NSA was that there were now such things as unbreakable codes, contrary to the old days when NSA not only intercepted every radio transmission, every telephone call, every electronic signal of any kind, including bank transactions, then processed the interesting ones through their massive Cray computers. Secret code went in one end and came out the other in clear language, ready for Intelligence analysts to read.

But today's NSA super powers, its almost magical ability to intercept all signals, is at the same time its bête noire. That is, the billions of bits plucked out of the air or from under the sea each hour of the day, every day of the year, year after year, were far too much to process by human observation. The advent of new, unbreakable secret code has caused the agency to become awash in its own massive information gathering system. Even with elaborate programming software designed around key words that alert the machinery and the Intel analysts to an item that needs special attention, humans can not keep up with the ever-increasing capacity of data production. An electronic sorcerer's apprentice has been unleashed. It is thus the case that some very important intercepts are made, processed into the belly of NSA's beast, never to catch the eye of a human being who must ultimately make the decision to act.

The second great advantage to having levered himself into the apartment in Manassas was Street's host's extraordinary Caesar salad. Somewhere between his undergraduate years at the University of Chicago, where he studied world history, and his electrical engineering graduate work at MIT, Wes had had no time to learn to cook except for making salad. The fact that August Street was not anxious to show himself in public unnecessarily in part led to their shared menu of french fries and hamburgers. Chilidogs were a specialty of the house when Street cooked, but good red wines improved their otherwise grinding diets. Still, the days flew by while Street wrote and Wes worked black magic at the H. P. Carlisle Foundation.

They had struggled through a complete dinner of frozen Thai food which, when doctored with enough soy sauce, tasted almost good. Street was accustomed to regular exercise. Not weight lifting, although he had flirted with that, too, but jogging was enjoyable to him and he was very aware of the benefits for his heart and lungs. He had been active over the past weeks but not in the kind of activity that gets one's heart up to 150 beats per minute and keeps it there.

"Want to do a run?" he asked Wes.

"Run? Run for governor? Run as in first you walk and then you run? Run from the cops? No."

"No to everything?"

"That's right." Wes belched.

"Think I will."

"Wait a minute, August. Don't go out."

"Why not?"

Wes slowly placed a cold french fry in his mouth and chewed deliberately.

"Your house got burgled," he said.

"Yes. I told you that."

Wes swallowed, then washed down the remnants with a cola that had become watery from melted ice.

"I could have told you," he said.

"Told me what? That my house got broken into? My bank account looted? That kind of stuff?"

Wes nodded his head. "That's right. Because we did it. We took everything you had."

Street sank slowly back to the cushion of the sofa from which he had intended to leave. "I don't understand. Who is we?"

"The Foundation. Think about it, August. Who knew more about you than the Foundation? We all have quarterly security updates but yours became weekly. Maybe daily. They knew everything about you. Who your friends were, what your investments were, who your mortgage company was. All about Linda. Everything public and private. And everything that's in your computer. Think about what you had in there, pal."

For a moment Street hit a blank. He had so much information in his computer that he couldn't remember even a fraction of it. Everything of any importance, including his code words and passwords to gain access to somewhere else were filed inside his computer under other coded passwords. Over the years he had merely acquired evermore sophisticated computer systems and larger hard drives and bigger memory chips to hold it all. Like most people, he didn't trust his own memory, especially about the really important things.

"You knew about it? All along? That they stole my identity."

Wes nodded. "They're after your life, man, if that's what it takes."

Street hardly knew where to begin. He knew Wes well but the relationship was not emotionally close. They had common interests, especially in their educational backgrounds, their political points of view, and such abstruse things as theological arguments. But that was an intellectual connection, not blood bonding. Street shrugged, trying to put it into a perspective he could accept.

"Well, it was your job."

"Sure was, wasn't it? What good is a friend if you can't buy him or sell him? I mean, that's what we do there, isn't it? We're a spy organization. So I spied."

"I always wondered," Street said, "how much they paid you."

"Low six," Wes said. "You?"

"Me, too."

A familiar face appeared on the television screen. It was a news anchor on a cable channel. The audio was muted but the words the news man was saying ran in white on black fonts across the screen for the hearing impaired. Neither Wes nor Street was reading them.

"We took it all apart. Your computer. Probably had ten people going through it for a week. I don't know who they were because I was the only guy from the USA."

"Where were they from?" Street asked.

"Don't know, man. I'd tell you if I did."

"Do they know I'm here?" Street almost choked as he spoke.

Wes nodded his head. "I don't think they'll touch you while you're with me. It'll still take them some time to go through all your stuff. Run checks on it, too. But if you go out..." Wes shrugged.

"Out of your sight, you mean. You're the watcher," Street finished for him.

Wes's silence confirmed what Street had guessed.

"I'm leaving tomorrow," Street said. The call from Guy Virgil had come that afternoon.

"Yeah. I know."

Of course he did.

"Your documents. In your computer. Would it help if you could get it back?" Wes asked, his eyes lifting to meet Street's.

"Are you kidding? Almost three years worth of work on *Raven* alone. It could save me a hell of a lot of time overseas."

"Well, for, ah, what it's worth, you can have it. I made a backup."

"How much of it?"

"Probably got it all."

Street could feel his heart beat faster. What a coup if he could get his hands on his lost treasure.

"Wes..."

"There's a company called WhereTo that puts out GPS road maps of the world. I formatted their discs and used them to put on your stuff. Sitting right on top of my desk. Ain't nobody gonna find 'em there."

"If you give me the discs it means you've just quit your job as a watcher."

"That's it. Tell me where to meet you tomorrow and I'll be there."

Wes could sense Street's hesitation.

"That's okay. I can just leave them for you somewhere, or..."

Street suddenly felt embarrassed. "Hell, no, Wes. That isn't it. I was just trying to think of a safe place."

He gave Wes the address of Personal and Business Credit Repair. "I'm going to meet a guy there at 11:00 A.M. I'll be out again in twenty minutes."

"I'll see you then. I'll be the guy with the jai alai basket in my hands. I think it's about time I learned to play Brazil's favorite game."

"Hello, Felicity," Street said to the receptionist. The single waiting chair was still empty as she put aside her People magazine.

"Oh, hi, Mister ah..."

"Brightmeyer."

"Yeah. Mr. Virgil is expecting you. Wait."

Felicity stepped through the door behind her then reappeared a moment later. She was smiling as she held the door for him. "Come in."

This time Guy Virgil rose to his feet as Street entered. The two men shook hands briefly.

"Hey, you look okay," Virgil said, sticking to his edgy persona.

"So do you."

"Yeah, well, I was always the best-looking kid on the block. Sit down. How'd you like Dean Minor?"

"The detective?" Street shrugged. "Okay. We didn't socialize much but he seemed like a good man."

"Did you know that he was the best baseball hitter ever to come out of the state of Iowa? Wouldn't know it to look at him, because he's smarter than a retired con man, but he would have put Mickey Mantle or Cal Ripken to shame if he hadn't torn up a shoulder in the minor leagues."

"Is that so?" Street said, trying to appear interested.

"Yeah. Two things he hates, crooks and banks," Virgil said, chuckling at the obvious irony. "And credit card companies. He doesn't see any difference, see? Between crooks and them. That's what it is."

Virgil's desk was clean of all impediments; even the telephone rested on a back bar. Virgil took his time in appraising his customer in what might have been a final assessment. Street was not insulted by the frank regard he was given by the man in front of him who, if his judgement was flawed in the least, could find himself facing a good many years in prison. So Street waited patiently. He felt strangely relaxed.

Virgil opened a drawer and came up with a large plastic Ziploc bag. Opening it, he emptied its contents onto his desk. They looked familiar to Street. His wallet, or at least the one he shared with the real Art Brightmeyer, was among it all. Virgil selected a three-inch-by-five-inch booklet that had PASSPORT stamped in gold letters against a blue background, along with the emblem of the United States of America. He passed it across the desk to

Street who opened it to the first page. His photograph stared back at him, as well as his "name," Arthur Brightmeyer, birth date, physical description, and words that stated that the passport had been issued at the National Passport Center. On the next page the document said: *The Secretary of State of the United States of America hereby requests all whom it may concern to permit the citizen/national of the United States named herein to pass without delay or hindrance and in case of need to give all lawful aid and protection.*

Street quickly flipped through the remaining pages noting that the color-coded paper looked quite correct as best as he could recall, and that if it ever got to the point where the document was the subject of official scrutiny his game would likely be up, anyway. He raised his eyes to meet Virgil's.

"Looks good."

Virgil grunted what was probably agreement, then pushed three credit cards toward him. Street looked them over closely. They, too, looked good. He had not copied the numbers of the cards before he gave them to Virgil but he was sure that they would be different. As though reading his mind Virgil confirmed his assumption.

"Different numbers but same account. The bills are going to go to this address." Virgil passed a hand-written memo across the desk. "You're going to get a paper bill to that address, and you're going to be able to access the account online. Everybody can do that, right? So if you want to keep the cards current, check online once in a while and pay something on 'em."

Street nodded his head. He could do that.

"So, how much do I owe you, Mr. Virgil?"

"Six thousand. You thought I was going to say six large, huh? That's how they do it in the movies but we're a business. Hey, wait. Six large."

"Okay," Street said, "that's fair, but you know, probably better than I know that I don't have that kind of money. At least not now."

"Sure you do. Write me a check on one of those accounts. Anybody's got a credit card gets checks along with 'em. They send those things out almost every month hoping you'll write one. So this month you don't disappoint them. Write it for cash."

Virgil produced the check and held aloft a ballpoint pen. Street signed "Art Brightmeyer".

Their momentary silence was interrupted by the sounds of sirens nearby. It was not an unusual cacophony in any city and neither man paid the slightest attention to the noise. A fire? Ambulance? Police?

"Now look, ah, Art. You can go a long way on these plastic slugs. Don't go nuts at the high end but you don't have to sleep in flop houses, either. Use ATMs and sometimes you write yourself out a check for cash. When the bill comes at the end of the month, all you pay is three percent of the balance. If you owe the credit card company two grand, you send 'em sixty bucks and you're good for another month. It's a Ponzi scheme and it can go on for one hell of a long time. Use all three cards, know what I mean? Hey, before the black hole closes up you might even have some money."

Street stuffed the wallet full of cards and cash. They were strangely comforting. And they increased his sense of desperation, as though a clock had begun to tick. He was aware that his heart was thumping harder than usual. He took Virgil's hand. Virgil's grip was strong and he maintained his pressure on Street's a little longer, unwilling to release him just yet.

"Where was it? I'm pretty good at finding out who people are, especially when I've seen 'em before, but not you. So, who are you?"

Street again felt the nagging sense that he should deny Virgil's request out of safety for all concerned.

"How about I tell you when we become cell mates?"

Virgil laughed in appreciation.

"Okay. You're smart. Don't go out that door. Go this way. Somebody else is waiting for me out there."

Street left by a side exit. That explained why there was only one waiting chair in the outer office.

He again ignored the elevator in favor of the faster stairs. When he arrived at street level he began to walk toward the northeast corner of a nearby intersection. As his pace drew him closer to the traffic lights he could see that a crowd of people had formed and was growing larger. The multiple sirens heard minutes ago were likely caused by whatever had happened here. It was easy to pick out the Metropolitan policemen, all wearing identical uniforms regardless of their specialties within the departments. It was his intention to meet Westbrook in this area so Street lingered, slowly gravitating toward the curb.

A pedestrian was struck down. Street listened to the undertones from the crowd, the witnesses telling their varied stories of the event to newcomers. A truck hit the man. That one over there. Street looked up the block in the direction the storytellers indicated. It was a ten-wheeler, diesel, with a big box. Didn't even stop. The intersection was completely blocked off for automobile traffic while police investigators made measurements, drew chalk lines, and took reports from various witnesses.

He looked around for Westbrook. He glanced again at his wristwatch, the minute hand now seeming to crawl. Twenty minutes to twelve. How long had he been with Virgil? Thirty minutes? No, less. Much less. Oh, where does the time go when you're having fun?

Street moved his feet again, now circulating, only glancing occasionally at the scene of the accident but scanning the ever-increasing crowd for Wes Claridge's blonde mop. *The man was waiting for a bus*, he heard a witness say. *No*, another person corrected, *busses don't stop there. Well*, the first said, *he was waiting for something. I don't think so*, a third person said, joining in the colloquy, *he was just walking down the street, from over there. He crossed there, against the light. That's why he got hit.* Then a lady spoke. *It was like he jumped off the sidewalk, like he wanted to get a head start on the light. Must have been a fool*, she said. *Looked like he was pushed*, said another.

Street found himself irritated. He felt like he was being forced to hear commercials on a television channel without a mute button. It was almost noon and no Westbrook Claridge. Street debated about whether he should return to the apartment and wait for Wes. No, that would be dangerous. They would be watching. Should he just leave? Maybe Wes couldn't get the backup disc out of the building. Street thought he could wait until he got to Europe, then get in touch with Wes from there. It began to make more sense.

He turned and walked north. He would get away from the jammed intersection where traffic was flowing again, then hail a cab. Near his shoulder he clutched the strap of his light bag. He made a brief mental note that he would buy himself some clothes when he arrived in England. He would need slacks and a sports jacket and a couple of neckties, he thought. And a suit. Yes, he would buy a suit to wear on occasions when he needed to speak with a public official and it just wouldn't do to have the other fellow better dressed. Their minds worked that way. Give them a chance to look down on someone and they will.

The police were still taking statements from the public, Street could see out of the corner of his eye as he reached midblock. The medical technicians were taking charge of the body. They unzipped a heavy-gauge rubber bag and laid it neatly next to the prone figure, then removed the temporary blanket the traffic policeman had placed over the lifeless form. The med techs then worked together to roll the full-sized corpse, first onto one side, then slid the bag underneath, then rolled it onto its opposite side. The bag zipped up easily. It was to be Street's last view of Westbrook Claridge.

Chapter 9

Christopher Brooks burned his tongue on hot coffee, the cup radiating heat as he looked downward from his office window onto the Thames below. Shipping always fascinated him. It was the colossal size of the sea that awed him and ships that could navigate the world were giant in scale to man. Barges pushed by tug boats and loaded with everything from gas to coal to wines from all countries plied the river below. They seemed to move in slow motion, a sense distortion caused by his relative distance and height from the business far below. There was another man in his office. The other man, Tyre Jones, stood virtually motionless but his eyes and ears were always alert. If anyone took notice at all of Mr. Jones, they might assume he was a functionary at a city water bureau. With an absence of sharp features in his rounded face, wire-rimmed glasses, slumped shoulders, and a physical frame he purposely covered with drab clothing, there was nothing about Jones that would draw a second glance. All but invisible in a crowd he would not be remembered, the perfect face and body for an agent. Jones was not his real name because he was an outside man, a field operative, where real names did not matter. Tyre Jones's genuine identity did not rouse Brook's curiosity in the least. It was only his performance that concerned him. If it was action that spoke more eloquently than words, then Jones's career with SIS had always provided dependable reportage. Until now.

"No one disappears," Brooks said.

Jones said nothing.

"It is a magician's term, making things disappear. We're not dealing with silk hats and white rabbits." Brooks turned slowly to regard Jones. The veteran field man was not intimidated by Brooks's rebuke because the field man could understand his boss's dilemma. Were positions reversed, Jones would feel precisely the same, and because of that he also knew that Brooks would gain nothing by firing one of his best outside men.

"Of course not, C. We lost him in Washington D.C. We had two very good men on him. That doesn't include the Claridge chap—"

"Who?"

"Westbrook Claridge. An employee of the H. P. Carlisle Foundation."

"Jesus. Them."

"They've always been reliable and quite professional," Jones reminded Brooks. When Brooks returned to contemplating the window without enlarging upon his objections to the H. P. Carlisle Foundation, Jones continued.

"Street went to a business that advertizes that they can provide clean credit histories. You've seen the kind."

Brooks grunted his assent.

"It's a scam, of course. The owner's name is Guy Virgil, aka Robert Ellis, aka Joseph Whitman, aka Lucky Joe. We're certain that Street got new documents there. Credit cards and the like."

"Passport?"

"Probably."

"Damn. Under what name?"

"We don't know that, yet."

"Driver's license, credit cards, Social Security. You don't know any of those?"

"No. We're looking for new licenses issued to California residents in the past weeks. Chances are good that he's among them."

Brooks delivered a withering stare at Jones. Jones shrugged. "California authorities feel no particular need to cooperate with anyone. They call it their DMV, Department of Motor Vehicles. They hate everybody," Jones said.

"How about Virgil?"

"We've had him detained, of course. The American FBI has seen to that. But it isn't the first time the man has been arrested and he doesn't like to talk. He has an office worker—"

"Who?" Brooks snapped.

"Her name is…" For the first time during Jones's audience with his superior,- Jones resorted to refreshing his memory by looking at a small notepad. "Felicity. Felicity Lourdes."

"Is that a joke?"

Jones flashed a smile but it disappeared quickly. He shook his head.

"No, sir. Not a joke. She is from Ames, Iowa. Her mother and father own a farm there. Ronald Moore Lourdes and Betty Jean Orson Lourdes. She has three sisters, two younger, one older. They—"

Brooks waved his hand, halting the recitation. The Lourdes family were anything but a hot lead.

"Can we get this…Virgil, away from the Americans?"

"I doubt that, sir."

"Then I'll send an interrogator over there. Now, what was this Claridge fellow going to do with August Street?"

"We're not sure. We had his apartment wired but he is in the business, you know."

"He found your bug?"

"Yes."

"Well, you don't suppose they were going to have lunch together, do you?"

"No, of course not. But neither was there anything to suggest the man would not simply return to work."

"To the H. P. Carlisle Foundation?"

"Yes, sir."

"Was there no other way to deal with Claridge?" C wanted to know.

The agent shrugged again. "I suppose it was a value judgment made on the spot."

"And what did we recover?"

"The contents of Street's research. They were on discs made to appear as electronic road maps."

Christopher Brooks sat heavily into his chair. He had spent five years in the field, less than half the time that Tyre Jones had been at it. He had no advice to offer the man. Uncertainty urged that he make a decision.

"The Rose Hawkins woman…"

"Yes?"

"Shouldn't you pick her up?"

"We considered that, C, but we don't think she knows where Street is. We're hoping that Street will go there to see her. He almost has to, doesn't he?"

"All right," Brooks conceded, terminating the interview. As the outside man turned to go Brooks said, "Do you have enough men?"

"I suppose so, sir. If we had any more they'd be bumping into one another."

Rose Hawkins lingered a few moments in one of the two upstairs bedrooms, trying to recall August Street's directions exactly. She was careful not to make the place appear too neat, leaving her bed tended but not tidy. She left her toothbrush conspicuously on the top of her washbowl. She had packed an overnight bag but thought better of it. She retrieved it from a corner of the small closet she maintained off the bathroom and took everything out of it, even returning the one dress she had packed to a hanger. She could not bring herself to leave a pair of hose and a change of panties behind, so she found a place for both in the pockets on either side of the warm jacket she wore. She had never fancied jewelry. With no regret, she left it all behind until she reached the bedroom door, then returned to the small box on her handmade dresser and picked out a gold chain bracelet. It was the only thing of monetary value given to her by her mother. She left her bedroom door open, then walked a few paces to the second bedroom door and opened it.

"Are you awake, mother?" she whispered

"No," came a snappish response from the bed.

Rose hesitated. She could make out a nearly full glass of water by the old woman's bed. She was certainly in no distress. Well, it wouldn't be long in any case. Rose closed the door gently.

As she had been told, she stuck to the established pattern of riding her bicycle to town twice each week, once to shop and once to volunteer at the animal shelter. She was punctilious and open about everything she did. Making herself a creature of habit was not hard, since she was precisely that.

They would expect her to leave the house by the side door, so that was the way she began, making it easy for them. She made no attempt to open the large garage door. She knew that if she took the car they would be sure to follow. Instead, she wheeled her bicycle out of the garage side door as usual and, pausing only long enough to tie a scarf around her neck, pushed off in the direction of the village.

The road to Thorntenet was only three miles by car, but one could shave a bit from that distance by crossing the pavement at Ruffery's Ferry, then passing under the bridge that had long ago displaced the ferry boat, then following the well-worn dirt path to the edge of Houge township. As she pedaled along in the afternoon mist she took care not to look over her shoulder. She did nothing suspicious as she crossed the road, taking care to look for traffic when she did. If there had been a vehicle to her rear she did not see it but, rather, respected those who did the watching to be more clever than she in hiding themselves.

She arrived in the village slightly ahead of the schedule she would have kept to on the main road. To be certain that her followers had not known of the shorter route to town, she went to a cluster of buildings rented mostly by professional groups: a dentist, a solicitor, a chemist, two doctors, and a public accountancy. She rode her bicycle down a narrow pathway separating various offices, then abruptly dismounted and pulled it into a community bicycle rack. She waited a short time near a hedgerow before she ventured a look around the corner. Apart from normal business activity by village citizens, several whom she recognized from a distance, she saw nothing untoward.

She walked directly north from the town center, staying as close as possible to the residential sidewalks, now cast darkly in late afternoon shadows. Four streets from the village center she arrived at an unprepossessing brick cottage. Its owner had planted a flower garden around its grounds, as other residents had done, but these flowers had withered from lack of attention or succumbed to heartier weeds. Rose knocked on the front door, resisting an urge to look over her shoulder. The wait that seemed interminable was actually brief as another woman, slightly younger than Rose, opened it only far enough to peer curiously at the person on her porch.

"Yes?"

"Hello. Marjorie. It's Rose Hawkins—"

"Well, of course it is. I didn't recognize you, Rose. Please, come," the sixtyish woman said, stepping back for Rose to enter.

"I'm so sorry I didn't call first. I saw the advert in the paper about your car for sale."

Rose felt a sense of relief as she stepped quickly inside the door and heard it close behind her.

"Would you like a cuppa, Rose? I'll put the kettle on," Marjorie McBurney offered, still put off stride by unexpected company. Her cat's food had begun emitting the unmistakable odor of over ripeness, and the animal's dining area, partially covered by the page from a newspaper, had a collection of food residue next to the water bowl. Rose had long known that Marjorie viewed tidiness as a virtue only when guests came by, and that was not often.

"No, please. I'd rather… Why, yes, Marjorie, I would indeed. About the car you advertised…" she said, following her host into a cramped kitchen.

"This is Birdy," Marjorie said of her tortoiseshell feline who was rubbing herself across Rose's legs. Birdy's body was a bit twisted, as though she had once been kicked very hard. When she mewed, the sound that came out of her was more like a chirp.

"She's wonderful," Rose said, touching the animal gently. "Uh, your car…"

"Oh, that thing. I don't drive, you know. My eyes. When Seldon died—"

"That was five years ago."

"Yes," Marjorie sighed. "When I lost Seldon I lost my driver. It's an old machine, I'm afraid. Seldon hated to pay the price for a new one. He was very firm about it. Total waste, he always said. He was a mechanic, that one. Anything he put his hands to ran very well. Our washer is over twenty years old. Our dryer is not much newer. He did them both, as they required his attention. He would put a belt onto this one or tighten a fastener on that one. I am helpless about those things myself. Aren't I, Birdy?"

"It's a Morris, isn't it, Marjorie?"

"Yes, I think so. Isn't this a lovely cup and saucer? It's Limoge. I like the orange. I don't have a collection. Some people in the village say that I do but I don't. Here is some chocolate. My mother drank her tea through a sugar lump."

"Many people do—"

"People don't do that anymore. Chocolate is wonderful. I like nuts in my chocolate but I had to back away from it, you know." She tapped her teeth.

"Ah."

"Look at this yellow. Isn't it just divine?" Marjorie presented the cup and saucer from which she intended to drink.

"Limoge?"

"No. I'm not going to tell you." Marjorie glanced in the direction of the tea kettle as though it was a trifle late with its signal.

"I'd like to write you a draft for your Morris," Rose said, producing a bankbook from her purse. "How much was it, again?"

"Oh, well, let me see. Isn't that silly? I don't recall." She covered her mouth with one finger as if to suppress her embarrassment.

"I believe the newspaper ad said two hundred pounds."

"It did? Well, then that must be right. I asked Mr. Carstairs to tell me what it was worth. Not that I would buy a car from that man. Nor would I sell one to him. Seldon would spin in his grave, you can believe that. They are crooks going in both directions, those car dealers. When you buy and when you sell. Seldon was very, very firm about that."

Rose was already writing the check.

"Don't you think you should try the car first, my dear?"

"The advert said it was in good condition."

"To be sure, but one never knows. You are a neighbor and very dear friend. I cannot imagine how I would feel if the old thing went bad."

They were not very dear friends, Rose silently corrected, and while Marjorie would be conservatively correct in most cases, Rose wanted nothing more than to escape at once.

The steam whistle on the tea kettle began to screech. The near proximity of the kettle set Rose's teeth on edge.

"I think the water is ready, Marjorie."

"Well, of course it is. One would have to be deaf not to hear it." Marjorie turned off the gas underneath the kettle then, using a potholder, wielded the stainless steel kettle toward awaiting cups and tea bags. Involuntarily, Rose leaned her body back, away from the table. She tore the signed check out of her book and passed it over to her host.

"There you are, Marjorie. Do you have the key?"

Marjorie was about to take a seat at the kitchen table in front of her cup but Rose's eager manner seemed to indicate that she was in a hurry. She opened a nearby drawer which contained dense clutter. She pushed aside loose rubber bands, odd-sized spoons, canning lids, an oyster knife, tattered pot holders, a wealth of grocery coupons, and a spilt box of toothpicks before fishing out an automobile key attachéd to a chain.

"Here it is. I have another one, somewhere. I'll find it for you, Rose. Now let me see..."

"I won't be needing it..."

"I might have put it in one of my hideaways. You know, I don't always remember where they are. The hideaways. I suppose that could be good, couldn't it? Before I put the advert in the paper I had the car serviced. Ah, I remember, now. I put it with the papers, the ownership documents. I set them... right over there."

The old woman pointed in triumph to a small dining area off the kitchen, more like a nook. Rose followed her across the room to a buffet, on top of which was a cut glass vase. Like the clogged kitchen drawer the vase had become a waste receptacle for letters, cards, old colored wrappers, paper clips, string, and a roll of clear tape. Marjorie pawed through these items before finding the car's title afloat near the middle of other detritus.

"I'm off to Saxlingham," she said to Marjorie with forced gaiety as the two ladies made their way to the attachéd garage in the rear of the cottage. .

"Is that so? Taking Mother Hawkins with?"

"Oh, yes. I'm going to pick her up now."

Rose had no intention of picking up Mother Hawkins. Nor was she going anywhere near Saxlingham. Instead she drove northwest, watching carefully in her rearview mirror. She stopped twice at teahouses for refreshments. It gave her an excuse for being out and about in the event her followers caught up with her. At the second stop, almost two hours from the outset of her trip, she used a public telephone to call the local social services. Without giving her name she reported that an old woman was living by herself at the Hawkins farm at Burton Heath and that she needed looking in on. She replaced the receiver on the telephone and returned to her automobile. It was now quite dark and she had one hundred eighty kilometers yet to London.

Chapter 10

As Street stood in Lufthansa's ticket line at JFK Airport, he had a niggling feeling in the back of his neck. He did not expect armed police to monitor all of the entrances and exits looking specifically for him. There were many, higher-priority desperadoes to occupy the attention of police agencies in this country than August Street. No, there were other threats to his life and liberty, many quite subtle. As the line inched along Street passed the time by watching his fellow ticket buyers. He tried to guess which would be more carefully scrutinized than others for their ethnicity. Dark-skinned people would set off subconscious lightbulbs in the heads of security personnel, especially those of Semitic features. Street was definitely not dark-skinned, his hair somewhere between blonde and brown, his eyes green, not brown.

His name, now Brightmeyer, was most likely not on a watch list. They almost certainly had not connected Street and Brightmeyer.

Faces.

"Next."

It was, he realized, his turn for the open window among the six ticket stations working through a waiting public. He picked up his bag and carried it toward the counter knowing that if Lufthansa was equipped with feature-recognition machines, his discovery would not come in this line but after. His luggage was examined and he presented his purchased ticket at the security check station. That was where the scanner would pick up his image and, at the speed of a photon, match his facial features against the airline's watch list.

As he stood in front of the smiling face of a ticket seller, he almost backed away. He could make an excuse, any excuse, for leaving the area.

"Sir?" the ticket seller urged.

"Sorry about holding things up."

"Not a problem," she said, using a mindless response that Street had come to find increasingly irritating. "Name?"

"Arthur Brightmeyer. I have no reservation but I want to be on the next flight to London," he said.

The ticket girl knit her brows as she worked her computer keyboard. Street was aware that more than fifty flights per day left New York for London and that there was almost no way that all of the flights, provided by a number of airlines, would be fully booked. That was not the problem.

"I have a flight departing at 7:00 P.M., Mr. Brightmeyer, but it goes to Gatwick Airport, not Heathrow," she said, eyebrows rising to frame the question.

"That would be just fine."

"Round trip?"

"One way."

"All right…" After several moments of operating her keyboard she was ready. "That will be seven hundred eighty-eight dollars."

Street handed the ticket girl his unproven credit card. She swiped it through her electronic processor, waited, then frowned.

"Hmm. Doesn't want to take it."

Street's stomach muscles tightened. "It's a new card," he said, lamely.

Without further comment the girl swiped the card again. And waited.

"There we go," she said. "Happens a lot."

She passed the card back to Street who began breathing again.

The young lady handed him a ticket and attended to his check through luggage, a bag still lacking a full wardrobe.

"Flight eight one six," she said, stapling his baggage check to the ticket jacket. She told him the departure gate and added, "The equipment is a Boeing 737-700. They'll start boarding at about six twenty-five, Mr. Brightmeyer. Have a nice trip."

He had a wait of almost three hours but Street wanted to test security now rather than worry about it. Carrying a small bag containing nothing more ominous than two writing pads, a paperback novel, a bottle of aspirin, two pens, and a package of chewing gum, Street removed the reading glasses from a zippered pocket of his suede jacket. Their magnification was plus one, hardly enough to alter the apparent size of distant objects, but the frames did wonders to change his appearance. Or so he thought. Most security lines were open and as Street opted for one near the middle, he hoped its operators would be sufficiently tired to pass him through without a second glance.

He first placed his carry-on bag into a plastic tray, then kicked off his loafer shoes and placed them in a second tray. He watched as the three items were carried away on a conveyer belt for X-ray while waiting his turn at the metal detector. Immediately behind that and directly at the end of the conveyer was the lens at which all passengers were required to pause.

"Remove your glasses, please."

Of course, Street thought. Idiot. What good did they do him now? As required, he looked into the scanning lens.

"Thank you," a laconic security man said.

It was that easy.

Retrieving his shoes, bag, and jacket, and feeling like a man reprieved, Street walked with new purpose along the pedestrian walkway toward his terminal.

Chapter 11

The return to Wales was a journey of sadness for Street. Thomas MacQueen was a man of gravity and his friendship with Street, however brief, had been intense. Street admired everything about the man—his courage, his insight, his sense of duty and, most of all, his great kindness to others, which he tried unsuccessfully to hide. What the man had endured for Queen and country, Street could not hope to fathom. We all have to die sometime, he thought, but Street had hoped that somehow MacQueen would manage to cheat the reaper for a much longer time.

The route to Saundersfoot was fresh in his mind; he might have passed this way just last week. He drove his hire car through the green hills and ever-gray clouds toward the Western Sea Approaches, since the Middle Ages, England's life blood. They had been guarded with unmatched skill and ferocity by the salty, unequaled British navy.

It was late in the evening when he arrived at the Cliff House on Wogan Terrace. In the crush of his arrival and nervousness about hiring a car at Gatwick Airport he had not taken the time to call ahead for reservations. He need not have worried for it was the off season and the omnipresent gray clouds of the coast carried with them a consistent cold rain that kept tourists away. He asked the desk clerk for the same room overlooking the bay that he had occupied more than two years ago. It was taken but a nearby room, also overlooking the bay, was available. He signed the registration, gladly.

Street deposited his light suitcase in the room, and quickly washed his face and hands, anxious to get on with his mission but with a certain sense of dread. He left his hire car at the hotel. He walked with his coat buttoned and collar turned up, unmindful of his body's discomfort. He passed by the marina, eyes down, head pulled into his shoulders, the cold wind and rain soaking him and discouraging a leisurely look at the boats.

By the time he arrived at The Wise Pelican the rain had turned to mist but the cold wind, unabated, pushed him through the pub's wide door. The outside of the building was essentially unchanged, as far as Street could tell, but as he walked through the front door, he could see that the interior of the place had been altered. The semicircular bar was in the same place on the far side of the room but Street noticed that instead of one, there were now two bartenders. Both of them were moving quickly to serve drinks to waitresses delivering to tables as well as customers sitting at the bar. There were now more tables than he remembered; they were smaller, and more people were sitting at each.

The crowd was a younger one. Rock music played on a stereo system. The noise level was high. Strangely, however, on closer look at the patrons Street noticed a number of people, middle-aged, who might have been present during one of his several visits in the past. For the most part, they sat at the bar sipping their drinks, cigarettes hanging from their lips, unsmiling. The one thing that had not changed was the smell of cooking oil and the unmistakable aroma of fish and chips. Street realized that he had not eaten since dinner served aboard the trans-Atlantic jet. There were no unoccupied tables but he found a place at the bar. He waited patiently until one of the bartenders asked him what he'd have. He said that he wanted a lager beer, whatever the bartender had on tap, and an order of fish and chips.

Street would have recognized the man who, acting upon MacQueen's orders to fetch the best Scotch whiskey in the world, had opened the door on the floor behind the bar that led to the basement had he been there, but these were two men he had not seen before. As he sipped his beer and waited for the arrival of his food, Street wondered if MacQueen would have approved of the change of clientele in his establishment. Probably not, Street decided. The place could have operated as it is now when the old veteran was still running it.

"How are ye, sir? The place don't look the same, does it?" a voice behind him asked.

Street turned on his stool to behold a missing link. He was a man whose age was difficult to judge except that it was probably between forty and fifty. One of his two front teeth was crooked, slightly overlapping the other. He might have lost a few hairs on his head since the last time Street had seen him, but it was still black and it was kept in place with oil. He was well under six feet in height but for the first time since Street had seen him, he was on this side of the bar instead of the other. In his hand he held a drink.

"Well, hello. Stupid of me, I forgot your name," Street said, offering the fellow his hand.

"Don't know that you ever got it, Mr. Street. Old Thomas never was much on social niceties. Specially around the hired help. Name's Louis."

Louis accepted Street's offer to shake hands. He was very strong, not the kind of grip one would expect from a man who made his living behind a bar. Nor was the hand soft. Rather it was coarse, the kind of hand that had done hard work without gloves.

"But I remember you well, Louis. You once plunged into the basement from behind the bar to came back with a bottle of the best Scotch I've ever tasted."

"And you had your drinks with old Thomas," Louis said.

"A good man," Street said.

"Did ya think so? The crotchety old burr? Ya could really stand to be around him?"

"I could. Damn right I could stand to be around him. And if he were here now..."

"The place wouldn't look like this, would it? Listen to that God-awful noise. Terrible hard on the ears."

The current musical offering was hiphop. This particular onslaught was an affront to all of Street's musical tastes.

"Is this a day off for you, Louis?"

Louis took a deep quaff of his drink, a darker brew than Street's.

"I don't work here anymore."

"Did you quit?"

"I suppose you could say that. I work at the bicycle place, now. Kinda temporary but I've always been into bikin'. I'm with a lady. Over there at a table. She'd like to meet you."

Carrying his beer in one hand, Street followed the ex-bartender to the far side of the room. The table, hardly providing room for three, was however located next to a window that offered a view of the bay.

"Meet Nina Crandall, Mr. Street. She knows who you are, dontcha, Nina?"

"Yes. Don't we all," Nina said, not offering her hand nor looking Street directly in the eye. She seemed far more interested in pulling the last bit of smoke from her nonfiltered cigarette and making sure that the city street lights were in working order. A drink at her elbow was hardly touched, Street noted.

Thus discounted as an object of her interest, Street took his time in looking her over. He guessed her to be about thirty, although it was his curse to frequently judge women to be younger than they actually were. Her hair color, what would be referred to as dishwater blonde, seemed a chore she was unwilling to deal with. It was pushed generally away from her face and most of it was fastened in the back. Tonight it was held together with a rubber band but it might have been any kind of clasp tomorrow night. Her nose was aquiline. It might have been broken at one time, but its slight hook was not unattractive. While she was sitting down it was not easy to judge her height but she was certainly not short. Her arms, covered by a wool cardigan, were on the thin side. Her raincoat was dropped carelessly over the back of her wrought-cane chair, a head scarf tucked into one of the armholes.

"Very glad to meet you, Nina," Street said.

"Yes? Why is that?" she asked, this time her eyes unflinchingly fixing his.

"Well, I... that is, any friend of—"

"Any friend of my good ol' pal Louis is a friend of mine, eh?" she said.

At an utter loss for words, Street looked to Louis. The barman's face was unchanged by their dialogue. He seemed almost disinterested.

"I'm sorry if I've somehow offended you. Maybe this isn't the best time for me to interrupt your, ah, party." Street shifted his weight in his chair as though to rise.

"Relax, Mr. Street," Louis said, evenly. There was a certain authority, certainly confidence, in the man's words that caused Street to check his notion of leaving the table.

For what to Street was a very long moment, quiet prevailed at the table. Neither Louis nor Nina seemed particularly interested in his presence.

"Well, since we're on the subject," Street began, awkwardly, "I'm not traveling under the name of Street. Uh, not August, either."

Louis snorted. "I should hope not. The name Brightmeyer won't win you no awards either, Mr. Street."

"How did you know that? Brightmeyer. I didn't tell you that name."

Louis withdrew a handful of peanuts from a pocket of his leather jacket. He began to place the nuts in circle on the table. After he had completed one circle, he placed still another circular peanut line inside the first. Then he began to eat them one at a time. Nina might not have noticed. Or, if she did, she accepted the peanut circles in their totality.

"No need to wonder, Mr. Street. There was a man in here last night looking for a Mr. Arthur Brightmeyer. The night before that as well." Louis selected a nut from the outer circle and began to chew. His mastications were deliberate. The nut, to watch him chew, was savory.

"Really?" Street asked, idiotically. He could think of nothing more insightful. Then, he said, "Is he here now?" He successfully resisted the temptation to turn his head and scan the room.

"Not tonight, and not tomorrow night, neither." Louis said with certainty.

"You'll have to get rid of that trash you're carrying around in your wallet." Nina said. She thumbed the wheel of a gun-metal gray Zippo lighter and held it under a fresh cigarette.

"The cards? They were hard to get. Not only that but my money was lost, my personal money, that is, and the cards—"

"Don't be an ass. What good are the cards to a dead man?" she asked.

Street suddenly wanted something stronger to drink. He motioned to a nearby waitress.

"Scotch," he croaked.

"Scotch it is. Any particular kind?" the slightly overweight girl wanted to know.

Street naturally looked to Louis to help him with his choice but the smaller man's attention was elsewhere.

"Hallard's," he said, picking the brand from an advertising sign hanging on the wall behind the bar.

"You can't stay at your hotel," Louis said. "It isn't safe."

"All right," he said, dumbly. He tried to imagine how he would execute his plan of action without a room in which to sleep or credit cards to find another, but there was no doubt in his mind that Louis and Nina were giving him life-saving advice.

"MacQueen was murdered, wasn't he?" Street said.

Louis nodded his head.

"How?"

Louis leaned forward in his chair as though examining his remaining peanuts with greater focus.

"Very simple, Mr. Street. A mixture of prussic acid and vinegar. Either can be bought at a chemist's shop. The stuff can be put into an atomizer to make a mist. Wrap a newspaper around it and you have an innocent-looking deadly weapon. Put the newspaper under a person's nose and give 'em a squirt. Just a whiff of the stuff is instantly fatal. Looks like a heart attack. Thirty minutes later there ain't a sign of the chemicals in the body. No trace at all."

Street was certain that Louis knew first-hand how to whip up a batch of the killing solution and probably other formulas as well.

"I take it, Louis, that you haven't spent your whole life working behind a bar."

Louis did not respond.

"And do you know who did it?" Street pressed.

"Oh, yes. The same people who will get you when the time is right."

"Another for you, Louis?" the waitress asked, placing a short glass of Scotch in front of Street.

"Not me, love. Time to go. Got to be up in the morning to get the worms, you know."

Nina emitted a grunt. "Perceptive devil, aren't you?" she said to Street.

"There was a time when I thought I was," Street said, self-doubt obvious in his tone.

"All right," Louis said, "let's be off, then."

Street tossed off his neat glass of Scotch, rising with Louis and Nina.

"After you see me step into the loo, Mr. Street, put your arm around Nina's shoulder and move toward the front door. Let Nina step outside while you stop at the loo yourself."

Louis finished off the last bit of his drink, then rose from the table and walked off.

Without questioning his new and unexpected relationship with Louis the bartender, Street did as he was told. He placed his arm somewhat awkwardly around Nina's shoulder. His sense was not to make the charade too emotive. For her part Nina made no display of affection but merely tolerated the arm. The couple, it might seem, were merely going to continue their evening together in another location.

Inside The Wise Pelican's washroom Street availed himself of the utilities while Louis merely rinsed his hands at a sink. Saying nothing until the last customer left, Louis turned to Street. In his hand he had a good number of large-denomination British pound notes, American dollars and euros. He passed them to Street.

"This will last you a good while if you're careful. Put your cards and passport into the bottom of the trash right here," Louis said, nodding toward a can stuffed with paper towels. "Someone back in the States must have told on you, old boy."

Street removed his wallet from his hip pocket and began to open it.

"My passport," he said.

"Everything," Louis said, briskly.

"My bag at the hotel. And the car," Street said.

"Forget the bag. I'll see to the car. Walk out in front of me. Nina will be waiting in a car out back."

"Where are we going?"

"Go now."

The wind had not waned and rain had resumed its downpour when Street descended the brick steps from The Wise Pelican's door to the driveway in the rear. The car waiting in front as promised was an unremarkable ten-year-old Fiat. He was glad to get out of the weather as he took the seat next to the woman about whom he knew nothing. He looked at her fully as he fastened his seatbelt while she, without waiting for him to finish his chore, accelerated out of the parking lot and into light traffic. She drove through the middle of town, the only part of the town with which Street was even vaguely familiar, and onto the main thoroughfare, then turned northwest on Valley Road, Carmarthen Bay behind them. He caught a glimpse of a signpost that said they were moving toward Pentlepoir. The name meant nothing to Street. The visibility was poor in the driving rain through the Fiat's windscreen. He gave up trying to navigate.

"How far are we going?" he asked.

"Not far. My house."

"You didn't strike me as a local lady," Street said.

"And what does that group look like?"

"Short and fat."

Street believed, for a fleeting moment, that he saw the beginnings of a smile at the corners of her mouth.

It seemed to Street that they were driving fast but when he looked at the speedometer it registered only seventy-five, and that was in kilometers, not miles. It was the rain and the wind which, in gusts, caused the Fiat to sway precariously. Wherever they were going, however, they were not traveling direct. Nina would make sudden turns, perhaps three consecutively, only to stop at the end of a block, lights off, engines running. She reversed herself several times before she was certain that they were not being followed.

When they finally put the town behind them, they drove in silence for more than thirty minutes until they arrived at another small town near the Irish Sea, not unlike Saundersfoot but less elegant. This village had no marina that featured fine sailing boats; rather it supported a small fishing fleet. Nina parked the Fiat on a side street within two blocks of the waterfront. They then walked four more blocks to a place where there was a sign that read Cozy Nook Cottages. The cottages were in sad need of repair from the ravages of high winds and sea air. He followed Nina to the side of one of the cottages at the end of a row. Nina led the way up four steps with Street close behind. She paused at the top long enough to unlock the bolted door. Were the house truly Nina's, she would not have needed to try two or three keys in the lock before it opened.

Closing the door behind him, she waved his hand away from a light switch. She peered around the side of a curtain, from the darkness of the room into the darkness of the street beyond, her eyes searching thoroughly for movement from a presence that might be out of place. After several minutes she backed away from the window and, reluctantly, Street thought, snapped on a low-watt lamp.

The room they entered offered no surprises to Street given the circumstances. It was cold, sparsely furnished, and what there was in the way of furnishings was dated and well worn. The entrance opened onto a kitchen furnished with a wooden table and three unmatched wooden chairs. There was an aging electric range placed near a sink, which dispensed hot and cold water from two faucets. The floors were linoleum continuing, Street would soon learn, throughout the apartment. The second room was the main room. There was no TV that he could see and the walls smelled moldy. There was an overstuffed mohair sofa that looked invitingly comfortable to Street, a rocking chair that was tattered but also serviceable, a standing lamp, and two unmatched end tables, one of which supported a radio. The radio was an inexpensive but new model, probably built in Asia. There was an open door beyond which, Street could see without entering the room, was a bed. Still another door, set between the main room and the bedroom, Street guessed would reveal the lavatory. There were heavy curtains covering the windows.

"Don't do that," Nina said to Street as he reached to open them.

Street complied but moved to one side so that he glimpsed a small and obscured view of the multi-pane opening to the outside world.

"The electric heater will get the place warmed up," she said, operating a switch that turned on a radiant heater, then walked into the bedroom where she repeated the process with the same kind of old yet efficient reflection heater.

"You sleep out here," she said, dropping a pillow and two blankets on the sofa. "Louis will be by in the morning."

"Do you suppose we might have something to drink?" Street asked.

"Tea, most likely."

"And, if it isn't asking too much, a bite of something? I never did get my fish and chips at The Wise Pelican."

"Let's see what we've got," Nina said, now shedding the fleece-lined jacket and, after glancing about, hanging it in her room on a brass bedpost.

As Street watched her move about the apartment and its kitchen, opening one cabinet door after another to peer inside, his suspicion was that this was not her house was confirmed.

"What's your last name, Nina?"

"Not important," she said, pausing to light a cigarette as she worked to open a can of tuna fish.

"Those things will kill you, you know," he said.

She turned to him squarely. "What I do is nobody's business. I smoke where I want and when I want."

"I wasn't talking about cigarettes. I mean the tuna. They're full of lead."

For a very long moment she continued her unblinking stare at him. Then, the corners of her mouth twitched and she smiled.

"Okay, Mr. Street. That was funny."

"August."

"August. I won't be calling you August very long. Louis will have a new name for you tomorrow."

"Who is Louis? Why is he helping me?"

"There are people who worked for the Crown who merit lifetime protection. Louis is one of those who protect. And he's very good at it. Ex-SAS," she said.

"I've never worked for the British government. Why is he doing this for me?"

"Because of your book, for God's sake," Nina said, turning to face Street. "You named names. You opened up a very big secret. Louis was Thomas MacQueen's bodyguard, you see."

"Ah," Street said, thinking hard. "MacQueen never said—"

"Because he never knew. He would have sent Louis away if he had known Louis had been assigned to watch over him."

She found an onion in one of the cupboards and diced it.

"Interesting. But if the Crown, and its allies, are out to close me down, and Louis is an agent of the Crown, isn't that a conflict?"

"Yes, it is. Very complicated. I think you should keep your fingers crossed, August."

"And you? Why are you helping me?"

He noticed her face quickly clouding and wished that he had taken another, less direct tact at getting to know her.

"That is my business and none of yours."

She opened a fresh jar of mayonnaise with ease. She placed two spoonfuls of mayo with the onion and mixed it into the tuna. Street moved from a chair at the table to the aging refrigerator.

"May I?" he asked.

"Sure. Help yourself," she said.

Inside the box was a dozen eggs, six lager bottles of beer, breakfast rolls, a cube of butter, a tin of coffee, and a package of precooked potatoes. In a lower compartment there was a package of prepared salad and a sealed dressing to put on it.

"Beer?" he asked, taking one for himself.

"I've got tea started for myself."

Street placed the bottle of beer back into the refrigerator.

"Sounds good. I'll join you."

Nina cut two sandwiches in half, placing them on small dishes. She also poured tea into cups, placing one in front of Street's plate. She opened two more drawers before finding napkins.

"This is going to have to do," she said.

"It's wonderful."

And it was. Street was famished. Well before he had finished his sandwich he was thinking about building another for himself.

"Eat mine," Nina said, pushing her plate toward him with another half of a sandwich untouched.

"No, that's yours."

"I'm full," she declared, reaching for a nearby cigarette pack.

Still chewing, Street accepted her largesse.

"What happens after tomorrow?" he asked between bites. "After Louis gets here, that is."

She answered first with a shrug of her shoulders, but then decided to talk.

"That's up to you, isn't it? I mean, here you are, stumbling about the countryside with a sizable number of people who want to get their hands on you. Not to give you an award of any kind. Not for your writing. But to make sure you die. You do realize that, don't you, Mr. Street? So you better have a plan. And don't count too heavily on Louis. You're not alone in all of this."

"And Louis? Is he alone in all of this?"

Slowly Nina shook her head.

"No. He's not," she said.

The last bite of tuna fish sandwich suddenly became unappetizing to him. It had not occurred to him that he not only needed a plan but he needed one that would work. He had been busy congratulating himself on being clever, in stealing another man's identity and thinking he had gotten away with it when clearly he had not. He had warned Rose Smythes Hawkins that she was in danger, but had he done the right thing?

"Rose Hawkins," he said quietly as he tried to think.

"Yes? What about her?"

"Do you know who she is?"

As Street watched Nina for a reaction he was grateful that she did not roll her eyes.

"Yes, of course."

"She's in London. At least I hope she is. I told her that they were after her, too. At least I believed that to be the case."

He had Nina's attention.

"Where, in London?"

"In Putney. Near her old address on Hammil Lane. I rented a flat for her."

Nina slowly leaned back in her chair as she mashed the stub of her cigarette in a saucer. "Well," she said, "it might have been worse. She might even still be alive."

"I know I did the right thing."

"I have to go out."

"Where?" he asked.

"I may be late. Bed covers are in that cupboard," she said, nodding to a small door adorned with a tarnished brass handle.

And with that she was gone.

Chapter 12

Clay Waldon had not eaten lunch despite the late hour. The Russian ambassador insisted upon seeing him even though he was not on Waldon's calendar. Perhaps that was why he had no appetite, he thought.

"I allowed thirty minutes for your meeting with Ambassador Khoklov," said Waldon's secretary. "His chief of staff did not want to say what it's all about so I rescheduled your four o'clock appointment with William Fell and James Gleason. They won't mind being kept waiting if you run over. Happy to have the audience in the first place, you know."

"Thank you, Gregory. Am I going to have time to pee between the Russian and the fundraisers?"

"No, sir."

"Ah. Can you get me something to eat? I'm not hungry but I should eat something. Maybe just a bowl of soup and a little salad."

"Of course. I had the navy bean and ham soup today and I recommend it."

"Fine."

"And a Caesar with corn bread," the secretary said with a certain note of finality.

"Perfect. Butter for the corn bread," Waldon said. Maybe the meeting with Khoklov wouldn't be so bad and he'd get his appetite back.

As it happened, the Russian's office called to ask the prime minister's indulgence. Ambassador Khoklov would be just a few minutes late and offered his most profuse apology. Waldon intended to use the unexpected delay against the Russian but was in fact delighted for the extra time to dawdle over what turned out to be a tasty and delightful lunch. He poured himself an extra half-glass of red wine, a bottle from one of the many given to him from French friends. By the time Khoklov arrived Waldon was fully rested and, at least so he thought, back on his game.

"Good afternoon, Mr. Ambassador," Waldon said to the Russian as he was shown in to the prime minister's office. The absence of the more familiar Sasha was meant by Waldon to keep the meeting on a business basis.

"Mr. Prime Minister," Khoklov responded. For the first time in Waldon's memory, neither man offered the other his hand. It was as if each was overworked, needing to get on with business, and so dispensing with nicety.

"I'll get to the point, Mr. Waldon. One of our attachés from our London embassy has disappeared. Murdered, it is safe to say."

"That's a terrible thing, Ambassador Khoklov," Waldon said, slowly retaking his chair and, with a gesture, inviting the Russian to sit.

"Yes, isn't it? And in such a civilized country as Great Britain. We are hoping you might be able to shed light. Reveal for us what you know." The ambassador, though sitting, leaned forward, quite clearly in no mood to relax.

"Well, of course we'll tell you what we know. Scotland Yard will be totally cooperative. And so will MI5. Alexander, being honest, I assume your man was an agent, eh? Not that it matters at all except that to admit it might get us to the bottom of the event much quicker."

"I can assure you categorically that he was no such thing. He was a cultural attaché who had an appointment with one of your citizens, Thomas MacQueen."

"How do I know that name? MacQueen," the prime minister mused aloud.

"I think you know the name very well. He was one of your decorated commandoes in the Great Patriotic War."

"Ah. A character in one of those thrillers? My wife told me about the book, as I recall."

"The man dies of a so-called heart attack on the same day he was to meet with our attaché, who was staying in a hotel three blocks away and who suddenly disappeared. I must tell you, Clay, that the attaché was a close friend to President Breznichian. Very close. I cannot tell you how seriously we are taking this event," the Russian said.

"You're leaping to very big conclusions when there may be no problem whatsoever. This MacQueen fellow dies of a heart attack and—"

"Please don't insult our intelligence, Clay. MacQueen was liquidated. On your orders."

"Now, look here, Alexander—"

The prime minister was stopped mid-sentence by the Russian's upraised palm.

"We had a man watching. He saw. You think we do not know what is happening with this Raven Operation you are trying to cover up? Your people have gone too far. I have to respond to President Breznichian by this time tomorrow. What will I tell him, Mr. Prime Minister?"

"I assure you nothing could be further from the truth, Alex. Believe me. I'm entirely flabbergasted at this news. And I can assure you that—"

"Do not reassure me, Clay. Help me. I cannot let this pass. He was a senior man. Highly respected in our foreign office. Not a thug, if you understand."

"Of course."

"I know how these things work. A problem arises. The boss tells the little men to take care of the problem. The boss does not want to hear how the problem gets taken care of, he just wants to hear nothing further about it. This is what I think happened with our man."

"And he was…?"

"His name was Viktor Villapov. He was not known to you, personally, I am sure."

"No, you're correct. Well, I can categorically assure you that your surmise about some kind of problem being taken care of does not exist here. We don't have those kinds of problems between our two countries anymore, Alexander. You know that."

Waldon's assured pronouncement brought a deep sigh from the Russian.

"I had hoped it would not come to this, Clay. I am trying to be candid. Mr. Antipov will not tolerate this assassination—"

"Disappearance," Waldon quickly interjected.

"—of a man he personally knew to be a non-Intelligence embassy man," Khoklov lied evenly, "carried out by your Military Intelligence personnel."

Prime Minister Waldon felt his knees suddenly tremble even though he was sitting down.

"Oh, come now. Isn't that a huge leap? You're suggesting that I ordered an assassination? I'm afraid I don't know how to react. What you have said is objectionable, Alex, on more than one level."

For a very long moment the Russian regarded his British host in silence. Then, still without a response of the kind the prime minister expected, he pushed himself slowly to his feet.

"Thank you for this audience," he said coldly.

Waldon, now on his feet but looking at the ambassador's back as he let himself out of the office, swallowed words of conciliation that had tried to made themselves heard. He cursed under his breath, then cursed again, louder. Angrily, he picked up his desk telephone and mashed the autodial button that would put him in touch with C.

"Hello? Who the devil is this?"

"Rupert Hesslik, sir. The chief is out of the office. I will have him located at once," a voice on the other end assured the prime minister.

Edward Wiles, chased out of his Scotland sinecure, had chosen the south of Spain for his temporary refuge. He had avoided airports and automobile agencies in favor of more inconspicuous travel by train. European train transport was the ultimate leveler for all social strata, containing its own class system by virtue of accommodation bought with one's ticket. It was the most egalitarian mode of transport that attracted the least attention. He had never enjoyed travel by any means in a life that had forced movement upon him often and usually at some peril. This trip through the Pyrénées was no exception. He had long ago reached the time in his life that he longed for a family, someone near and warm with whom he could communicate on the simplest terms. He had a family, or what was left of one, but it was anything but simple. And communication was only a technical event, not a soulful experience.

He had traveled, as always, a circuitous route. He had passed through Portugal, through a number of villages and towns along the Iberian Peninsula, before changing trains at Castro Verde in the Faro province. He boarded when passengers were notified, found an empty seat in the second class section of the train, then stepped off again with less than two minutes until departure. He lit a small cigar, watching carefully those milling about the train platform. A good watcher was difficult to spot, especially for Wiles who, while spending his entire adult life in the espionage business, nevertheless had not received the kind of acute field training required to operate at high levels. Even so, he thought his intuition was still keen. The collection of people remaining at the station appeared benign. *Ah*, he sighed, *that was exactly the way a watcher would seem.* He reboarded the train just as the conductor was closing his door. He walked through the now gently swaying cars until he reached the first class car. His ticket entitled him to a seat there in a well-padded four-chair compartment, but for some undefinable reason, he retraced his steps toward the rear of the train. He found an empty chair in a third-class car and sat.

He hoped this trip to Spain would be smoother than his travel in nineteen forty-seven. His wartime comrade, Stephen Dietrich, was arrested by Spain's secret police in Madrid. Dietrich had just been released from Allied Army's custody but was still considered a criminal to Generalissimo Franco's regime. His tiny apartment was searched and all his belongings were confiscated. He was then thrown into a cell with counter-revolutionaries. Wiles knew of Dietrich's handwritten diary. Those papers had fallen into the hands of Spanish authorities and the SOE, meaning Wiles had to get them back quickly and at any cost. Wiles had recovered the papers by paying off low-level police functionaries which, at the time, was the way most business was done. He had returned the diary to Stephen in exchange for a promise that they would never be made public. Now, fifty-eight years later, those same papers were priceless.

A young lady, hardly out of her teens, entered the compartment and moved toward the rear of the car looking for a seat. She was flirted with by two young men as she moved along, one of whom rose from his seat and offered to squeeze her into a space between the two of them. Annoyed, she turned away without speaking to them. Wiles had taken an aisle seat. The girl paused, and nodded her head toward the window seat without speaking. Wiles rose, ushering her to a place next to him. Out of a lifetime of habit, he had touched the edge of his wool beret, a gesture few men would now make and the girl was amused.

The disappointed young men made comments that Wiles and the girl could hear, but they were not offensive.

There was, he guessed, about two hundred twenty miles to travel before reaching Seville. Though the train was sleekly modern, the trip would not be made at high speed. For several minutes he feigned interest in a paperback book while he examined each face and each profile of his fellow passengers. As the train picked up speed leaving the coastal region and heading for mountainous terrain, Wiles felt a rare sense of well being. He felt the need to close his eyes.

He opened them some time later when a vender was passing through the car selling food of various descriptions from a cart. The thought of tea nudged Wiles's fancy, and the idea of a croissant and cheese sounded even better. He regarded his young fellow traveler for a moment and asked, in Spanish, if she would like something from the cart. A beverage, perhaps?

"I will have a wine," she said in a surprisingly cultured speech, "but I will not let you pay." She reached to her side where she kept her purse.

He was amused. "You'll not deprive me of the pleasure," he said, indicating to the vendor that they would have two wines, pastry, and Brie cheese, the notion of tea suddenly seeming pedestrian.

Her name was Carla del Vega Milagros. She was a graduate history student at the Berne Academy. He told her his name was Adrian Small.

"English," she said, poking a piece of her croissant at the soft Brie cheese.

"Welsh," he said, switching from Spanish to English.

"Oh. You lost your kingdom." She, too, was fluent in English but with an accent of Europe, not necessarily Spanish.

"What's that?"

"In fifteen thirty. You were annexed by England."

"Not to put too fine a point on it, it was we Celts who allowed the British Crown to join us in empire building," Wiles theatrically arched an eye and sniffed. "And it was fifteen thirty-three."

"And you are one of them. An empire builder."

"Certainly. I take great pride in the empires I've built. Are you tired of school yet?"

"Yes. Because I am not a good student. And it seems like I have been there forever. I want to get out and work. With history, what will I do but teach?"

"You might be surprised."

Wiles signaled to the vendor, when he passed through, for two more wines and was pleased that Ms. Milagros did not object.

"Do you think it is a good reference for my resumé?"

"Why not? What a prospective employer wants to know is how well you think. Some people are better at it than others."

"Then I will be a failure. I am a bad thinker."

"I know you are teasing me. But it's true, thinking at complex levels takes training."

"Like you?" she laughed at him.

"No. I was cheated by Providence," he said, enjoying time spent with the girl.

Wiles opened two more bottles of what had become tolerably drinkable Burgundy. There was still a bit of Brie cheese left, which they wordlessly agreed to divvy up.

The train traveled more slowly as it climbed through the Sierra Morena mountains. The scenery was quite beautiful, its colors in the setting sun remarkably enhanced by the tranquilizing effect of the wine. Wiles and Carla shared the warm effect in easy quiet.

"Do you have a man in your life, Carla?"

The girl did not answer immediately. She seemed to consider, first.

"Yes. But…"

"But what?"

"Well. More than one."

Wiles was entertained at the light in the girl's eyes. It made him remember his own youth.

"Do your parents know that you are, ah, involved, with more than one man?"

She shrugged. "They ask me, like you. In Switzerland there is a lot of skiing, for instance, and where there are skis, there are girls and boys. You can't avoid it, you know. Besides, I'm a woman."

"Hmmm."

"Sometimes I think you Englishmen need more snow on your slopes. You can be so uptight."

"We should have girls in our sporting lives much sooner," Wiles observed.

"Yes. I think so."

"I couldn't agree with you more."

"And your wife? Where is she, now?"

"She's waiting for me in London. I'm looking for a vacation house to buy in Spain, but Emma doesn't like to travel," Wiles lied without restraint. Emma. How did that name pop into his head? As far as he knew there was no Emma in the long ancestry of the Wiles.

"That's too bad. She's missing a lot."

"Oh, I don't know. She has a very fulfilling life. She's something of a social lion. Or lioness."

"My mother and father like to travel. I think that's why they sent me away to school, so they could go places without me."

"I'm sure they did nothing of the sort. Where do they live when they're not traveling?"

"Malaga. My father made very much money in beef. And my mother spends the beef money," Carla said as she drank fully from her plastic cup.

"Does your father approve?"

"Oh, yes. They have been married for almost thirty years. They do everything together, including spending beef money."

Carla's eyelids sagged. The sight of them subconsciously caused Wiles's to droop as well.

He might have napped. When he became alert again they were near Seville.

They rode the escalator from the boarding platforms to the main lobby of the modern station, called Santa Justa. The beautiful old one was now a shopping mall. She paused near the corridor that would take her to the baggage claim, and here they bade each other goodbye. While Wiles carried his light travel bag by its shoulder strap, Carla still had to claim her several bags, she said, and he should go on without her. Her mother, or someone in her family, would meet her. Wiles had enjoyed their meeting and told her so. Still, he was glad that she did not ask for his company to the baggage claim area because he would have found an excuse to decline.

The old man and the young woman stepped off of the train, neither having spoken more than a few words of truth.

Outside the station Wiles waited for a taxi. There were many in front of the train station, all of them wanting his business, but Wiles waited for the right one.

"Taxi, Señor?"

Wiles looked at the driver stepping out of his cab.

"Yes, thank you," Wiles said, cheerfully, as the driver hurried to relieve Wiles of his bag. The driver opened the rear door of the car for Wiles to step inside.

"Did you have a good trip, Mr. Wiles?" the driver asked.

"Yes, it was very nice, Ramon. I met a young lady." Wiles smiled wistfully at his own foolishness. "How have you been, Ramon?"

"Very good. And we like Spain. Plenty of sun."

"*We?*"

"I'm married. Again," the driver said, smiling along with Wiles. "Not traveling with Louis, sir?"

"Louis had business to attend to at home. He'll be along."

"We have a place for you on the Calle Luis Montoto, Mr. Wiles. Do you know the street?"

"Good heavens. Near the Jesuits? Aren't you afraid I'll contaminate them?"

The two men shared a moment of laughter.

Wiles had always loved Seville. He hoped he would be able to visit one of the great museums or perhaps spend time in the cathedral in the old city. He had only once seen the Giralda tower from the inside. From there, he knew, the view of the city was wonderful. Only blocks from the university of Seville, Wiles realized that the pangs he was feeling inside were not caused by his lost youth and necessary separation from Carla, but by hunger. A good restaurant not far from the campus was, he recalled, very near.

"Ramon, I want to have a bite to eat. Why don't you drop me at La Taberna del Alabardero? I can walk home from there," Wiles said.

"I'll wait for you," the driver said, slowing as he turned a corner on the street that would lead to La Taberna del Alabardero.

"Nonsense. I'll be perfectly safe. You go ahead."

Ramon gave the apartment number to Wiles.

"Can you remember the number, sir?" Ramon asked.

"Of course I can remember it. I'm not senile yet."

Wiles patted Ramon on the shoulder as he exited the cab.

Ramon watched the elderly man enter the restaurant. Once he passed through the doorway, Ramon drove to the address on Calle Luis Montoto. He drove by slowly, giving it a very long look. He continued around the block watching, this time around, the street, the traffic, and the people in the area. It was all quite peaceful, as it should be. The safe house was chosen carefully by himself. Ramon parked his cab as far away from the apartment house as possible, but near enough so that he could watch the entrance at all times. He slumped in his seat, allowing the brim of his hat to slide down onto the bridge of his nose. He appeared to be napping.

Inside the restaurant Wiles ordered from desire rather than discretion. He had his waiter bring prawns in a shellfish sauce and garlic bread. He drank a preferred local red wine. For his entrée he was served a red mullet cooked with leeks and black olive oil. He was not halfway through the meal before he realized he could not finish it all. He declined the waiter's offer to bag what was left for home consumption. He paid his bill and, still carrying his travel bag, began to walk toward Avenida Remurdo.

He walked without hurry, pleasantly stimulated in the warm Spanish weather, but when Wiles let himself into the tiny apartment and climbed the stairs to his room, he felt deeply fatigued. He quickly dropped his carry case and removed his clothing before falling into bed and immediately to sleep.

Ramon remained parked up the street, watching the house for an hour after Wiles's lights winked off. A police patrol car passed by slowly. It was a reassuring sight for Ramon. He started the engine of his car and left the area.

It was after 3:00 A.M. when the door to Wiles's apartment was struck by a heavy, two-man battering ram. The locks on the door simply exploded, fragments of the door and its framing still falling well after the men entered the room. The psychological impact of such a catastrophic event can hardly be understood. All animals, including humans, have a deep subconscious belief that they are safe in the places where they lie, else they could not close their eyes. Further, there is a certain natural-occurring drug produced in the brain that literally doses us to sleep. The technique of smashing in a door during sound sleep is designed to shock the senses and create mental paralysis.

Its effect on an eighty-eight-year-old man can only be imagined. Among shouts of *police!* and *arrest!*, Wiles could offer no resistance, even when strong men had roughly thrown him to the floor, handcuffed him, kicked him twice in the hips, and pulled a hood over his head. He was jerked to his feet and hauled, his feet dragging, down the narrow stairs to the street. He was clad in nothing more than his underclothing. As his awareness began to return, he was sickened knowing that under enough pain he would talk.

Chapter 13

In his dream he was running away. His feet could fly. In the twilight between wakefulness, between fear and audacity, he sensed he was no longer alone. He did not hear the door opening but he knew Nina was back. He could smell her presence, a combination of pungent nicotine and her shampoo was in the air. Now he could hear the sensuous rustle of her removing her clothing as she prepared for bed. He imagined that she was wearing nothing but her bra and panties as she pulled the covers over her. Perhaps he was wrong. She might be wearing nothing. He ached.

Morning, when it came, was anticlimactic for Street because he awakened to the smell of freshly brewed coffee and the soft exchange of cautious voices. He was reminded how lucky he was that his military duty did not require him to stand guard, at least over anything important. If he had, the battle would have been lost.

"Good morning," Nina said, pouring black coffee into a mug. "Cream?"

He shook his head. Sugar was not offered but he would not have used it, anyway.

"How do you feel?" she asked.

"Okay."

"There's a shower in there," she said, jerking her head toward the bathroom.

Louis sat at the kitchenette table, saying nothing. Then, turning to Nina, he asked "Did he go anywhere last night? No? You're sure?"

Then he turned his gaze back to Street.

"How about it, Mr. Street? Did you go anywhere before you dropped off?"

"No."

"Maybe just to see where Nina was off to?"

"Of course not. Why?"

"It's nothing," Nina said.

On Louis's forearm Street could make out a tattoo. It was a shield behind an upraised sword and the words inked into his skin read *Who Dares, Wins.*

"That's right, it's nothing," Louis said, shrugging into his jacket. He got to his feet and went to the door.

"When will you be back?" Nina asked Louis.

"Four days if all goes well," he said. "You know what to do." And he was out the door.

"I suppose I'm not to ask where he's going this time," Street said, not very disappointed with the bartender's departure. Explosives can come in small packages, he recalled.

"There are complications," Nina said, not answering his question directly.

"What kind?"

"They have taken one of our people," she said, simply. "Do you like eggs?"

"What? Yes, of course. Who is he and who took him?"

She shrugged. "If Louis wants you to know he will tell you. We have no morning newspaper. I'll cook."

Street was uncomfortable with the past day's accumulation of dirt on his body. The shower water never achieved much beyond a tepid temperature, but the results were no less invigorating for Street who felt renewed as he dried himself. He tried to catch a glimpse of his body in the wall mirror. It was a small mirror and he had to stand on his toes to see much of himself below the chest. In spite of his pre-middle years he had little fat on his body, a fact that he consciously worked at by walking, running, and avoiding sweets.

The thought of wearing yesterday's underwear appealed to him not at all. While considering his options he opened a nearby drawer to find an unexpected solution to his hopes. In a cabinet drawer were two sets of men's underwear, still contained inside store wrappers, three pairs of sox, a handkerchief, a toothbrush, and toothpaste. There was also a comb, a small travel kit containing a razor, shaving cream, aftershave lotion and a small spray can of antiperspirant. Things were suddenly looking up.

Nina had already served up his scrambled eggs. The fact that most food does not stay warm long, not even scrambled eggs, didn't bother Street. He was hungry. As he dug into the food on his plate, he could see that Nina had finished hers and had already lit the inevitable after-meal cigarette. Right then he didn't care that the eggs were lukewarm or that Nina had filled the small amount of air in the apartment with smoke.

"These eggs are terrific," he said, and meant it.

"My secret recipe. I dice up French fried potatoes. The frozen ones that they dip in batter first..."

"Yes?"

"They taste like llama dung if you follow the manufacturer's directions, but if you sauté them in olive oil at a high heat until they are crisp, add a little onion, then scramble the eggs over it all, you have something special."

"Fabulous," he said. His toasted bread had been lavished with melted butter. "Thank you."

"I do crepes, too."

"I mean thank you for helping me."

She knew very well what he had meant when he said it.

"I'm helping myself. I don't care much about you, Mr. Street. If you benefit by what I do..." She shrugged her shoulders.

"And what *do* you do, exactly?" he asked.

Nina looked at him for a long moment before stubbing out her cigarette and reaching for another. She glanced back at his eyes and decided to postpone her next tobacco fix.

"I choose sides in issues. It happens that you are on the side I agree with. Simple, isn't it?"

"And what side is that?"

"The right one, of course."

"And how do we tell which that is?"

"I don't like Socratic questioning, Mr. Street."

"Oh," he said, "is that what I was doing?"

After a suspended moment of incredulousness, they broke into laughter.

"Sorry," he said quickly. "I didn't mean to do that. And please don't call me mister."

"August? Does that sound better?" Nina asked.

"Yes," he said. It had never sounded better. There was something about the woman's intellect that enhanced the sound of his name when she spoke it. In fact, almost everything that attracted her attention also arrested his. "Well. Still, may I have an answer?" he asked.

"To what? The sides? Does it really matter to you? What side you're on?"

"Absolutely. The world is driven by moral imperatives."

"Nonsense. In the first place the world isn't driven. Rather than being driven, it's like a wreck out of control. Morals are the rules we make up to play our games. Like Rugby. Or soccer."

"You're only partially correct. There are other rules that were here before us. Natural law. Some people call them God's laws." Street snorted. "I'm an agnostic but there are indisputable truths that are independent of man that simply exist in the universe with or without man."

"That's insane. When you die you are gone and your laws are gone with you. The universe will cease to exist for you," she said, reaching for another cigarette.

"So, whatever matters only concerns the here and now?" he asked.

She shrugged again. "Nothing matters."

She looked him fully in the eyes, not daring him, but quite certain of her own perceptions.

"You're a nihilist," he said.

She laughed. "Isn't that better than an idiot? If you must have names for everything—"

"We have to have names in order to understand what things are—"

"Stop it," she said.

He poured himself a second cup of coffee. The ensuing silence was not entirely uncomfortable.

"I agree with you about one thing. It is wrong for the strong to oppress the weak. If there are such things as moral laws of nature, that must be one of them."

"And to torture others," he said, softly.

"Yes. I hate them for that."

Street's agreement was his silence.

"You're staring at me," she said.

"Are you married?"

"I lived with a man. I will tell you something, August Street. I loved him more than I can tell. He has been dead for seven months and the reason he is dead is because of you. It is very hard for me to sit here with you, to protect you, when Paul has been murdered."

Street felt a chill in the pit of his stomach. "Who was he?"

She shook her head. "You wouldn't know him. His name was Paul Glenn Wiles. But you would know of his grandfather—"

"Edward Wiles," Street finished.

Nina nodded her head.

"My God. Wiles has been dead for years."

"No. Edward Wiles is still alive. Paul wanted to help. Edward tried to talk him out of it but ..." She shrugged her shoulders. "It was dangerous. Paul would have done anything for his grandfather; they both knew that. But he was caught."

"Caught doing what?"

"Trying to contact you but they reached him first. He had the proof you need but they never found the papers."

"What papers? You mean for the *Raven* account?" Street asked, his heart beginning to pound.

She nodded her head. "The Hess transcripts."

Rudolph Hess. The closest thing Hitler ever had to a friend. Rabid personalities both, Hess helped Hitler lift the Nazi party from its twisted roots scattered incoherently across the beer halls of Germany, appealing to social misfits, into the most powerful political machine in the nation. Then in all of Europe. The Nazis did it by fighting, literally, in the streets, giving speeches wherever a crowd might gather, and taunting Germany's government in power. After attempting a second putsch to seize control of the government and failing, Hitler and Hess were, in 1923, sentenced to Landsberg prison. In the two years Hitler and Hess were imprisoned, Hess worked slavishly to copy onto paper Hitler's ravings, later to be published under the title of *Mein Kampf.*

When Hitler and Hess were released from prison in 1925, Hess remained closely attachéd to Hitler. He was designated the number-three man in the Nazi party and, at the time, was perceived to be Hitler's most intimate friend. Whether either man had the capacity for such a spiritual association with another human being has for many years been the subject of speculation. But no one questioned Hess's dogged loyalty to Hitler and Hitler's high regard for the man who became his secretary for party affairs.

It was, therefore, a shock to the world, indeed a numbing event to the

German Reich, when in 1941, on the eve of Hitler's invasion of Russia, Rudolph Hess fled to England. No one was more surprised than the British when a report from a farmer was received at an aerodrome in Scotland that a German pilot had landed by parachute and had demanded an audience with his "old friend," the Duke of Hamilton. Hess had met Hamilton briefly during the Berlin Olympics in 1936.

There were rumors that persisted after the war that Hess was taken in by an elaborate plot created by British Intelligence. There was a cabal organized to overthrow the Churchill government, the authors of the ruse were reported to have said. They had the means of informing a gullible Rudolph Hess that a coup was to go forward aimed at toppling Churchill's government, and that his presence could do much to improve its chances. There would be a peace between Germany and Great Britain, now allies, who would take on the Russian Communists. Hess, the SIS account maintained, was known to be an astrological believer and the British story about a plot was buttressed with references to planets that were properly aligned to ensure the scheme's success.

August Street never bought it. Hess, he was sure, was not a stupid man. While he had personality idiosyncracies, he was neither insane nor naive as the SIS wanted the world to believe. It was, Street believed, a story made up after the war as part of the bodyguard of lies favored by SOE and Churchill to cover their Raven tracks.

Street believed that Hess was the only man in Germany who knew that Adolf Hitler was dead and that his place had been taken by a British imposter. Armed with this knowledge, Hess was ready to assist the British in the deception but he had a list of concessions to which he expected the British government to agree in exchange for his cooperation. Whether this was true or not could only be revealed in the transcripts of Hess's interrogations.

"Where are they now? The transcripts?" he asked Nina.

She slowly shook her head.

"Never mind." He knew how it could be done. "I need a telephone."

Nina considered for a moment, then rose from her place at the table and dug into her handbag. She found what she was looking for.

"Here," she said, passing him a cell phone.

"This call may be intercepted," he said, pausing for her reaction.

Nina shrugged. "We won't use it long. They are easy to throw away, you know."

He did not recall the number from memory but it was no trick to ask an information operator for the public phone access. He then dialed the number for the SIS.

"I'm returning a call for Debbie Mears," he said to the operator.

"Her extension number?"

"There was no number left, only her voice on the scrambler," Street said.

There was a substantial pause before the operator spoke again.

"Hold the line, please," she said, then the line went silent.

Presently another voice came to Street through the ether.

"Mears."

"I have an intense craving for Bhutuwa chicken and mamoco with a bottle of ninety-six Pauillac. Are you interested in joining me?"

After a moment that seemed to Street to go on forever, the voice said, "Where did you get this number?"

"They were handing it out to all of us leaving the ship down at the Navy pier," he said.

"You fox. Always know my hot buttons."

"Remember where we ate masco bara?" Street asked, mentioning the name of an excellent black lentil hors d' oeuvre.

"How could I forget?"

"Nine o'clock?"

"I'll be there panting when you come in."

"Wait for me at the bar," Street said, and clicked off.

Nina looked for a cigarette in an empty pack.

"Debbie Mears works in archives. She was my contact person when I did my assignment two years ago at SIS."

"What kind of assignment?"

"I worked for the H. P. Carlisle Foundation in Virginia, USA. The Foundation does specialty work for the U.S. Defense Department. My job was to assist in declassifying MI5 and SIS documents from World War II. That's how I discovered the Raven file," Street said.

"Brilliant of you," she said, at last finding a crumpled cigarette in her purse.

"What's that supposed to mean?"

"It means that you didn't find anything," she said. "Want to play cards?"

"I don't understand," he said.

"What kind of cards do you want to play?"

Street was silent for a long moment while he studied her face. She had tightened her jaw muscles. Body language.

"I don't care."

Nina dealt out two hands. Street put his in ascending order by suits.

"You go first," he said.

"Threes," Nina said.

"Threes what?"

"Give me all your threes."

"What are we playing?"

"Go fish."

Chapter 14

The desk called at three o'clock. They had understood that Mr. Dietrich would be checking out at noon. Had there been a change of plans? Still in his skivvies and a sweater, Dietrich acknowledged that he was staying on another night but would be gone the next day. His response to the desk clerk had elicited the same attention as chewing gum did from a jogger. He had never let the sheaf of papers out of his hands while he talked on the telephone and had never quite stopped reading. He had finished his first run through the material in the early morning hours and had started again from the beginning. The call from the desk had, however, done him the good turn of reminding him that he had not eaten in twenty hours. He called room service for breakfast only to be informed that breakfast was no longer being served, but anything on the lunch menu was available. He ordered a BLT sandwich and coffee.

While his attention was diverted, he helped himself to a shower, then to a clean change of clothes. He was back reading the papers delivered in the box while seated at the room desk, furiously making notes this time around. To his mild irritation he was interrupted by the arrival of room service. He had no cash for a tip but signed a room check leaving one. By nine o'clock that evening Dietrich had eaten only half of the sandwich but had finished his second reading of the documents and had finished copious, if scrawled, notations.

Even while the myriad of lights from New York's cityscape cast his room into an eerie glow and he closed his eyes to ease their burning, he considered what he had just read. His grandfather, after whom he had been named, was a whole person at last. His biography, written for the most part in his own hand, interspersed only with occasional typewritten sheets, was the most fascinating thing he had ever read. Not only that but the fact that it was hand-drafted placed it on approximately the same level as a legal document such as a last will and testament, needing no official witness as to its provenance.

The story told of a young man on a trip through pre-war Europe, of his prolonged stop in Berlin during the summer Olympic games, and of his acquaintanceship with an Englishman, Edward Wiles. Wiles was older than Steven Dietrich but the two men shared a passion for airplanes as well as for Berlin's exciting ambience. Berlin at the time was the capital of the world, not just of Germany, and Adolf Hitler was considered a genius, the man of the century, as judged by millions around the globe. Under Hitler's rule Germany had been the first nation to regain its economic equilibrium from the crippling effects of the Great Depression. The German people were again proud of their heritage, proud of their great Führer, and totally unashamed of their aggression.

Edward Wiles was not in Germany simply to treat himself to the Olympic festivities, as third-year Yale student Steven Dietrich came to learn, but to take a more military assessment of the Fatherland. Although Dietrich was politically naive at the time, it did not take a great deal of sophistication to realize that Adolf Hitler's plans for Europe included all-out war. When Wiles asked young Dietrich to remain in Germany to serve not only Great Britain but America, too, there was much appealing in the proposition. Dietrich's father had been born and raised in Germany. Steven spoke German himself and felt completely at home among his ethnic roots. He was bored with college and would have preferred to devote all of his time to flying high-performance aircraft.

Of course it mattered for whom one did one's flying.

Dietrich, the biography related, contacted his parents and announced that he was staying on in Europe for an unspecified period of time. He had already notified the Yale registrar's office of his decision. There was simply too much of the Continent to see in a few weeks, he explained, and added that he was certain that they would understand. He felt cowardly for wiring this information to his family rather than speaking with them on transatlantic telephone. His father wired back that he was greatly disappointed that he, Steven, had opted out of university when graduation was so near. He considered Steven's decision ill-conceived, but if his mind was made up then his father and mother would support him financially insofar as they could and, of course, would always love him fully and without reservation.

Steven had become friendly with other young Germans and had remained in Berlin long after the Olympic games had ended.

Book II
1936-1940

Chapter 15

The fact that Steven Dietrich was American gave him a certain cachet wherever he went. Affable and intelligent, he fit into almost any social group. It was pleasing to his German friends that he had chosen to live in Germany when, even during the 1930s, America was a desirable, even glamorous country in which to reside. It gave them additional affirmation to support their already growing sense of superiority vis-à-vis the rest of the world's population. America, to be honest they said, was mongrelized and in the long term the nation would be torn apart from within. Jews and Blacks were America's Achilles' heel. Everybody knew that Jews were already running the country and controlling its wealth. Blacks were and would always be a permanently dependent underclass. Someday they would rise up in revolt as they were already beginning to do in Africa. Americans would be slaughtered in their beds.

Dietrich reminded himself that he was not there to argue politics or to reject racist philosophies, no matter how ludicrous. One way to place one's self outside of Germany's social circles, no matter how small their individual orbits, was to speak ill of the Führer or to seriously challenge the German leader's harangue against Jews. Dietrich had never thought much about Jews in any case and, if he were to be quite honest with himself, he supposed he had never cared for them as a group. Like the American Negro, he could take them individually but collectively he felt estranged from them. As time went by in his life in Germany he would come to change his attitude about these matters from detached indifference to great passion. It was one thing to hear rumors about concentration camps or mass deportations, and still another thing to witness inhuman events as they occured. Within the next nine years, Dietrich would find himself shocked to the depths of his soul by savagery he had never imagined could exist among humans sharing the same planet.

That would be later. But now, in 1936, he needed a job.

"Why not work here?" Bunny Hartung said to Steven Dietrich as they lounged at a boulevard table at The Faucet Café or, in German, Das Wasserman. It was the early days of October and, while the weather was still warm, late afternoons contained a bracing nip in the air. Dietrich could sniff football weather. He wondered how he would bear the coming season three thousand miles from the games.

"Yes," Frederick Friedel offered in support of the idea, "this is where I started, you see. History will record it."

"He has a load of bombs he wants to drop," Hartung said, jerking his head toward Friedel. "Tell us, Leutnant Friedel, will you kill women and children as well?"

"No one escapes," belched Friedel, his uniform tunic straining the buttons of his waistline. His dark blue Luftwaffe uniform bore the cuff title of *Geschwader Hindenburg,* inscribed with aluminum thread. There was a silver eagle worn over the right breast pocket, a swastika gripped by the bird's talons. His epaulets were gold and silver, while his lapel badges were gold. Over his left breast pocket was another bird of prey, gold, wreathed in carefully woven aluminum thread. It was the Bomber Gold Clasp. Uniforms look good on almost everyone but, Dietrich thought, attention must be given to preserving the waistline, a challenge for Friedel.

"What war are we talking about?" Dietrich asked. He loved the German lager beer. Perhaps it was only his imagination but it somehow tasted better than beer that came from Milwaukee.

"Any war. We are ready. Pinky!" Friedel shouted for their waiter. "Where are you, you swine? Ah. Isn't it time for the house to buy?"

"But you've just finished a war," Dietrich said.

"What? Finished? Don't be stupid. We are...what you call resting..."

"Taking a break," Dietrich offered.

"Exactly. Breaking, and then we will be right back in the game," Friedel was more than confident.

"But the Locarno Treaty. You don't suppose England and France will allow you to break the treaties and just walk away?" Dietrich was at a loss to understand either Teutonic confidence or real politics. Probably both, he thought.

"It is already done," Hartung said, his mouth pulled into a lopsided grin. "I will hand it to our Leader. He can read minds. We are back in the Rhineland and they only talk. Just talk."

"But they'll only talk for so long," Dietrich said. "Look what happened last time."

There was a long moment of silence while both uniformed German officers looked at him.

"The last time does not count," Friedel said, softly. "The only time that counts is this time. And this time we are ready."

Dietrich knew very little of the Locarno treaties, a series of seven agreements designed to make western Europe secure at the end of the 1914–1918 war. The signatories—Belgium, Poland, England, Germany, and Italy—agreed to respect national boundaries and to establish a neutral zone. Germany was to respect the Rhineland as a demilitarized zone. Hitler, after consolidating his power over the army in 1936, marched troops into the zone in abrogation of all agreements and began building fortifications.

Dietrich turned toward Hartung, a man who seemed to have a better-than-average intellect despite the fact that he tried to hide it.

"So. What happens next? If this is all your leader wants why is he still building more tanks and guns?"

"To catch up," Friedel said, fielding the question.

Hartung said nothing.

"Well?" Dietrich wanted an answer from the SS officer.

"It is very simple, Steven. Women are attracted to uniforms. The more uniforms we have, the more women we attract. The Führer is no fool," Hartung said.

"Ah. Now we are making sense," Dietrich said, nodding.

Pinky, the waiter, stood stone-faced, while the Leutnant turned his beer mug upside down to demonstrate that it was empty.

"Yes," Bunny Hartung quickly agreed, "we must not be publicly embarrassed in front of our American friend here."

"You mean you can't pay your bill," Pinky said.

"Not at all," Hartung said, dismissively. "But you see, timing is everything—"

"And we are out of time," Friedel finished for him.

"Let me buy," Dietrich said, reaching into his pocket. "Make mine Scotch this time."

"Look at what you've done, Pinky." Hartung said. "Now we will have to let our friend pay the bill. You have no shame."

Dietrich dropped several marks onto the waiter's tray. The waiter, a cigarette hanging from the side of his mouth, insolently held the bills up to the light from the sun. He grunted his reluctant satisfaction and walked toward the bar inside.

"You see how well he handled that?" Friedel said to Dietrich, nodding his head toward Obersturmfuhrer Hartung. "It is important to maintain class distinction. We must not soil our hands."

"We learn that in officer's school," Hartung confirmed.

"I think one is born with that kind of power," Dietrich said, facetiously.

"You may be right," Friedel snorted. "It is what separates us from the common people. Remember Elicia's mother? She loved me for what I was," Friedel said, his eyes rolling back in reverie.

"Fat?" Hartung laughed.

"I wasn't fat then," Friedel said, his eyes closing.

"Ah," Hartung said, "the drinks have arrived. Have one for yourself, Dietrich."

"I shouldn't," Dietrich said, reaching for his tumbler of Scotch.

"Where are you staying, Dietrich?" Hartung asked.

"At the moment I'm at the YMCA. Apartments are hard to find. At least at the prices I can afford."

"Maybe you could join the SS," Friedel suggested to Dietrich, dropping a generous handful of beer nuts into his mouth. "Then you could be Bunny's roommate."

"Did you live in a house in America?" Hartung wanted to know.

"Of course."

"Of course? Does every American live in a house?"

"No. I didn't mean that. We are what is known as middle class. Many people, most, I suppose, rent a house. Or apartment. We happen to own ours."

"The Jews own most of the apartments in America," Friedel said, as though it was a point of known fact.

"That's nonsense," Dietrich said.

"The Führer said so," the bomber pilot said.

"He's wrong."

Hartung's eyebrows shot up. "The Führer is never wrong, Dietrich. You must learn that."

Dietrich started to open his mouth but managed to keep it closed.

"He is a superman," Friedel said, taking a long pull from his stein of beer.

"Exactly," Hartung agreed. "Therefore, Dietrich, use the Führer as a guide for all of your actions while you are in Germany."

"Or even if you go on holiday out of the country," Friedel suggested.

"Do you suppose he farts?" Hartung asked Friedel.

"Certainly not." Friedel belched.

"You see, Yank? When you feel the urge to pass gas remind yourself that supermen have no need to engage in flatulence. Sit on your farts, Dietrich."

"I think I am beginning to understand," he said.

Not many would want to be the roommate of an SS officer, Dietrich thought. Hartung's rank of SS Obersturmfuhrer was equivalent to leutnant in both the American and the German army. They were known to be handpicked men, fanatic in their loyalty to Hitler and the Nazi cause. Their profile for physical fitness was demanding and they would become known for their fearlessness in battle as well as for atrocities they committed in the course of waging war.

Yet "Bunny" Hartung seemed not to fit that profile. He had no natural enemies, or at least that's what he had told Dietrich when they first met. He had joined the SS because he had counted on his commanding general, Wilhelm Beckman, to keep him out of war. And he didn't think he would be very good at it, anyway, he said. Besides being self-effacing he was insouciant, tall, blonde, and appealing to women. To that part of his life, Dietrich would learn, Bunny Hartung was dedicated. His contradictory personality was a puzzle to Dietrich as he regarded this man whose field gray uniform with black collar tabs showed the silver runes of the SS and his "Schirmmutze" (peaked) hat contained a small skull, the Death's Head.

"If you don't mind me saying so," Dietrich said, leaning forward in his chair, "you don't seem exactly the kind of man I thought would be attracted to the SS."

Hartung arched an eyebrow. He looked around cautiously, as though to make sure they could not be overheard. Leaning forward, he lowered his voice. "At the formation in Magdeburg, there were thousands of us. We swore a blood oath to our Führer. It was at night, Dietrich. There were aeroplane search lights surrounding our troops. The important leaders of the Reich were there. Himmler, Göring, Goebbels, and of course Hitler himself. I tell you, it was dramatic. You can appreciate it, ja? When they administered the blood oath, Dietrich, I had my fingers crossed."

Hartung's eyelids narrowed as he once more looked about their table

"Incredible," Dietrich said.

"If you betray my secret, I will hunt you down like a dog."

"And if you have ever been hunted down by a dog, you know the feeling," Friedel confided to Dietrich, pulling on his elbow. "You are dry. Pinky!"

"No, I've had enough," Dietrich said, already having trouble feeling his toes inside his shoes. "I need to get back to my room. Business."

The two German soldiers watched Dietrich's back as he walked unevenly through the iron gate of the bistro's table area and onto the street.

"We've got to get our American friend out of that filthy hole," Hartung announced.

"Yes, and into a hovel," Friedel agreed finishing his beer. "It is time to see if there are any vacancies, eh? Your friends would know."

"If I had any friends, Freddie, I would have no use for you."

The Berlin YMCA was not, of course, a filthy hole. It was quite clean and the price for a room shared with three others was more than reasonable. The cafeteria-style food that was offered was uninspired but it was within the means of a frugal traveler. Even though there was a time limit placed upon its clientele, Dietrich had no desire to push those limits. He had received one hundred fifty dollars from his parents only last week, a tidy sum given that year of universal need, but Dietrich realized that he would have to drastically reduce his habit of drinking good wines and eating Germany's ever-tempting food. Living with three other men, plus those who habituated the recreation room, small library, and other on campus facilities at the YMCA, was getting old fast.

Dietrich was returning from the community showers, a towel tied around his waist and another draped over his shoulders, when he spied the unmistakable form of a uniformed SS officer near his door. Other residents, Dietrich could not help but notice, attempted to avert their eyes from the intimidating keeper of the Death's Head insignia in their midst. Obersturmfuhrer Hartung leaned easily against Dietrich's door jamb as the American approached.

"Greetings, Steven. Get dressed. We are off!"

"Off to where?"

"What do you care? You are being rescued. That is all that matters. I'll help you pack."

Hartung snatched Dietrich's towels away leaving him naked in the hallway. Dietrich maintained his dignity long enough to step into clean shorts and trousers. As he pulled a sweater over his head, Hartung was already tossing articles of clothing into his only suitcase. Sensing that argument was neither warranted nor appropriate, considering his circumstances, Dietrich gathered up his remaining possessions from the sink and his few books in a box under his bed. Within minutes he was ready to go.

"Where's Friedel?" he asked as the two men departed the building through the lobby. Dietrich headed for the desk but Hartung steered him away.

"They have been told you are leaving. Freddie is out dropping sandbags onto an empty field from seven thousand feet. And I have to do the same. Not sandbags, mind you, but I am already late reporting for duty."

Dietrich knew that Bunny Hartung was assigned to part of Hitler's vast security detail, a force of more than battalion size. Dietrich seemed to recall that his duties involved route planning or coordinating units as they were needed. It was as close, Bunny said, as he ever wanted to get to real operations.

They rode across the city in an old but presentable Daimler car that had once belonged to a dear friend. He had sold it to Hartung when he unexpectedly changed employment and had to leave Berlin. As they drove along the River Spree, Hartung swung over to a wide boulevard that bordered the Tiergarten, the city's centerpiece park. He gave a brief monologue about the park's many advantages, including its six acres of lakes and ponds, its cafés and beer gardens.

"You will need to know this," he said.

They passed the Berlin Technical University, *Technische Universitat Berlin,* on their right. Dietrich turned his head as they continued on, interested in taking in the campus of a great university. Construction was in progress, he could see, which would combine new buildings with others that had probably been there when the school was founded in 1870.

"Not far, now," Hartung announced.

He turned the car south on Leibnizstrasse, drove for two more short blocks, then turned into an alley, Ragenstrasse. Hartung parked the car and shut off the engine. They were still in the university district, an old part of the city but treated tenderly over the years by students and supporters of the school.

"Bring your bag," Hartung said, removing his gray uniform gloves and looking upward at the surrounding flats. The buildings were brick, the newest perhaps a half-century old. Still, as Dietrich hoisted his bag in one hand and incidental kit bag in the other, he liked the quaint elegance of the area.

"Your new home. You don't deserve it, of course, but you have bought your share of drinks. That was the test, you see," Hartung said as he led the way up a flight of stairs in the rear of a four-story building.

At the top floor, he paused in front of a doorway at the end of the hall, while a puffing Steven Dietrich caught up.

"Here, my friend," Hartung said, producing a key from his pocket. "This is your new room." He unlocked the door and stepped aside for Dietrich to enter first.

The door opened directly into what could be called the living area. It was small, like the rest of the apartment. It contained a mohair sofa, a freestanding lamp, a side table covered with a tattered doily, a threadbare area rug, an unupholstered rocking chair, and a steam radiator, now cold. There were two doorways, only one of which had a door attachéd to it. Through the other, Dietrich could plainly see a kitchenette. Glancing within he spotted an icebox and a surprisingly modern gas range and oven positioned next to a single-tub sink. A table large enough for two completed the room's utilitarian ensemble.

The other door, opened by Hartung, was the bedroom. The SS officer allowed himself to bounce demonstratively on its springs. The double bed was clearly soft and comfortable. There was a kind of closet, or a place where a closet might have been, where clothing was hung. There was also a small chest which, Dietrich assumed, contained someone's clothes. He assumed this because a woman's articles of clothing could be seen here and there in the room as well as personal items like a photograph of a little girl with what appeared to be her parents, a Raggedy Anne doll, as well as a single woman's mid-heel shoe partially hidden under the bed.

There was no bathroom in the apartment. Dietrich by now was accustomed to community bathrooms more common in Europe than in America. Or at least in the part of America from whence he came.

"Someone lives here," he said simply to Hartung.

"*Did* live here. Frauline Shpetner is moving. You might as well take advantage of the good fortune."

"Is that so?" Dietrich said, looking about. Small though it was, the place was cozy and well kept. Its location was excellent. It was no doubt one of the many student apartments that existed near most universities in the world and that catered to attendees of the institution. "She still hasn't packed," Dietrich observed, glancing casually inside a chest drawer.

"But she will."

"Maybe I better wait, then, and come back later when—"

"Don't be an idiot," Hartung interrupted, dropping the keys on a night table. "I'm late," he said as he let himself out the door.

Given the circumstances, Dietrich told himself, he would indeed be foolish to leave—at least before discussing the issue with Frauline Shpetner. Apartments in Berlin were scarce at the best of times. Coffee shop talk revolved around the subject of places to live. And the situation would get worse before it got better with Berlin's increasing importance as the center of a world power. Like Adolf Hitler or not, the man was an enormous force.

Then there was the question of his connection to Edward Wiles. Dietrich's fascination with Germany, with Berlin, with Adolf Hitler and the entire menu of a determined rising military power quite aside, Dietrich never forgot that he was an American first, an Anglophile second. His German blood was a distant third. If push came to shove or, to use a more appropriate metaphor, if bombs began to fall, there was no question on whose side Dietrich would serve. He had made no promises to Wiles, no agreement of any kind, but he was under no illusion that Wiles represented the crown in some Intelligence capacity. Wiles had urged him, in effect, to become associated with the new German Wehrmacht for the purpose of reporting to London.

Dietrich was not drawn toward the world of intrigue. There was no fascination on his part for espionage, the ingredient of betrayal lacking in his personality. Even as a child he never could abide his those who were designated "hall monitors" so that they could report on their fellow students for deviant behavior. Nor did he care for those who were given keys to a projection room or gym lockers or school supplies, the tacit suggestion being that these keepers of the keys also bore assumed authority over the others. There were born snitches, he felt, and those who could never be. He regarded himself among the latter.

Dietrich considered whether to unpack. There was probably no reason not to, yet he hesitated. Since Frauline Shpetner had not yet left, it seemed presumptuous of him to simply settle in. Besides, until she removed her own clothing from the closet and bureau, there was no room for his things.

In a niche in one corner of the bedroom, Dietrich noticed a Victrola. Most homes, at least in America, now had electric record players but there were still plenty of the windup sort about. His grandmother, he recalled, still had one. Out of curiosity Dietrich looked closer. He found a number of records, apparently in good condition, kept neatly within brown envelopes designed just to protect them. Most of them, Dietrich could see as he thumbed through the stack, were classical. He liked classical music, appreciating its complexities and, in most cases, he was familiar with the stories or premises behind the pieces. He selected a selection from Strauss. He placed the record on the felt surface of the turntable, cranked the handle on the side of the machine, and placed the needle onto the record. He thought the sound was not nearly as true as the new electric annunciators but the strains were pleasant.

He wandered through the small living room then into the kitchen. He began to open drawers and cupboards only for amusement, he told himself, but in reality he was looking for something to drink. It need not be alcohol but something to remove the dryness from his throat. He looked around until he found tea in one of the cupboards. He also found a loaf of rye bread in his explorations and even butter wrapped in butcher's paper. He put water on for tea while managing to toast a piece of rye loaf he had sliced off for himself. While the whistle began blowing on the kettle Dietrich was still rummaging about for jam or marmalade to put on his toast. In the process he burned an edge of his bread, creating an evil smell in the apartment. Undaunted, he scraped off the blackened bit, smeared butter on the bread, and began to provide himself with something like a breakfast meal.

His shaving kit was atop his suitcase so, careful to lock the door behind him, he visited the end of the hall where bathroom conveniences were provided. There were two doors side by side, one for ladies and one for gentlemen. The men's facility was still damp on the floor from the ablutions of the last man but there was no shortage of hot water for Dietrich to lather and shave. He brushed his teeth and returned to his new room without seeing anyone else in the hallway.

The restful music Dietrich had playing on the Victrola had transmuted into a repetitive scratchy sound, the needle needing to be tended. He removed a bit of lint that had accumulated on the stylus then shut the machine off. He settled down on the small sofa to read an aviation magazine, his feet propped up on a stool. He was pleasantly aware, just before the event, that he was drifting off to sleep. The magazine was still upon his chest when he woke up hours later. He was considering whether or not to find a grocery store in the neighborhood or, failing that, a café where he could get a bite to eat. He was accustomed to eating more than a single piece of toast for breakfast. He had just got to his feet when he heard the rattle of a key in the lock. The door swung open to reveal a young woman about Dietrich's age.

"Oh," she said.

"You, ah, must be...I'm sorry I don't know your first name," Dietrich said.

"Monica."

Monica clutched an old black leather bag in one hand. He could see that it contained books and a round loaf of rye bread similar to the one in the breadbox.

"Monica," he repeated, stiffly.

"Monica Shpetner. I know who you are," she said without offering her hand. Instead she marched into the bedroom where she dropped her bag on the floor.

"I'm pleased to meet you, Monica," he said.

"If you didn't mind," she said, emerging from the bedroom, "I would like to wait until tomorrow morning before I leave. I can sleep on the sofa."

"Why should I mind? And you won't sleep on the sofa. I'll sleep there. That is, if you don't mind."

"It isn't my apartment anymore, is it? How could I mind?" she said, her words clipped, suppressed anger flashing in her eyes and in the set of her chin.

"Well, you weren't expecting me. So soon, that is." Dietrich felt somehow embarrassed. "I'm sure your new place will be just great. Better than this."

Monica had no verbal response but looked him squarely in the eye, her anger quite evident.

"Well, then, I suppose your new apartment isn't ready, huh? Moving around the city these days is a mess. It is for me, anyway. I've been staying at the YMCA."

"Does it matter?" she said. "You are here, now."

Monica turned her back once more as she entered the bedroom and sat on the bed. Dietrich was somewhat at a loss as to what to do. He supposed that he should follow up on his idea of shopping but discarded the thought of bringing groceries here. It might be better to have something out. He moved awkwardly to the door, his hand on the knob, before turning his head slightly to tell Monica where he was going and that he would be back. As he did, he could see that her head was down and her shoulders shaking.

He moved at once into her bedroom and stood for a long moment trying to find something to say.

"Monica," he said as gently as he could, "you're crying."

"I am not," she said, choking.

"Come on. I know better," he said, moving closer to her, not wanting to frighten her. "Tell me what's wrong."

"It's nothing. I'll get over it. Thank you," she said, her voice losing strength.

At a loss, Dietrich was uncertain what to do next. He wanted to touch her but in her distress it might alarm her. Though he knew her not at all, his first impression of Monica was that there was nothing weak about her. She should not have been in tears, he felt. She was attractive, with high cheekbones, and her hair was brown. Her neck was perfectly shaped. Though she wore a plain skirt that fell well below her knees he could not help noticing that her ankles were slender and well defined. He thought that even into a long life she would remain beautiful because her looks were classic.

She had stopped crying but began looking for something to wipe her eyes. Dietrich carried a handkerchief but it was not clean. He looked around the room for something, anything, to serve the purpose, but Monica beat him to it by angrily throwing back the bed covers and using a large corner of the sheet to bury her face.

"Please, Monica. Talk to me. Maybe there's something I can do," he said.

She gathered herself together. She took a deep breath, then turned toward him.

"Really, there is nothing. If it was not you it would be someone else."

"Me? What about me?"

Her smile was wan but she had lost little of the fury that still smouldered like embers in the back of her eyes.

"Why are you trying to be so concerned? You don't have to act like a fool."

"I'm not a fool. I don't need to be insulted. We've just met, for God's sake," he said.

She rose to her feet to look first out of the window at the Ragenstrasse below.

"You really don't know?" she asked, turning toward him again, her arms crossed against her chest.

"What's to know? Want me to guess?" he said, trying to lighten the mood.

"I am being thrown out of this apartment. Compliments of the Nazis. I am a Jew, in case you didn't know."

Her simple statement took the breath out of him. He shook his head.

"Oh, man," he said in disgust. "The Jewish thing again. They're making you move because you're a Jew? That's it?"

Her answer was silence.

He sat slowly onto the bed. In the distance they heard the sounds of laughter. A group of students, perhaps. He became aware of music somewhere on the alley. Someone practicing a piano, done well. It was, under the circumstances, obscenely gay.

"You are American," she said at last.

"Yes."

"Your German is very good."

"So is yours."

Her lips twitched in appreciation for his humor, but there was no joy for either of them.

"Your parents?" he asked.

"They live in France, now. At least they are safe. That's where I'll go," she said.

"Yes, that would be good," he said weakly, disliking the very sound of his voice for agreeing with her.

"Are you a student? I saw the books in your bag," he said.

She nodded. "It won't last much longer. They are getting rid of non-Aryan professors. Soon it will be students, too. Maybe it's just as well."

"Bullshit," he said in English.

"Pardon?"

"It's an American expression. When things aren't going well or somebody is lying to you. Things are bullshit."

"Yes, I understand."

"Well, we're not going to let things happen this way," Dietrich said, realizing that he was speaking from a position of complete ignorance. "There must be someone who can countermand an eviction order."

"No one."

"I'll find out who it is," he said, as though he had not heard her speak. "Then I'll straighten it out. Don't worry."

"I'm not worried, I think. In the back of my mind I have known it was going to happen. So. I will do fine."

"You are going nowhere," he said, pointing his finger directly at her. She smiled for the first time. "You're staying here, just like always, and I—"

"You'll stay here, too."

"Okay," he said, relieved that she was not frightened at the prospect. "The couch will do very well."

Well or not well, it was the only alternative to a cold, hard floor. Monica bustled about preparing it for him. She had two pillows and gave him one. There was only one more clean sheet. She offered to take one of the two from her own bed but Dietrich stoutly declined. One would do nicely. It would have to be doubled over, anyway, and he could get by with but a single cover on top of that. She had a Dresden quilt that her mother had made, and she had a knit comforter which, while not long enough to serve as a total body cover, Dietrich could nevertheless put on top of the Dresden piece. He would be fine, he reassured her once again.

He later learned that there was nothing fine about one's feet hanging over the edge of a sofa or, to compensate, bending one's knees for long periods while lying on one's side. It was dark by nine o'clock that evening and both were in their separate beds shortly after. Dietrich managed to get through the night, waking each time the ache in his legs required him to shift positions. And he was cold. He promised himself that if there was to be another such night he would supply himself with sufficient covers, perhaps even a sleeping bag, and put himself onto the floor. He could endure the hardness if he was warm and could stretch out.

"How did you sleep?" Monica asked him in the morning when she found him sitting at the table looking out of a frosted window.

"Wonderfully," he said.

"No, you didn't. This won't work, you know," she said.

He watched her open a cupboard and retrieve a small bag of ground coffee and two cups.

"Yes, it will," he said with more certainty than he felt.

"Would you like an egg? You can have two. I have three."

He recalled the day before having looked into her ice box. There had not been much there. Today was Friday, not the best time to begin a battle with the bureaucracy in any city. Monday would be better.

"What are your plans?" he asked.

"Do you mean for the day?" She shrugged. "I have one class, at ten o'clock."

"Skip it," he said, the aroma of percolating coffee stimulating his senses.

"Why?"

"I don't know. I just don't think you should go to school today. We'll do something else."

SS-Obersturmfuhrer Bernard Hartung clicked his heels as he reported as ordered by SS-Standartenfuhrer Gert Earhardt, SS-Oberfuhrer Wilhelm Beckman, and SS-Gruppenfuhrer Hermann Fegelein. General Fegelein would one day marry Eva Braun's sister, thus becoming Adolf Hitler's brother-in-law. These high-ranking officers were gathered in General Fegelein's office located at SW 11 PrinzAlbrechtStrasse in Berlin.

"Is this the man?" General Fegelein asked of General Beckman.

"Yes," Beckman said, pouring himself a snifter of brandy from Fegelein's private bar.

Fegelein looked Hartung over carefully.

"They call you what? The Bunny?" The general had difficulty keeping his face straight.

"Yes, sir," Hartung said, still standing at attention.

"Why do they call you that?"

"I am not sure who gave me the name, Herr General. It may have been my mother, but I have answered to it all of my life," Hartung said.

"Well, that is good. We will unleash a Bunny against the enemy, eh?" The general said glancing around the room. The others chuckled along with him.

"General Beckman tells me of the good work you have been doing, leutnant. He says you are a fighting man, Bunny Hartung. Because of that you have been recommended to transfer to a new arm of the SS. Just in the planning stages, of course, but we are looking for the right people even now. We will be the Waffen-SS. How would you like that, Herr Bunny?"

Hartung glanced sideways at General Beckman whose influence had kept Hartung in the background of the SS and out of harm's way, a condition Hartung dearly cherished. All eyes were on the young Leutnant Hartung and not on the smiling face of Beckman. Beckman was immensely enjoying Hartung's discomfort.

"I can only hope I won't disappoint the general, sir," Hartung said crisply.

Later, in a hallway, Hartung allowed himself to fall in stride next to General Beckman as he exited General Fegelein's office.

"I want to thank the general for recommending me to higher command," Hartung said, acidly.

"Don't mention it, Bunny boy. Life could be much worse for you. Say, Christina is at her mother's for two days. Why don't you call a couple of your girls and we'll have a party," Beckman said, tapping his felt gloves on Hartung's chest, a smile still pasted upon his face.

"At the Faucet?" Hartung suggested, facetiously.

"Why not? Like old times. We could get Freddy, too. No, never mind. He would only scare the girls. Say, my son is in the Hitler youth, now. You should see the little girls they have to play with. My God," General Beckman rolled his eyes.

Before Beckman was a general in the SS he was the owner of The Faucet Café, along with its slot machines and other gambling devices. There was a time when then Wilhelm Beckman was known as the "slot machine king of Berlin". He had been arrested but later freed by his fellow Nazi party members. He was appointed to an office in the SS and elevated in rank by his fellow sociopaths. Hartung, one of Beckman's few trusted employees, had something of a soft spot for his former boss, but could not understand how he could abide some of the more thuggish members of the group. One of the worst was Beckman's old drinking pal Bruno Gesche, Hitler's bodyguard commander. Gesche was sadistic and insane even when he was sober which, even Himmler knew, was not often.

"What's this Waffen-SS all about? You know I don't want to crawl around in the mud," Hartung said.

General Beckman slowed his pace. He patted Hartung firmly and affectionately on the shoulder.

"It is in the future, Bunny. They are building a Führer field headquarters in Tannenberg. Do you want to go there? You were on the list. You would have to work for the first time in your life. This way, between now and when the so-called Waffen-SS goes forward, anything can happen. Say, let's start early tonight."

Hartung thought for a moment before nodding his head.

"All right. I'll meet you at nine o'clock. I might need your car."

"Not my staff car. I'll get another for you."

Hartung watched his boss, old and current, as he continued jauntily down the hallway toward his own office.

Having left Monica at her apartment, Dietrich spent part of the day shopping for the essentials of sleeping more comfortably. He bought a thin mattress at a secondhand furniture store, the kind usually found on a camp cot. It rolled up easily, and he tied it with twine before leaving the store. He drew sideways glances as he made his way through the city on a combination of streetcars and subways. He must have appeared to be a well-dressed bindle stiff. He stepped off a trolley within two blocks of Ragenstrasse, an easy walk even with the items he carried. As he passed a small grocer he hesitated, then went inside. He bought a baguette of French bread, a slice of Brie cheese, a handful of Mediterranean olives, and a bottle of Italian wine. He was able to sling the mattress over his shoulder to complete the picture of a drifter, but carried his food purchases in a small net bag provided him by the man behind the counter.

He kicked on the door gently with his foot but got no response from inside. Placing the food bag on the hallway floor, he knocked with his hand. When there was still no answer, he fished through his pockets until he located the key supplied to him the day before by Hartung. He opened it and went inside.

"Monica?"

There was no answer. She might be at the end of the hall, he reasoned. But he called again, rapping lightly on the door that led to the bedroom before opening it. The bed was made but Monica was not on it, nor was she in the room. He dropped everything he was carrying and, leaving the apartment door open, walked quickly to the end of the hall where the bathrooms were located. He knocked on the one marked for ladies.

"Yes?" he heard a woman's voice.

"Ah, Monica? Is that you?"

There was no immediate response but after a few moments the door opened to reveal a woman about Monica's age who otherwise bore no resemblance to his Jewish friend of twenty-four hours.

"I'm sorry," he said. He might have been embarrassed but for the fact that he was now worried. He had asked her to stay close to the apartment and not go to school. She had agreed. What if the Gestapo had come back to ensure that she had vacated the premises as ordered? What would they have done to her for disobeying their commands? Dietrich had heard all sorts of rumors about people being "resettled," especially Jews. He had no idea what resettlement involved but it could not be anything good.

He noticed others moving about on the floor, most of them students, he presumed, judging by their age and demeanor. They were two young men who greeted him and still another young woman whom he could see through a door that was ajar. He could also hear music from more than one source, and part of a news broadcast that was obviously coming from a radio.

But upon his return to the room there was still no Monica. A fast look around indicated that nothing had been packed. Her clothes still hung in the closet or filled the drawers of her bureau. He sat on the edge of a wooden kitchen chair considering his options. She might have decided to attend her class after all but it was just after three o'clock in the afternoon. Certainly Monica's class would long be over since it had begun, she said, at ten o'clock in the morning. There were all kinds of places she could be with good reasons for being there. He should wait calmly, he told himself. If she was not back by, say, five o'clock he would act.

What kind of act? To whom would he go? Where would he look?

Suppose she was still gone at midnight? In America she would have been missing and he would have reported her so. But in Germany, appealing to the police was out of the question. A missing Jew would not so much as raise an eyebrow. On the contrary. He had no friends upon whom he could call who would be of any assistance, except perhaps Bunny Hartung. Or Freddy Friedel. Even then, he reconsidered, they were German officers and seemed not to have love for Jews.

He had not eaten since early morning and became aware of the gnawing feeling in the pit of his stomach. It was the result not only of no food in the belly but of the churning acid of worry. The idea of eating a meal while not knowing Monica's whereabouts seemed obscene. At last he was unable to remain in a chair or continue to pace the small apartment. He had to do something. He had to go out. He buttoned his leather jacket to the top, his wool turtleneck sweater reaching above the collar. He checked his pockets to make sure he had his key as well as his wallet, then left the room.

Again in the hallway, he decided to ask Monica's neighbors before launching into the streets. He knocked on the nearest door. It was opened by a middle-aged woman.

"Pardon me, madam. My friend who lives next door. Monica. Ah, she does not seem to be at home and I wonder if you would know where she might have gone?"

"She is gone? I thought she would be leaving," the woman said, knowingly. "So. Good riddance."

And she closed the door.

Dietrich moved farther down the hallway before knocking on another door. There was no answer so he moved on to another.

"Yes?" a young man asked, as he opened the door to Dietrich's knock. Dietrich could see another young man in the background, almost certainly a student.

"Sorry to bother you but my friend…" Dietrich said, indicating with his finger toward Monica's apartment door.

"Monica?" the young man interrupted. "Yes?"

"She was supposed to be here. Waiting for me but, ah, she isn't. I thought you might know…that she might have left word. Or something."

The young man smiled either at Dietrich's obvious distress or at the emotional reaction of a man whose lady acquaintance had decided to jilt him.

"We know Monica," he said. "Don't we, Wolfgang? But she doesn't let us know where she goes. We all come and go, you see."

"Yes, I know, but…"

"If I see her, who shall I say called?"

"Ah, Dietrich. Steven Dietrich. Never mind. Thank you," he said. He turned away from the door and took the stairs two at a time that led to the street below. He hesitated outside the doorway and considered his next move. Common sense told him to stay put, to give Monica a chance to return to the apartment. Ignoring his own counsel, he stepped onto the narrow sidewalk and began to walk east.

"Steven."

A soft voice, almost a whisper, emanated from the shadows of a doorway.

"Monica?"

"Yes," she said, materializing from the edge of the building. She glanced about. He reached for her hand and pulled her toward him. He resumed a casual pace and with the pressure of his hand around hers, brought her along. They strolled like other couples who walked in the evening.

"Why did you leave?" he asked.

"The man from the Gestapo came. I heard his voice down the hall so I went out the window, down the fire escape."

"The one who ordered you out of your apartment?"

"Yes. But now he knows I am still there. I had no time to get my things. That's why I am back."

He could feel her hand tremble.

"You came back because you still live here," he said, controlling the frustration in his voice. "There is no reason for you to leave now. The apartment is in my name. I officially registered for it today. We'll be roommates. That is, ah, I'll sleep on the floor. I bought a mattress. I hope you agree."

"Impossible. I could not do it," she said.

"Well," he began, suddenly embarrassed that his solution would appear so simplistic that Monica would dismiss it out of hand. "Naturally I hadn't thought about appearances. Your family wouldn't like it at all, I suppose. Even your friends..." He shrugged his shoulders.

Monica stopped walking to study his face.

"I wasn't thinking about that. It is the danger. For me and for you, too. They will come back, you know."

"So what? It is my apartment now. Right? What can they do?"

Monica shook her head at his naivete.

"Anything they want, Steven. That is Germany today. The law is whatever they say it is."

"I'm an American citizen. If they try to bully me they'll get one hell of a surprise. Got any better offers?" he smiled.

"I suppose not. No, of course I haven't."

"All right. That's a relief that we don't have to spend the rest of the night arguing about it. Hey, are you hungry?"

"Well..."

"Of course you are. I'm starving myself. Let's go get something to eat. Ever been to The Faucet?"

A streetcar took them to within a block of The Faucet. It was only Wednesday but the place was crowded, typical for The Faucet's night trade of food and spirits. There was no sidewalk table available, and Steven sensed that Monica would prefer something more secluded inside. He left his name with the maitre d' who, Dietrich later learned, was really a part-time bartender pressed into service for the night. Dietrich put his arm around Monica's shoulder, keeping her close to him while he led them through a sea of bodies toward a place at the bar. He waited patiently until he caught the eye of one of the two bartenders, Richter Mülls. Through Bunny Hartung, Friedel, and of course Pinky, Dietrich was becoming one of the "in" crowd. Also, Richter liked to talk about airplanes, a subject Dietrich knew something about. Richter immediately left the far end of the bar to stand in front of Dietrich.

"Greetings, Yank."

The nickname bestowed upon Dietrich was offered with undisguised respect. It often became a conversation piece among new people Dietrich would meet.

"Hello, Richter. This is Monica, my..." Dietrich said, wanting to finish but not sure what should come next.

"Welcome, Monica," Richter said smoothly. "I have lost five Reich marks on your account. We have made bets that the Yank could not find a girl who would go out with him."

"You mean I have ruined the whole night?" she said.

"Well, not for him, of course. And maybe I think losing my bet was a good thing," he said.

"We are going to have dinner so maybe we will drink wine, eh, Monica?" Dietrich asked, turning toward her.

"Oh, how nice. Maybe just some..."

"A good Bordeaux," Dietrich said, giving no thought to thrift. "You choose the bottle for us, Richter."

"It will be a pleasure," he said and moved off.

"Steven, please don't think I am ungrateful, but the expense of French wine these days…"

"My family is terribly rich, Monica," he lied cheerfully. "They send me so much money every month I hardly know how to spend it all."

"Is that why you are staying in a small student apartment?" she said.

"Yes. I want to see how the poor people live. I think it would round out my character."

He could not take his eyes from hers even though he realized he was staring at her. They were brown, like her hair, and he imagined that they contained fascinating secrets, even deep passion.

Richter showed Dietrich his selection. Dietrich was entirely ignorant of the chateau that appeared on the label and had the good sense to not pretend that he did. He merely bade Richter to pour the wine.

"Have one for yourself," Dietrich said.

"I'll be off soon. Maybe I'll stop by your table."

"To friendship," Dietrich said in toast, his glass touching hers.

"You're a nice man, Yank," she said.

By design or accident, their table was just what was required. It was set for two, against the opposite wall from the entrance and out of the way of service traffic. Apart from a chalkboard set up at the entrance and more or less the same selections written in chalk above the bar, there was no menu offered to the public. They decided on a simple Mediterranean dish of roasted Brie cheese, garlic cloves, Greek olives, and green peppers with seasoned toast for dipping.

"I've never tasted anything so good," Monica said.

"It will make you fat," Dietrich said.

"Are American women fat?"

"Not all of them."

"Of course not. But you know what I mean."

Dietrich shrugged. "I suppose that depends. Upper-class women worry about their appearance so they eat less, I think. The fat ones just don't care. That's the way it seems, anyway."

"What are you doing here in Germany? Are you going to stay? I would rather be in America," Monica said, her eyes lowering to her dish.

Dietrich's gaze wandered over The Faucet's patrons—mostly young people, college age for the most part. They might have been in America. But there were many uniforms. Perhaps as many as fifteen to twenty percent wore some kind of official dress. Germany seemed to have a uniform for everything, from a building inspector to a streetcar conductor to a hunting club member. Eagles and swastikas were everywhere; on peaks of caps, arm bands, tie pins, and lapels. These often included women's clothing.

"America is different," he said, turning back to her eyes. "More relaxed, I think."

"Even in New York?"

He smiled at the thought of the city. "New York exists by itself. There is no place like it. I suppose New Yorkers are not very relaxed, now that you ask. More like Berlin. Very busy."

"So, are you going home soon?" Monica sipped her wine, clearly enjoying it while some of the fear drained slowly from her furrowed brow.

"I don't think so. I like Germany. Not everything about it, of course, but a lot of these silly things that governments do when they are trying to reconstruct themselves can be corrected in time."

"Silly? Is that what you call it?"

He lowered his voice and leaned forward. "Monica, what good would it do if I left? If I stay, I may be able to do something worthwhile."

A smile crept slowly across her face. "You are not such a bad-looking man, after all."

"Is your mother as beautiful as you?" he asked.

"Are you telling me I am beautiful?"

"Without any doubt. Did I forget to say so? I only wanted to add that you will always be so and that I would bet your mother still is."

"How wonderful of you. I'll tell her that you said such a thing about her. Yes, she's lovely."

They turned their attention to finishing their food, nothing more than scrapings on the bottom of their small pottery bowls. It was near midnight and the second rush of late-evening diners were pressing to get inside. There was a theater nearby and, Dietrich thought, many of the new people were arriving from one of the shows.

"Shall we go home?" he asked.

He could see her involuntarily stiffen.

"Monica, you are not to worry. I told you, they can't get to you while I stand in their way."

She nodded slowly. The fear had still not left her eyes when Dietrich held her coat. He wanted to wrap his arms around her, hold her tightly. Instead he took her hand firmly and began to lead her toward the door.

"Yank!"

They turned as one to look behind them. Richter was no longer behind the bar but beside it. He held a bottle above his head and with his free hand pointed to it. His intention was clear: would they like to have a drink with him. Dietrich waved his hand but shook his head. Leaving a crowd for the quietude of the night with a beautiful woman on his arm was far more appealing than sharing yet another bottle in a hot bar. Even Richter must understand that.

They stepped off one of the last streetcars of the night near the Tiergarten and walked along its pathways. They passed a small lake, dark and quiet, the ducks and swans now hunkered down on the banks, heads tucked under their wings.

"What will you be when you graduate? An engineer?" Dietrich asked her.

"University has been very difficult for me. I am the only woman in virtually all of my classes. Not that I mind competing with men, but it is clear that I am not always welcome. Young Germans have become, what is the word? Supermen. And there are no superwomen."

The Technical University had graduated such illustrious students as chemist Carl Bosch and physicists Dennis Gabor, Gustav Ludwig Hertz, and Ernst Ruska. It was clearly a male-dominated student body and faculty.

"I understand. We have a lot of that in our colleges, too. Male superiority. It's hard for us to put our egos aside," Dietrich said, still holding her hand as they strolled.

"This is different. It is not just competition, not the girls against the boys kind of game. It is deeper than that. More sinister. I don't expect to graduate. Not because I'm a woman but because I'm a Jew."

He stopped walking, and by doing so caused her to halt and face him as well.

"You know what I think? I think you should go. Leave Germany for somewhere else. England. Or America."

She leaned forward and touched her lips to his.

"It isn't that easy," she whispered.

Chapter 16

By early spring of 1937 Dietrich had been working at the Gustaf Autowerks almost six months. He had begun sweeping floors, washing cars, and cleaning oil traps. He soon graduated to doing simple work on automobiles brought in by customers looking to keep the old family car running another year. He would repair or replace muffler systems, tune distributors, and adjust fuel flows. He developed a knack for overhauling carburetors, a talent even some of the veteran mechanics never mastered. He then progressed among the other eight mechanics to working on engine overhaul and occasionally assisted in tuning the company's Porsche race car. Dietrich liked every aspect of his work, finding the whole experience surprisingly stimulating.

The fact that he was American made him a kind of minor celebrity, a persona that none of the other shops with whom the Autowerks competed had. With one or two exceptions, he was easily accepted by his fellow employees.

Things were getting more desperate for Monica. She found it difficult to buy foods as most stores refused service of any kind to Jews. Dietrich began to do more and more of the shopping until he was doing it all. Signs over shops read "Jews Not Admitted." It made him think shamefully of places in America where signs just like those refused admittance to Negroes.

Germany had signed a so-called Anti-Comintern Pact with Italy and Japan. It was symbolic, Dietrich found out, and did not commit one country to come to the military aid of another should war break out, but it occurred to Dietrich that Japan was not America's ally. If it was true that one is judged by the company one keeps, then Hitler was creating for his citizens a shabby reputation.

Dietrich did not feel the same about Italy. Mussolini struck him as a comic opera clown but he still found the country beautiful and most of its people good company. Like most nations, Italy was emerging very slowly from the grasp of worldwide depression but its citizens concerned themselves with music, art, and the pursuit of a good party. Dietrich and Monica had made a trip to Rome where they spent five wonderful days, but their travel was marred by an incident on the return train that frightened Monica. At the frontier she was informed that her papers were not in order. It would not have been so bad if she had simply been refused reentry to Germany, but it looked like she was about to be arrested. Acting quickly and out of instinct, Dietrich took aside an Italian train official and placed fifty American dollars into his hand. As a result Monica was quietly removed from the train at Merano and diverted to another that crossed the Swiss border near Susa. Monica was all but inconsolable. She was a burden to Dietrich, she said, and was embarrassed that she had been stripped of her humanity.

Without her knowing, this had been the catalyst that solidified Dietrich's plans and, indeed, his entire life. This was a wrong that needed to be made right. He held her in his arms virtually the entire way back to Berlin. Though he was warmly welcomed back to the Autowerks he was not the same man who had gone on holiday just a week before. By the end of 1937 he had joined a soaring club, spending all of his free hours, especially weekends, flying gliders. It was fine sport but everyone in the association was aware that their club was the sheerest form of deception. It was a stepping stone for young men to enter more formal training in the Luftwaffe, Germany's air arm, that was rebuilding at a frantic pace in anticipation of war. What war and exactly when nobody could say, but the day was coming and it could not be far off.

Hitler was by birth an Austrian. In 1938 he demanded of Austria's chancellor, Schuschnigg, a list of requirements he sought for Germans who were residents of that country, a list which was not only impossible to meet on any sane basis, but which was in fact a demand for the surrender of the country's autonomy. Hitler massed his troops on the border. Schuschnigg resigned his office and was succeeded by German puppet Seyess-Inquart. Seyess-Inquart was, naturally, amenable to Hitler's aggression and allowed Nazi troops to march across the border into Austria. England, France, and Russia did nothing.

Persecution of the Jews in Austria began at once. Opponents of the Nazi regime were rounded up and jailed, tortured or executed. That included former Chancellor Schuschnigg who was jailed, then sent off to a concentration camp. Even Dietrich's political naivete could not allow him to escape the conclusion that Germany was headed for war and that Hitler, whose word among other national leaders could not be trusted, would never be satisfied.

In December of 1937 the mood in their apartment was somber. Monica had been notified that she would not be allowed to return to the university for the winter term in the interest of Germany's racial distinction laws. It was something the two of them had expected but, nevertheless, it was still a shock to their psyches when the notice finally arrived.

"They are monsters," she said into her soup bowl, avoiding his eyes.

Dietrich could not disagree.

"I know why I am here, Steven, but not you. Why don't you go now?" she asked.

"It won't always be this way."

"No. It will become worse," she said, lifting her eyes to meet his, but his gaze was fixed upon his meal.

He shrugged.

"Well?"

"Well, what?" he said.

He knew very well what she wanted to know. She did not know that he had made application for Luftwaffe pilot training. He was going nowhere except into the German military. Neither could she know that he had placed an advertisement in the *London Daily News* that he was willing to sell a silk hat at a bargain price.

"You'll have to go. We've talked about it but you can't wait any longer," he said. It was true. All Jews were being arrested and sent to camps. There was a newly completed, large, concentration camp in the east called Buchenwald where many Jews and political prisoners were being sent. Only a week before, the last of Monica's Jewish friends had gone. A young husband and wife, Laura and Yev Abernathy, had been caught in a Gestapo net and had disappeared. Monica had not left the apartment since.

Monica suddenly froze. In the hallway came the sound of heavy knocking on one of the apartment doors. Then a voice could be heard. Dietrich had paid no attention; students, the bulk of the building's population, were often boisterous. But this was different. It was relatively late in the evening and all should have been quiet. Monica slowly put down her spoon.

"It's him," she whispered.

"Who?" he asked.

For an extended minute Monica said nothing, her eyes closing as though to block out the vision of a nightmare. Dietrich was now aware of what Monica had heard. A man's voice, not deep, not resounding, but rather shrill as its speaker was forceful. Then, footsteps in the hall. Stopping at their door. The knock, not a rap made with the knuckles of friendly fingers, but with a fist.

For a long moment Dietrich and Monica looked at each other across the table, neither moving but the deep sadness reflected in her eyes. The pounding came again.

"Open! Official business!"

Dietrich rose from his chair. He had hardly turned the knob when the door was pushed rudely open and a man in a leather overcoat stepped by him and into the middle of their apartment. His hair was blonde and, Dietrich noted, despite his instant hatred for the man, he was quite handsome. He had even, white teeth, and full lips which contained the natural color of rouge. He was in his early to mid twenties, but affected a swagger and self assurance that was far beyond his years. He was taller than Dietrich but did not have the Yank's shoulder width. In one hand he held aloft a small, stainless steel identification badge.

"Gestapo," he said, dropping the badge casually into his pocket. He surveyed the room without deigning to regard Dietrich. "I am Agent Duerfeldt. Where is she?"

"She?"

"Yes, she. The Jewess."

"Well, ah, you mean Monica, I suppose," Dietrich said, stupidly. He quite realized he was dealing with a martinet but the man was dangerous. Dietrich's knees were watery and he used all of his willpower to resist the Nazi's intimidation.

Agent Duerfeldt paused to fix a withering stare on Dietrich.

"Are you the perfect ass you appear to be? Do not simply stand there and repeat my questions rhetorically. You know perfectly well who I mean." With that the Gestapo man turned on his heel and kicked open the bedroom door. While Monica was not immediately visible even Dietrich knew where she had to be hiding. And so did Gestapo agent Duerfeldt. The agent flung up the mattress from the bed, then the bed itself to reveal a cowering Monica beneath. With studied nonchalance he reached down and with his gloved hand grabbed her by the hair and pulled her roughly to her feet.

Dietrich, reflexively, moved forward.

"Stay back," Duerfeldt snarled.

Dietrich halted in his tracks.

"Well, what have we here? So this is your Jew whore, eh, Dietrich? Well, you'll just have to go down into the gutter and get yourself another one," the agent chuckled. Now ignoring Dietrich altogether Duerfeldt tightened his grip on Monica's lush hair, pulling clumps of it painfully from her head in the process.

The Gestapo agent seemed to enjoy her stifled screams of fear and pain. Fear and pain were the real coin of the secret police's realm and their treasure chests were bottomless. While the agent opened the apartment door with one hand, he maintained his grip on Monica's hair with the other. His intention was no doubt to drag her from the apartment and down the stairs to the street below.

Dietrich could only imagine what the Gestapo man must have felt as the ice pick in the heel of Yank's hand was driven to the hilt into the German's skull. Dietrich started the tip at what he thought was about the base of the brain and put his weight behind the blow. The Nazi did not die immediately. He spasmed, his right hand releasing Monica. His head snapped back and Dietrich could feel the Nazi try to turn his body but Dietrich had him pinned against the apartment door, now slammed closed, and did not let him move. Rather than pull the ice pick out of the head and jam it in again, Dietrich simply increased the pressure on the hilt and rocked the steel pick from side to side.

When the Nazi tried to scream Dietrich snatched at the man's exposed neck and closed his fist, snapping the larynx. The Nazi fell to the floor. The body convulsed once then lay still. The whole execution of Agent Duerfeldt took less than a minute.

Dietrich turned to Monica. Her eyes were wide, unblinking, as she looked down at the prostrate body on their living room floor. Dietrich assumed that she would be panicked, certainly terrified out of her mind. She was not.

"I am sorry he is dead," she said in a monotone. "I would like to kill him again."

Dietrich understood. While he did not find pleasure in what he had done he found great relief. It was easy. And he knew he would never lose sleep that the world no longer had Agent Duerfeldt to guard its ramparts.

"I've got to get him out of here," Dietrich said.

"*We* have to get him out."

"Yes. We need a car."

They discussed the possibility of finding a car into which they could load the body. They knew of no one they could trust to lend them a car with no questions asked. There would be lots of questions, especially at this time of night. The more they talked about it the more they realized that a car to use for body disposal was impossible.

Cut up the body? Not only irrational but even for a beast as totally loathed as Duerfeldt, it was not a course of action they could stomach.

"Let's have a drink," Dietrich said.

Monica smiled at the thought. They had a half bottle of brandy which she fetched from a cupboard. She poured one glass which they shared. Dietrich took the first swallow then passed the glass to Monica. Monica took her share, drinking fully, then returned the glass to Dietrich. There were about three full swallows of the burning fluid for each and neither hesitated their turn. After several minutes, without speaking, Monica put her arms around Dietrich's neck and kissed him passionately, deeply. Tearing at each other's clothing they lurched into the bedroom, falling upon the mattress that was still on the floor where the Gestapo man had tossed it. Their lovemaking was frantic, made all the more so by the grisly corpse close by.

By 2:30 A.M. there was no solution at hand.

"Do you have a needle and thread?" he asked her.

"Needle?" Monica responded, sleepily. "Yes, of course."

"And a pair of scissors." Dietrich knew she had those. "Yellow cloth. The hand towel in the bathroom. That will do."

While Monica was gathering the articles Dietrich required, Dietrich removed the Nazi's leather outer coat. He then went through Duerfeldt's clothing and removed everything including his wallet, Gestapo identification, and miscellaneous papers he found in the lapel of his suit. The agent also carried a gun, a Walther PPS 9mm pistol. Dietrich put the weapon into his own pocket.

With those tools at hand, Dietrich cut a crude form of the Star of David from the hand towel. He then stitched it loosely onto the front of the late Gestapo agent's suit. When he had finished he ripped a piece from a cardboard box, onto which he wrote the word JUDEN in large letters using a fountain pen and retracing the letters until they stood out.

"Got a safety pin?" he asked of Monica. Having watched him with fascination, Monica left the front room for the bedroom and returned with the pin. Dietrich began roughing up the dead agent's clothing, tearing it here and there, ripping at the seams, so that it looked as though he had been attacked by more than one person.

"Go into the bedroom and close the door," he said to Monica.

"No," she answered.

"Do as I tell you. I don't have time to argue."

Reluctantly she withdrew to the bedroom and closed the door.

Dietrich placed an old newspaper under the head, then turned the Gestapo man's face upward. He stomped the heel of his foot downward into the face as hard as he could, then again, and again. The Nazi's face was pulverized beyond recognition. Dietrich kicked the body on the side to break bones and did the same on the head and neck. There was very little blood because the heart had stopped long ago. What little spatter there was could be easily cleaned up later. The bedroom opened just as Dietrich was putting on the Nazi's outer coat and hat. He put his fingers to his lips, then quietly opened the door to the hallway. There was no one about and the single lightbulb at the end of the hall provided just enough illumination to make out one's way.

Grasping the Gestapo man's coat by the collar, Dietrich began to drag the body. It was surprisingly easy to do, the corpse sliding along on polished wooden flooring. The task became even easier as he started down the stairs. The steps were covered by threadbare carpet but it was enough to muffle most of the sound as Dietrich easily allowed gravity to help him pull the body to the bottom three flights below. It was now after 3:20 A.M. and no one, at least in the apartment house, was about.

Before pulling his gruesome cargo into the Ragenstrasse, Dietrich looked up and down. This time his load was much harder to move and Dietrich was beginning to sweat heavily as he dragged the body down the concrete allee. His aim was only to reach the far end of the block, probably sixty meters more, then simply leave it. Now pulling with both hands and moving backward to maintain best traction Dietrich looked up to see two young men watching him in amazement.

"What are you looking at?" Dietrich snapped. He withdrew the stainless steel I.D. tag from his pocket and waved it in front of the men. "Gestapo. How would you like to take his place, huh?"

The magic combination of evil and violence worked once more as the two men, Dietrich cared not who, lit out at a fast pace and did not look back. Dietrich at last achieved his objective, a storm drain at the intersection. He looked about carefully once more then pushed the body into the gaping drain hole. It was a tight fit. So tight, in fact, that the entire body would not pass through. Just as well, Dietrich thought. One more Jew found beaten to death in the city streets of Germany would hardly raise an eyebrow. The body would be burned along with city trash and forgotten.

When he returned to the apartment he stripped to his shorts and washed himself, not daring to use the community bath at the end of the hall. Monica wordlessly helped him in the process, tenderly washing and drying his back and parts of his legs. While he was gone she had looked for places on the floor that needed to be cleaned. By the time he had dried himself and pulled on a nightshirt they could go to bed with some confidence.

They fell asleep in each other's arms.

Chapter 17

Considered a "natural" pilot of gliders, Dietrich made application to the Luftwaffe for pilot training. In April of 1938 he was notified by mail that his request for admission into the Luftwaffe had been approved. He was given two weeks to put his personal affairs in order before reporting to primary induction and training.

"You have to leave, Monica. Tomorrow," he said, looking out of the bedroom window into infinity.

"I can find another room. There are places in the city where they would never look." Monica's voice lacked conviction.

"It wouldn't work. Sooner or later they would discover you. Even if you could hide somewhere else you wouldn't have a real life. I don't want that for you," he said.

"I love you, Steven."

"I know you do. And I love you, too. That's why you have to leave. Not just for you but for us both."

"Why can't we leave together? You are American. You don't belong here with these evil people."

Dietrich wanted to smile at the irony but could not.

"I have papers for you," he said. "A new name for you to travel under." The documents had cost him almost every penny he had. Even at that, Richter had worked on his behalf to reduce the price of the black market product. "Your train to Amsterdam leaves at seven ten. When you arrive go to the

American Express office. There will be an envelope with your name on it. In the envelope will be a money order you can cash right there in the office. There will also be a ticket on a Royal Dutch Lines ship leaving in three days. Finally, there will be the address of my parents who live in Maryland. Memorize it then burn the paper it is written on. They're expecting you."

"Please, Steven," Monica said, tears welling in her eyes, "don't make me go without you." He touched her gently with his hand.

"Someday, who knows, I may just turn up—"

"No! Not who knows," she said, burying her head in his chest.

"Yes. You're right, Monica. I'll find you for sure. I'll begin looking for you in Maryland."

"I'll be there. I promise."

When a young Edward Wiles was dispatched from his junior post at SIS to "nose around" Berlin during the 1936 Olympic summer games, he had no idea he would meet anyone quite like the American Steven Dietrich. It was an easy friendship to fall into. They had similar academic backgrounds and, both loved airplanes, the faster the better. They also shared the same sense of humor. Dietrich, Wiles believed fervently, had a strong inner direction, a sense of moral outrage which would certainly trigger itself the longer he remained in Germany. The fact that Dietrich was German himself and that he spoke the language better than most Germans, was a huge advantage in the business Wiles hoped Dietrich would undertake.

Despite the fact that he was an American citizen, or perhaps because of it, German nationals seemed to go out of their way to include him in their affairs. They were proud of what they and their Fatherland had accomplished and wanted others, from outside Germany's borders, to see and appreciate what they had done. Their Führer, Adolf Hitler, had worked economic miracles for his people that brought them out of the world depression well in advance of other European countries, indeed, even ahead of North America. Wiles had not been specific in his invitation to Dietrich back in 1936, neither about what would be expected of him nor about how they would proceed working together. But there were no illusions in either man's mind: there would be a war and both would be a part of it. Nor was there any question about whose side Dietrich would be on. He was an American and a lover of freedom.

When Wiles returned to London and his work at SIS, he began every single day of his life by scanning the personal columns of the *London Daily News* in search of a silk hat. He had said not a word to anyone about meeting Dietrich. Dietrich had not agreed to a thing nor, for that matter, had Wiles asked him to do anything specific. He only asked that he resume their contact sub rosa. And despite Wiles's personal confidence that Dietrich would work for the Allies, there was no promise attachéd. Also, and Wiles had to be honest with himself, it was safer within SIS to say nothing. Dietrich would not be betrayed either through a double agent or by accident if Wiles was the only person in England who knew he existed.

Wiles executed all of his assignments with skill and discretion. He rose steadily through the ranks of professional spies, doing occasional field work competently, seldom making mistakes. While he lacked nothing in imagination he developed a reputation for dependability, an enormously important asset in a business that was known to attract a surprising number of half-baked people. SIS, was, as indeed all spy agencies in the world were, a bureaucracy. As such, exceptional vision was not always encouraged. One was expected to do a great deal of "getting along." As in all feather merchant employment, one could expect to persevere from induction to retirement without advancing ideas that would make one's superiors look as though they were asleep at the switch. Wiles had a talent for recruiting and developing agents, including women, from unexpected sources and making it appear as though he was simply carrying out the directions of his superiors. It was a quality that endeared him to everyone. Wiles took personal satisfaction from watching a well-functioning machine run even better. He sublimated his ego to the mission, a rarity among people of any profession, not least of all government security work.

It was an early spring morning in 1938, as Wiles was riding the tube across the city to Semley Place, that he opened his newspaper. He had only a few minutes to spend during his commute to read nonofficial material and he was anxious to scan the football scores. He was tempted to lay aside the advertisements and go straightaway to the scores but habit won out over personal desire. His eyes flitted quickly along the briefly worded sales, want to buy, offerings to sell, then the personals. After so many years the message was so unexpected that he blinked several times and read it twice before believing his eyes. There it was. A man was offering a silk hat for sale at a bargain price. Interested parties could call for details. The telephone number listed, Wiles knew, was Germany.

Arriving at his new office location in Belgravia, Wiles went directly to one of the special telephone booths operated by SIS. They were "clean" telephones, unconnected in any way with the government communications system. If necessary, any of the clean phones could be a civilian business with a "secretary" answering an incoming ring, or a "home" phone that could be answered by a housewife or the Intelligence officer himself posing as the home owner. It was necessary for Wiles to place his call through the Continental operator. As he waited he resisted the temptation to drum his fingers.

At last, at the other end of the line, he could hear the ringing telephone answered by a German-speaking man. His voice sounded like that of a young person and there seemed to be a good bit of noise going on in the background. Wiles's German was good enough to hear the man at the other end explain that if the operator would hold on, he would knock on Dietrich's door and tell him that he had a call.

Wiles waited.

"Steven Dietrich speaking."

"I'm calling about the silk hat you have for sale," Wiles said.

"Then you are in luck," Dietrich responded. "I haven't much time to get rid of it. The price will be in your favor."

"Where do you live, Mr Dietrich? Perhaps I could meet you."

"I live in Berlin. Is that difficult for you?"

"Why, yes, it is. Much too far to travel for just a silk hat. Still, if I had your mailing address I might be able to send you the price of your hat and you could mail it to me."

"Why not? My address is 411 Ragenstrasse, in the Tiergarten."

"And your price, Mr. Dietrich?"

"Three Reich marks. But in two weeks I will be gone."

After hanging up the telephone Wiles sat back in his chair to think. He knew that every call from England to Berlin was added to the Gestapo's records. There were thousands each week, impossible to record by wire, and impossible to send an agent to investigate each one—unless the subject being called was already on their watch list. Dietrich required a personal call. Not Wiles. Someone else. It required an embedded agent in Europe to make himself known to Dietrich. To make a move of this gravity Wiles would need approval from the top of SIS. The head of SIS, or "C" as he was called, was Admiral Sinclair. Wiles knew him only superficially but was not totally impressed with what he saw. There was another senior officer in SIS in whom Wiles had more confidence. He was William Schuyler. Schuyler was already in his late sixties but to call him an old man would be a mistake. Crusty to be sure, skeptical, always, but Schuyler had vision. He also encouraged young intelligence officers, in whom he correctly saw SIS's future, to step forward on their own. Schuyler had been knighted following his behind-the-scenes, never-publicized, diplomatic action in Russia during the Great War.

Also, William Schuyler was accessible.

"Well, it must be very important to make you climb the stairs from the basement," Schuyler teased Wiles. Schuyler folded and refolded his gangly legs under his desk, never a comfortable place for the elder spy to be. The man stood almost six and a half feet tall and had not an ounce of extra weight on his frame. Had the man lived in America, he probably would have been a star basketball player, Wiles thought.

"Thank you for seeing me on such short notice, Sir William," Wiles said, taking a chair the older man offered with a wave of the hand.

"Still haven't got yourself a girl yet, eh, Wiles? I'm beginning to worry about you, lad. Working too hard or do you not find the opposite sex to your liking? It's too early in the day for a real drink but I can offer you tea."

William Schuyler was famous for his barbs but they were meant to keep people off balance. And he aimed his stingers indiscriminately, regardless of rank. It was, everyone agreed, why he had not long ago been named C.

"Thank you, sir, but I pass reluctantly on both. Time being of the essence in both cases."

"Ah. Then let's get on with it," Sir William said, clasping his fingers behind his head.

"As you might recall I was in Berlin in nineteen thirty-six," Wiles began, aware that a good many British intelligence agents had used the cover of the Olympic games to poke around Nazi Germany, "and while I was there I met a young American. His name is Steven Dietrich. It took some time for me to realize that Dietrich was not German, his language was that good. Turned out that Steven was born in Berlin while his father was going to school there. When I met him almost two years ago he had one year left before graduating from college."

"In America?"

"Yes, sir. Yale."

"Hmm."

"I regarded Dietrich as a young man of good character and strong moral compass. Because of that I encouraged him to stay in Germany. I pointed out that one day we would be at war with Hitler and when that time came he could serve his country well."

"Meaning who?"

"I beg your pardon, Sir William?" Wiles said.

"I said, meaning who? Germany?"

"Why, America, of course. And Great Britain, as well."

"You say of course, but years spent in Germany for a young man like that might appeal to him, might convert him to the Nazi cause. How do you know?" Schuyler shifted uncomfortably in his chair, stretching his legs out to the side of his desk, then allowing his head to fall into the palm of one hand.

"I take your point, sir, but isn't it always the case when you recruit a spy that the same risk is always there? If we turned our back on all possible doubles our ranks would be virtually empty."

"But you like your chances with this chap."

"I do."

Schuyler let his eyes drift absently about the room, once a library, now his "personal cubbyhole," as he called it. Curtains to London streets below were always tightly closed and no one had ever seen Schuyler so much as peek out from behind them.

"So. What do you want of me, Edward?"

"Before I left Germany I gave Dietrich a way of reaching us. An advertisement in the *London Daily News*. This morning I received that message and I called him from a safe phone in the basement."

Wiles was gratified to see the old man's eyebrows raise in surprise or interest or both.

"He is living in an apartment near the Tiergarten. In the background I could hear sounds of others on the same floor. The university is nearby so it is likely a student population in the building. Dietrich said he is leaving in two weeks. My going there to meet him would be dangerous for both of us. I would like your permission to use Gustav for the contact."

Intelligence agents were awarded various levels of importance to their reporting agencies. Most important was their veracity, or reliability. Second was their access, that is to what level in the enemy camp would they be able to penetrate? A secretary, for example, might have access to the secret paperwork produced by the Foreign Office or a building superintendent might have access to blueprint information for battleship production or in submarine construction. Rankings generally ranged from one to five, five being the highest level both in veracity and access. The man code-named Gustav was a level-five. He was of inestimable value to the Crown. Gustav was brought into the service of British SIS immediately after the Great War by no less a person than William Schuyler himself. Such agents were very rare and hard to replace. They were not employed incautiously.

Few people within SIS knew of Gustav's existence, and those who did certainly did not know the man's background. He was "run" by Schuyler. If Sir William did not have a specific mission for Gustav the man merely continued his very low profile, almost what is called in the trade a "sleeper." Edward Wiles knew only limited information about Gustav. He knew that he was in his early- to mid-sixties, that he was German, and that he was a Jew. His "take," or Intelligence information, was always of high quality. Gustav possessed a shortwave radio furnished him by SIS but the man had a healthy respect for German mobile intercept operators and used the transmitter only when necessary. Most coded messages sent to Gustav were imbedded in BBC broadcasts.

"And how do you propose Gustav contact your man?" Schuyler asked.

It had been Dietrich's last day at the motorwerks and his fellow workers gave him a small sendoff in the form of beers after closing hours.

"You will probably crash," one of them said to Dietrich, referring to his upcoming flying program.

"Hans, you stupid ass," said another. "What kind of encouragement is that, eh?"

"Well?" Hans, said, "isn't it like saying good luck, or something? You know, they say those things on stage."

"You're exactly right," Dietrich said to Hans, knowing perfectly well that the teasing remark was meant in the best spirit. "I may have to crash a few of them before I get the hang of it, anyway."

They all laughed.

"The war in Spain, Steven," another worker said. "Maybe you will be posted there."

The same thought had occurred to Dietrich. The Condor Legion had been sent to Spain by Hitler to support Franco in the civil war raging even now. It was good combat training for Luftwaffe pilots, Field Marshal Göring had said. But there was also talk about the town of Guernica, about how the primary target, a bridge across the river, was ignored in favor of massive bombing of civilians, killing and wounding thousands. The dead were mostly women and children. Dietrich was grateful he had been spared at least that.

He shrugged. "Well, one goes where one is ordered, eh?"

"Dietrich," an older man, Otto, said "do you have your bag packed? There was nothing for us to pack in the last war." Otto began to laugh at the memory but the laughter turned quickly into deep coughing. Otto had very little hair, not lost because of age but as a result of poison gas. The wind had shifted and blown the stuff back into their own lines. Hundreds of his comrades had died. Otto had lost his hair and burned his lungs. He breathed only with difficulty.

"Nothing has changed, Otto. We are told to bring nothing but the clothes we are wearing."

On the way back to his apartment Dietrich's head was a psychological kaleidoscope. He had not heard news of Monica, a matter of concern even though it was too soon to expect that she had boarded the ship. Events in Germany were spinning ever faster, its citizens almost delirious with excitement, fear, and pride. Even Dietrich felt an inner sense of elation when Hitler and his government managed to pull off yet another international coup. Almost daily the population appeared in ever more uniforms until it seemed that civilians were the rarity. He also found himself eager to arrive in Augsburg where he would begin his training.

As he left the streetcar and began walking the remaining two blocks to his apartment he felt that he wanted to celebrate. Perhaps he would go to The Faucet. He could drink some beer. Or brandy. And have a frankfurter and kraut. He was beginning to enjoy basic German food. Then his mood changed. He would not feel entertained without the company of Monica.

It was fully dark by the time he let himself into the apartment. And it was cold. He struck a match and touched it to the small heater that was attachéd to a gas line coming through the wall. He pulled a chair under him and sat in front of the anemic fire, his jacket left on. He had been reading a book, an American mystery about a private investigator by the name of Marlowe. He picked up the book intending to finish it that night but the characters were no longer clear in his mind. He felt distracted and edgy.

It was quiet in the building, typical for the midweek when most of the tenants were faced with classes the next morning. Still, Dietrich thought he should have heard footsteps in the hardwood hallway before the knock on his door. He quivered. He rose quickly to his feet, debating with himself about his next move. Fight or flee? Yet the rap on the door was almost gentle, just loud enough to fetch someone from inside but not loud enough to alarm a neighbor. Dietrich realized that whoever was on the other side was probably not the

Gestapo. He opened the door.

"Mr. Dietrich? My name is Schmidt. I have been asked by a friend of ours to complete the purchase of a silk hat."

The man framed in the doorway was, like Dietrich, not tall. He was perhaps fifty, and when he removed his fedora he revealed a pate that accommodated only wisps of hair. He wore thick, gold-rimmed glasses that had a tendency to slide forward on his nose. Above his generous mouth was a full mustache that obscured his upper lip. Schmidt's face was more round than oval and his cheeks were quite full, reminding Dietrich of a cheerful chipmunk.

"Ah. Yes, well, please come in, Mr. Schmidt," Dietrich said, glancing down the hallway before closing the door behind his guest. "Sit down. May I take your coat?"

"That won't be necessary. I won't be staying long," he said in a soft, almost melodious voice.

"I see. What should we do now?"

"If you don't mind, I'd like to ask you a few questions." Schmidt arched his eyebrows as though requesting permission to proceed.

"Certainly."

"The name of our mutual friend, please?"

"Yes. He is Edward Wiles," Dietrich said.

"And where did you meet Edward Wiles?"

"It was here, in Berlin, in 'thirty-six. I was here for the Olympic games."

"Here from where?"

"From America," Dietrich said, a hint of surprise in his voice.

"And where in America?" Schmidt pressed.

"Well, New Haven, Connecticut. I was an underclassman at Yale at the time. My family doesn't live there, of course. And I—"

"Could you describe Edward Wiles for me, Mr. Dietrich?" Schmidt interrupted smoothly.

"He's about six feet, I would say, about middle twenties or close to it. Blonde hair, combed over to one side. Brilliant white teeth and he likes to smile. Not heavy. Slender, in fact."

A quiver at the corners of Schmidt's mouth gave Dietrich a feeling of relief, somehow, as though he was doing well on his oral exam.

"Now," Dietrich said, "there are some questions I would like to ask you."

Schmidt shook his head. "Sorry. Not allowed."

"I see."

"Mr. Dietrich, Edward Wiles works for SIS."

"I assumed it was something like that."

"The fact that you contacted him must mean that you will, in some way, help the Allied cause from within Germany. Are we correct in that surmise?"

"You are. Are you interested in knowing why?" Dietrich asked.

"Not unless you want to talk about it. I am only a lowly coordinator. It was convenient for me to contact you because it was impossible for Wiles to appear in the flesh."

"Sure. That figures," Dietrich said. "So, what should I do?"

"Nothing for the time being, Steven," Schmidt said, using Dietrich's given name for the first time. It was, in a sense, an unofficial signal that Dietrich was now inside the loop. "You indicated that you were leaving here very soon. Where are you going and why?"

"I applied for aviation training in the Luftwaffe," Dietrich said, suddenly worried that he had made a serious mistake. "I report tomorrow for induction. Officer's training school will go along with flight training."

"Excellent," Schmidt said. "Very good, indeed. It would have been preferable, of course, to have been able to train you in England in the craft. Spycraft. But the fact that you were not may be a blessing in disguise. You will not carry the baggage, so to speak, of an agent, so you will have nothing to hide. We think that your contact with London should be quite minimal in the beginning. We want you to feel very much at home in Germany. Very comfortable. In the present case you will be free to concentrate on becoming an efficient member of the Nazi war machine. Flying airplanes cannot be a simple task so you will need all of your wits about you."

Dietrich found himself nodding as Schmidt spoke.

"Someday, maybe months, even years from now, you will be contacted. It may be me or someone like me. It may even be a woman. You will know this person when he or she tells you that he or she is a lover of all dogs except bulldogs. Later in the exchange the person will admit that his or her dislike extends especially to the English bulldog. Easy to remember, eh?"

"Yes, of course."

"Then I'll say goodbye," Schmidt said, rising to his feet.

"That's all? How do I contact you in an emergency?" Dietrich asked.

"You cannot," Schmidt said with simple finality.

"Well, there could be a complication..."

Dietrich quickly sketched his involvement with Monica and finished with the killing of her Gestapo tormentor.

Schmidt accepted the information as though being quoted the price of a new shirt.

"What did you do with the man's effects?" he asked.

"I dropped his coat in a municipal garbage can at the Tiergarten. His identification badge I tossed into one of the lakes there."

"And his pistol?"

Dietrich hesitated only for a moment. "I still have it."

"Were you going to shoot it out with the police when they came for you?" Schmidt asked without humor. "Give it to me."

Dietrich fetched the Walther automatic from a bedroom drawer. Schmidt dropped it into his pocket without glancing at it.

"Good luck, Steven," he said, and was gone.

Chapter 18

Dietrich found officer-cadet training demanding but nevertheless stimulating. Physical fitness consisted of one hour of calisthenics each morning at dawn and a two-mile run later in the day. It was November and he found himself in shorts and a light shirt doing jumping-jacks in freezing weather. He and seventy-nine other pilot candidates were part of a *Staffel*, or squadron. A *Gruppe* usually consisted of three *Staffeln* and a *Geschwaderstab* had under it three *Gruppen*.

The days were divided into rigorous physical activity, academics, Wehrmacht protocol, and familiarization with basic aircraft. Military bearing was unrelenting. Cadets learned to march and to march very well. Cadets were made to drill while carrying rifles as well as backpacks. The units went everywhere in a group; to classes, to mess hall, even to the flight line when flying basic trainers.

Dietrich was quite up to the academics part of the program since Yale curricula was demanding in itself. As part of the academics for those among the Staffeln who were part of the commissioned officer program there were extra demands. Officer cadets were expected to conduct themselves with almost ramrod precision, to be able to take orders without question and to display courage along with military bearing. While instructors did not call it hazing, Dietrich nevertheless was subjected to extremely trying demands upon his time. There was military law to learn, military history, political theory, all of which revolved around Adolf Hitler's edicts and philosophies. Dietrich could see through the obvious propaganda goals of the indoctrination but found himself genuinely interested in fourth century hordes such as the Huns, the Ostrogoths, and the Visigoths who preceded the great German leaders of history such as Otto von Bismarck, Kaiser Wilhelm, and others. Despite the rigors of officer training Dietrich looked upon the whole ten-month course as a great learning process.

His consistent effort, his keen intellect, and his apparent dedication to his adopted country did not go unnoticed by his superiors. He was given marks that put him in the top five percent of his cadet class on the academic side. He made no reference to his previous flying experience in the United States and when it came time for him to try his hand at flying a basic two-seat instruction airplane, the Fieseler F5, he did not disappoint. Sitting in the front cockpit he was told by the instructor to advance the throttle of the HM60 engine and to keep the plane headed down the middle of the field by using his rudder pedals and holding the stick back in his lap. As the aircraft picked up speed, Dietrich allowed the stick to work its way forward, about in a neutral position, then pulled gently back.

Once airborne Dietrich and his instructor made a gentle left turn away from the field and found a place ten kilometer distant where they could do what was called "air work". The instructor, speaking to Dietrich through a tube, demonstrated a stall. He eased the throttle back while simultaneously pulling back on the stick with increasing pressure. The aircraft developed a nose-up attitude and, no longer pulled ahead by its engine, began to shudder. The shaking of the aircraft was not excessively violent but when it fully stalled, meaning that the aircraft stopped flying, the nose dropped quickly down. To recover from the stall the instructor pushed the throttle full forward, increasing the engine power, then slowly pulled back on the stick. Dietrich had done this maneuver many times and when told to reproduce the stall effect, executed the power-off stall perfectly. Next came the power-on stall, a more active maneuver with a steeper angle of attack before the wings lost lift and the nose of the aircraft once again suddenly dropped below the horizon. Dietrich had no trouble with this exercise, either.

"Very good, Cadet Dietrich. Now, bank to the left, then turn one hundred eighty degrees in the opposite direction," the instructor intoned through the speaking tube.

Dietrich looked over his shoulder first to the left, then the right, then began his turn. At the completion of a ninety-degree turn to port Dietrich moved the stick across the cockpit to the right side, kicked in right rudder, then neutralized his stick while the Fieseler began its turn to starboard. Throughout the turns Dietrich easily maintained a constant altitude.

"All right, Dietrich. Would you like to land the aircraft for me?" the instructor asked, his sarcasm mixed with a dash of humor.

Dietrich turned the plane in a southeasterly direction at three thousand feet. Finding an airport in unfamiliar countryside is no automatic thing. As he looked in front and below him Dietrich could see nothing resembling an aerodrome. He saw many farms, a number of third-class country roads, lots of hills, an occasional hamlet. He was about to inform his instructor that he was lost when he caught a glimpse of another aircraft ahead. Then there was another. Both aircraft were executing what seemed to Dietrich to be landing approaches. Dietrich corrected his heading by several degrees according to his compass, dropped down to one thousand feet AGL (above ground level), and began a downwind approach.

The landing was uneventful. Dietrich loved the way the Fieseler handled. It was an aerobatic aircraft, one patterned after the Fieseler F2 Tiger with which Gerhard Fieseler had won the European Aerobatic Championship in 1934. Dietrich had been a fan of the aircraft then and still was.

"Well, Cadet Dietrich, that was a nice little trick you did to us."

"Trick, sir? I apologize, Herr Instructor. I intended no such thing."

"Obviously you have flown before. You said nothing to us. It is not on your records," the flying officer said, not amused at all.

"I was not asked, sir."

"Hmm. Well, I can assure you, Dietrich, tomorrow we will fly again, you and I. And then I will know how good a pilot you are."

The instructor turned on his heel and strode off leaving Dietrich with his hand in the air saluting the officer's back.

Despite his hard work throughout the day Dietrich had no appetite for the evening meal. He sat with his fellow students in the mess hall looking down at his plate. The word had leaked out.

"Dietrich," Rudi Helger said, "Oberstleutnant Werner doesn't like you. He is going to kick you out of the program."

The others around the table watched for Dietrich's reaction, some grinning widely, others looking quite sober, even sympathetic.

"You have only one hope," Helger said. "You must not show him up tomorrow. You must pretend that you have exhausted all of your skills today. Try to be as dumb as you really are, Dietrich."

Dietrich's eyes did not rise from his untouched plate.

"Nonsense, Dietrich. Don't listen to Helger. The way out of your problem," Cadet Rheem suggested, "is to show him what you can really do. He will only respect you if you exert yourself, yes? Give the son of a bitch a good hard spin and show him what you are made of."

"Nothing will help," another cadet put in. "You have lied. Omission is lying, isn't it? Well, you are not fit to be an officer in the Luftwaffe."

"That's right. But wait, you can go back to America. The American Army will take you even if you are a liar."

The last remark came from Cadet Bregan Höltz, a man Dietrich did not trust and did not like. He especially disliked the insinuation that Dietrich lacked honor. He felt that he could not let it pass. He looked up from his downcast position. Höltz was bigger than Dietrich.

"What would you know about honor, Höltz? Everyone at this table knows that you cheated on your navigation examination. You are not only dishonest but you are stupid as well."

Conversation at the table ended at once. All eyes swung to Bregan Höltz. Höltz went rigid except for his eyelids, which narrowed.

"You filthy swine. You will meet me behind the gymnasium. You are overdue to learn a good Nazi lesson."

With that Höltz stormed away from the table, leaving his plate of partially eaten food to be picked up by lower ranks. Dietrich felt a sudden familiar weakness in his knees, as though they had turned to water. Clearly the man he was about to fight was determined to beat him to a pulp and Dietrich could imagine no reason why he should not succeed. Nevertheless, Dietrich stood and followed the bigger cadet toward the exit. Others at the table followed discreetly, careful to draw no unnecessary attention to an upcoming event that could get both men kicked out of the program if they were caught.

The eastern corner of the gymnasium was lit by nothing more than the dim glow of light within the building itself. The night was dark and cold. If Dietrich were not already shivering from fear, he certainly would have been shaking from the freezing temperature both men found themselves in. Despite the cold they removed their uniform tunics. It would be hard to explain the damage done to them had they worn them to do battle.

There was a ring created by other cadets of the Staffel, perhaps two dozen in all. Höltz moved into the center, his hands raised in the air in a fighter's stance. He was well muscled, as most of them were, but Dietrich was giving away fifty pounds not to mention reach. Höltz was not less than five inches taller than Dietrich and had the long arms to match. Dietrich knew that his only chance was to get inside the bigger man's arms and hit the body hard and often.

That was the plan. But when Dietrich made his first move to go inside, Höltz moved deftly to one side and let Dietrich move into a left hook. Dietrich immediately saw stars on a cloudy night. He staggered and wondered how many aspirins it would take to make his head stop hurting. When his vision cleared he decided to stay with his battle plan—only this time he would watch out for the left hook. He feinted one way, moved the other, then took a jab step inside to get at Höltz's middle. This time the big man dropped a right hand behind Dietrich's ear, which began an entirely new corridor of pain inside his head. He felt himself wishing that Höltz would hit him in the body.

Dietrich backed away, tried to dance a bit to gain some sort of momentum while allowing his ears to stop ringing and his eyes to clear. Slowly he felt his strength coming back. The pain lessened and his fists felt excellent. After all, so far they had hit nothing. He moved in again. This time he got a straight shot in the nose and could feel it break immediately upon impact. He now found himself inside his opponent's long reach, actually against his body. Dietrich put everything he had into three shots with his right hand into the man's kidneys, while hanging on to Höltz's middle with his left arm.

Dietrich could not understand why Höltz did not fall, or at least did not backpedal to get away from the onslaught. Had Dietrich seen his effort from the circle of cadets surrounding the combatants, he would have understood. There was nothing behind the blows. To put it into recognizable fighting vernacular, Dietrich could not have broken an egg. He was literally knocked out and did not realize it.

Höltz merely pulled Dietrich's arm from his waist and, hardly glancing at Dietrich, began to walk away. The ring of cadets looked at Dietrich, a bloody mess who would be lucky to get out of hospital in a month.

"Höltz," Dietrich said through swollen lips, "come back here and fight." When there was no answer and the bigger man continued to walk away, Dietrich said "Don't make me come after you!"

This made Höltz stop. He turned and looked at Dietrich. Then began to chuckle. The group of cadets began to laugh as well. Höltz did come back but it was only to help the thoroughly beaten Dietrich into his tunic, then support him on one side as the others pitched in to help him back to the barracks.

"My God," Oberstleutnant Werner said the next morning when he laid eyes on Cadet Dietrich. "What happened to you?"

"Begging the Leutnant's pardon, sir," Dietrich lisped through his swollen lips, "I foolishly fell down the barrack stairs in the dark."

Oberstleutnant Werner peered more closely at Dietrich's face. His nose, now no longer bleeding but clearly plugged with congealed blood, had gone sideways. It needed to be set. There was a gash above his ear where the upper part had been partially torn from the side of his head. His jaw was swollen on one side making his entire head appear lopsided.

"You've been beaten."

"With apologies, Herr Leutnant, it was my own clumsiness. I tripped when—"

"Damn it, Dietrich, stop that stupid story of yours. There are only four steps leading out of your barracks. Are you saying you hit each one of them?"

"Yes, sir, I believe I did."

"Dietrich, I warn you, don't compound your problems by lying to an officer. I will ask you one more time. Who did this to you?"

"I have no intention to lie to you, sir. Nor do I intend to lie to any officer in the entire gruppe." Dietrich then closed his mouth. It was clear that he had said all that he intended. After a protracted moment, while Oberstleutnant Werner studied Dietrich's face, he drew a deep breath and exhaled.

"Very well, Dietrich," Oberstleutnant Werner said in a much softer tone, "report to the dispensary. You need medical attention. If they ask you what happened tell them to contact me. I will back up your ridiculous story."

"Yes, sir, Herr Leutnant. Thank you, sir."

Dietrich barely managed a salute without falling down.

He returned to his barracks late at night, having refused to remain in a hospital bed. His entire head was swollen, his nose was heavily taped but at least straight once again. There was a large bandage over his ear. The entire barracks fell silent as he entered and closed the door behind him. They watched, virtually speechless, as he made his way to his bed and allowed himself to carefully lie upon it.

"Dietrich." He tried to turn his head as he heard his name spoken softly. "Don't move," the voice said. "It's me, Höltz."

It was good that Höltz had told him not to move because it was the last thing Dietrich wanted to do. He could feel the man sit gently on his bed.

"You were right, you know. I am a cheat. And now I am worse. I'm a bully. And you are the hero."

Dietrich formed the word "no" but was not certain if the word came out of his swollen mouth.

"I do not have your skills. So I stole from my comrades. I'm confessing these things because I want you to know that I am not entirely what you believe me to be," Höltz said, trying to maintain his voice. The fact that he was overheard by others in the staffel bothered him not at all.

Dietrich did turn his head and looked out at Höltz under his puffed eyes. He did not speak but his hand touched the bigger man's and he squeezed.

For the next four days Dietrich did not get out of his bed except to visit the open latrine in the barracks. He did not shower because Höltz gave him warm sponge baths in his bunk. The others in the barracks kept his uniforms cleaned and pressed, and his boots shined, always ready for inspection. But for some mysterious reason their barracks were not inspected until the fifth day. That was the day that Dietrich was back on his feet, his face and head sufficiently reduced in swelling that he could wear his flight suit and buckle on a parachute.

Oberstleutnant Werner arrived at the aircraft on the flight line shortly after Dietrich. He took his time appraising the young cadet. The hint of a smile flicked briefly across his face.

"Well, you weren't very handsome anyway. Can you fly?"

"Yes, Herr Leutnant," Dietrich said, snapping to attention.

"Hmm. We'll see. We're not going up in the Fieseler today. Do you know the Bü 133 Jungmann?" he asked Dietrich.

"Yes, sir. I have never flown one, of course, but I know the machine." Dietrich could see the 133 on the line. A biplane, the 133 Jungmann was a two-place version of the 131, an advanced trainer with a strong radial engine. It was a solid performer but not complicated to fly for Dietrich, who had flown a Steerman while in college. They were comparable machines.

"Good. You will fly in the front seat," the Oberstleutnant pointed at the 133 on the line. "We have radios today."

Dietrich pre-flighted the aircraft, checking the control surfaces including aileron traverse, horizontal stabilizers, rudder. He checked for water in the fuel tank, draining off a small amount. He checked the engine oil, the propeller, paying special attention to its leading edge. Dietrich was acutely aware that his instructor was following his movements with a critical eye. When he had buckled himself into the cockpit in front he turned his head to make sure Oberstleutnant Werner was himself secure before signaling to the ground crew that he was ready to start the engine.

He primed the engine several times, pushing in then pulling out the primer plunger, then switched on the ignition.

"Contact," he yelled and made a twirling motion with his hand. Two members of the ground crew began cranking on an inertial starter, which worked like a crank handle on an old car before electrical starter motors were invented. When the rpm on the inertial wheel was optimum, Dietrich engaged the starter. The two-bladed prop turned, passed four blades and coughed, missed, and coughed again as white smoke, a burn-off of excess gas in the cylinders, was forced through the exhaust system. The engine caught, and began to rumble smoothly.

Dietrich allowed the engine to run at 900 rpm for almost a minute before signaling to his ground crew to pull the chocks from the wheels. When this was done he advanced the throttle and taxied into takeoff position. He turned into the wind, and advanced the throttle once more as he checked his magnetos, watching for a maximum drop of one hundred revolutions on each side. The drop on the left was fifty, on the right about forty. Very good. He checked his compass setting, tickling in two degrees. There was no control tower, so Dietrich checked for other aircraft in the pattern. He waited a short while to allow another aircraft to land. When it had put down safely and began to turn off the grass runway toward the hangars, Dietrich advanced the throttle on his 131 and began his roll.

Because of engine torque he found he had to put in left rudder, a normal condition. The big radial, however, slung more torque than Dietrich was expecting simply because he had not flown the aircraft type in almost a year, but he increased his leg pressure on the left rudder pedal to hold the nose of the plane steady down the middle. As the aircraft picked up speed and its tail lifted naturally, the torque lessened accordingly until it took only light pressure to maintain his heading.

As the 131 lifted off the ground Dietrich automatically began to trim the control surfaces by adjusting a large trim wheel inside the cockpit on his right side. Suddenly he lost all power. As the engine died everything became very quiet except for the rush of air over the wings and through the wire struts holding them together. They were less than three hundred feet off the ground and there were only scant seconds to make ready for the crash that was about to occur.

There is a mantra for all pilots with at least ten minutes experience in the cockpit. It is *fly the plane!* No matter what else is going on around the pilot, his first obligation is to keep the wings level, and maintain the optimum glide angle to prolong the aircraft's flight time. If there is enough altitude the pilot will try to restart the engine. In this case, however, there was not, and not enough time. Nor was there enough altitude to turn the airplane around and try to glide onto the hospitable runway he had just left behind him. There was nothing that could be done but keep the aircraft gliding straight and hope he could find a reasonably flat space ahead of him. These things he did simultaneously and without panic.

As the aircraft got lower to the ground, less than one hundred feet from gently rolling hills in front of him, the engine magically turned itself on. Power surged through the plane, it picked up flying speed rapidly, and Dietrich made sure he achieved enough speed before coming back on the stick to make the 133 climb again.

There are several ways to stop an engine. One, of course, is to "chop" the throttle. If the instructor in the rear seat was to kill the engine in this manner the student would immediately see his front cockpit throttle retard. Another way to stop the engine is to pull the mixture control, robbing the engine intakes of oxygen. A third way is to close the shutoff valve to cut the flow of fuel to the engine. This is what Werner had done from the rear of the aircraft. He wanted to see how his student would react to an emergency, in this case, the loss of takeoff power.

Dietrich had done well.

They climbed to 5,000 feet as Oberstleutnant Werner directed Dietrich to a practice area about ten kilometers from the field. After making two turns, one left and a longer turn right in order to make sure they were alone in the sky, Werner gave the order.

"Dietrich," he said over their intercom system, his voice crackling in Dietrich's earphones in the front cockpit, "give me a spin to the right."

Rather than respond verbally Dietrich merely nodded his head. Dietrich brought the nose of the plane above the horizon and kept coming back on the stick. When his angle of attack passed through forty-five degrees he cut all the way back on his throttle. Thus robbed of forward propulsion, the aircraft began to shake, the portents of a stall. Just before the aircraft stopped flying altogether Dietrich put in right full rudder. The right wing stalled before the left, the left wing came "over the top," and the aircraft began falling from the sky, nose down, spinning to its right, in the direction engine torque pushed them.

Dietrich was not told how many revolutions to allow before bringing the plane out of the spin, but for safety's sake he allowed only two. He then put in opposite rudder to the spin, to the left, and moved the stick in the same direction in order to level the wings. The 133 responded well, the spin slowing until the aircraft was moving directly ahead. Dietrich recovered from the spin the same way one recovers from a stall, by applying power, waiting for airspeed to pick up once again, then coming back on the stick until level flight was achieved.

"To the left now, Herr Leutnant?" Dietrich asked into the intercom.

"A hammerhead, Dietrich," Werner said from the rear cockpit.

Dietrich had very little aerobatics training. The spin one must do to avoid an unexpected disaster. But he was very aware that the long hours of practice one must do to become proficient in aerobatics was not part of his experience. Once again Dietrich pushed the throttle to the limit building up maximum airspeed. When his 133 was indicating 113 knots, he came back on the stick, pointing the nose upward until they reached vertical. The airspeed bled off very rapidly until the 133 had literally stopped flying. It was now merely hanging on its prop. Dietrich then kicked hard right rudder to turn through 180 degrees, the plane's nose turning from straight up to straight down. He turned once again through a quarter loop to bring the aircraft to level flight.

"Dietrich," Oberstleutnant Werner said from the back seat through the intercom, "I am glad we are alive. You were not level at the start. You were not vertical at the start and the finish of your stall turn. So you could not be parallel to your entry path. When you recovered you were two hundred feet from your entry path."

Dietrich's heart sank. He had reached his maximum skill level. And it was not very far.

"Watch me," Werner said, shaking the stick as a signal to Dietrich that he would be flying, now.

Like Dietrich, Werner built up airspeed, then came smoothly back on the stick, keeping the vertical line perfectly straight. He input the rudder smoothly but decisively, bringing the nose over the top and back down, retracing his pattern on the bottom and bringing the aircraft back to level flight at exactly the same altitude at which he had begun the maneuver.

Dietrich was impressed.

"Now I want you to do a slow roll," Werner said from the rear cockpit. "One revolution."

Dietrich took over the stick once again and, from a straight and level flight, tried to hold the nose of the aircraft at a consistent spot on the horizon as he moved the stick to the left causing the ailerons to lift the wings on one side while forcing the opposite wings to go downward. Dietrich tried to maintain the nose position with a touch of rudder pedal throughout the roll but came out of the maneuver with his nose too low to the horizon.

"Too many changes, Dietrich. Watch again," Oberstleutnant Werner said, taking over the controls. "We don't want a snap roll, Dietrich. We want a slow roll. Use less than maximum aileron traverse. Seventy percent is about right. That will slow the roll." The plane began to roll smoothly as the instructor was speaking. "Now, as we approach inverted, apply a little down pressure on the elevator. Just a pulse," Werner said as he worked the stick. "It will compensate for your loss of lift." The aircraft continued rolling until it came back to the horizontal, straight and level.

"How do you feel?" Werner asked his student.

In fact Dietrich was beginning to feel good for the first time in days. The slipstream was blowing open his sinus passages, which had been painfully filled with pieces of mucous, dried blood, fragments of who knows what. The forced oxygen to his brain relieved him of his constant headache. And the need to concentrate on the task at hand took his mind completely away from pain.

"Never better, sir. May I try the roll again?"

This time his roll was very good. From the back seat Werner ordered several more of the same but almost smiled when, on Dietrich's third try, it was as good as he, Werner, could have done himself. They went on to other aerobatics including Cuban eights, Immelmann turns, and inverted flying.

"The fuel, Dietrich," Oberstleutnant Werner said over the intercom. "I don't want to push this thing back to the field. Why don't you fly us there?"

Werner made a long series of notations on Dietrich's flying records. He was far ahead of all other students, even a few who had previous flying experience. What was unique about Dietrich, Werner put in his remarks, was that Dietrich could see or be told what needed to be done in the air and then execute the maneuver correctly. He needed to be told nothing twice. He was, in addition, cool at all times. While Dietrich had a long way to go in his pilot training in order to familiarize himself with advanced instrument training, high-performance aircraft (such as the ME-108), and Luftwaffe procedures, he was an exceptional student who should be watched.

The Luftwaffe wanted pilots. It did not want to discourage good men, but at the same time, for those who were undergoing officer's training, the combination of discipline and academics was meant to weed out unsuitable candidates. The failure rate of Dietrich's staffel was forty percent to all causes.

Of the remaining percentage several were graduated pilot sergeants, some of whom would spend the next eight years of service in the non-commissioned officer grades. One of those who succeeded in graduating as a qualified pilot and an officer was Bregan Höltz.

Dietrich and Höltz, now inseparable friends, were facing each other while inspecting the other's uniform prior to the graduation ceremony.

"I cut a handsome figure in my uniform, don't you think, Dietrich?" Höltz asked, his chin held high.

"No doubt about it," Dietrich said, flicking pieces of lint from Höltz's uniform shirt.

"We'll go out tonight. Maybe I can find a girl for you. A small one, just your size."

Dietrich leaned forward to speak more closely into the taller man's ear.

"Bregan," he said, "the truth is that I don't care much for girls. It is men I crave. Big men, like you, Bregan. Forget the girls, we can rent a hotel room and sleep in the bed together. You and me."

Höltz sprung back like he had burned himself on a hot frying pan.

"Don't say those things," he hissed, flustered.

"But why?" Dietrich stepped nearer Höltz. "Would you turn me in? Are we not friends anymore?" Dietrich worked his lips theatrically, fish-like.

"You little ass," Höltz said, picking Dietrich off the floor of their barracks and spinning him around in circles until they were both dizzy.

Chapter 19

By early 1938, when Dietrich graduated from flying school, the ME-108 was the advanced trainer for those pilots assigned to fighter units. It was a joy for him to fly with its 270 horsepower engine, 20,000 foot ceiling, quick response to control inputs. The cockpit was snug, literally touching Dietrich on both shoulders. Dietrich was assigned to Luftlotte 3, VIII Fliegerkorps where he oriented in the ME Bf 109E. He received nine weeks of further training in combat flying techniques. Here he learned tight formation flying, dog-fighting, and air-to-air and air-to-ground gunnery. The E model 109 was equipped with two machine guns and two 20mm cannons. It had a maximum speed of 348 mph at sea level which, while it was not as fast or powerful as the later model Me-109s would become, it was a thrilling plane to fly and a very effective gun platform. It was by then late August 1939.

Since the beginning of the year Hitler had been complaining publicly about another creation of the Versailles Treaty, the free-city status of Danzig, a German city. It was a thorn in Hitler's side and the Reich's citizens, indeed the world, heard the German leader rant more and more about the injustice visited upon Deutschland. The Poles, against whom his diatribes were aimed, treated Hitler's comments with contempt and made no secret about it. They were made of stronger stuff than the Czechs, who had fallen apart in March, as Hitler would learn if he chose to use military muscle to back up his threats.

British Prime Minister Chamberlain, meanwhile, declared that if France were attacked Britain would go to its aid. France, with Britain's full support, declared that it, and Britain, would likewise go to Poland's support if it was attacked by Germany.

Hitler did not believe them.

While Dietrich was flying as many hours as he could that summer and fall, Hitler was in secret meetings with his military chiefs. He revealed to them his intention of going to war against Poland. He told them that the city of Danzig was only part of the problem with Poland. Germany needed living space and dependable food supplies from the east. He wanted to attack, he said, at the first opportunity. He was not concerned with the prospect of intervention from the Soviet Union. They would do nothing, he said. As events would play out, he was right about Russia. If France and England were to become involved, they would fail, he said.

Even so, Hitler hedged his eastern bet by entering into a non-aggression treaty with Russia wherein it was agreed that Germany would carve out enough of Poland and other areas in the east for their needs while Russia would then be free to chew on the bones of the corpse. This kind of political back-stabbing appealed to the avaricious Russian dictator, Joseph Stalin. The non-aggression pact was signed in August, to the shock and consternation of the world, since Hitler had long railed against the Soviet Union and Communism. The following month, on the first day of September, 1939, Hitler invaded Poland. World War II, as it came to be known, had begun.

Hitler's armies crossed the Polish frontiers with forty-four divisions. Hitler's generals, determined never again to become victims of attrition while bogged down in trench warfare, launched lightning strikes by using eleven tank divisions as the vanguard for its infantry. While the Germans used four motorized divisions, Poland had none. Their cavalry was still mounted upon horses.

The Luftwaffe acted as airborne tanks and artillery, maximizing the effectiveness of the Stuka JU-87 dive bomber. So accurate was this machine that before war's end Hans-Ulrich Rudel would be credited with destroying 519 Russian tanks, more than 800 motorized vehicles, and 150 artillery pieces. Germany employed 850 bombers, including the Stuka, and 400 fighters. Among the 43 fighter aircraft pilots in the newly formed Luftlotte 2, VIII Fliegerkorps, Stab (Staff) I/JG 27, was Leutnant Steven Dietrich.

Initially staging out of Leoben, Dietrich flew the wing Hauptman Heinrich Kuhl, a seasoned fighter pilot first bloodied in Spain. Dietrich, a precise pilot, was more interested in the success of the Stab, previously referred to as the *Schwarm* (four aircraft) and ultimately the Staffel (12 to 14 aircraft) than in soaking himself in personal glory. And, he realized that he had much to learn about combat flying, so he locked himself under Kuhl's wingtip and did his job. His assignment was to make sure no enemy got close enough to Kuhl to harm him. Dietrich watched the sides and the rear while Hauptman Kuhl did the shooting. When his element leader ran out of ammunition or nearly so, Dietrich would assume the forward position while the leader took on the rear-protection role. Hauptman Kuhl liked it this way very much. It gave him the peace of mind that it took to focus on a target without having to worry about watching his back. The follow-the-leader formation suited Dietrich as well because he got to watch an expert at work.

Unfortunately for the Poles, who were the equal of any pilot in the world, thoroughly trained and valiant to a man, their equipment, with a single exception, let them down. The front-line Polish fighter, the PZL-P11, was a parasol-wing aircraft and had no chance to keep up with the swifter, deadlier Me-109. In anticipation of the invasion, the Poles had dispersed their aircraft in camouflaged revetments around the country so that they lost relatively few aircraft in the first week of the war. Most of those destructions were air-to-air victories scored by the Luftwaffe. When it was at last discovered where the enemy had hidden their aircraft, however, pilots like Kuhl and Dietrich destroyed them on the ground.

Dietrich was flying a minimum of four sorties a day, bringing back his Me-109 just long enough to refuel and re-arm, then fly off once again to the front. The front was advancing so rapidly that on the fourth day of the conflict their gruppe was moved forward, or east, to what was literally a flat spot on the map south of Leszno. Ostensibly, Dietrich's staffel was to occupy an operational flying field, but even had the retreating Poles not sabotaged the runways and support buildings—POL, for example—the field would not have been usable because of the bombs and strafing done by the Luftwaffe. So, for several days Dietrich and his staffel used the flat grass surrounding the field to land and take off while their support organization, the fuel bowsers, ordnance handlers, and mechanics worked from trucks parked nearby. Sleeping was done in tents.

German engineers attempted to reconstruct the bombed-out aerodromes but no sooner would they get a runway back into usable order then the gruppe would move off, deeper into Poland. The relatively short range—410 miles—and combat time for the Me-109s required that they continually moved closer to where the fighting was being done. Later variants of the Me-109 would increase range to over six hundred miles but even a 50 percent increase was not satisfactory to Luftwaffe pilots.

On September 17, Hauptman Kuhl and Dietrich had located a network of Polish aircraft, most of them PZL P-37s, a very good medium bomber. Kuhl had exhausted most of his machine gun ammunition and more than half of his cannon rounds. Wanting to save some for the flight back to their base, Kuhl felt it was time to move Dietrich to the front.

"Black-Cat Two, take the lead. I'll fly your wing," he said into the radio throat mike.

"Understand, leader," Dietrich acknowledged briefly. Dietrich rolled his fighter over, then put back pressure on the stick until the nose of his plane dropped below the horizon and moved inexorably toward its ground target. He was always aware that his inverted twelve-cylinder engine was fuel injected and would never suffer from fuel starvation as it went through an inverted maneuver, unlike the British Spitfires and Hurricanes which still used carburation systems that could handle no sustained upside-down flying. As he maneuvered, Kuhl dropped neatly behind and followed the shooter, now Dietrich, down.

Dietrich made no attempt to approach his target at red-line speed. The faster one flew downward, the more the aircraft wanted to lift, and when it did so, without compensation to keep the nose pointed down, gunfire would land beyond the target instead of right on it. So Dietrich maintained a steep dive, but when the Me-109 wanted to pull itself faster toward the surface of the earth, Dietrich eased his throttle back just enough to stabilize the aircraft. The result was a solid gun platform when he opened up from fifteen hundred feet with his 20mm cannons.

The first P-37 exploded after the first burst of fire, then Dietrich allowed the nose to raise slightly as he pumped yet another burst of cannon fire into the second revetment. As he pulled back on the stick to clear the tree tops at no more than fifty feet, Dietrich could look behind him to see the second plane on fire as well. Swiveling his head to the port side of his plane he caught a glimpse of Kuhl, steady on his wing, giving him the thumbs-up sign.

Dietrich made two more passes at targets on the ground, setting ablaze one more aircraft plus one fuel truck that was trying to hide beneath camouflage netting. The fuel truck went up in a large explosion. Dietrich was still low but rolled his wings into a tight inside turn to avoid debris from the big bang. He was getting low on fuel and, even though he had used only a bit more than half the ammunition in his machine guns, he knew that it was time to return to base. Turning again so that Kuhl could see him, Dietrich motioned in the direction of home. He saw Kuhl nodding vigorously, confirming that he was equally short on fuel.

They began streaking west for their temporary field in Zalesie when Dietrich felt his aircraft buck violently. He knew immediately he had been hit but not, he knew, by another aircraft. It had to be ground fire. All at once he could smell the acrid stench of oil and other composite aircraft material on fire, then he could see the flames licking at the fuselage from under the engine cowling. Dietrich quickly actuated his engine compartment fire extinguisher but it had no effect on the flames. He pulled up on his cockpit canopy release, the slipstream ripping it away. He knew that he was too low to bail out but that option was better than burning alive in the plane. He was barely two hundred feet above the ground but still making about two hundred miles per hour. He pulled back on his control stick until the nose of the plane pointed upward, achieving about a 60-degree vertical angle. He released the straps that held him in the airplane and tried, using all of his strength, to exit the burning fighter.

The awkward angle, the confines of the cockpit giving him no leverage, and the g-forces on his body kept him inside the plane. Flames from the engine licked over the top of the canopy and into the cockpit, searing his face. Dietrich felt that he was about to die, that he had tried everything he could think of to exit the aircraft when there was another explosion. The left wing disintegrated causing the aircraft to roll completely over and drop Dietrich out. He felt instant relief that the searing heat from the fire had ceased. His second conscious reaction was to pull the handle on his parachute. Kuhl, now in a tight turn above Dietrich's stricken fighter, said later that the chute was still filling when Dietrich struck the trees.

Kuhl had precious little fuel to loiter over his downed comrade but managed to get a firm navigation fix on Dietrich, which he radioed to army units on the ground. Dietrich was found by forward elements of the 1st

Leichte Panzer Division. Dietrich was in and out of consciousness until he could be taken by ambulance to a Wehrmacht field hospital. He suffered a compound fracture in one leg and had second-degree burns on the lower part of his face. One arm and hand was heavily bandaged, the result of flames licking his arm as he pushed himself away from the flaming aircraft.

"You will not be able to play with your weenie now. It will be good to give the poor thing some rest," a familiar voice parted the fog of sedation.

"Bunny? Is that you?" Dietrich said.

"Yes. Who else would interrupt their busy day to see you? I have a war to win, you slacker."

Dietrich blinked his eyes repeatedly, unaware that they had been treated with a soothing fluid by doctors. Still, he could make out the image of a tall, blonde man standing next to his bed. He had never seen Hartung in combat clothes before and said so.

"I hope you never do again. This war business is quite loud. They shoot guns out there."

Dietrich could see that Hartung wore the black beret of the SS-Panzer Gruppen, Waffen-SS. Upon his belt he carried a holstered 9mm pistol but no other arms. Even if he did not feel like a warrior, Hartung looked the part.

"What happened to you, Dietrich? Do you remember anything after you went to bed with your mechanic?"

It hurt Dietrich's face to smile.

"Most of it I'd like to forget. Hey, there's something different about you. You got promoted," Dietrich said. "Congratulations."

"SS-Hauptscharfürer. I wanted to be a general but this was all that was left," Hartung said.

Hartung glanced around at the others inside the medical tent. It was large and they were in the part of the tent that was reserved for officers. Nurses flitted about while doctors were less evident, but in terms of warfare, the Wehrmacht medical service was not stretched to its limits. Hartung reached inside his camouflage tunic and brought out a silver flask. He unscrewed the lid.

"Would you like a drink of excellent French brandy?" he asked Dietrich.

"I sure would," Dietrich said, lowering his voice.

Hartung unscrewed the lid, lifted the flask to his lips, and drank deeply. He put the lid back on the flask and returned the flask to its place under his jacket.

"I'll bet you would," he said.

"You swine," Dietrich said.

"You see? You never loved me as you said you did," Hartung said, smugly.

"I could change my mind again. For a drink."

"Ah. That's what I was waiting for," Hartung said, producing the brandy flask once more. "Here."

He removed the cap so that Dietrich could hold the flask and drink with his free hand.

"Ahhhhh," the pilot said. "The French are good for something after all," Dietrich said, then drank again.

"Well, I hope that does not include fighting wars."

"Why?"

"Because we are at war with them now. England and France declared war on us poor Germans. Can you imagine?"

"Damn," Dietrich said, almost to himself.

"Luckily you are not involved," Hartung dead-panned.

"It wasn't our fault," Dietrich said facetiously. "Everybody knows that."

"Just because fifteen hundred Luftwaffe bombers leveled Warsaw. With Friedel at the controls I am surprised any bombs hit the city," Hartung said, hardly hiding the bitterness in his voice. He leaned close to Dietrich. "Yank, wouldn't you like to be having a glass of wine at the Faucet, right now? Maybe with your young lady. What was her name?"

"Monica."

Dietrich felt Hartung touch his shoulder gently. He then slipped the brandy flask under Dietrich's sheets where he could get to it with his good hand.

"I'll see you tomorrow, Steven," Hartung said, and then he was gone.

A nurse appeared at his bedside shortly after Hartung had left.

"What is that smell?" she sniffed.

"What smell?"

"Alcohol," came the response.

"I've been smelling alcohol ever since I woke up," Dietrich said, wrinkling his nose. "I suppose all hospitals smell the same, eh?"

The nurse did not immediately answer but set to work gently changing his bandages.

"I was here earlier but you were sleeping," Hauptman Kuhl said as he approached Dietrich's bed. He was munching on an apple. He was still wearing flying boots but they only made him and his sky-blue uniform with aluminum threads look even more dashing. On the right side of his chest Kuhl wore the prestigious Spanish Cross with Swords. Around his neck he wore the Knight's Cross and the Luftwaffe officer's eagle stitched above the right tunic pocket.

"Thank you for coming, Hauptman Kuhl," Dietrich said.

"Dietrich, I think you can call me Heinrich if you like. After all, you have been promoted," he said. "And you will be awarded the Iron Cross."

A surge of excitement and pride went through Dietrich.

"Promoted?"

"Yes, you are a first Leutnant, now. You see what wars can do? I wouldn't feel too good if I was you, however. I was promoted, too."

"Well. Well, congratulations Herr... Heinrich. You deserve it, Major Kuhl."

"So do you, Steven. You have a new plane. You won't be flying it soon, of course. It is the E6 model but with a supercharged engine and four machine guns."

"I feel honored," Dietrich said, torn between his feelings of genuine pleasure that his piloting skills had been recognized and the very vivid knowledge that he had helped in the subjugation of a helpless nation. He had seen a limited amount of the carnage from his single-seat fighter aircraft, but the smoke and the dust and the long lines of refugees on the roads below him told him more than he wanted to know about the German war machine and Hitler's aims.

"I am being posted to the west," Kuhl said. "We are fighting the French, now. I'll ask for you, if you'd like. They are pretty good at sending pilots back to their old outfits from hospital."

One week later Dietrich was taken by ambulance for evacuation back to Germany. He would be flown out on a JU-52, the tri-motor workhorse of the Wehrmacht. But first he was taken to his new fighter that would be flown back to Germany. Dietrich walked on crutches with some pain and great difficulty, but it was worth the trip. On the side of the Me-109E6 was the word "Yank".

While on medical furlough in Berlin, Dietrich divided his time between the officer's quarters at Templehoff, the club, and occasional trips to a movie house. Airplane traffic of every conceivable kind was going non-stop around the clock at Templehoff so that the sound of high-performance engines became a part of even his thinking process. He could have watched films on the base but he preferred the quiet of the city. Berlin gave him a chance to feel less militarized. There were more uniforms than ever, literally everywhere one looked, but there were also diversions that one did not have on base. On his

Luftwaffe tunic he wore not only the pilot badge, but also the silver "wound badge." He also displayed the Silver Class Day Fighter Operational award for sixty missions. Dietrich was shot down on his sixty-third. Hauptman Kuhl advised him that he would receive yet another award for that feat. If so, it was a hard way to win a decoration, he thought.

In his second month of convalescence, Dietrich was beginning to get along with only a cane for support. He had spent a good deal of the day reading a novel and, needing further distraction, was debating whether or not to go to the officer's club when he was told he was wanted on the telephone.

"Are you still sitting on your fat little ass, Yank? The war is almost over and you will sleep through it all!"

"Friedel!" Dietrich said, his spirits immediately brightening. "Where are you?"

"Templehoff, Base Operations. Just got here."

"From where? Oh, never mind. How much time do you have?"

"Just passing through. We're leaving in the morning," Friedel said, obviously in good spirits.

"Then come here. You can spend the night with me."

"God, I hoped to have better luck than that. Well, it could be worse. I could be a prisoner."

They agreed to save time by meeting at the club. The Luftwaffe officer's club at Templehoff was quite large, seating several hundred. There was a wide stage and dance floor with the best entertainers in Europe booked to treat Germany's most prestigious uniformed men. Fighter pilots walked with a special swagger, a personality trait not exclusive to the Luftwaffe, but to all single-engine pilots of all countries. Dietrich was self-effacing by nature, yet his decorations and the use of his cane got him an unspoken edge over most other club members. He was shown to a good table and the waiter paid him special attention, even bringing Friedel to his table so the wounded Dietrich would not have the stress of monitoring the front door.

He rose to his feet when amicable Freddy arrived, throwing his arms around the bigger man's shoulders.

"You haven't grown an inch, Yank," Friedel said, standing back to look at his friend.

"You have. Around your gut. You must wear out a lot of belts," Dietrich said. "And promoted!"

Friedel was now a *hauptman*. Captain. Dietrich also noticed that his friend wore the cuff title of the Hindenburg Geschwader stitched with aluminum thread. He also wore the gold lapel tabs, as Dietrich did, which designated him among flying personnel. German flying personnel wore their class-A uniforms to battle, merely adding flying boots and suits and helmets overall. During the Spanish Civil War, fighter pilot Adolph Galland of the German Condor Legion, who would later become a general and head of all Luftwaffe fighter forces, once wore his undershorts and undershirt on a combat mission.

Friedel looked better than Dietrich would ever let on. He now exuded confidence and a certain maturity that he had lacked more than three years ago when Dietrich first met him in Berlin.

"Tell me what you are flying, Freddy," Dietrich asked even before their drinks arrived.

"Dornier 17Z-2. Good airplane, Steven, but a little slow. We are about four hundred kilometers per hour with a tailwind. The JU-88 is faster and has more range. Of course in Poland it didn't matter. But someday it will. When we go to London. That's when it will matter."

Their drinks arrived along with cheese and bread. Friedel, always hungry, ordered another round of drinks and food even before the waiter left their side.

"Might as well stay ahead of the rush, eh?" he said.

"So, what kind of targets did you have? Did you hit anything?" Dietrich asked.

"Yes, of course. They all hit the ground," Friedel laughed at his own joke. "Rail centers were a priority, of course. Airfields. We flew at least two missions a day and never ran out of targets."

"How about Warsaw? Were you on those raids?"

Friedel slowly stopped chewing. He swallowed hard.

"Yes. Everyone was," he said, his voice dropping low.

"And?"

"And what?" Friedel turned toward Dietrich.

"What was your target there? In our gruppe we heard the city was leveled," Dietrich said, his voice non-judgmental.

Friedel hesitated for a long moment while he chose his words.

"It was Schrecklichkeit." Frightfulness. "That was our mission, to make the civilians afraid. Afraid so they would surrender."

Dietrich waited.

"Well..."

"Yes?"

"There are no yeses. They are targets. That's what I drop my bombs on. Targets. How about you, Dietrich? How did you feel about shooting down your allies?" Friedel snapped.

"They're not my—"

"Nonsense!"

"Allies." Dietrich finished.

"This is not your war, Yank. The British support the Poles. We are at war with the British. America supports the British. You cannot escape the irony, Steven."

Dietrich thought for a long moment.

"You are right. They are targets. I never think of people inside the machines I shoot. I just shoot the machine," he responded, honestly. He never allowed himself to think beyond the technique of placing his aircraft into attack position and pulling the trigger. It was a flying exercise that quite frankly fascinated him.

"It has to be done, Dietrich. War is not a pretty business. We all knew that, didn't we? But it will be for the better in the end. The war must be made short. That's what I think. And the really smart people have thought about all of this. Not you and not me. So I load up my plane and I drop my bombs."

"For a better world," Dietrich added.

"Are you mocking me, Dietrich?"

"Of course not. The more bodies the better." Dietrich said, draining his glass of cognac.

Friedel dropped his remaining piece of bread into his plate.

"I think I am tired. Maybe I'll sleep early tonight, Steven," the bomber pilot said.

"That sounds good to me, too. You're going to stay in my room tonight," he said.

"Perfect. I want to hear about your war in Poland."

At the BOQ Friedel dropped his flight bag onto the floor and immediately began to remove his uniform.

"Shower?" he asked.

"In there," Dietrich said, nodding his head toward a door leading off from the kitchenette area. Dietrich's attention had been distracted by an envelope that had been delivered under his door. It was covered with stamps of all kinds. He knew at once it was from America. Sure enough, the return address was Randallstown, Maryland. At a glance he could see that the envelope had been opened and then resealed. He hesitated a moment before opening it yet again, lest he inadvertently tear the letter inside. The paper was powder blue and very light to the touch, written clearly in small letters with a black ink pen.

Dearest Steven, it began, I hardly know how to begin this very difficult letter. I suppose the good news should come first. Your friend has safely arrived. I'm sure you know who I mean. She is quite lovely and I can see why you are attracted to her. Your father and I tried to get her to stay with us but she insisted that she could not. Heavens knows we have the room what with you gone and your sister long since married and out of the house. She left yesterday for the Chesapeake area where she says she has prospects for a job. Shipbuilding in America has suddenly revived.

We had to twist her arm to take any money and the small amount she did accept she insisted was a loan. We'll see about that later.

Steven, I can't tell you what effects your conduct has had on your father and me. A great number of your father's patients have found other doctors. We reel between wanting to withdraw from social activities and our own attitudes about the rights that we have to live our lives as we deem fit. Your picture was in Life *magazine and it has appeared in a number of newspapers across the country. It seems that the Nazis are quite proud of you.*

Steven, we love you, your father and I. More than you can know, but we simply cannot imagine why you have aligned yourself with people whom we regard, frankly, as despicable. We know you to be a kind, loving, bright young man. This turnaround, if that's what it is, is flabbergasting. Your friend refuses to discuss it with us because, she says, she simply doesn't know herself and will not speculate. Nothing good can come from you staying in Europe with a war clearly looming on the horizon. I speak for your father as well. I beg you to come home, dear son.

—Your loving mother.

The letter had been written on August 29, 1939. What would his mother think now that Germany had invaded Poland? Dietrich read it for a second time before folding it and putting it into his pocket to be read again later.

"A letter? Something from that girl, what's her name?"

"No, not from her," Dietrich said, purposefully omitting Monica's name. He felt foolish; she was out of the reach of the Gestapo. Nor would Freddy betray her. At least not purposely. "My mother."

"Ah. The matriarchal family. What does mother have to say? Is she proud of you?" Friedel asked, still wiping water from his hair with a towel.

Dietrich did not respond at once.

"No, she isn't," he said at last. "She and my father don't agree with Nazi party politics."

"Ach, well, that is so for many people. They don't understand, yet. But they will, Steven. When they realize what the Führer has planned they will all stand up and applaud. Even your mother," Friedel said, sitting on the edge of the spare bed facing Dietrich.

"Are you sure about that, Freddy?"

"Of course. Aren't you?"

Dietrich shrugged. "I'm politically naive. You and Bunny keep telling me that."

"Naive, but not stupid. Look at what we've accomplished so far. My God, we have pulled Europe together for the first time in a thousand years."

"It wasn't together a thousand years ago," Dietrich corrected.

"Well," Friedel waved his hands in the air, "one hundred years. Fifty. Who cares? The point is that we are the mightiest nation in the world, now. And we will get stronger every day. Tell your mother that."

Again Dietrich did not respond.

"Well, Steven," Friedel said, his tone conciliatory, "I take that back. Mothers are supposed to worry about us. God bless them. And what do they know about politics? But your father, he must be proud of you, eh?"

"Sure. He must be just popping his buttons."

"Popping buttons?"

"That means expanding his chest," Dietrich demonstrated by inhaling deeply.

"Oh, I see," the bomber pilot said, stretching out on the bed. "You have a very good father, I can tell." Friedel closed his eyes and quickly drifted off to sleep.

Dietrich found his personal stationery supplied to him by the Luftwaffe. He was absolutely certain that his mail would have been read carefully by the Gestapo. It would have to be answered. He also knew that whatever he wrote would likewise be opened and read before it was sent on. He took pen in hand completely aware that his mother and his father would be further alienated, that he might cause them real harm, if not to their health certainly to their psyches. Yet he could think of no other course of action.

> *Dear Mother, he wrote. You and dad need to understand that what we are doing here in Germany is for the good of the whole world. Don't believe everything you read in the newspapers. There is no one else in history quite like our Führer, Adolf Hitler, and it won't be long before the world realizes his true purposes for the people of Europe and, particularly, for the Jews. What I am doing now, flying for the Luftwaffe, is something I had to do. I really had no choice and I hope you and father will understand.*
>
> *The war will be over some day and we'll be together again. That fact that you and father have suffered socially because of my actions is devastating to me. You are innocent victims of events over which you have no control. Try to remember that your real friends, your true ones, will continue to care about you as always. Until I see you again, you have all of my love, [signed] Steven*

Dietrich purposely omitted any mention of Monica, even by inference.

Best to allow that subject to die. If the Gestapo wanted to question him about her he would make something up. He had run into an old college flame, he would tell them. Something.

Chapter 20

Dietrich had, for the most part, healed from his wounds by February of 1940, although he now walked with a slight limp. He managed to get himself reassigned to an operational fighter gruppe stationed near Cuxhaven. He was delighted to strap himself into the cockpit once again, his nostrils filling with the rank but somehow intoxicating smell of fuel, oil, and coolant mixtures. He flew the first five or six orientation hours by himself, practicing various aerobatic maneuvers, tight turns, spins and snap-rolls and slow rolls. A fighter pilot's longevity in the sky depended upon his ability to make a tighter turn than his opponent and to hold that turn under a high G load longer than the enemy. The fighter pilot had to avoid blacking out, a condition caused when the forces of gravity cause blood to pull downward into the body and out of the brain. Dietrich made violent turns to the right, to the left, and held them until he "grayed," recovering just before the world turned black. Continued practicing began to show results; he was able to hold the tightest possible turn for longer and longer periods.

Finally he took a wing man up with him and dusted off the technique of attack flying in formation. Pilots doing this kind of work are constantly adjusting throttle settings and control inputs to maintain precise distances and positions from the other aircraft. It is a tiring way to fly but absolutely necessary to success in aerial combat.

Like an athlete allowed to work at his own pace, Dietrich finally announced that he was ready to return to combat status. He was at once assigned to lead a stab, an element of four fighters.

Very soon, April 9, Germany invaded neutral Norway, ostensibly to protect its vital supplies of strategic war materials, including essential iron ore. The fear was that the British Navy could and would cut off the flow of these goods by sea blockade. Hitler was probably quite correct in assuming that he had to make a bold move to the north and do it without delay. He was not supported enthusiastically by his general staff and particularly by the Kriegsmarine. Hitler saw his OKW composed of timorous leaders in uniform and remedied the problem simply by naming himself commander in chief of all armed forces, wehrmacht, and ordered war plans for the occupation of Scandinavian countries to proceed.

Dietrich was part of a large air armada which flew north to support the army's invasion. The British Navy made its appearance as the German admirals feared but their attempt to put enough British troops ashore (they did succeed in doing so at Trondheim, Bergen, and Narvik) yielded only minor gains. The reason the British were driven back to the sea while their navy elements were sent sailing back to England was because the German Luftwaffe arrived with enough fighters to gain air superiority over the RAF and enough bombers to send the British Navy packing.

It was in this action that Dietrich got his first kill as a fighter pilot. Leading his stab at 19,000 feet northwest of Stavanger, Norway, Dietrich spotted a flight of six British Hurricanes flying east over the coast at approximately 16,000 feet. Unwilling to give their presence away by using the radio, Dietrich motioned to his wing man on his right that he was about to begin an attack. The other two aircraft in the stab monitored Dietrich's signals and when Dietrich rolled in on the target aircraft his stab was right behind him. The Hawker Hurricanes had not yet seen the Germans coming from their four o'clock high. The German stab lined up abreast so that each aircraft had free range with his guns. When they were within fifteen hundred feet of the Hurricanes the British spotted their attackers and broke left and right. Dietrich's eyes never left his target, the aircraft trailing their flight leader. While the element leader broke hard left his wing man, Dietrich's target followed. The Me-109s had superior speed to the Hurricanes and the fact that the Me-109s were in a steep dive made it no contest. The Hurricane suddenly loomed large in Dietrich's gunsight and, wanting to make sure of maximum damage to the target, he pressed his 20mm trigger.

Made of mostly of fabric that could often allow small-caliber ammunition to pass cleanly through it, the Hurricane, in this case, took the first cannon hits in the engine compartment and at least one in its fuselage gas tank because it blew up in a ball of black and red flames. Dietrich was instantly through the fireball and out the other side when he pulled into a steep right turn, back where the other aircraft should have been. Because he was now climbing and because turns drastically reduce an airplane's speed, Dietrich had pushed his throttle to the stop trying to increase the 250 kph shown on his airspeed indicator.

Craning his neck in all directions Dietrich could see no aircraft nearby. He was about to turn a few degrees to his port side when he caught a flash of movement at his seven o'clock position. Without ascertaining whether it was friend or foe, Dietrich kicked his Messerschmitt into a hard left turn and held the stick back in his belly as hard as he could pull. Then he kicked opposite rudder and held his fighter in an extremely hard right turn as tracer bullets flew past his canopy on their way out to the north sea. He knew the Hurricane could not turn inside him and he knew something else about the British fighter; that it could not fly inverted for long.

Dietrich pulled back on the stick again, pushing his throttle to the stop without thinking that his throttle had been set at battle position throughout the attack, pulling thirty-four inches of mercury on his manifold pressure indicator. As he rolled out of his right turn he fed in a touch of left rudder and came back once more on the stick, putting his aircraft into the top half of a loop.

The Hurricane followed. Rather than pull through the maneuver, however, Dietrich allowed his Me-109 to remain inverted while, he knew, the British pilot made the adjustment to line up his gun platform with the Messerschmitt. Dietrich counted on the fact that the British pilot would not half-roll his Hurricane back to level flight lest he miss his opportunity to shoot the German fighter. Dietrich, hanging in the cockpit from his shoulder straps, watched while tracer bullets flew ineffectually under and past his cockpit. As the tracers continued to pass lower and lower, Dietrich knew he was out of danger for the moment. The British pilot had to roll his fighter back level to accommodate his carbureted engine.

As the Hurricane began its aileron roll to the right, the pilot taking advantage of propeller torque in the counter-clockwise rotation of his propeller blades, Dietrich did his own roll over the top of the RAF fighter and came down on its tail. The Hurricane filled Dietrich's gunsight, a scant one hundred yards away. Dietrich pulled the trigger just once and the 20mm cannons blew away the fabric tail, then exploded its engine.

Dietrich turned away immediately intending to round up his stab. He looked above him, around him, and saw nothing. No planes anywhere.

"Eagles Four, this is Eagle Leader. Do you read me? Over."

"Eagle Leader, this is Eagle Three."

"Anybody hit? Good. Fuel critical. Make your way home independently." They would all save fuel by heading right for base without first loitering in the area to join up as a group.

One by one he received confirmation from each of his stab. Their flight back to base would take a minimum of thirty minutes and take them to the limit of their flying range. Dog fighting sucked even more time and gallons from the aircraft so when Dietrich and his pilots arrived back in Germany, they would be landing with little more than fumes in their tanks.

Dietrich was on a heading of 171-degrees magnetic on his way home. He had leaned out the fuel mixture as far as possible, even at the risk of damaging his Daimler-Benz engine, running it hot but saving fuel in the process. He was at 6,000 feet when he happened to look upward. Flying across his course line was a British Sunderland bomber. The Sunderland seaplane, with a crew of thirteen, was approximately 3,000 yards ahead, at his ten o'clock, about 500 feet above. Given the bomber's speed of approximately 190 mph and Dietrich's speed of 300 mph, if neither aircraft changed directions the intercept would be perfect for a zero-deflection shot. Dietrich watched with fascination as the lumbering four-engine bomber continued its plodding course, apparently without seeing his small silhouette in the sky. The convergence course stayed unbroken as Dietrich switched his guns from the off position to armed, then pulled gently back on his control stick to raise the Messerschmitt's nose just slightly. He depressed both triggers, his two 20mm cannons as well as his twin 7.92mm machine guns. With a flick of his rudder Dietrich placed his rounds at the Sunderland's nose and allowed the bomber to fly through an extended burst.

Both starboard side engines burst into flame. Dietrich dropped his nose so that he passed almost directly under the Sunderland. He retarded his throttle so as not to overshoot the target too far. As he rolled back to a parallel course to the bomber he was now able to put a burst of cannon fire into the port side wing. He fired only a few rounds because the bomber was even now rolling to its starboard side, right wing solidly aflame. He immediately threw his fighter ninety degrees to the left, leaning back his engine once more, almost angry with himself for his second approach to the Sunderland that was already going down. If he ran out of fuel and had to bail out, it would be his own fault. He watched with regret as the beautiful, graceful Sunderland plunged into the sea below.

Twenty-eight minutes later, Dietrich was flying with his canopy opened, anticipating that it would save time if the engine stopped. His fuel gauges were on zero. He could see the field ahead, approximately five miles. He did quick mental calculations factoring in altitude, glide ratio, and airspeed. While he did the arithmetic he experienced the first rumble from the engine. His engine rpm began to drop as the engine coughed. His altitude was five thousand feet but the nose of his Messerschmitt dropped with each lost rpm. He pushed his mixture control full rich to pump any remaining fuel from his fuselage tank. The sink rate in the fighter was rapid. Dietrich determined to bail out when his aircraft reached an altitude of two thousand feet, but he passed through two thousand feet almost before he realized it was there. By the time he had reconsidered his options his propeller had stopped turning and the increased drag brought him dangerously close to a stall.

He dropped his nose even more in order to pick up the necessary airspeed to avoid the stall, a point at which the aircraft would simply fall out of the sky like a rock. Dietrich actuated the toggle switch that put the gears up and down but there was no response. It was clear that he was not going to make the runway and there was simply no time to crank down the gears manually. The distance from where Dietrich and his stricken Me-109 was passing and the fence that separated the runway from a civilian road was about six hundred meters. Suddenly he could feel the aircraft shake violently, the precursor to the stall. From reflex, Dietrich pulled back on the control stick to avoid hitting the ground nose first.

The Me-109 hit hard, sending pain shooting up Dietrich's spine, and sliding into and through coils of barbed-wire fence surrounding the airfield. The wire may have saved Dietrich's life or at least reduced serious injury, acting as an effective brake on his forward progress on the ground. The aircraft slid on its belly only a short distance before it was pulled to a complete stop. The danger of fire was minimal since there was no gasoline on board to burn, but Dietrich immediately turned off the master switch inside the cockpit. Aside from the discomfort in his back from his bruised spine, Dietrich was quite in one piece. For a long moment he simply sat in the cockpit of the aircraft, totally exhausted, then slowly began unfastening his harness straps. All the while, indeed even before impact, fire equipment, an ambulance, and other assorted vehicles were driving toward Dietrich at high speed down the side of the runway.

Within minutes eager hands were gently helping him out of the wrecked fighter and into an ambulance. Dietrich might have winced once or twice when he was forced to move his back because he heard stern voices command others to be very careful as he was moved. Later X-rays taken at the medical unit confirmed what he had assumed all along: there were no breaks in the bones of his back but rather some serious bruising had occurred.

Dietrich asked about his stab even as he was gulping pain pills prescribed by a Luftwaffe doctor. They were all back, he was told, and waiting outside the building. He asked if he could get up and see them but was forbidden to do so even as the words were coming out of his mouth. They could come in but he was going to spend the night immobilized in one of the medical unit's beds for observation. He would be evaluated the next morning.

What was evaluated immediately, however, was Dietrich's gun camera film.

To have shot down three enemy aircraft in one day, in a single sortie, was a great accomplishment, and one that put aside any question of the American's allegiance in Germany's war. Secondly, and of vastly more serious consequences, the Sunderland bomber that Dietrich brought down was carrying twenty-seven passengers in addition to its crew. Aboard were Edvard Hylland, leader of Norway's ruling political party, along with his wife, Antonia, and their four children. Halvard Nansen Hastrup, Minister of Defense, his wife, name unknown, and their two children. General of the Army Karl Ernberg was aboard as was King Haakon's Intelligence chief, Gustav Peterson.

There were many others on board the Sunderland, en route to Norway's so-called government in exile in London. It was a huge victory in the air, not only as a blow to the Allied cause of continuing the war but an even greater propaganda ploy. The Ministry of Propaganda in Berlin wasted no time in going on the air and into every paper around the globe announcing that the leaders of the Norwegian government, like their cowardly King Haakon, were busy saving their own skins by taking their families and mistresses to safety from the advancing German army.

Dietrich was instantly promoted to hauptman and decorated with the Knight's Cross, which would always be worn around his neck. It was a very handsome award indeed, Dietrich thought, for having a big, slow moving airplane fly unwittingly into his gunsights.

A nurse appeared at his bedside to place a thermometer under his tongue.

"No talking. Mouth shut," she said, her fingers lightly on his left wrist. After an appropriate amount of time she entered his heart rate on his chart. She was stocky, about forty years of age, hair mouse-colored. Her accent was not quite German, Dietrich thought. Dutch, perhaps.

"My God," she clucked, looking down at him and shaking her head. "You are very poor looking, Hauptman."

News travels fast, he thought. Even the hospital staff had heard of his promotion only hours old. She gently removed the thermometer from his mouth, read the results and wrote them onto the chart.

"Do you know what you look like? Eh? You look like some dog attacked you. Like a bulldog bit you on the butt. I hate those things. English ones are the worst."

Dietrich opened his mouth to speak but closed it again when all words failed him.

"You will be examined again in the morning. Tell the doctor when he is finished that you would like to go for a little walk outside. You and I will walk together." The nurse plumped his pillow and was gone.

Under SIS the British had formed the SOE, Special Operations Executive, whose business it was to bring the war to the enemy by any means possible. SOE personnel were carefully chosen for their expertise in a wide variety of occupations that might be useful in conducting sub-rosa warfare. The organization had need of document forgers, safe crackers, commando teams, parachutists, explosives experts, and spies. Intelligence gathering and analysis was a critical part in planning any operation, and the SOE put no limits on the size of the mission or its target. Among the best and the brightest drawn upon when the organization was chartered were Sir William Schuyler and his junior but very bright colleague from SIS, Edward Wiles. Part of their inner circle was retired general Maclean Elliot, DSO. Elliot appeared every inch the product of Eton that he was: ramrod straight, bright blue eyes glistening under a still thick thatch of white hair, and a baritone voice that would bring angels to listen. Elliot was a no-nonsense military planner who, young Edward Wiles always suspected, remained skeptical of their very purpose for existence: to confuse and confound the enemy.

The three men were meeting very early in the morning, a time that did not suit William Schuyler, who had walked from across the street in his house slippers to the house they now occupied at Semley Place in Belgravia. His ankles must be cold, Wiles thought, as he sipped his tea. Mac Elliot fidgeted with his cup, interested in devouring his scone.

"Can't we get anything to eat?" he asked.

"It's coming, Maclean," Wiles said. "I have Sergeant Lamar's personal guarantee."

"Is that so?" Elliot remarked, clearly cheered by the news. "I didn't think Sergeant Lamar came in this early."

Sergeant Dennis Lamar was simply the best cook in the entire British Army.

If he was a civilian, a possibility which seemed to be a long way off, he would be a head chef in any fine restaurant. He was never cheerful, always disrespectful of rank. Sir William added Sergeant Lamar to the SOE staff after rescuing him from an army group general who was going to have the man shot for insubordination. When Sir William ensconced the cook in Semley Place having snatched him from the hands of a firing squad, Sergeant Lamar did not mutter so much as a thank you.

No matter. When he cooked he was worth the misery that he brought as baggage.

"You can't be serious about this man," Elliot said in connection with Steven Dietrich, nodding toward the steel safe built into the wall where his file was kept.

"I am quite serious, Mac," Wiles said. "By the way, you are one of only three people in the world who knows of his connection to us."

"Yes, yes, I'm aware," Elliot said, somewhat testily. "The man is high risk."

"I don't want to seem cavalier, but that is, after all, the business we're in," Wiles responded, reasonably.

"I think that's my point. It's risky enough without inviting an unprincipled man like that into our organization," Elliot said, stubbornly.

Sir William said nothing, Wiles noted, but was listening with interest.

"We're hardly giving him the keys to the front door," Wiles said. "Ostensibly he will be serving us rather than the other way around."

"What can we do if he betrays us? Eh? Even his mother and his father see him as a traitor, and I dare say they know him better than all of us."

Wiles arched an eyebrow.

"And how do you know that, Maclean? About how his parents feel about him?"

Elliot looked Wiles squarely in the eye. "He is the most common topic of conversation in all of Boston. There is no question that they are mortified about his conduct. Steven Dietrich already has a fat file at the FBI."

"Hmm," Wiles said. "Yes, but for the wrong reason. Sir William? You've been unbearably silent. I don't think I can take any more of it," Wiles said, smiling.

"I tend to agree with Maclean. Did you see yesterday's dispatches? He is a fast-rising star in the Luftwaffe. He shot down one of our Sunderlands. Imagine. He did immeasurable damage to the Norwegian government here in London. It could have just as easily been the Royal Family itself."

"I understand entirely, Sir William, but isn't that exactly what we would have ordered him to do? Become a very trusted and highly competent part of the German military establishment?"

"Yes, but we didn't order him to do it. We didn't order him to do anything," Elliot said.

Wiles thought Elliot's utterance lacked coherent logic. It certainly lacked imagination. He wondered once more how Maclean Elliot found his way into the SOE.

"On the other hand," Sir William said, looking upward at the ornate walnut ceiling of the Semley Place house, "we would be terribly remiss if we did not at least go to the next step with this man. Let him prove we're wrong, so to speak." He cocked an eyebrow at Elliot for expected agreement. He was not disappointed.

"I suppose, if we used every safeguard, protected ourselves as we go, it could turn out to be a decent harvest. At least nothing will be lost if our suspicion about him was correct."

"Your suspicion, Maclean, not mine," Wiles stipulated.

"To be sure, Edward. And good job, digging up the man as you have. I hope I'm quite wrong about him," Elliot said, pushing himself out of his chair to his feet. "Where the devil is our breakfast?"

Chapter 21

Dietrich felt a bit foolish leaning on the arm of nurse, Hildegarde, pretending more pain than he had. The discomfort in his back was now a dull throb, easily removed by swallowing two aspirin. But many uniformed man walked with or were pushed in a wheelchair by nurses, so the two of them blended in perfectly with their surroundings.

"Would you care to sit for a moment?" Hildegarde asked him in her best professional tone.

"Er, yes. I suppose that would be nice," Dietrich responded.

They were fifty meters from all others as they sat on a wooden bench under a tree. There was a more or less constant roar of aircraft engines but none that interfered with their conversation.

"You are very valuable to certain people in London," the nurse began without preamble.

"You mean Edward Wiles."

"Yes. He asks that you deliver certain information that can be used by the Allied cause."

"I don't suppose it would do any good to ask who you are?"

She shook her head. "There is no need. The less you know the better. You should get used to the idea. If one is arrested and tortured by the Gestapo, one cannot reveal identities one does not know."

"I understand," Dietrich said.

"Good. There are certain ground rules to be passed on to you. Try to remember. First, never write anything down unless it is absolutely necessary. Work very hard on training yourself to memorize everything. Second, it has been decided that you are not to have a camera or a radio. They are extremely dangerous. The Germans are very good at radio direction finding."

Dietrich nodded. "I'm aware of that."

"Third, speak to nobody unless you have been instructed to do so by London. That is, unless you were approached by a person whose bona fides are vouched for by London, you are not to respond. Do you understand that?"

"Yes, I think so."

"Not good enough, Hauptman. You must be absolutely one hundred percent clear. You are not to respond."

"Of course. No question about it," Dietrich said, feeling chastised.

Hildegarde regarded him for long moments, looking deeply into his eyes before satisfying herself that there was no confusion or question on Dietrich's part.

"You will be controlled by Edward Wiles and Wiles only. His code name will be Fox. Easy to remember; the Wiley Fox. Your code name will be Viking. If you need to contact Fox you will do so through me. There are any number of reasons to visit the medical unit. You can ask for aspirin or liniment for your back. We will arrange to talk, like friends. If either of us is asked by an official what it is we talk about we will say only news of the war. Nothing else. We are watching Germany's glorious victories everywhere we look. That's what we talk about."

"Understand," Dietrich said. "There is something Wiles needs to know. That is that I will never betray my staffel in combat. I will lead them to the best of my ability and I will do everything in my power to protect those who fly with me. Pass that on to Fox."

Another couple, a wounded airman, and a nurse were passing nearby.

Hildegarde and Dietrich got to their feet and began strolling in the opposite direction.

"Very well, I'll see that he gets your message. Fox is interested in Luftwaffe unit assignments. Also information on new weapons systems or navigation devices. Four days from now you will return to the medical unit. Tell me at that time what you have learned. Be careful. Don't be too anxious or eager to play the spy. You must not draw suspicion to yourself. Understand?"

"Perfectly," Dietrich said, soberly.

At first it seemed his assignment was ridiculously easy. Hauptman Dietrich merely walked into the administration office at his gruppe headquarters and asked to see the disposition map. After all, the large map display with small flags stuck into it existed for the benefit of pilots, and the sergeant in charge of the administrative staff merely clicked his heels as Dietrich swept by and entered the briefing room. Dietrich stood before the map, staring intently, memorizing everything that he could, until, twenty minutes later, he had saturated what he believed was his ability to recall units and stations. He added this information to other bits he had picked up listening to air crews as they ate their meals and relaxed at their clubs. When he returned to his quarters, he repeated silently to himself the information he had digested from the map display. Four days later he paid a visit to the medical unit.

"Tell me," he said to the pharmaceutical NCO at the dispensary, "what do you have for muscle spasm? My back, you know."

"Yes, sir. One moment, please."

As the corporal went off to look for the correct liniment Dietrich bided his time, pacing slowly, looking up and down the nearby hallway.

"Here you are, Herr Hauptman," the NCO said, holding out a bottle of yellow liquid. "The directions are on the bottle, sir."

"Ah. Thank you," Dietrich said.

As he turned away from the counter he almost ran into nurse Hildegarde.

"Hauptman Dietrich," she said, obviously delighted to see him. "How are you getting along, sir?"

"To be honest, the back is giving me a little problem. Nothing serious, mind you, only a little soreness in the muscles."

The two of them walked slowly toward a doorway leading to the outside. As they walked they animatedly discussed war news as it was reported in the newspapers and on German radio.

The date was May 2. Out of hearing distance of others Dietrich began to recite information to nurse Hildegarde.

"We have been ordered to support two Luftflotte: Luftflotte 1 and Luftflotte 2. Action will commence on 10 May. Luftflotte 1 will have six Heinkel 111s, four JU88. These staffeln will operate from Kassel-Rothwesten. From Döberitz, Me-109. That is my stab. Luftflotte 2 will have 205 He111 at Farberg, Gütersloh, Delmenhorst, Quackenbrück, Varrelbusch and Vechta. Number IV Fliegerkorps, also He111, 351 aircraft at Hannover-Langenhagen, Delmenhorst, Wunstorf, Oldenburg, Marx, and Düsseldorf. VIII Fliegerkorps with 492 Dornier 17s, Junker 87 Stukas and Me-109 at Dusseldorf, Werl, Koln-Ostheim, Nörvenich, Köln-Butzweilerhof, Duisberg, Lauffenberg, Gymnich and Mönchen-Gladbach."

Dietrich paused for a breath and to look around him. Nurse Hildegarde was struggling mightily to remember as much as possible of what was being passed on to her.

"There is considerably more," he said, "but you will get the idea. Two air fleets will support an attack against France. I don't know the order of battle for the army and the panzers, but my understanding is that more than two thousand tanks will spearhead the attack. I would think the generals will send one hundred fifty divisions into the low countries. But I don't know that for certain. Now, Hildegarde, remember what I tell you next. We have built a radar code named Freya, named after a Norse goddess. We are building sites to make a complete system along the English Channel. It operates on 1.2 m bandwidth and is quite good. We are working to increase the band to 2.5 to 2.3 meters /120 to 130 MHz. That will make early warning very efficient. The Allies should target this system. Have you got that?"

Hildegarde had her eyes almost closed, her lips moving just slightly as she repeated the numbers to herself.

"Yes. Go on."

"Not much more. We are trying to mount an airborne radar for night fighters. So far not so good. I think the high command does not believe we will need them so there doesn't seem to be a hurry. But London should watch the developments."

As they parted company Hildegarde had an instant headache. There was no way she could remember verbatim what Dietrich had passed on to her. The man needed a more efficient system of communication than she could provide.

May 10, 1940, was a seminal day for the Axis and for the Allies. Indeed, for the world. On that day Prime Minister Chamberlain was forced to resign. A new government was formed under Winston Churchill. It was also the day that Hitler's order to launch operation Yellow began. The Wehrmacht had assembled 135 conventional Heer divisions, ten Panzer divisions, four motorized divisions and two air fleets consisting of 1,500 fighters and 3,500 bombers.

Opposing Hitler was the poorly equipped Belgian army supported by the Allied armies consisting of ninety-five French and British divisions of the BEF (British Expeditionary Force). The vaunted Maginot Line—a series of reinforced concrete fortresses strung along a line between France and Germany, guarding alpine passes and festooned with tank traps—stood between the West and the German General Staff. The Allies' armor, about 2,500 tanks, equal in number to those of the Germans, was distributed among brigades, battalions, and regiments with no central control.

In the air, opposing the Luftwaffe, were one thousand French aircraft and seven hundred British, all based in France. The Allies' fatal strategic assumption was in believing the Germans would attack through the flat countryside of Belgium, just as they had in 1914. But having learned a bitter lesson from the prior war and boasting young and daring tactical Panzer commanders, the Germans went on the attack in another way. As they did in Poland, the Germans employed tanks in the van against the enemy while Panzer infantry units followed through holes in the line created by the armor attack.

The Germans skirted the Maginot line, ignoring its manpower and heavy artillery, and advanced through neutral Holland and Luxembourg. The Dutch government, and Queen Wilhelmina, fled to London. On May 13 German armor, with close support by the Luftwaffe, broke through the Ardennes Forest to Sedan, exactly where the Maginot line ended. The Blitzkrieg was rolling through France just as it had through Poland nine months prior.

The entire British expeditionary force and three French armies marched northward into Belgium and directly into a German trap. Exploiting the Somme valley pocket to its maximum, Panzer armies drove spearheads to the English Channel at Abbeville, thus isolating the Allied armies at the beach. French general de Gaulle, attempting to engage the German Army further west, was merely pushed aside.

Hauptman Dietrich led a staffel of twelve aircraft in the action against France. Dietrich personally downed a Dewoitine D.520 fighter, France's new top-line fighter, as well as two Arsenal VG-33 fighters. In twenty days of continuous fighting Dietrich's staffel accounted for thirty-six enemy fighters and bombers, including nine British fighters and two Beaufighters. They also destroyed a number of ground targets including trucks and armored personnel carriers. Dietrich personally did not like the air-to-ground role he and his comrades were asked to take on because of his experience in Poland with ground fire. But he did his work very well and if he flinched when he went in for a strafing run it was not noticeable.

Promotions would come fast for Germany's Luftwaffe pilots. Adolf Galland was a captain on June 10, 1940, the day Operation Yellow began. One month later he was promoted to major and awarded the Knight's Cross. In August he was promoted to Kommodore of Fighter Wing 26. In September he was awarded Oak Leaves to the Knight's Cross and two months later, in November of 1940, he was promoted to leutnant-colonel. A promotion to full colonel followed ten months later and Galland, an excellent fighter pilot, would attain the rank of General Leutnant and was named General of Fighters.

Other capable officers had rapid rises through the ranks, especially when the war slowly turned against Germany and Luftwaffe losses became heavy. Experienced pilots, especially group leaders, were at a premium. Dietrich was among this group. Following the escape of the British Expeditionary Force at Dunkirk, Dietrich was promoted to major.

"Confound the man," Sir William said as he rocked on his heels and toes in Wiles' office. "I won't deny his information is excellent—"

"Better than excellent," Wiles said, calmly. "Priceless."

"Well," the impatient spymaster said dismissively, flailing a long, bony hand through the air, a gesture resembling the labored flight of an albatross trying to get off the ground. "That's a bit dramatic, Edward. Yes, very good. But look at what he's done. If he keeps up at his present rate as a group leader in the Luftwaffe we might very well lose the war!"

"Who's being dramatic now?" Wiles said, studying his fingernails.

"I don't know, Edward. I have always regarded myself as a keen judge of men. My instincts are almost without fail when it comes to people in our business, but the Viking chap has the better of me. Eh? And you think we should use him to run Raven?"

Wiles shrugged. "Who else? We can't use Gustav. I mean, on what possible grounds could we have the leader of Germany interact with Gustav? Or anyone else we have working in that area? Viking is the perfect man."

Schuyler fell heavily into an overstuffed chair, hands and feet in a tangle.

"Well. To be candid I don't think Raven has much of a life expectancy, anyway. Do you? No, I thought not. So it isn't likely that we would lose much if Viking turns out to be a double agent." Schuyler sat for a very long moment thinking about what he had just said. Wiles privately had to agree with him. A British actor taking the place of Adolf Hitler was the longest possible shot one could invent. Yes, it was only a matter of time before Archie Smythes was discovered for what he was. By sending Viking they had nothing to lose.

"Very well," Wiles said, relieved that the senior man agreed with him. "In that case I think it's time I put Viking into the picture."

With the fall of France, Dietrich's gruppe had been moved out of Germany and into France at Calais. Bombers were now flying regular raids over England. Fighters accompanied the bombers. The slow-flying JU87 Stuka dive bombers that had been so effective in Poland and France had become easy pickings for the much swifter Hurricanes and Spitfires flown by RAF fighter command. The JU87s were pulled out of combat over England, but not before Dietrich received the news that his one-time nemesis and later close friend, Bregan Höltz, had been shot down and killed over the Channel. That night in the officer's mess, Dietrich found himself shedding tears into his food. It was the first time he could remember crying in years.

Listening to foreign radio broadcasts was forbidden for all Germans, including the military officer corps, but the proscription was not rigidly enforced against those of higher rank. It might not have meant much if

Dietrich were thus discovered listening to the BBC, but he preferred to do so in private. At the end of certain programs there were always passages broadcast from London that were coded messages to agents operating throughout occupied Europe. For Dietrich it was easy. He merely sat in the cockpit of his Messerschmitt, turned on his radio, and tuned it to the correct BBC frequency.

"And," the British radio announcer said, following the war news, "here are personal messages for our friends in Europe.

"The cat is out of the bag. The cat is out of the bag.

"Sister Racine has come down with the flu. Sister Racine has come down with the flu.

"The poetry reading for Friday night has been postponed. The poetry reading for Friday night has been postponed.

"Johnathan has been working too hard and should rest. Johnathan has been working too hard and should rest.

"Friends of Tommy will be happy to know he is well. Friends of Tommy will be happy to know he is well.

"A new book is now available from the library. A new book is now available from the library.

"Viking has developed a backache. Viking has developed a backache."

Dietrich sat bolt upright in his cramped aircraft. The message was clear. He needed to contact Hildegarde. But how? He had no idea where to find her since he had left his last aerodrome in Germany. He felt it would be dangerous to inquire of her whereabouts so he would keep it as simple as possible. As a start he would go to the base dispensary in Calais.

Dietrich had flown three missions over England the day before, the last one ending at night. He had lost two fighters and the bombers they were trying to protect had taken much heavier losses. They had attacked RAF bases in southern Britain where there were stationed the greatest concentration of fighter units. They were not scheduled to fly again until afternoon but Dietrich dragged himself out of bed at 0600 and walked a half mile to the aviation medical unit on base. He looked about the complex for a nurse resembling Hildegarde but no joy. He shuffled about, asked twice by medical people if they could help him. He finally said that he was trying to find the pharmacy. At the window he told a female volunteer that he had a backache and needed a liniment. While she was away putting together a bottle of the stuff he needed, Dietrich looked around him. Still no sign of Hildegarde. He regarded the chances of her being here as slim in any case. He would have to figure out some other method of contacting her. He took the bottle over the counter given him by the volunteer. It looked like the same stuff he had used before. He would find out later. He left the medical complex and trudged toward Base Operations a few hundred meters away.

When he arrived he perused the mission board, confirming his gruppe's first sorties three hours away. He greeted several fellow pilots, briefly exchanging gossip with one or two, then waited a few minutes outside the building for the crew transportation taxi. His billet was less than ten minutes from the field. It was a large French house confiscated by the Luftwaffe for the duration of the war. The house had four bedrooms, a spacious dining room, a library, a large kitchen now manned by two enlisted men, an obergefreiter who did the cooking and a gefreiter who served the food and helped with most of the other housework. Dietrich was the senior officer of the four assigned to that house. There was a hauptman and two leutnants, all fighter pilots of 51 Jagdgeschwader. Dietrich was also the oldest at twenty-four. He was expected to sit at the head of the table when the four had dinner or luncheon together, to instruct the others about what wines to drink, even to lead them by example in music and general deportment. Dietrich was no master at any of these things but he enjoyed the games that derived from trying his best.

His room was the largest and it was comfortable. The house was fully furnished, just as it had been when it was occupied by the French family to whom it had once belonged. Dietrich had run across a family picture in a gilded frame and placed it at his bedside. He hoped it would still be there when the war was over and the family, God willing, returned. He was sitting on his bed pulling off his boots when there was a rapid knock on his door.

"Come," he said.

The door was flung open, much like a teenager would do, and a head and upper body appeared sideways.

"Herr Major," Leutnant Karl Bötta said, "how is your back?"

"My back?" Dietrich almost said it was just fine but he instantly changed his mind. "Sore. I bailed out in Poland—"

"Yes, sir. So you said, sir. Well, there is a nurse downstairs. She says she is here to rub your back. Shall I send her up?" The fighter pilot's eyes were shining brightly, the large grin pasted across his face indicating that his back might be sore as well.

"Yes, of course. Send her up at once."

As Leutnant Bötta disappeared from the doorway Dietrich pulled the suspenders up over his shirt and waited. Moments later Hildegarde appeared at the top of the landing. Without waiting to be invited she stepped into Dietrich's room.

"God, how did you...?"

Hildegarde held her finger to her lips.

"The flight surgeon at the base was worried about your back, Herr Major. I am experienced in massage," she said in a normal speaking voice.

"Ah. Very good of him. Very good," Dietrich said, moving to the door and placing his ear against it. He listened carefully but could hear no one outside. A radio tuned to the forbidden BBC was turned on in the next room bringing the sound of American jazz throughout the house. It was Bötta's favorite music and no one in the house complained.

"Take off your shirt, please, Major. Lie down there. That's good. Let me put this pillow under your shoulder just so." Hildegarde poured a generous amount of liniment into the palm of her hand and applied it to Dietrich's back. As she slowly began to rub the lower part of his back she spoke again quietly into his ear.

"The Fox needs to meet with you urgently. Impossible for him to come here. There is a secret field for you to land west of the town of Deal, in England, preferably at night."

"My God, there must be thirty RAF bases in that area!"

"This will be a grass field. It will be marked with blinking red and blue lights from dusk until 2200 hours every night this week. As you approach the coast fly at minimum altitude with your navigation lights on and your landing lights on. When you pass over the coast you are to lower your landing gear. The strip will be outlined with ten blue lights and they will blink on and off every five seconds. Is that clear so far?"

"Yes, but..."

Lowering one's landing gear was the international sign of surrender for aircraft. It was just one added precaution, Dietrich supposed, against an interception.

"The coordinates are fifty-one degrees twelve minutes north latitude, one degree seventeen minutes east longitude. Once on the ground you will remain only ten minutes. Shut off your engine but remain in your aircraft. A special service crew will be there if they are needed."

"Well, I hope Fox has thought out—"

"How does that feel now, Major?" Hildegarde asked in a normal voice.

"I think it's worse," Dietrich said.

Hildegarde laughed aloud.

"Do you mean I am not doing my job?"

"No, of course I don't mean that."

The two were silent for several minutes while she continued to rub his back.

"I think that will help you. Just remain in bed for an hour or so."

"Thank you, nurse."

Hildegarde let herself out of the room. Dietrich rose from the bed, his back never feeling better. He replaced his shirt and was buttoning it up when he parted the lace curtains and looked down at the street. There was a car with two men at the curb as Hildegarde arrived. They stopped her and began to speak. He could not hear the exchange of dialogue but the two men were almost certainly police, probably Gestapo. The Gestapo had a certain look about them, the leather coats and hats, all designed to intimidate their prey. One of the men took Hildegarde's elbow and with his other hand opened a rear door of the car. Hildegarde suddenly pulled herself away from the man and began to run. She was quickly caught by the second man and was struck in her face by his fist. She continued to resist, albeit much more weakly, and was struck again and again in the face and body by the agent.

Dietrich rushed out of the door of his room and down the stairs.

"Stop that woman!" he yelled as he ran out to the curb.

Still holding the nearly unconscious woman by one arm, her head sagging from her shoulders like a rag doll, the two men looked up from their handiwork.

"Yes? Who the hell are you?" one of them said. Like his partner, he was a man of medium height but very lean, almost cadaverous. His hat had fallen on the sidewalk as he lunged for Hildegarde and Dietrich saw that his hair had prematurely grayed. His mouth was thin, his eyes almost black as they flicked up and down Dietrich's form. Dietrich thought the man was actually handsome.

"I am Major Steven Dietrich, Luftwaffe. And who are you?" he demanded.

The man came out of his pocket with the now-familiar Gestapo metal identification tag.

"I, uh…" Dietrich's head was spinning. He had only wanted to stop the beating of this good woman. "I did not pay her," he said, vacuously.

The Gestapo man smiled wickedly.

"Is that so?" he asked as Dietrich fumbled in his pockets for Reichsmarks. He held them in his hand awkwardly. He bent over Hildegarde and carefully placed the paper money into her lightweight coat pocket. He wanted to take her in his arms to protect her, comfort her. "Here, madam," he said softly. "It was a wonderful afternoon. Thank you."

There was an unmistakable flicker of a smile through her swollen lips and bloody, flattened nose. Then she bit down on something inside her mouth. She suddenly grimaced, doubling over while lying on the pavement near the street. Her body convulsed.

"What is that?" the other Gestapo man said, quickly bending over her. He slapped at her face hard, then grabbed her shoulders and began shaking her violently. But Dietrich knew that she could feel nothing.

"She is dead, Hans," the Gestapo man told his partner.

"Too bad," Dietrich said, trying his best to make his voice sound indifferent. "Well, she was good sex, anyway. Worth the money."

"A prostitute, Major Dietrich?" the Gestapo man asked.

Dietrich nodded his head, looking downward once more on the courageous woman at their feet.

"Yes. Of course," he said.

"I doubt that. Prostitutes do not have cyanide capsules implanted in their dental work."

Dietrich wanted to say something but words failed him.

"She is an agent. We are sure of it," the Gestapo man said. "How did you know her?"

"She… she called me on the telephone. She said that she knew my back was hurting me. She said she could make it feel better." Dietrich shrugged and cleared his throat. "I agreed. That's all."

"You are an American."

"Yes."

"You are the one they call the Yank," the Gestapo man said.

"Yes."

"Your German is excellent. I would not know that you were not German. But you are not. You are American." The man's eyes squinted as he continued to look at Dietrich without blinking.

Dietrich nodded again.

"I have to fly a mission," he said but did not move his feet.

"Well, then, by all means, major, you must go. And good luck," the Gestapo agent said.

Back in his room Dietrich sat on his bed and covered his eyes with his hands. He could feel the tears seeping through his fingers.

Chapter 22

He had chased a lead Hurricane from its attack formation at 28,000 feet and began turning and rolling with it in frantic maneuvers that took both aircraft down to the deck. Dietrich had the slower, less-agile British fighter in his gun sights more than once but did not fire. He not only admired the skill of the RAF pilot but on this date in August, Dietrich had far more urgent business to attend to. It was late in the day and the last rays of the sun were settling over the coast of Britain when Dietrich allowed the Hurricane to slip away to the northeast and, presumably, the safety of his own field. Dietrich did not turn 180 degrees in the direction of Bergues, France, where he was stationed, but dropped onto the deck and, a scarce twenty feet from the top of the cold whitecaps, flew at full throttle on a predetermined course for England. As instructed, he reduced speed and lowered his landing gear as he passed over the English shoreline.

Within a few short minutes he gently pulled back on the stick of his Me-109 and, almost clipping leaves from trees as he flashed over British countryside, began to look for a secret airfield near Northiam. Dietrich peered hard through his clear plastic windscreen for the landing markers that he had to locate within a few minutes lest his lack of fuel force him down onto a plowed field, wrecking his aircraft in the event. He pushed his flying goggles back onto his leather helmet and, circling low, at last located the critical landmark, a farm silo with blinking blue lights, five on each side of the field. Not daring to break radio silence, Dietrich changed his propeller pitch and gunned the

Messerschmitt's engine three times. As if by magic a large haystack became illuminated at its top and runway lights winked on and off at either end of an unimproved strip, then remained on. Dietrich lined up his fighter for a final approach knowing that the lights would be lit for less than a minute. His first attempt would have to be perfect.

He reduced engine power, then snapped on the toggle switch that would lower his hydraulic flaps. Immediately the high-performance fighter began to sink. Dietrich calmly added more power as he simultaneously pulled back on the stick, raising the aircraft's nose and "hanging" it on its prop in the execution of a short field landing. As he flared the fighter he could feel its three wheels touch ground simultaneously and he began to gently brake the machine. After a short roll out, Dietrich kicked hard left rudder, spinning his airplane around on the runway. He taxied to a location which supported camouflage netting, impossible to spot from the air.

He cut the fuel supply to the twelve-cylinder Daimler-Benz engine and, disregarding instructions to remain in the cockpit, was climbing out of the airplane even before the propeller had stopped turning. He was quite aware, as he stepped onto the wing root, that his legs ached from cramps and his body was sore from the strain of pulling continuous Gs during a long day of combat flying. But he had much to accomplish before he could find his way back to the comfort of the officer's mess in Bergues. And a couple of smooth cognacs.

His feet had hardly touched British soil when a fuel bower pulled up next to his aircraft and two RAF mechanics opened the fuel caps of his machine.

"Not too much. I don't want to arrive back from a sortie with full tanks," he cautioned the refuellers.

"And how much, sir?" one of the ground men asked.

"About two hundred litres should do it," he said, removing his flying gloves.

"Have a cuppa."

Dietrich turned toward the voice of Edward Wiles, who stood holding a thermos bottle and a large mug in one hand. Wiles extended his free hand to Dietrich.

"Hello, my friend," he said.

Dietrich squeezed the man's hand with force. "I hope to hell this is important, Eddie," Dietrich said, mangling Wiles's given name, continuing a tease that was now four years old. "First things first. Have your men fire a few holes into my ship. Make damn sure they don't hit anything vital. Put a couple through the engine section but take the fasteners out, first, and open the cowl."

"Right. You can supervise the job," Wiles said. Wiles noted, with satisfaction, the growth of maturity in Steven Dietrich, the German commanding squadron leader, from the callow college youth of only four years ago. The young Dietrich, awed and wonderfully stimulated by the huge wide world before him, was playfully indecisive, often uncaring of the planet on which he frolicked. Now, hard of eye, his deft intellect straddling the complex intelligence work of two warring nations, Wiles could only admire the American's ability to remain focused.

Dietrich wore his Luftwaffe uniform, a blue one-piece cotton flying suit lined with synthetic fur, black leather jacket with gold epaulets, an embossed metal eagle over the right zippered pocket, a wide leather belt around his waist that supported a holster for a 9mm pistol and a compass. In his hand Dietrich held an inflatable life vest that he had removed for comfort while on the ground. He could not help but wonder what must have been going on in the minds of the British ground personnel who were obliged to service a Nazi fighter aircraft and take orders from its pilot.

The ground crew were hand-picked personnel, as were the entire complement of the two dozen men who operated the tiny, ultra secret airstrip for SOE. Their discretion could be absolutely counted on and their skill levels were at the top of their fields. It took only a few minutes for the bullet holes to be fired at angles into the Me-109 to make it appear that a following aircraft had done the damage.

"You," Dietrich said to one of the mechanics, "cut this oil line. Then bind it up with tape. It needs to last for the flight back."

One more bullet was fired, this one cutting the chosen oil line. There were two ways Dietrich could return late to his Jagdgeschwader without arousing suspicion. One was by bailing out anywhere over France, allowing himself to be picked up by the occupying army. Or he could damage his airplane, then later claim that he had landed in a grass field, repaired the machine himself, then continued back to Bergues. There were risks in either case. Contrary to what some people might believe, bailing out of a fighter aircraft was inherently dangerous with a good chance of being killed or badly injured as part of the exercise. Dietrich had been forced to leave his plane when a Spitfire had shredded his vertical stabilizer and he had lost control over Calais. He had barely two thousand feet of altitude when he managed to free himself from his safety harness and drop out of the very tight cockpit. It was not an experience he cared to repeat again unless there was no other choice. So he would carry through with the more elaborate scheme of choice number two.

Dietrich turned back to Wiles. "I don't know that I can do this again."

"I can't express to you the gratitude of the Crown, Steven. The Prime Minister himself asked me to tell you that."

"Is that so? How is Winnie?" Dietrich said, drinking deeply of the tea which was only lukewarm. But it tasted wonderful.

"He is not sleeping well. Your bombers keep him awake."

"Ah, well, then, we'll just have to ask Göering to stop it all," Dietrich said, leaning tiredly against a fender of the fuel truck. "It must be a hell of a strain on him."

"As a matter of fact, it is," Wiles said.

"I'm sorry, Eddie. It is a crummy war. Sometimes..." Dietrich's voice trailed off.

"Sometimes what? Hard to remember which side you're on?" Wiles asked.

Dietrich smiled. "I fly with men, not animals, Eddie. They are courageous. They're good fun to be around. They like girls, just like you and me. Well, maybe not like you. Anyway, it isn't pleasant to see them die."

"No, I'm sure you're right. I sit at a desk while you do the fighting and killing?" Wiles said.

Dietrich knew that if Wiles could have it the other way around, he would leap at the chance.

"What happened with your people in Pilz? I went to a hell of a lot of trouble to get you that information," Dietrich said with a trace of disgust in his voice.

"It worked out very nicely, Steven. Better than we had hoped."

"It did, huh? Well, we flew air cover around some little town down there where Hitler was recovering. So you wrecked a train and killed some troops, but Hitler survived. This war is still going on," Dietrich spat. His life was always at stake, not just flying fighter aircraft in battles over British skies, but in gaining vital intelligence from under the noses of the Gestapo and paranoid Nazi party members and transmitting the stuff back to London. Having a hash made of his work was doubly disheartening.

"That's why you're here, Steven. He didn't survive."

"Nonsense. He is back, hard at work killing the Jews and attacking your country," Dietrich spat. "And I hope it was worth the life of Hildegarde."

"It was worth it," Wiles said. Something in the way that Wiles made the simple statement made Dietrich listen. "The commando mission succeeded. Hitler is dead."

It took Dietrich most of an entire day to locate the whereabouts of Hauptman Frederich Friedel at his current station of Foucarmont, forty kilometers from the French coast. Like many forward bomber bases, Lufflotte II, KG 4 flew from grass runways. As Dietrich made his base leg turn onto final approach he knew that the Luftwaffe High Command assumed their Channel bases would become unnecessary by the time fall weather made unpaved fields unusable. The battle for air supremacy would be all over by then, with Germany the winner. Reichsmarshall Göering had personally promised as much to the Führer.

After parking his Me-109 in the place directed by ground crews, Dietrich removed his parachute, as well as his helmet and life vest, and dropped them onto the seat of the plane. He declined the offer of motorized transportation to flight operations in favor of walking the short distance from the maintenance area to administration. He asked one of the duty sergeants the whereabouts of Captain Frederich Friedel and was told that KG 4 was on operations but should return from their mission within fifty minutes. Dietrich knew that precise forecast meant that Friedel's He-111 would have exhausted its fuel supply by then. It would either be back on schedule or it would likely never return. Dietrich left word for Friedel that he would be at the officer's mess.

He had not seen his boisterous friend for six months, their duty assignments being the cause. So Dietrich was anxiously looking forward to the reunion, brief though it would have to be. He felt guilty that his real objective was to find and speak with Bunny Hartung as soon as possible, but the situation presented to him the night before was urgent in the extreme.

It was warmer inside the mess than outside and Dietrich, removing his leather flying jacket, was pleased with his decision not to wear a flying suit over his uniform for the short hop from Bergues. There had been no need to climb to altitude. There were less than a half-dozen officers eating or drinking in the mess, none of them giving Dietrich more than a cursory glance as he sat alone at a table. The place would fill up, he knew, when Friedel's unit returned from its mission. He recalled that he had missed lunch, his orderly allowing him to sleep late the first morning of his leave. He ordered a roast lamb sandwich and a cup of coffee. A slaw that came with it was surprisingly good. Dietrich was developing a taste for cabbage in its many forms uniquely prepared by German cooks.

He finished his third cup of coffee, his mind reeling with possibilities presented by yesterday evening's extraordinary revelation by Edward Wiles. He tried to imagine what he might do if he were in the boots of this man, Archie, who now occupied the Reichschancellery and controlled the mightiest system of armed forces on the face of the Earth. Well, he wouldn't simply issue an order to stop the war, would he? Edward was quite right that it couldn't be done that way. Hitler, Archie, would have to nibble at the problem, at least in the beginning. He had already succeeded, according to Edward, in causing the German Army to remain on this side of the Channel. Or so they thought. Dietrich, personally, was skeptical about the claim. His unit was still battling desperately for air superiority in the skies over England, an absolute must before an invasion could be mounted. So, if Archie had succeeded as Wiles claimed, why was the air battle still raging? Wiles had said that Archie almost certainly did not know what to do.

The actor's real identity might well have been discovered by the time Dietrich was able to get to him, if indeed it was possible. Archie was not, after all, a military man, and had no idea how desperately the British military was being threatened by the continuous pounding of RAF air bases. And by the heavy losses being inflicted upon Fighter Command. Unsustainable, Wiles had said. As a Luftwaffe pilot, Dietrich experienced a strange feeling of elation to hear the highly placed British master spy make such an admission. Dietrich's ostensible business as a Luftwaffe pilot was, after all, to shoot down British aircraft. And he was succeeding! But Dietrich was, on the other hand, in opposition to the continued success of the Third Reich, and his exhilaration was short lived.

He had no direct access to information on overall Luftwaffe losses other than for his own unit. According to the Ministry of Propaganda, German planes and aircrew lost in battle were very light, certainly far more favorable than that of their opponents, the RAF. Dr. Göebbels predicted a very short war, indeed, and from Dietrich's limited perspective, the chief of the Nazi's information agencies might be correct. England was all alone, that was for sure, and Germany was more than a match for Britain's armed forces in almost every respect, save naval units.

Dietrich was gazing into the bottom of his empty coffee cup when Friedel lumbered through the door, his helmet, goggles, and life vest still carried in one hand. He hung these impediments on a wall hook at the same moment he spotted Dietrich seated across the room.

"Good God!" he hollered for all to hear, "Look who is taking a day off from the French whorehouses."

Heads turned to see the object of Friedel's accusation as Dietrich got to his feet to put his arms around the larger pilot. Still in a bear hug, Friedel was not yet done baiting his friend.

"No! Please, no! He is a major, now. Every man in his squadron must have been shot down. We are losing the war," Friedel said, throwing his head back, leading gales of laughter at Dietrich's good-natured expense.

"Guten tag, you drunk," he said.

"Sit down, Yank, and I'll buy you a man's drink. Vegan," he called to the locally born bartender, "two brandies here. You remember Pinky, Steven? At Das Wasserhahn in Berlin? He is a corporal in the Wehrmacht and you will never guess what his job is, eh? He runs the officer's mess at Neubiberg."

"At last the Army finds a fully qualified man for the job," Dietrich said. "I can't drink with you. I still have to fly."

Dietrich was struck by the dark circles under Friedel's blue eyes, the cheekbones made more prominent from loss of weight and, no doubt, sleep. Dietrich noticed Friedel's left hand, kept rather low and out of sight, had been burned and two fingers had become shriveled stubs, not yet fully healed. They must have caused him great pain.

Friedel followed Dietrich's gaze. "I never played with my weenie with that hand, anyway. So I am lucky. There must be a God. Prosit!" he said, raising his glass.

"I'm sorry about your hand, Frederich, but as long as you can wipe your ass you can still stuff your face with schnitzel. How have you been, otherwise?"

"How do you suppose a handsome Luftwaffe pilot can be? I am a part of the greatest force in the history of the world. We are just finishing off the pesky little Limeys and then soon I will be fucking their sisters right in Piccadilly. How could I not be wonderful?"

"I couldn't be happier for you, then," Dietrich said, watching while Friedel gulped down his brandy.

"Vegan, bring two more," Friedel said.

"No, really, I can't, Freddy." Dietrich demurred.

"Bring two anyway, Vegan, one for my other hand," Friedel laughed. Friedel appraised his American friend with studied interest. "By God, the war suits you, Steven. You are not a little boy, anymore."

"I might have grown up even without the war," Dietrich said.

"You must be what, a gruppe leader?" the bomber pilot said. "Congratulations. You deserve it more than most. I'll never live to see it for myself.'"

"Don't be silly. It will all be over, soon," Dietrich said, rhetorically.

"Yes? Then I am greatly relieved. The way we are losing men and machines I would have thought our factories could not keep up."

More than one head turned toward Friedel's voice. Friedel leaned forward toward Dietrich. "In three days this month we lost one hundred ten of our planes. Think of it, Steven. Three days."

Dietrich knew exactly what Friedel was talking about. Those black days were only last week and the fighter command had lost thirty-five. It was not reported to the public, of course, but the word among pilots and ground crew went around the squadrons like a gasoline fire.

"Still," Dietrich said, "the RAF is losing."

Friedel's voice dropped even lower, to a near whisper. "You don't believe that, Yank."

Dietrich shrugged. "We have more planes than they. You don't need a slide rule to figure it out."

But Friedel was right. Germany was losing its best pilots to the RAF Fighter Command because of stupid planning at the top. JG-52 had lost all three of its squadron commanders escorting the cumbersome Ju-87 dive bombers on raids over England, sacrificing the superior speed and altitude advantage of their Messerschmitts to stay with the dive bombers. They were easy pickings for the Brits who waited for them at 30,000 feet. Still, the British could not afford to trade aircraft with Germany because she would lose.

"Are you still flying the He-111?" Dietrich asked.

"Yes. A little too slow and too little bomb load to do much damage. We did a very nice job in Spain, you know," Friedel sighed. "Nobody shot back at us. But against fighters that are 150 kph faster..." Friedel merely shook his head as he finished his third glass of brandy.

"Are you still after shipping?" Dietrich asked, aware that Freddy had hunted British merchant shipping the last time they had met.

"Airfields. And shipping, too, but mostly airfields, for whatever good it does," Friedel scoffed. "They simply repair them again."

"So," Dietrich said, getting to the point of his visit, "I have a few days off. I wanted to find Bunny. Do you know where he is?"

"Of course. He is fucking his way through the entire city of Paris. Where do you suppose he would be? He has been here to see me twice, already."

"How is he?" Dietrich wanted to know.

"He is no longer an aide to that filthy wretch, Beckman. Did you know that he is now a hero of the Reich? Not Beckman, that asshole. Bunny. It's true! He commanded a Panzergruppe against a French strong point in the Ardennes and knocked it out from the rear. He wins an Iron Cross Third Class, the stupid clod."

Dietrich could clearly see in Friedel's eyes the pride for his childhood friend. "And this was the man who joined the SS to stay out of the war," Dietrich said.

"And like you, he is promoted. He is now SS-Sturmbann Führer Hartung."

"Well, then he will survive. There is nothing left to fight over. Hitler will be satisfied with what he already has. France is no small prize, you know," Dietrich said, believing that the two belligerents, Britain and Germany, would somehow come to terms.

"You think so, Yank? Good, then I will have a drink on it. Vegan! Bring me a bottle so you don't have to run your legs off."

It was quite dark when Dietrich left his Me-109 under the vigilant eyes of German sentries who guarded all of Orly airport in Paris. He was able to arrange transportation from the motor pool that took him to the West Bank. Knowing that he was not far from the street he needed to find, Dietrich dismissed the car and driver in favor of walking the old streets of the city. Paris was in a state of quasi-blackout in recognition that there was a war going on, but no bomb had been dropped on Paris from either of the warring parties, so there was enough illumination to make navigation easy.

Like any other tourist following a city street map, he craned his neck as he walked along the Quai De Celestins, taking in the façade of Notre Dame. Unable to spend the time to look inside, he turned left on Henri IV to Avenue Saint Antoine. Rather than taking a slightly longer way around the Place des Vosges, Dietrich walked through the narrow Rue De Birague. The square of apartments by which he strode included one which had been lived in by Victor Hugo, but Dietrich had no time to appreciate the historical significance of that fact. He emerged at the literal doorstep of the address Friedel had scribbled on the back of an envelope: Pavillon De La Reine, 28 Place des Vosges. De La Reine was a building six hundred years old, now a hotel, and also now the residence of SS officers of the 1st SS-Panzer Division, Leibstandarte Adolf Hitler.

As he stood before the gates of the hotel on Rue Des Francs Bourgeois, he became aware of civilian pedestrians watching him. Parisians, when he looked their way, quickly averted their eyes, but not before Dietrich recognized hatred in their glares. He tried to rationalize how he would feel if he were French and his country had been overrun by an invading army, especially a German one. Their enmity was not hard to understand.

He was saluted by the SS guard at the entrance to the hotel's courtyard. At the end of the stone walk the door to the lobby was opened for him by a white-uniformed attendant whose sight was fixed on a place in space. Dietrich stopped briefly at the desk to enquire the room number for SS-Hauptsturmfuhrer Hartung. The clerk showed only the slightest hesitation before obliging Dietrich with the second-floor number, but also adding that the Hauptsturmfuhrer Führer was "entertaining" at the present time. Would the major like to be announced?

Please.

Sounds of loud music, and male and female laughter reverberated throughout the hotel despite the thickness of the old stone walls. Hartung's room, as he opened the door, appeared to Dietrich to be incredibly small, and the lady of Bunny's choosing, although in bed, seemed to be practically in Dietrich's lap. Bunny, embracing his American friend, did not want to release

Dietrich from his clutch, insisting on tossing him to and fro until he let him go with a fling onto the bed.

"Meet Doniele," Bunny said, referring to the giggling French lady who, without a stitch of clothing that Dietrich could discern, occupied the middle of the bed.

"Well?" Doniele said to Dietrich in French. "Is that all that you are going to do, sit there and twist your fingers?"

Dietrich's French was at first awkward but there was no question that he was being invited into, rather than onto, the only bed in the room.

"You are too kind, miss, but my mother would not understand," he responded to gales of laughter from both Doniele and Bunny.

"God," Bunny said, reaching for a full bottle of wine, two others nearby quite empty. He poured two glasses to their brims. "How long has it been? Let's see, were we at peace or war? Friedel called to say you were on your way. Another girl is coming. What is her name, Doniele? No matter, Dietrich is a rich American. She will love him. We all love him. I got you a room in this hotel, Steven. It was full, you know, but I had a full colonel kicked out on his ass. A quartermaster officer. He keeps the units supplied with rubbers here in Paris." Hartung paused long enough to swallow half the contents of his glass. "Drink, Steven. I will order another bottle."

The wine was superb and Dietrich had no more flying to do that night. Dietrich broke off a piece of rye bread and dipped it into the red wine. Delicious, he thought. And it was just as well that Bunny was well into the grape.

"Do you and Friedel have the same mother? You're alcoholics. He probably takes his cognac on missions in his Heinkel," Dietrich said, pretending disgust.

"Remember that we were drinking when we met in Berlin. It just tastes better, now. I think wars are good for liquors. It elevates even the worst to a much higher level. What a relief to discover French wine."

"Your glass is empty," Dietrich said. "Doniele, would you be wonderful and get us another bottle? No, make it two more bottles,"

"I can have it brought up," Hartung started to protest, then caught Dietrich's imploring eye. "But," he said, turning to the girl, "maybe it would be faster?"

Doniele pretended to pout, but her sense of humor remained high as she slipped into a dress and, without hose, high-heeled shoes. Hartung admired her with lecherous eyes. He stepped to the door with her. "Take your time. This lion of the skies and I need to talk privately. I'll call you."

After the door to his room closed Hartung put his glass aside, not bothering to take the last swallow. "All right," he said, dropping onto the bed wearing only his shorts, stockings, and an Oriental silk robe that was at least two sizes too small. His fine, blonde hair hung loosely over his ears, conflicting with the firmly enforced regulations of the Schutzstaffel. "What is it you have to say that you cannot say in front of my precious little French whore? Actually, she loves me. She says she will continue to work while I am off fighting the war. Now, is that love or is it not?"

"Bunny, I need a favor," Dietrich said.

"Name it, *mon ami*"

"I need to meet Adolf Hitler," he said.

"Adolf Hitler?"

"Yes. The SS guards him. Everybody knows that. I hope that you can arrange it," Dietrich said.

"This is a joke, isn't it?" Hartung said but without laughing. "Ask me to do something else. As a matter of fact, I am willing to give up Doniele for as long as you are in Paris. Will that do?"

"I'm serious, Bunny. Can you do it?"

Hartung shook his head as though to clear it.

"No. Of course I cannot do it."

But if mere words could sober a soldier, invoking the Führer's name would accomplish the trick. It was true that the SS was a close fraternity and it was more than possible that Bunny might know someone assigned to the Reichschancellery. Or knew someone who knew someone.

"Steven," Hartung said, "I am not willingly into your business. I like you. You're a little queer, and maybe that's why I like you. But you have to tell me some reason why I should even try. Do you understand? Consider how many people want the Führer's time. Heads of states. Gauleiters, generals. I need a very persuasive reason to even try. And I am sure I cannot do it even then."

Dietrich knew the question would be asked. The only answer he had, however, was itself an act of desperation. He wanted to open his mouth to say the words but he hesitated, knowing that the next step would place him in a position from which there would be no retreat. He might very well be the instrument of his own death.

"So?" Hartung asked, not really eager to hear his friend's response.

"I know who supplied the British with the information about the Führer's train from Munich," Dietrich said, evenly.

For a long moment Hartung remained expressionless. He had known one of the officers aboard the train as well as one of the other ranks.

"Steven, do you know what you are saying? Do you have any idea what could happen to you if you said this to anyone but me?" Hartung said, his voice lowering.

"Yes."

"What you are saying is true?"

"Yes. It is absolutely true. But I will inform no one but the Führer himself. That is my requirement for revealing the spy," Dietrich said, feeling his mouth go dry at the sound of his own voice.

"God damn it, Dietrich, you stupid son of a bitch!" Hartung said, his anger flashing as he got to his feet. "Think of where this puts me! I don't want to be involved but I am. Unlike you, I'm not crazy. I can't withhold information or blab it out loud just as I please. And neither can you, except you're too stupid to realize it."

"I'm sorry to involve you, Bunny. There isn't any other way. If there was, I would have done it. I promise you."

Hartung's anger ebbed. He put his arms around Dietrich. "This is not America, my friend," he whispered into Dietrich's ear. "The closer you get to the power in Berlin, the less your life is worth. In trying to save Hitler's life, you might lose your own."

Chapter 23

The occasion was a reception in the great hall of the Reichschancellery for the observance of the 1933 Enabling Act. Decreed by Hitler only seven years prior, the Nazi party became not only the official representative of the German people, but was also the only political party allowed in the nation. It was the epiphany for the party from which all growth in modern Germany could be traced. The huge room, with its giant chandeliers suspended from the high ceiling, ornate tapestry gracing two walls, and hand-crafted furnishings made in Salzburg occupying the outer edges of a giant carpet, was now set with tables covered with linen cloths. Elegant foods of all description graced a service line, which included sculpted ice as its centerpiece. Among the invited guests was the handsome young architect and builder of the New Reichschancellery, Albert Speer, recently appointed the new Reichsbuilder. Although totally obsequious to his patron, Hitler, Speer attracted admirers as he sipped champagne in one corner of the vast room.

Other dignitaries included Foreign Minister Joachim von Ribbentrop, a coarse, one-time wine salesman turned anglophobe; Joseph Goebbels, Minister of Propaganda and his wife; Secretary of State Dr. Stuckart and his wife; Reich Minister of Justice Freisler; Foreign Office Secretary Otto Luther and other party members, including Martin Bormann, Hermann Göering, and Heinrich Himmler.

Archie had made his entrance as late as possible, putting it off partly out of fear and partly because he wanted a full room that would allow him to leave one group of people for another should they become uncomfortable to him.

He was tense as he moved among the guests of the Third Reich. He recognized most of those he would be expected to know by their photographs contained in the now-massive number of dossiers supplied him by Standartenführer Hebert and Bormann, and acknowledged new faces as they were introduced. Uniforms were de rigueur and they began to blur as he greeted his guests, shaking hands, forcing a smile, then going on to the next. He took no particular note of a young Luftwaffe major whose hand he shook but, as he turned away, thought he heard the word "Archie" called softly behind him.

It was such a shock to his system that, after an instant, he believed it was nothing more than his imagination. Even so, he did not turn to the source, if indeed there was a source, but continued to move about the room. He felt his body tremble again and wondered if his agitation was visible to others. He placed one hand over the other as he sat in a comfortable chair and nodded agreeably to a white-coated waiter who, after a slight bow at the waist, asked the Führer if he would care for tea and lemon cake. He said that he would, grateful that there was a table nearby on which he would be able to place the cup without spilling its contents.

A knot of people coalesced about him, straining to remain at a respectful distance but, after all, meaning to make their Führer comfortable among their warm friendship. Joseph Goebbels was nearest and seemed quite pleasant. He was, it seemed to Archie, genuinely concerned about the Führer's physical comfort. It was perhaps, Archie thought, because of the propaganda minister's own uneasiness of having to live with a club foot all of his life and suffering emotionally from his subsequent failure to do military duty in the last war. Archie knew Goebbels to be a man with an abiding interest in the theater, an activity Archie would have given much to discuss with him but feared he would somehow give himself away in the event. Still, Archie was paying attention to an idea that Goebbels had for a dramatic new film that would feature not actors but real fighting men, and to be done by the incredibly talented female director, Leni Reifenstahl.

Out of the corner of his eye Archie could see yet another uniform, also in a dress white tunic like his and others in the room, and with the silver and gold wings of the Luftwaffe. It was, yet again, the young pilot with whom he had shaken hands minutes ago and who had, Archie believed, almost stopped the very blood from flowing in his veins. He turned slowly toward the sandy-haired major and looked into his blue eyes and sandy colored hair. Smiling broadly, the major allowed himself to move closer to the Führer than perhaps protocol would permit but said in German, "Having a good time, Archie?"

Others standing back, including Goebbels, did not clearly hear the words of the decorated Luftwaffe officer, but Goebbels was near enough to clearly pick up the word "Archie". The minister of propaganda turned quizzically toward the pilot, regarded him appraisingly, then glanced at the Führer. Hitler seemed not in the least upset at whatever it was that the pilot had said so that Goebbels merely believed that he had heard incorrectly. Arch? What kind of arch? Still, not wishing to be rude, the propaganda minister returned the pilot's smile.

"I don't believe I have had the pleasure, Major ...?" he said.

The major clicked his heels and, bowing slightly at the waist, said "Dietrich, Herr Minister. Steven Dietrich. Forgive me, sir, but the fellows in my squadron made me promise to extend their deepest best wishes to our Führer. I hope I have not been impertinent."

Dietrich seemed to be a poster image of what the German fighter pilot should be. He wore the prestigious Iron Cross 1st Class at his throat, as well as the Silver Class Day Fighter awarded for sixty combat missions, and the German Cross in gold placed upon his right breast. He might have been a few inches shorter than the ideal matinee idol but he had a fine physique, broad shoulders and just the hint of swagger that one would expect of a hunter of the skies. The Führer, too, seemed taken with the young fighter pilot, apparently not able to take his eyes from him. Goebbels felt compelled to break the silence that ensued sensing a unique moment of military opportunity.

"I see by your badge that you are in Fighter Command, major," Goebbels said.

"Yes, sir. I have the honor to command 44th Staffel, Jagdeschwader3, Fightergruppen West."

"And you are stationed where?" Goebbels asked.

"Bergues, France, Herr Minister," Dietrich said, still holding an empty champagne glass in his hand.

"Fill the major's glass," Goebbels said to a passing waiter. "What machine do you fly?" he asked, turning back to Dietrich.

"The Me-109. We have just been upgraded with the E model. An excellent aircraft, we think."

"Tell me, Major Dietrich, what do you think of the British pilots?"

"They are flying Hurricanes and Spitfires, and the Spitfires are a very fast, very maneuverable aircraft. The Brits are well trained and they are courageous."

"Ah, chivalry. It is good to respect one's adversary," Goebbels observed, turning to Hitler for confirmation. The Führer seemed, strangely, to be following the conversation closely but contributing nothing. It was uncharacteristic for the German leader to remain unopinionated on the subject of war and warriors.

Goebbels continued. "So, when will you finish them off?"

"With respect, Herr Minister," Dietrich said and, turning toward Hitler, "my Führer, I am only able to shoot down the one who is unlucky enough to fly into my gun sights. It is for the generals to tell us when we will win."

"Your answer shows keen tactical insight. Thank you, Major," Goebbels said, dismissing Dietrich since he had taken up quite enough of the Führer's time.

Dietrich took one step back, clicked his heels as he nodded his head in a military bow, and turned to go.

"I would like to hear more about your airplane, major," Archie said, at last rousing himself from some inner place and time.

Dietrich turned back.

"Have you seen the Mosaic Hall? They are made of Saalburg marble. Come," he said, rising from his chair. Archie took the Luftwaffe ace by the arm and led him out of the ballroom.

The interior of the Reichschancellery was all but deserted save for the omnipresent SS guards stationed at key places within the grand walls.

"Did you see the sculptures representing the Army and the Party as you entered? You came through the Honor Courtyard, ja? They are among the most beautiful ever created in Germany," he said as they strolled along the block long hallways of the chancellery. "Ah, here we are. You see? The mosaics were designed by Professor Kaspar." Archie was not yet sure with whom he was talking. The major might be more than a Luftwaffe pilot; he might also be assigned to the Gestapo. Or the dreaded SD. Or any of the myriad agencies of betrayal and death spawned and cultivated by totalitarian regimes.

"You said that you have a friend by the name of ..." Archie looked over his shoulder once more, assuring himself that they could not be overheard.

"Archie," Major Dietrich supplied. "Actually, he's not a relative." Dietrich switched to English. "He is a British actor. And he is either quite brave or very foolish."

"Foolish," Archie said in English, "is charitable. I am a coward. My knees are weak even as we stand here speaking where we can't be heard. I often feel that I am about to cry and at this moment I wish to God I was sitting in The Lion's Den on Pinkney Street having a glass with my mates. Are you really a major in the Luftwaffe, or did you steal the uniform?"

Dietrich smiled, and when he spoke again he reverted to German. "I am what I told Minister Goebbels. And I fly missions against the British. I'm sorry about that part of it but it is vital to my deep cover."

"You're British! Thank God! Can you get me out of here?"

"I'm not British, Archie. I'm American. But I work for the SOE in London. And I can't get you out of here," Dietrich said. There was a moment of sad silence as Archie knew at once that Dietrich was lying and Dietrich knew that Archie knew better. "Not yet, anyway. I have directions for you that come from London. From time to time I will receive orders from there and I will pass them on to you. It will work the other way as well. I will get certain information from you and I will relay that information back to London."

Archie nodded balefully. He had expected something like this. Or death before the people at home could reach out to him.

"How?" he began. "I mean, what will be the mechanics? How will I contact you?"

"You will take an interest in me. You will enjoy hearing my tales of aerial combat and from time to time you will have your adjutant or secretary summon me from my unit to come to wherever you are for lunches or dinners or even weekends at Obersalzburg. We will go for walks as our friendship develops. Whatever happens, make no notes. Trust nothing to paper or film. Spies and counter-spies are everywhere," Dietrich warned.

"Why don't I just appoint you to my staff here at the Reichschancellery?" Archie asked.

"That would put me in too much scrutiny. For now I have to drop out of sight for hours or even days at a time. If I were in Berlin, here in this building, it might be dangerous to arrange," the Luftwaffe pilot said.

"Yes, I see," Archie said, a feeling of disappointment pulsing through him.

"By the way, Archie, the prime minister conveys to you his personal congratulations. He sent word to have me to tell you that you have not only saved lives in this war but might have saved the British Empire itself."

Archie only nodded, at a loss at how to express his gratitude for Churchill's great compliment. In his uneven career as a professional actor, he had received very little praise.

"Now, Archie, listen carefully. You must order the Luftwaffe to change its primary target campaign," Dietrich said.

"What? I don't understand," Archie said.

"The bombers are hammering British airfields. The losses of planes and pilots is too great. If Germany keeps it up the RAF will not be able to sustain itself. Do you understand?" Dietrich said calmly but forcefully.

"I think so but how...?"

Archie and Dietrich became aware of a presence in the hallway. It was Martin Bormann.

"They are waiting for your speech, my Führer. When should I tell them you will be ready?" Bormann asked, his eyes not missing Dietrich standing by Hitler's side.

"I'll be along, Martin," Archie said.

After Bormann withdrew Dietrich smiled. "If you don't mind, Führer, I'll skip the pep rally."

Pep rally? Archie thought on his way back to the Reception Hall. What was a pep rally?

Archie was about to make his way to the dais when he felt a light touch on his arm. It was Bormann.

"Führer," he whispered, eyes shifting among others in the huge room, then back to Archie, "the Luftwaffe officer you were with..."

"Major Dietrich," Archie said, impatiently.

"...is an American. I have a very large file on him," the deputy party secretary said.

Book III
The Present

Chapter 24

Nina spotted Debbie Mears easily by Street's physical description. She was the tallest woman in the bar, even taller than most of the men. She had long, naturally blonde hair that touched her shoulders and her body was the envy of every woman in the place. The restaurant on Eversholt Street was called Great Napalese. Her eyes flicked about the room while one foot tapped impatiently in a high-heel shoe. Nina watched while Debbie finished her martini and casually flicked the empty glass back at the bartender. Nina had the impression that Debbie was about to order another before Nina touched her elbow.

"Debbie Mears, I presume?" Nina said.

"That's me," Debbie said, looking down. "Who're you?"

"I'm little Augie's pal," Nina said.

"Little Augie, huh? I like that. Wasn't there an American gangster once called Little Augie? So, where is Little Augie now?"

"He's outside. He's worried that if he comes in he might meet somebody he knows."

"Good ol' Little Augie. Lot smarter than he looks. Okay, lead the way," Debbie said, casually throwing her lightweight coat over her shoulder as the two women exited the restaurant. They walked a block and a half while Nina paused in doorways to check behind them for a tail. Debbie looked over her shoulder, mildly alarmed.

"I hope this is just for practice," she said to Nina.

"Just a little fun," Nina said, moving out to the sidewalk again while holding Debbie's hand.

Half way down the next block Street pulled up to the curb, stopping for them to get in. Nina sat in the back seat to allow Debbie a more intimate position near Street.

"Thanks for coming, Debbie. Good to see you again," he said.

"I wouldn't have missed this for the world. I can't tell you how boring that place can be. People think SIS stuff is thrilling but all we do is push piles of papers and pictures from one desk to another and wait for the whistle to blow. God, you look great. How do I look?"

"You always look terrific," he said.

"Are you lying to me?"

"No. Not at all."

"You're not just trying to say nice things, pour a couple of drinks into me so you can take me to bed, are you?"

"No. I promise, not at all."

"Then why am I wasting my time?" Debbie asked.

Street looked into his rearview mirror and for the first time in over thirty-six hours he saw Nina laughing.

"I'm always horny," Debbie said to Nina. "Men just don't know what they're missing. Absolutely kills me."

"Every man in that bar was simply drooling in their drink over you," Nina said, not able to wipe the grin from her face.

"Yeah? Then we should have stayed. To hell with the risk. Turn around, Little Augie, I'm wanted back there."

"You're wanted more right here," Street said driving along slowly in rush-hour traffic.

Following Debbie's directions they arrived at a brasserie not far from Finsbury Circus. They were a bit early for the dinner crowd so their service was prompt from the moment they walked in the door. Street asked for and was given an out-of-the-way table where, even when the place began to fill up, they would still have privacy. Debbie waited for Street to order the wine. He knew what she expected.

"Do you have Paulillac, nineteen ninety-six?" he asked their waiter.

The waiter appreciated customers who were discriminating in their wine orders. He did not know if they still had that bottle, he said, but he would be more than happy to look.

Nina retrieved a package of cigarettes from her pocket and put one into her mouth. Street said nothing but Debbie leaned forward.

"Not here. They're a bunch of swine."

Nina's eyelids dropped but she tossed the cigarette aside, not bothering to replace it into the pack. Street was used to the fact that Nina was not looking to make new friends. The lady had an attitude.

The waiter returned with the wine and fresh bread and butter.

"We'll need another of those," Street said, referring to the wine.

For some time they chatted about pedestrian things, Nina adding little.

"So, how are things at SIS?" Street asked, hoping to sound casual.

"Like what?"

"Like anything. How about Jean Scheerer? What's he been up to?"

"He's never around the office much. He must be somewhere else a lot."

Debbie was smart. She was also coy.

"He is on our side, isn't he? I mean, he hasn't sold out to some foreign power, has he?" Street said, making no effort to hide his impatience.

"Gee, I wouldn't know about that," Debbie said, ripping off a piece of bread.

"Have you heard anything about me at the office?"

"Yeah. I have."

Debbie's nonchalance caught him off balance.

"You have? What?"

"Look, I'm just in this for sex. I'm not interesting in blabbing secrets. People get shot for things like that. I think they still do it that way," Debbie said to Nina.

Their food arrived. They began eating in silence.

"They're looking for me," Street said.

"Yep. I'm going to see how the night goes before I turn you in myself," Debbie said.

"Do you know why they're looking for me?"

"The book, I guess. You made a lot of people very unhappy. Everybody including the cleaning people at SIS has read the bloody thing. If it's true, it's devastating," she finished, forking a piece of meat into her mouth and washing it down with red wine. "God, that stuff is good," she said.

"We need help, Debbie," Street said.

"We?"

"Yeah. We. I am about to be burned. Strike that. I have already been burned. I had my identity stolen along with my money and I'm fairly sure that the next thing that's going to happen to me is that I could soon be dead."

"Isn't that always the way? I just know I'm going to get stuck with another dinner bill."

When no one laughed Debbie sobered.

"Are you pulling my chain? Putting me on?" she said.

"We've already lost two people. Thomas MacQueen was one, if you read the book you know who he is. And my friend Westbrook Claridge."

Street told Debbie the whole story, how he was asked to sign a statement that his work was fabricated, that the people he interviewed didn't exist, how he snuck out of America. "I think when they have me completely erased they'll kill me," he concluded.

Debbie had stopped eating.

"What kind of help?" she asked.

"We think that Rudolph Hess told everything to his British interrogators in nineteen forty-one," Nina said. "The transcripts are still classified. We'd like to see them."

"And you want me to get them for you," Debbie said.

Nina and Street nodded their heads solemnly.

"Well, I'm sorry. I'm not in the document-stealing business. Especially classified ones," Debbie said.

"I respect your position, Debbie," Street said. "Thank you for listening. I know you'd help if you could."

Nina said, "I don't respect your fucking position."

The rest of the meal passed in silence.

Edward Wiles expected to be taken to the main police station. When the drive stretched into the better part of an hour he knew better. The Policia Nacional has its headquarters in the heart of the city, only minutes from where Wiles had been staying. Still blindfolded and lacking intimate knowledge of its streets there was no way he could keep track of the driver's turns nor estimate his changes in speeds. The automobile finally stopped, the doors opened, and Wiles was roughly pulled out of the backseat. His bare feet stubbed painfully against a curb, even while he could feel a cold and wet sensation. He had stepped in some kind of gutter.

He was pulled and pushed up a flight of perhaps a dozen stone steps, wide enough so that his escorts could hold either side of him as they ascended. A door opened and closed behind him. The temperature dropped many degrees as they left the pleasant warm outside air. Still another door was opened, Wiles was propelled through, then he heard it close behind him. He stood still, his hands still handcuffed behind him, trying to pick out pieces of the conversations among his captors. They seemed disciplined for their comments were short and clipped. They must have done this sort of operation before, Wiles thought.

All at once he felt a heavy blow on his left arm near the shoulder. He was propelled almost off of his feet to his right, striking a stone wall. The rough wall hurt even more than the blow that put him there and he fell to his knees, only to be jerked sharply upright again, strong hands under his elbows. The pain in his shoulder joint was so sharp and so strong that he heard himself yelp like a dog.

One of his wrists was freed from the cuffs while the hand that was still manacled was attachéd to the stone wall. The temporarily free hand was recuffed and attachéd to another part of the wall. Wiles was now spread into a crucifix position.

"Take it off," a commanding female voice said.

The blindfold was snatched from Wiles's head. He blinked into an array of blinding lights. It was impossible to look into the high-intensity beams but it was equally impossible to avoid them. There were four across in three banks, twelve lights in all. They were positioned less than six feet from his face so that even with his eyes closed their powerful light penetrated his eyelids and created pain underneath. Their heat was uncomfortable.

Wiles felt a searing pain under his left armpit. He had been struck by what he guessed might have been a bamboo cane. The cane was designed to cause maximum pain with minimum damage to the body. It was important to his interrogators that he remain alive long enough to tell them exactly what they wanted to know. The person wielding the blow was only a blur, a ghostly movement among the blinding lights. Wiles tried to stifle a scream, managing to create a moan instead.

"Let the old bastard have another one," the female voice said. Wiles felt two more searing strikes against his body. He gulped to catch his breath, which had been driven out of him by the stark pain. He recognized the voice.

"You," he said.

Carla moved near his face, the high-intensity beams behind her creating a monster from light refraction and shadowing.

"Look at the worthless old man," she said, laughing at him. "The old spy. Still playing his games. Edward Wiles, alias Adrian Small. You were so pathetic. Buying a little girl a glass of wine. Who did you think you were fooling, you old fart? Now, you are going to tell us what we want to know. You realize that, don't you, Mr. Adrian Small. Who did you give the diary to? We are not going to be patient, Mr. Adrian Small."

It was not a good thing that the woman called Carla had shown him her face. He knew then that he would never leave the room alive to identify them.

Carla pulled back from the lights and nodded her head toward one of the men. The bamboo cane was wielded viciously under his upraised arms. Wiles cried out loud and gasped, gulping for air to refill his evacuated his lungs.

"Very quickly, now. The diary. Who did you deliver it to?"

Wiles wanted more than anything to tell them what they demanded. He knew he could not indefinitely endure their brutal strokes. He was too old. His heart would not take it. He knew that. They knew that.

When Debbie Mears settled into her desk the next morning she was distracted. She slept very little the night before, her meeting with August Street heavy on her mind. She liked August Street. He was a fine, decent man. August had been in the trade for a good many years. He had probably seen more secret material than she had, so why were they out to ruin his life? Or kill him? The Hess interrogations. God, it was old, old stuff. Who cared, anymore? Debbie turned back to her work, which was converting old audio, video, and written archives into retrievable computer data. She had nine assistants working full-time whom she directed and would have four more after the start of the next fiscal year. She could hardly wait.

Distracted and unable to concentrate, she finally rose from her workstation and walked without knocking into the cubical occupied by Aubrey Ainsworth. Ainsworth was older than anyone this side of Operations, perhaps the oldest man in SIS. He wore a grotesque brown hairpiece that sat atop his head like a large bird nest. Ainsworth's nose was pinched together at the end, ironically creating a bird-like look. Debbie loved to tease and were it anyone else she might have ribbed Aubrey Ainsworth but she pitied the man who, he had once admitted, had nothing else in life but his work. His wife had passed away years ago.

"Aubrey, I need the Hess interrogation transcripts," she said.

"Yes? Well, why do you ask me for them?"

"Because they are not in the master files," she said. "I just looked."

"Are you quite sure, Debbie? Perhaps they are still classified. Need to know. Something like that."

"Then I should have found that notation in the files," she said.

Aubrey Ainsworth sat, motionless except for, lightly tapping a pencil on the hard surface of his desk.

"Well?" Debbie prodded.

"Well, what? If you can't lay your hands on them at the moment, I suggest you simply work around them and come back to that subject matter at a later time."

"I need them now," she said, stubbornly.

"We've had them sixty-four years, Debbie," Ainsworth observed. "Can't your program wait another week or two?"

"If I can't find them now why should I think I'll find them two weeks from now?" she asked, virtually gritting her teeth in frustration.

Ainsworth continued to tap his pencil, a sound that was now aggravating to Debbie. Determined to wait her out, Ainsworth did not respond. Debbie's personality did not allow for the patience it took to win such a battle. She spun on her heel and slammed Ainsworth's door as she left.

Back in her office she began to think. There must have been more than one transcript made of Hess's interrogations. They would have been far too valuable to lose. She picked up the telephone and dialed a four-digit number.

"This is Marcia Priestly in C's office. Who is working the Raven project?"

Pause.

"No. Support," she said into the phone.

Pause.

"Doren who? Lattimer. Would you transfer my call? Thank you."

Pause.

"Doren Lattimer? C wants to look at the Hess file. He says you still have it. Right. No, I'll have Deborah Mears pick it up. Would you meet her at the door? Fine."

Debbie hung up the telephone and took an elevator from her subterranean office to the fourth floor.

The S-3, Operations floor, was accessible two ways: by eye-scan or by passing through a guard station. Debbie had neither authorization. To pass through the guard station she would have to be escorted or her name would have to be entered on an access list. She had arranged the easiest way. She waited at the guard desk for Lattimer to appear.

Lattimer was a taller than average man, with brown hair and droopy eyes. He reminded Debbie of a big dog so relaxed he looked like he wanted to get back to his nap. He looked at her identification tag and the picture she wore around her neck.

"Hello, Deborah," he said with a tired smile. She liked him at once. "Sign here, please," he said, offering her a small clipboard with a property slip attachéd.

She did so with a flourish and accepted the folder which was heavy manila, secured with a twist of wire. It was marked Top Secret on the front and back.

"TS for a sixty-five-year-old doc?" she asked to Lattimer.

"We always worry that the Nazis are going to make a comeback," he said, dryly.

"Can't be too careful, I guess."

She turned to go.

"Ask Brooks to call me after he reads it. Something in the transcripts I want to discuss with him."

Debbie was glad that she was already walking away. "Righto," she said over her shoulder.

Back in her office she removed the wire fastener and quickly scanned the documents. They were not originals, of course. There appeared to be more than one hundred pages. At first she had no intention of reading the material but after glancing at the first page she read the second. Then the third. Soon she was swept up in the dialogue between Hess and his interrogators.

"I never got the call from C so I thought maybe you forgot to tell him," Lattimer said. He was leaning against the doorway of her office, hands in his pockets.

"I…" Debbie choked, not able to think of a single word. She wished she could somehow swallow the documents she held in her hand.

He withdrew a slip of paper from his pocket and handed it to her. It was the document receipt that she had signed.

"You better keep this so they can't use it to hang you."

"When...how did you...?"

"I called C's office after you hung up. There was no Debbie Mears working there. Debbie Mears works in Archives. Amazing stuff, eh?" he said, nodding toward the documents in her hands.

"I just started reading it," she said, stupidly, as he languidly took a chair near her desk.

"Well, it is. Amazing stuff. Now that you have it you might as well finish reading it." He glanced around the room. "I see you have a copy machine. I suppose you'd need a good one in your line of work. If I came back in, say, fifteen minutes, would that give you enough time to finish with the papers in your hand?"

Debbie swallowed hard. "Yes. Fifteen minutes would be just fine."

Lattimer rose from his chair to his full height and moved to the door.

"Did you read the book? *Raven?*" he asked.

Debbie nodded her head vigorously.

"Everyone in this building read it, I should think. Tell August Street that I enjoyed it immensely, would you?" he said, his hand on the doorknob.

"Yes," Debbie croaked.

Lattimer turned before letting himself out. "If one of us goes to jail, Debbie, it's going to be you," he said, very softly.

Street and Nina exchanged questioning glances when her cell phone buzzed.

"Yes?" she said. Wordlessly she held out the telephone to August Street.

"Street," he said and waited. Then, "good God, how did you get this number?"

Hundreds of miles from Wales, Debbie spoke from a public telephone booth.

"I have the a wonderful sheaf of papers that you've dying to read."

"Where..." he began, then, "never mind. We need to meet." There was only one place she could have got it and that was someone who worked at The Wise Pelican.

"Yes, of course. I recall where you stayed when you first arrived in London. On your very first trip," Debbie repeated carefully.

"All right. I'll meet you there at..." He considered the drive time to London.

"At twenty-three hundred. The east side entrance."

"Got it," she said.

"One more thing, Debbie. Locate Jean Scheerer. Give him this number and tell him to call me, fast."

Her voice was forced, under stress, Street thought. There was one other place Debbie could have gotten the number of the cell phone. That location would be the Government Communications Headquarters (GCHQ) at Cheltenham who, in turn, had full access to the intercept base at Menwith Hill, near Harrogate in Yorkshire. He wanted to toss the cell phone but it was vital he first speak with Jean Scheerer.

Scheerer called within ten minutes. Street did not know where he was located nor did he care. What Street needed was a bodyguard, a bodyguard of a particular kind, and Scheerer was the man who could make the right contact. They talked cryptically, Street providing Scheerer with nothing more than a street in Westminster.

Street stopped in Gloucester long enough to get rid of Nina's car and rent a mid-size sedan, arriving back in London slightly behind schedule. He parked within three blocks of Brown's Hotel on Albemarle. He and Nina had discussed the pick-up between them. Street had wanted to go alone. Nina pointed out that "they" were after him rather than her, Nina, so she argued that she should go alone while he waited. Street agreed.

But he only waited until Nina was a half block away before he stepped out of the car and, walking on the opposite side of the street, began following her. As she turned left on Clifford it began to rain. Nina quickened her pace. Street did not increase his but cut across the street in a southerly direction, still remaining well back from Nina. Street look around, vigilant for followers but saw no one suspicious. Tyre Jones almost laughed at the amateurish maneuvers of his quarry. Jones could hardly have drawn it on a blackboard to make the persons, or person, behave more favorably to his needs.

Jones wore his drab, inconspicuous clothing as usual, and, thanks to the rain, had an umbrella to hide his face even if August Street looked at him directly.

Alaine Demiex was a born Guide Yost in Sterkstroom, South Africa. At the age of fifteen Guide Yost lied about his age to enter the military service of the Apartheid government. He was big for his age, had no fear, showed excellent aggressiveness, and was allowed into the highly secret Bier Regiment. Simply referred to as "the Regiment", its very existence was denied. Its personnel, extremely well-trained in all aspects of silent killing, wore no unit patches or identification of any kind, either on their uniforms or, more often, in civilian dress. They were, to a man, self-reliant, well-equipped, and dedicated to the supremacy of white skin over all others. The Regiment was not for the squeamish. Infiltration into the state's enemy camp was impossible for the racially pure members of the regiment but their Intelligence sources were either bought or extracted. There was no man in the Regiment who would hesitate to dismember an enemy under questioning while he or she was still alive.

Well before Nelson Mandela became president of South Africa in 1994, Guide Yost exited the country before he and his colleagues could be tried for a number of homicides and atrocities committed under color of authority. Yost made his way to Dakar in Senegal, western Africa, where he spent several months getting drunk and whoring. When his money ran out, he presented himself to the local French embassy as a recruit for the Foreign Legion. He remained idle for several days until he was sent to Aubagne, France. There he surrendered his passport as required, never mind that his was a poor forgery, and signed the obligatory five-year contract. The name he chose was Alaine Demiex.

Recruit Demiex was ideally suited to both the Legionaire's training and to its life. Even in the lower ranks he was paid well enough to buy whores on his leaves, which he took in blocks of a few days throughout the year. He excelled at the basic infantry training program and went on to advanced combat training, then parachute school at which he had considerable experience from his service in South Africa. He finally finished commando training in Mont Louis in the Pyrenées mountains. Instructors at every level liked what they saw in the young, ferocious but cool Legionaire and he rose steadily within the ranks. At the end of his five-year contract, however, Demiex left the legion with the idea in mind that the work he had been doing all of his life for the paltry pay of a soldier might be done for far more money as a civilian. Almost before he had spent his first civilian week in Paris, he agreed to work as a contract man for the Russian KGB, now called FSB. He became a reliable and resourceful operative for the First Directorate, foreign operations.

The FSB, like the American CIA, has three times as many contract workers as regular employees. The advantage to contract workers is that they paid a far higher wage for their work, usually piecemeal, than the regular worker listed on the public payroll. The advantage to the bureau who issues the contract is that the contract worker is paid "off the books," thus providing deniability all the way up the line if something goes wrong. Alaine Demiex's contracts had always gone well for the FSB.

Tyre Jones, who was following August Street with his deadly newspaper hiding pressurized prussic acid, was in the process of making the same mistake that August Street was making as he followed Nina. He had "checked six," his six o'clock position, that is to the rear, but only quickly and thus carelessly. Jones was watching an amateur and he became too relaxed. And target-fixated. It did not occur to him that he was not the only professional on the street that night.

Debbie Mears, standing in a covered area under the hotel overhang, recognized Nina when she was one hundred yards away. She was alone.

Despite the rain having begun falling harder, Debbie stepped onto the hotel's driveway and moved forward, a bulging, zippered document case under her arm. A man in a raincoat and hat stepped quickly from shrubbery bordering the driveway and laid hands on the document case. The narrow strap on the case had been looped casually over Debbie's forearm. It now caught in the crook of her elbow. Had she been a small woman the thief might not have been inconvenienced but Debbie Mears instinctively firmed the muscles in her arm and the would-be thief was stopped cold. By now Nina not more than a few feet away. She rushed forward to give assistance. A brief tug of war broke out. The thief was knocked off balance long enough by the two women that August Street arrived on a dead run to put a lowered shoulder into the man's chest. The thief flew through the air into the tangled arms of nearby shrubbery. Street was about to give the man a fist to the jaw when the man spoke.

"Lemme go, yer! C'mon, man."

Street hesitated long enough to look. The man was wearing no socks. His ankles were filthy and his shoes did not match. Wrappings of string around two belt loops in his trousers kept them from falling down. His overcoat, several sizes too large, covered a dirty undershirt.

Street slowly released his grip on the man's throat.

"Please," he said.

From ten meters away Tyre Jones was more than a little surprised to see his carefully choreographed interception of the Hess transcripts brought to ruin by a public bum. Jones quickened his pace, moving ahead of August Street and heading toward the women. He knew that he would have to deal with Street after the women but he expected to handle the book writer with little trouble. The shorter of the two women, Nina, now had control of the black bag. Jones touched her on the elbow with one hand, as though it was a helping gesture, and with the other hand-delivered a strong whiff of vaporized cyanide. Nina's knees immediately buckled, Tyre Jones deftly shifting the bag from the fallen woman to his own underarm. He turned to walk away but kept August Street in his peripheral vision. Although not comprehending that he had just witnessed murder delivered via a rolled-up newspaper, Street made for Jones and the bag he had just stolen. The Street distraction ironically saved not only his life but that of Debbie's as well. The Soviet agent Demiex had, in the dark, moved silently and unseen to Jones's blind side. It was his original intention to shoot the SIS man with a silenced pistol. The fact that it would be witnessed by at least three other people bothered him not at all, yet at the last moment he struck Jones in the under the base of the skull, behind the ear, with a custom-made steel knuckle. Demiex could feel the crunch of bone as the chop was delivered, a blow that would leave the British agent either dead or mentally dysfunctional, Demiex not caring which.

He easily removed the bag from Jones's grip and handed it to Street. Hardly the sentimental type, Demiex felt no compulsion to instruct Street what to do with the prize. Debbie knelt beside Nina, taking up her hand, pressing her ear to the other woman's heart.

"It is too late for her," Demiex said. "The police will be here soon. You had better go now. Leave them," he said, nodding toward the bodies of Nina and Jones.

Chapter 25

The taxi driver followed the abductors. There were too many for him to deal with alone. He had a satellite telephone in the luggage compartment but it lacked secure scramble capability. It would take him thirty minutes to return to his residence for that equipment. He debated only a matter of seconds. Even if he was intercepted it would take the listeners time to move people and equipment. Ramon trusted that they would remain at least one step behind. He used his satellite connection and called a one-time disposable number in England.

Carla peered closely into Wiles's eyes, using her fingers to open them.

"Turn out the lights," she said to one of the men. "We need him alive until he speaks. Take him down from the wall. Feed him. Give him plenty of water. And let him rest."

"Should we have a medic look at him?" another man asked.

Carla considered but shook her head.

"No. But put him on the cot and let him sleep. Then we begin on his feet."

Nine hours after receiving the call from Seville, Louis sat in the backseat of the same taxi that had delivered Wiles to his rendezvous with fate. A third man, Raoul, no more than thirty, left a doorway and walked down a narrow sidewalk to the taxi. He opened the passenger side front door and slid into the seat next to the driver.

"Are they still there?" Louis asked, referring to the house where Wiles was being held.

"Yes. There are five."

"Including the woman?"

Raoul nodded. "But how long he can hold out…" he shrugged.

Of course. That was what had been on Louis's mind for the past eighteen hours. Wiles was a very courageous man but virtually anyone will succumb to torture given the right methods and enough time.

"The woman. I want her inside," Louis said.

"To be sure. She is there now," Raoul assured him.

"Do you have a place to work?" Louis asked Ramon, the taxi driver.

"Sure."

"All right, then. Drive to a super store. One with a garden department," Louis ordered.

"There is one on the way."

It was all quite simple and quick. While the cab driver bought two fifty-pound bags of fertilizer in the garden department, in another part of the store Louis picked out a forty-gallon plastic garbage can and two dozen packages of sealing wax used in home canning. The two men then drove to a truck stop on the edge of the city where they filled a five-gallon gas can with diesel fuel. They then drove to an address only four miles from the truck stop, a borrowed garage, on route A-4 in the south of the city. Inside it took less than two hours to dump the fertilizer into the plastic garbage can and mix in ten pounds of black gun powder, the innocuous kind used for reloading one's shotgun shells. Into the mix Louis added a gallon of diesel oil. The final touch was made by melting the paraffin wax and pouring it over the top of the mass, sealing it tightly. The garbage can and its contents was placed in the trunk of the taxi. The driver dropped Louis off at a Hertz auto rental, then drove back to the location where Wiles was being held. He parked in a side street where he could keep the safe house in view. Louis arrived several minutes later, parking the new rental car nearby. Raoul had by now joined the taxi driver.

"Still inside?" Louis asked.

"Two have left," Raoul said.

"There must be three more inside," Louis said.

Raoul nodded his agreement. "The woman and another."

"They would go out to eat," Louis mused aloud. He looked at his watch. It was five-fifty in the afternoon.

"All right," Louis said. "We go in. We'll wait inside for the others to return."

The driver waited in his taxi until Louis and Raoul had walked entirely around the block and taken up positions on either side of the safe house. Then the driver started the engine of the cab, pulled into the street, and drove his car to the front of the safe house and parked. Before getting out of the cab he screwed a silencer onto the barrel of a 9mm Beretta pistol. He concealed this under a clipboard.

Inside the house a man was watching through the curtains.

"Who is it?" Carla demanded, munching on grapes from a tray of fruit as she leafed through a magazine.

"A cab driver. He is coming up the steps."

"Is he alone?" she demanded.

The man at the window looked up and down the residential street. Everything appeared normal.

"Yes."

"Get rid of him," she said, turning back to her perusal of the magazine.

The man inside held a pistol in his right hand, which he concealed behind his back as he waited for a knock on the front door. When it came he opened the door.

"What do you want?" he said to the cab driver.

"A taxi. Somebody called," the driver said.

"A mistake. Nobody called," the man said and started to close the door.

"Apologies, sir," the driver said. "The call came from this house. Look, I have it here on my order sheet." The driver held the clipboard higher so that the sheet was just below the man's chin. The driver pulled the trigger twice quickly. The weapon's suppressor spat, muffling the sound. The first 9mm bullet entered his windpipe, taking out his larynx. The second round penetrated through the wound left by the first, severing the spinal cord in the neck. The man behind the door was dead before his body hit the floor.

Louis and Raoul burst quickly into the house, guns drawn. Dropping her magazine on the floor, Carla lunged for a pistol atop a table nearby. Her move was far too late. Louis put a bullet into her leg before she could lay her hands on the weapon.

She screamed at the top of her lungs. Louis made no attempt to silence her, the walls being impervious to sound in either direction. A second man who had made a move for his pistol checked himself at once when he saw himself confronted by three more armed men.

"We are police," the man said. "Police. We are on police business."

It was obvious who they were. His badge was displayed, on his belt. Carla's was in her purse.

"You filthy swine. You'll go to jail for this!" she said, gasping in what must have been extreme pain, holding her leg. The bullet had smashed the bone above her knee.

Very quickly the taxi driver used their handcuffs to bind them together, then a second set of cuffs to attach them to the same fasteners that had held Wiles to the wall. Raoul stepped forward and roughly wrapped Carla's head and mouth with duct tape, and did the same for her confederate, the other policeman. He bound Carla's leg tightly with duct tape over the wound to stanch the flow of blood. There would be no need to loosen the crude tourniquet later, he thought. Maybe the leg would fall off. Raoul suppressed a smile as he moved away.

Louis knelt by a rough metal cot with a thin mattress. Wiles did not look good. His white beard had grown for several days, his thin hair was matted with blood. It appeared to Louis that the old man had had his nose broken and because of it was having trouble breathing. Both eyes were puffed and closed by dried blood. He examined the old man's feet. They were swollen, blood-filled, raw. Louis did not waste his energy on rage directed against Carla and her minion. That would come soon enough.

"Get me a cold, wet rag," Louis said to Raoul.

Raoul found a bathroom with towels. He wet one and brought them both to Louis. Louis carefully dabbed Wiles's face, speaking to him in low, comforting tones. Louis rinsed the towel several times before Wiles was sufficiently cleaned and his eyes gently opened.

"We are going to take you out of here, sir," Louis said. "Relax while we carry you." "Indeed," Wiles returned in a whisper, "relaxing is what I do best."

With Raoul on one side and Louis on the other, they managed to place the old spy into the backseat of the rented car. Louis placed a pillow behind the frail man's head and gently tucked a soft wool car blanket around him.

The cab driver drove his taxi into the alley, parking it directly against the safe house, literally touching it. The driver got out of the cab on the opposite side and closed the door. He opened the trunk, and wrapped two wires around a battery anode connected to an electronic device set within the paraffin-covered garbage can. There was a cheap, small black plastic briefcase in the trunk which the driver held in his hand while closing the trunk lid. He walked across the street to where Raoul and Louis were waiting.

"The Fox and I have a plane to catch. Can you finish up here?" Louis asked the two men.

"Oh, yes," the taxi driver said, touching the small black bag. "We have plenty of time to wait for the others. "Have a good trip."

Louis followed the signs to San Pablo International Airport northeast of the city where he had arrived only fourteen hours before.

Back at the house the cab driver and Raoul waited patiently. Within the hour the two remaining policemen they had been expecting returned. The taxi driver waited until they were well inside before he closed the circuit on the garbage can bomb.

The explosion was enormous.

Raoul dropped the remote detonation device and calmly walked away.

At 0800 hours Christopher Brooks's door was opened by Lucille Vickers.

"A Michael Callahan is on the telephone. He says it's quite urgent."

"Callahan? Is he on the list?" Brooks wanted to know.

"No, sir, but his call is coming through on a secure line from the American State Department."

"Hmm," Brooks mused. He was something of a stickler for protocol. If Michael Callahan was of very high rank in the American State Department he would know who he was. He did not like the idea of picking up the telephone for just anybody who decided he wanted to talk with the chief of SIS. Still, if the man said it was urgent, perhaps it really was.

"All right," he said to Vickers and picked up the telephone. "Brooks here."

"Good morning, Mr. Brooks. Mike Callahan speaking. Thank you for letting me interrupt your day," Callahan said.

"You're not interrupting a thing, Michael," Brooks said, affecting his most sincere tone. "We don't have much to do around here, these days. What can I do for you?"

"I'm calling about the Raven case..."

"Raven," Brooks interrupted. "Raven... Doesn't ring a bell."

"I think you've been coordinating with David Desmond at the CIA.

Desmond has been replaced and I've been assigned to clean up the loose ends," Callahan said.

Christopher Brooks cursed under his breath. He had known nothing of Desmond being replaced. And there was no way he could feign ignorance of any part of the operation at this point.

"Ah, yes. Of course I remember the Raven case. All about a spy book. Well, good to be brought up on events. How are things progressing?" Brooks said, his head falling into his free hand as he leaned forward on his desk.

"Not very good news, I'm afraid," Callahan said, his voice coming across the ocean as though he were next door. "It seems there is more to the story than we thought. We've been cooperating with you to keep this thing under control—"

"Yes, yes. Rumors, no matter how ridiculous, can do a lot of harm," Brooks said, squinting his eyes against a sudden headache that had come upon him.

"I suppose you're right, Christopher," Callahan said, using the SIS chief's given name in the spy's own tradition of encouraged collegiality, "but I think things have spun away from us. Did you know that this fellow Steven Dietrich, the one who flew for the Germans in World War II, kept a personal diary?"

"I beg your pardon?" Brooks asked.

"It's in his own handwriting. Gives it a very strong legal standing. Fascinating damn thing. Our handwriting experts haven't completed their investigation yet but they think the pages are going to turn out to be authentic. Steven Dietrich's grandson brought it in, pictures and all."

"Pictures?" Brooks gasped. "Did you say pictures? As in photographs?"

"Photostats, of course. The grandson kept the originals. Hello? Hello? Are you there, Mr. Brooks?"

"Yes. I'm here. Well. I can't tell you how much I appreciate you, ah, bringing me up to date. I'll... pass this along to the interested parties. Whoever they are. Historians, and such," Brooks finished in a weak voice.

"Naturally I'll copy you with the results of our confirmation of the documents and my assessment of our part in dealing with everyone concerned. By the way, would you have any idea how we could reach Mr. August Street?"

"No."

Chapter 26

August Street was arrested immediately by agents of Homeland Security as he deplaned at JFK International Airport. The charges against him were numerous. He was locked up at the Federal Correctional Center near Foley Square.

By contrast, Edward Wiles, traveling with a nurse and in the company of Street, was not detained but was taken by limousine to the Ritz-Carlton hotel near Central Park. He was ensconced in a suite of rooms overlooking The Pond.

At the detention center Street was read his rights, fingerprinted, had his picture taken, aliases noted, then booked. He was assigned a federal identification number and placed in a holding cell pending a plea hearing. This was on Friday. Monday morning his cell door was opened and he was escorted to the same place he had started forty-eight hours earlier. His personal belongings were returned. He was free to go, a jail official said.

Jean Scheerer was leaning against an iron handrail as Street emerged. Scheerer extended his hand and Street took it.

"I'd give you a big hug but you smell like...well, not too good, old pal," he said.

"I'm not sure I love you anymore, anyway. I guess I should thank you for getting me out, Scheerer," Street grumbled.

"You don't have to thank me for a thing. You never should have been in there in the first place. Stupid. Somebody didn't get the word. Matter of fact, that's typical for anything the government gets its fingers into, isn't it? I've been trying to retire for four years now and the main reason is because I was fed up with all the nut cases I had to work with. Of course, they probably thought the same about me," he said, laughing at himself.

Street was not deceived. Scheerer was one of the most effective espionage agents and controllers who ever served SIS and, in turn, supported the H. P. Carlisle Foundation. Street had no idea what Scheerer's job description was, but he was certainly no rube.

"Do you know what I brought with me, Scheerer?" Street asked, literally gritting his teeth as he snapped the words.

Scheerer held up the palm of his hand.

"Don't tell me. Not yet. First you get a hot shower, maybe a massage of some kind, a bite to eat. Then you can tell me and a couple other people what you have."

Scheerer took Street by the arm and pulled him gently down the steps from the Correctional Center to a waiting car.

"This is just delicious," Rose Smythes Hawkins said, savoring her garlic shrimp and grilled peas.

"And the Chardonnay?" Doren Lattimer asked.

"Heavenly," she smiled broadly. "Really, this has just been an amazing day." She paused briefly, then added "Of course, I'm not an wine afficionado, if that's the right word."

"Doesn't matter, Rose. What matters is how you like it. And I'm glad you do. This is also one of my favorite lunches," he said, pouring more white wine into her glass. After the first glass Rose no longer resisted his refills.

They were seated outside on a warm, early spring day. The café was called Joel's, just a bit upscale but not so much that it made clientele uncomfortable. Rose looked at the river, looked again up and down the street. The bridge was nearby. How many times she had played near its huge columns.

"It's so hard to believe," she said.

"What is, Rose?"

"Oh, this place. The neighborhood, I mean. I lived here once. Not two blocks from here," she said, smiling self-consciously. "It looked different, then."

"At 12-C, Putney Bridge, Hammil Lane," Lattimer filled in. He enjoyed watching the expression on her face.

"Good heavens, how did you know that?" she gasped.

"Well, like so many people in the world, I read the book about your father. I more than read it, actually, I studied it. Totally fascinating to me," he said.

"You're a policeman or something, aren't you, Mr. Lattimer?" she asked.

"Please call me Doren. I think we're good enough friends, aren't we? No, I'm not a policeman, but I do work for the government. I push papers," he said.

"Ah. You're a spy!" Rose said, lightly clapping her hands together.

Now it was Lattimer's turn to be surprised.

"What in the world gave you that idea?"

"August Street told me that when people who work for the government have unimportant jobs they tell you that they work on very important secret projects. When they really work on secret projects they say they only push papers."

"Hmm, well, for the record, I'm going to stand by my story that I only push papers."

"Now that you've found me am I still in hiding? I wasn't to tell anyone where I am. August said it was very dangerous," she said.

"You were only in danger when you gave our people the slip back in Burton Heath."

"That was pretty clever of me, wasn't it?" Rose asked, feeling the full effects of the wine.

"Yes, it was. Please don't do it again. Don't turn around but across the street there is a man watching us. He works for us. There's another person, a woman, on that corner over there," he said, jerking his head in a rearward direction. "They are assigned to make sure nothing happens to you, so please cooperate with us and don't make any rash moves."

"And August. If anything has happened to him, anything bad, that is, I want you to know that I will tell everybody everything I know. I will...I will spill my guts!"

"Tell me, Rose," Lattimer began with a perfectly straight face, "have you ever forgiven your father for your years of neglect? You and your mother's?"

Rose leaned back on her chair. Her eyes wandered a bit as though she was searching for something elusive in the air around her.

"No. I don't think I ever did. Or ever could. He led his own life, you see, and mother and I came a very distant second place. As a child I didn't realize I was suffering at the time. Kids just don't think that way. But I was aware that my mother survived only with difficulty. We were abandoned and her pain hurt me, too. That's what I cannot forgive Archie."

Lattimer digested this for a long moment.

"I think your father was a great man. A truly great patriot. A defender of the Crown, corny as that may sound. I happen to believe in those old values."

"Oh, yes. And I suspect you're right. But he was always gone, wasn't he?"

"Still," Lattimer pressed, "if man can rise above himself and do extraordinary things at extraordinary times, then Archie is that man, is he not?"

"Yes, but..."

"But?"

Rose Hawkins lips pressed tightly together, her eyes closing to keep out the afternoon sun.

"I understand you had a very rough time of it," Bradley Wallis said to Edward

Wiles in their Ritz-Carlton suite. "I was sorry to hear it."

Wiles waved his hand in the air as though his previous discomfort was nothing.

"Well," Wallis went on somewhat nervously, "you look just fine now, Edward."

"You're still a liar," Wiles said, his voice was weak but he was otherwise alert.

Wallis laughed fully, a bit forced, Street thought.

"August, meet Michael Callahan. Michael is with us today to put the official imprimatur on this whole affair," Bradley said.

"Unofficial," Callahan corrected, offering Street a somewhat unenthused hand to shake.

Callahan was just above average height, probably fifty years old, Street guessed. He had sandy hair and his speech was East Coast, probably Boston. Street noticed earlier that Callahan had quietly turned on the room's television set and set the channel to the Celtic basketball game but with the volume very low. He watched the game with one canted eye while keeping up with people and their conversations with his ears.

"CIA?" Street asked Callahan.

"God. No. I think they wear uniforms over there. Don't they? No, my boss is a very nice lady. Mind if I smoke?" he asked, producing a cigar.

"Yes," Street said as the Irishman deliberately snipped the end of his cigar and lit the other end.

Street opened a window.

"Let's see, you're considerably older than Edward, aren't you, Bradley?" Street needled, turning his back on Callahan.

"Very good, August," Wallis said, attempting to keep the atmosphere light for everyone in the room, "but I'm well beyond the age where I need to be sensitive."

"You've given up," suggested Street, still twisting the needle for his former boss.

"I keep telling myself that I'm going to do precisely that," Wallis said in a tone that momentarily caught Street off guard. The aging spy, head of the H. P. Carlisle Foundation, did seem tired at that moment. "I learned from this man here," he said, patting the hand of Edward Wiles. "If I've served my country well, if I've served America equally well, my model for integrity is right here with us in this room."

All eyes turned to Wiles.

"Thank you, Bradley, that's good of you to say," Wiles said, then spoke to the others in the room. "Bradley joined us for the Cold War. It was difficult then, at times, to know who was on your side. Some of our very top men, you know who they are, were traitors. One had to be on one's guard at all times, distinguishing friend from foe. Isn't that so, Bradley?"

Bradley Wallis nodded his head.

"But Bradley wasn't one of those. He was a rock," Wiles said.

"Here, here," Scheerer said encouragingly. He raised his whiskey tumbler to his lips. "Say, Callahan, got another of those?" he asked, nodding toward the man's cigar.

"Certainly," Callahan said, removing yet another stogie from his pocket and offering it too Scheerer. "Cuban," Callahan assured his shared sinner.

"Why don't we finish our business so we can go?" Wiles said.

"Go?" Bradley said. "Where do you want to go, Edward?"

"There are things to do in New York City," Edward Wiles said. "And I'm feeling stronger by the hour. And Ms. Woods," Wiles nodded toward the adjoining room where his nurse awaited, "has never been here. Young people like to have a little fun, Bradley. You remember what fun is, don't you?"

"Happiness is overrated, Edward. You should know that," Bradley grumbled.

Street withdrew a thick sheaf of papers from a manila folder.

"Do you know what these are, Bradley?" he asked.

"I think I can guess," the aging spy said.

"They are the Hess interrogation transcripts. I'd like to read some of them to you," Street said, donning a pair of reading glasses.

Wallis held up his hand and shook his head energetically.

"I know what they say, August. I read them again yesterday. Personally I think you were conned. Those papers are as phony as any I've seen." He held up his hands again when Street opened his mouth to object. "They don't matter, anyway. You can use them for toilet paper if you like." Bradley Wallis settled heavily into a padded chair.

"The Dietrich diary. That was the key that turned the lock," he said, not without a hint of regret. "There never was a real Hess transcript. What you have there in your hands is total fiction. Real fiction. It's what SOE invented so that what Hess really said could be covered up. Oh, he talked about Archie the actor, of course. And of course Edward Wiles and his pals couldn't let that out, could you, Edward?"

"That was then, Bradley. Not now," Wiles said, the edges of his mouth tilted up to reveal a mood of optimism.

"You're wrong, Edward," Bradley said, shaking his head slowly.

Street was not about to give up. He held the Hess transcripts aloft.

"We'll see about that. We'll see what the media does with these. Fleet Street is just as notorious as the American media."

"Suit yourself, August," Bradley said, "but you've won. You are swinging after the bell, as the old saying goes."

"That's right, August," Scheerer said, languidly moving away from the window, no longer caring about his cigar fumes. "The Dietrich diary. That is what cashes in everybody's chips." Then Scheerer smiled as he turned to Wiles. "You got what you wanted, Edward."

Street thought about it for a moment. He knew about the Dietrich diary but had not read the pages himself. Yet even without them, Street knew, the

Hess documents were dynamite. They would describe in detail how Hess had caught on to England's phony Hitler, Archie the actor, and how Hess wanted to make a deal. He would be quiet about Archie the actor if the British and Americans would put him in charge of the Third Reich. Hess would return once more to Germany but this time with a written agreement in his possession signed by Winston Churchill.

Churchill ordered the man locked up and kept in solitary forever. That was why Rudolph Hess, a relatively harmless party functionary, was kept alone and locked up tight until he died a madman in his cell, the only prisoner in Spandau prison.

The result of forged transcripts? Is that all it took? The real transcripts, if there ever were any, simply destroyed to be replaced by phony confessions of Hitler's aide? A huge lie to cover up an even bigger lie?

"I want Linda returned to the U.S. from Canada," Street said.

"Of course," Scheerer said, a limp hand moving expansively in agreement.

"And I want my identity back," he demanded.

"That was an unfortunate episode. I want you to know that I argued against that course of action, August," Bradley said.

August thought he was sincere.

"With my finances returned. Well?" Street said, waiting.

"Certainly. I told you it was a mistake. Everything is changed, now. But August, we need your written statement that the Raven thing was total fiction. That the characters existed only in your head. We must have that, August, or we are back to square one."

Street had been thinking about that. He was convinced that his position would be upheld by history. Well, he had won. He had the evidence and he had the witnesses. Most of them, anyway. Enough of them. Why should he sign the damn paper? Yet in his heart of hearts he knew the answer. Nations, like people, do what they do because it is the only thing they <u>can</u> do. Britain had to save itself first, the world later. What was his pride next to that?

"Rose Smythes Hawkins has to be made whole as well," he said as firmly as he could muster his convictions.

"The Crown is prepared to recognize her father's war time service in, ah, the commandoes, Third Para. She will be entitled to full survivor's benefits. Pension, of course," Scheerer said, speaking with the confidence that spanned the Atlantic Ocean.

"Retroactive," Street said.

"Naturally."

"I'll be in touch with her, Jean," Street warned. "I intend to follow up."

"Indeed you should. As a matter of fact the Prime Minister ordered her protected months ago. You needn't have worried about her," Scheerer soothed.

"I shouldn't have worried about Wes Claridge, either. Should I?" Street said.

This time Wallis's lips became bloodless.

"Good people were lost in this enterprise of yours, August. I wouldn't consider myself altogether blameless if I were you," he said.

"Now, now, lads," Jean Scheerer said. "Let's all have another drink. To good friends."

He raised his glass.

"At last you've arrived at my area of expertise," Callahan said, joining in.

The End

Epilogue

Steven Dietrich, grandson of Steven Dietrich the Luftwaffe pilot, continues to live and work in Santa Monica, California. His grandfather's handwritten biography is in a secure place; copies have been given to the Administration and to the Central Intelligence Agency.

Louis Workman departed for sub-Sahara Africa after Edward Wiles's safe return to England. Unverified reports have it that Louis was employed as a military consultant to one of the quasi-democratic governments there.

Edward Wiles passed away of a massive stroke several months after his meeting with Bradley Wallis and Jean Scheerer in New York. He was ninety-one.

In making his full report to Prime Minister Clay Waldon chief of SIS Christopher Brooks filled in missing details. "We are still on the trail of the terrorists who killed the Spanish police, of course," Brooks assured his prime minister.

"We know they were Muslims?" Waldon wanted assurance.

"No question about it, Prime Minister. Al Qaeda fingerprints are all over this one. I only regret I asked those poor devils for their help."

"You can't blame yourself, C. Wiles probably only survived because of them. Filthy Muslims. I'll never understand that kind of uncivilized superstition."

Linda MacTaggart was allowed to return to the United States where she and August Street were married in a private ceremony. Bradley Wallis's promises to Street, speaking on behalf of the government of the United States, were only partially fulfilled. While Street was compensated in lump sum for his missing bank funds and other assets, his home in Lompoc had been sold to strangers. He was forced to hire legal counsel and file suit to recover those funds. To date he has seen none of the money. The man who took over Street's identity still resides in or near Cleveland, Ohio, and still represents himself as August Street, the author.

Street and Linda now live in the community of Stoneridge, Prescott Valley, Arizona. Their passions are their dogs, Jack, Shoe, and Jasmine—a Fox Terrier, a Husky, and a Dachshund—hiking, and supporting the Prescott Community Symphony.